Sir Robert Jones is one of New Zealand's best-known public figures, with a successful track record in many fields including commerce, politics, sport and writing.

Full Circle is not for the overly sensitive. For Jones leaves no sacred cows unslaughtered in this wickedly funny commentary on contemporary life. Beneath the humour, however, lie serious observations about human relationships and folly.

FULL CIRCLE

A MODERN MORALITY TALE

BOB JONES

HAZARD PRESS
publishers

Full Circle is a serious story written in a comic picaresque medium. It is in no part autobiographical, the characters and their conduct stemming from general observation and in every respect they are fictitious. Elements of fantasy arise in Part Three, notably with the behaviour attributed to the Archbishop of Canterbury and the Church Commissioners.

REJ
March, 2000

First published 2000
Copyright © 2000 Sir Robert Jones
Cover painting: *Unknown Journey*, 1989. George Morant.

ISBN 1-877161-76-4

Published by Hazard Press
P.O. Box 2151, Christchurch, New Zealand
Production and design by Hazard Press Ltd
Printed in New Zealand

Prologue

'N ot far now, sir, it's a splendid view from up here,' Mr Rutledge the estate agent remarked as he manoeuvred the car up the narrow winding lane to the summit of the hill. As they rounded each corner small clouds of pheasants rose fluttering into the air like colourful mini-explosions. Overhead a continuous canopy of ancient trees shaded the bright afternoon sun twinkling through the branches.

This was it; old England, timeless and certain England, civilised and venerated England, yobbo-less England; Len Edward's England during all his years of nostalgic exile, although like most expatriate sentimentalists, an England he had never experienced or belonged to other than in his mind.

Emerging from the shadowy moss-covered lane into the sunshine on the crest of the hill, Rutledge edged the car on to a grassy knoll. The two gazed in silence at the splendid panorama laid out before them.

Half a mile below, the river Wye sparkled in the mid-afternoon sun, bent round under the hill and stretched across the horizon. A mile downstream a tiny figure, waist deep in the water, could be seen languidly casting a line.

'His Lordship wasted no time, I see,' Rutledge remarked. 'The estate has eight miles of private salmon water. Many's the man would die for that.'

They had spent the previous three hours with Lord Melcup inspecting Wyebury. Dolefully, Lord Melcup had escorted them from room to room; first the great hall with its historic architectural features and Grinling Gibbons inlaid carvings, all of which he had painstakingly described, then the ancient library, the carved panels of the billiard room, large and small dining rooms, numerous drawing rooms, sunrooms, fifteen bedrooms, a glorious ornate ballroom, landings, balconies, a splendid sweeping main stairway, supplementary stairways, maids' rooms, bathrooms, dressing rooms, the pantry, a 'works room' with its modern central heating system and reserve generator; after an hour Len's initial confusion waned as the symmetry and flow of the interior design provided clarity and comprehension.

Outside they had inspected the stables, a glasshouse, a chapel, a cupola crowned, Ionic-columned summerhouse, the family cemetery with gravestones dating back nearly three centuries, a gazebo, the machinery shed and some ancillary buildings, the orchard, a croquet green, tennis court, flower gardens and a maze. When the inspection tour finally ended, a maid brought coffee, tea, sandwiches and cake to them in the conservatory.

Once seated Lord Melcup launched into a droning monologue.

'Two hundred and fifteen years my family has been here… two hundred and fifteen years and now it ends. It's all different today. The modern generation has no feel for tradition or sense of duty. When I was young I never questioned my role. But my son Philip won't come near the place. I blame the education system. There's no morality to it any more; all this self-centred rubbish about doing your own thing. One expects better from Cambridge. Some broadening tutorage, once over lightly with the classics, that sort of thing. But not so, not any more, no, it's all gone, all gone. I thought the boy had lost his senses. Five years at Cambridge and he returns as an oceanographic climatologist. Never heard such nonsense. We're eighty miles from the sea here, I told him. And anyway, what does it matter what temperature the damned sea is? Who cares and what can you do about it anyway? He had no reply to that, I can tell you; that had him stumped. But there's no stopping him so perhaps it's best I tidy things up while I'm still here'. And then after a pensive pause, he added, 'Well, I'll think about it, anyway.'

This last remark flushed Len with a deja vu resentment unfelt in almost forty years since leaving England. The message was clear. He was not, in his Lordship's eyes, a suitable occupant for the historic seat. But as it turned out, soon all became well.

'A friend of mine had a son who came home from university and announced he was a poet,' Len offered sympathetically.

'Good God!' Lord Melcup exclaimed, visibly shocked.

'It came out all right though. My friend bought the boy a motorbike. A week later he crashed and incurred permanent brain damage.'

'I say; what a stroke of luck,' Lord Melcup said, brightening.

At that Rutledge piped up. 'A chap in our office had a daughter who ran off with a black. They ended up in the Sudan building village wells.'

Lord Melcup glared at Rutledge. 'That's a gel,' he protested. After that Rutledge was silent while Len and Lord Melcup exchanged anecdotes of other acquaintances' misfortunes with their male heirs. Soon Lord Melcup's melancholy lifted.

There was the son who wore dark glasses night and day, another who incessantly talked into a cellphone; a merchant banker's eldest had become a clergyman, another a scoutmaster; yet another had married a thirty-eight-year-old grief counsellor with three teenage children; a hitherto sensible lad had grown a beard and joined Greenpeace. As horror followed horror a bond steadily grew between the two men.

Finally, Lord Melcup said, 'Look here, you might like to come down next week. We've a nice run of salmon in the river this year. I'm going in myself this afternoon.' Len had learned to fish in New Zealand and this invitation led to an agreeable exchange about the virtues of the wet fly over nymphing and dry fly fishing.

Later, on the drive up the hill, Rutledge had explained the background.

'The old boy's a widower. Only one son who's never there. I think it's all a bit much for him now so if we find an acceptable buyer he plans to live in London. Says he'll miss the fishing most of all. Can't say I blame him.'

The landscape stretched away into the distance; a vista of ancient forests, of rolling green pastures lush from centuries of tilling and grazing. Far in the distance the village church spire emerged above trees. Cattle grazed placidly on the rich, tree-dotted downs. Embedded centrepiece like an ageless rock of stability lay the great house, its classical splendour exaggerated by distance. It was a world unto itself, a civilised preserve of certainty far removed from the transitory coarseness of the England Len had returned to find.

The faint hum of an engine broke their idyll and from the steeply pitched cluster of stables a toy-like tractor emerged and puttered across the fields.

'Ah, one of the farmhands,' Rutledge said. 'Lord Melcup seems to have it well balanced. Two outside staff, three indoors and an estate manager and it all runs along nicely. Averaged over any period of time the farm income meets all upkeep; maintenance, heating, rates, wages; everything's covered. But what it doesn't do is produce enough to service any debt.

'It's the same old story. When Lord Melcup inherited it he was hit with death duties and the title deeds show he's increased the mortgage every few years. He's reached the point of no return now and has to sell. Our surveyors have a full audited report available for approved potential purchasers. I think you will find it satisfactory. Of course, you must use some imagination. As you saw the furnishings are tired and the gardens neglected. But these are matters easily put to right.'

'Six million pounds you say might do it?' Len hesitatingly enquired, his voice reduced to a nervous croak.

'Well, sir, as I have said, Lord Melcup was anticipating something more than that. After all there's 2200 acres and they alone would fetch a good portion of that. And how do you put a price on the house? They don't build those any more.'

Rutledge dropped his voice to a confidential tone. 'Between you and me, sir, we've told Lord Melcup he may have to lower his expectations. The Arab market has died since oil collapsed. These days the moneyed classes are different. It's all city living now,' he added mournfully. 'There's not the same respect for the old values which people like us appreciate.'

Len stood silently for a minute wallowing in the wonderland before him.

'I want it,' he said emphatically.

Part One

Home

1

Len Edwards last saw his mother on the morning of his first day at school. When he came home the five-year-old boy found his father waiting. 'Your mother's gone away for a while, son,' his dad said, and over the next few months he devoted such close attention to the lad Len eventually forgot about her. When he was ten the boy raised the subject through curiosity rather than any sense of loss.

'Your mother couldn't help it, lad. She was like a caged bird here. It was unnatural for her to stay in one place. It was in her blood.' His mother was the illegitimate offspring of a fleeting contact between a Norwegian seaman and an Irish gypsy woman, which mix provided a convenient explanation for her abrupt departure rather than the more plausible one of her marriage at eighteen when Len's father was already forty-eight. Nevertheless those exotic blood-lines were already showing in the boy with his brown eyes and dark hair but in his London Docklands home he was inconspicuous among his peers. Odd shapes and colourings, frizzy hair, Icelandic blonds, broad noses, Oriental features; the entire gamut of the human stock was on display in an un-English disorderly stew in the great city's port.

Len's father was a market trader without speciality, his activities depending on such supply opportunities as arose in the austere post-war years. They lived in a ramshackle flat above a small warehouse, the ever-changing contents of which amounted to a veritable Aladdin's cave for a small boy. By the time the lad was fifteen and had left school he was adept at trading whatever came his way. He knew the varying tricks of selling oranges and antiques, footwear and fabrics, watches and washing machines, conscious always of his father's oft-repeated instruction to look for the angles.

Sometimes his father took him to boxing matches in the Shoreditch Town Hall. Throughout he maintained a constant instructional commentary, seemingly viewing each contest as a metaphor for life. Brawling fighters were dismissed as fools who lived for the moment, reliant on optimism rather than strategy.

'There's a right way to do everything, son,' his father would preach. 'The trick is to add the extra angle,' for he would also condemn the correctly orthodox boxer who lacked this critical additional faculty. From time to time a star would emerge and his father would enthuse about the new hero's magic combination of orthodoxy with an ability to do the unexpected.

'There are opportunities everywhere, boy,' his dad would say. 'It's not hard to crack it. It doesn't matter what you do so long as you master the correct procedure, then lift yourself above the rest with an angle that's different from what everyone else is doing.'

The relentless repetition of this doctrine of unconventionality's reward, despite his father's inability to apply it personally, was never forgotten by Len who in later years, during times of frustration, constantly reminded himself of this maxim, looked for the angle and invariably found himself back in motion again.

As an only child he was naturally introspective, thoughtful and observant and in that sense an oddity among the cacophony of East London marketplace voices where opinions were never proffered but instead advocated with great force, a practice universally common to ignorance. At the age of twelve an event occurred which proved definitive in the boy's development. For reasons never explained a schoolmaster, Mr Gifford, shifted into the neighbourhood. As a suit-wearer he was a curiosity and Len observed the awe in which his father and other adults held the newcomer without any apparent justification for such deference.

More particularly he noted that while Mr Gifford might as well be a deaf mute, for he rarely spoke other than the most token greeting, he was referred to constantly in the most glowing terms as 'a gentleman' and 'a very, very clever man that Mr Gifford, make no mistake'. All of this taught Len a valuable but extremely un-East London lesson, being a truism known to the most successful journalists and politicians, namely that their silent, unopinionated audience will always be misread by the speaker as sympathy for their argument. For the rest of his life Len applied the Gifford example to his steadfast reward.

Leaving school at fifteen for the street market taught Len a great deal about people, their foibles, impulsive behaviour, vulnerabilities and stubbornness. He discovered some golden rules from his father and other stallholders who adopted the same parental patronage role towards him in the art of persuasion. 'You never know where your sales lie, lad,' was one such message never to prejudge any situation when people were involved. He learned the verbal persuasion skills of always placing himself in the purchaser's shoes and that it was always more fruitful to say 'I'll tell you what I'll do for you' rather than 'I'll tell you what I'll take'.

The subtleties of salesmanship he acquired were to serve him well in later life and when after a year he felt constrained by the small world of the street trader and told his father he wanted to expand his horizons, this was well received, to his surprise.

'It's good you should go, son, and it doesn't matter what you do so long as you learn the rules then look for the angles to take yourself above the mob.'

Fortune intervened when his friend Tom advised of a vacancy for another boy in The Palmerston; a Mayfair gentlemen's club where Tom was employed. For Len, knowing only the raucous street market, it was a strangely foreign environment of quiet understatement and unostentatious affluence. Such abrupt changes were to characterise his future years.

2

Introduction in 1882 of The Married Women's Property Act by the newly elected second Gladstone Ministry engendered such anger among men of affairs that the Palmerston Club was founded in response. This is a common phenomenon whereby a defeated government's natural supporters instantly lose faith in their existing leaders. Organisations are born in a welter of hand-wringing anguish outside the conventional system, ostensibly to combat the perceived malignancy now befallen the nation in the form of the new government.

So it was with the Palmerston Club, nostalgically named after the late Lord Palmerston who, in the eyes of the club's founders, epitomised, with his gentleman's breeding and his anti-radical, progressively conservative values, all that represented sound government. 'Must we do anything at all?' Lord Palmerston once famously asked after examining that day's Cabinet papers, which attitude reflected the sentiments of the Palmerston Club's founders' outlook on the world.

By the time Gladstone had fallen five years later the club's original raison d'etre was largely forgotten and for half a century it prospered as a haven for city gentlemen, Conservative parliamentarians and visiting country gentry. By 1930 a waiting list for membership extended to six years but this changed abruptly with the onset of the Great Depression which brought a dramatic drop in membership and a corresponding financial pressure.

Following a failed membership drive the Palmerston's management committee resolved to combine with another club but being late off the mark, found their preferred choices had already adopted similar survival actions. With its viability at stake the Palmerston in desperation entered into the improbable marriage of amalgamating with the London Exploration and Travellers Club. As is often the case with marriages of convenience, the relationship prospered, having the desirable ingredients of mutual need and an absence of friction arising from the total disinterest of each faction in the other.

The London Exploration and Travellers Club had been

formed during the prosperous expansionist late-Victorian era, its membership comprising sober-minded scientists, geologists, explorers, engineers, anthropologists, Orientalists, tea planters, colonial officers and others with lives bound up in far-flung places who desired a haven among like-minded souls when on home leave in London.

In contrast The Palmerston Club members were gregarious men of the world inclined towards excessive and noisy drinking sessions and the pursuit of money, possessions and pleasure.

By 1950 the club, which following amalgamation had retained the name the Palmerston but whose stationery still displayed in brackets the words 'Incorporating the London Explorers and Travellers Club', had been restored to its former glory. Its management committee was invariably drawn from the city members with one conspicuous exception in the wake of a much publicised call from Doctor Geof Cone, a junior lecturer at London University's biology department, urging the compulsory sterilisation of criminals, the unemployed and the mentally deficient. For the first and only time the city members embraced one of the LET group, resulting in the youthful academic being elected to the club's committee for a single term.

Despite its incongruous membership the Palmerston ranked among the top drawer of London gentlemen's clubs, largely due to its St James's location and its healthy financial position. This latter factor was attributed to its founders' astute foresight although as with many seemingly brilliant financial decisions, it lay more with chance and the passing of time. The founders had secured a forty-year lease on the five levels, early-Victorian building, at a fixed rental with an option to purchase it and the neighbouring identical property, at 1870 prices. The boom Edwardian years had allowed the committee to exercise both options and on-sell the neighbouring property at a figure yielding an outcome of debt-free premises and a sizeable capital investment fund.

One entered the club through a narrow entrance and passed a cloakroom before opening on to a large marble-floored, octagon-shape hall containing an oak centrepiece table with a bust of Lord Palmerston. Side tables bore large floral displays while a magnificent double staircase at the rear led to the first floor.

Around the central hall's oak-panelled walls hung oil portraits of the club's sixteen past presidents.

To the right lay the principal sitting room containing clusters of sofas and armchairs, newspaper-cluttered side tables and in a far corner, a bar. On the walls hung ornately framed, gloomy, Victorian pastoral-scene oil paintings which, like much of the club's decor, had remained unchanged and immune to all fashion since its formative years.

The dining room off the other side of the hall had a half-lit ambience and its walls were adorned with photographs of past committees and, inexplicably, First World War battleships.

On the first floor could be found the club secretary's office adjacent to which lay the billiard room containing two tables dating from 1830.

In one corner of the billiard room was a marble bust of James Figg, the first English heavyweight champion, while the walls were adorned with numerous sporting themes, spotted and fading photographs, all dating to the late-nineteenth century. With the exception of some Cowles regatta yachting prints, these all involved the slaughter of animals. Tiger shoots in India, beached salmon in Scottish lochs, African lion hunts, neatly filed rows of pheasants; all displayed as the centrepiece a past club member standing erect with rod or gun behind the corpses while to each side of him, with moronic wide-eyed subservient vacuity, stood African bearers, Indian beaters, Scottish ghillies and other such minions appropriate to the destruction. A fourteen-point antlered stag's head gazed glass-eyed down from above the entrance while high on the walls above the photographs, mounted salmon and the stuffed heads of numerous wild beasts were spaced around the room. At the end of the room was a redundant, heavily carved fireplace and on its mantelpiece stood an array of silver cups for long-abandoned sporting contests.

Opposite the billiard room lay a spacious library. Its shelves contained bound Hansards dating to 1870, Stock Exchange annual reports, a 1920 set of the Encyclopaedia Britannica, the memoirs of past members from the LET section, numerous bound scientific journals dating back half a century, atlases, every edition of Debrett's and Who's Who, a complete set of Wisdens and diverse other titles in an eclectic mix but with the common characteristic of rarely having been read. The walls were relieved by fading maps of English counties and former colonies and caricature sketches of past club presidents.

Three ancient oak desks were placed about the library at which could occasionally be found ageing LET members working on their memoirs. From this room had been spawned more than forty titles and with the exception of an unreadable scholarly tome on Talmudic inscriptions, all were of the Forty Years In the Kenyan Highlands, Life As a Colonial Officer, Lost Cities of Arabia and Memoirs of a Ceylonese Tea Planter genre.

The third floor, accessible since 1925 by a tiny hydraulic passenger lift, contained a cocktail lounge and meeting rooms available for hire and on the fourth floor, visiting members' bedrooms rentable for a maximum stay of one week. At the top lay the president's bedroom and private suite, which was rarely used.

Despite its anachronistic character club membership remained keenly sought and a five-year waiting list prevailed into the 1950s allowing a prohibition on foreigners, which definition included missionaries and applicants of Celtic and Jewish origin.

It was into this strange new world that the seventeen-year-old Len Edwards came as a club 'day boy'.

Len's duties, shared with Tom, included polishing the brasswork and wooden surfaces, replacing newspapers and magazines with newly arrived editions, taking drinks orders from members in the lounge, vacuuming and brushing the billiard tablecloths, dish-washing and drying in the kitchen and occasionally, the running of errands, a privilege available only to the club's committee members.

For two years Len remained at the Palmerston carrying out these tasks and building resentment at the starkly different behaviour of the membership towards him. The city gentlemen barked orders while seemingly looking through him. The LET set rarely sought his services and when they did, were hesitant and apologetic.

Conscious of his father's gospel to look, learn and find the angles, Len began taking home the club's old newspapers and magazines and studying these at night. Initially their contents were meaningless but through repeated reading and eavesdropping on the members' discussions, his eclectic education slowly began to take shape.

The overheard travellers' tales sparked a curiosity about foreign lands while the financial pages of the newspapers, the contents of which were the major source of conversation among the club's city members, if confusing in their jargonese, induced a desire to become a man of means.

The scientific and exploration magazines particularly fascinated Len, even when the material was beyond his comprehension. On the other hand Tom quickly grasped much of the financial newspapers' and journals' contents and would endeavour to explain these to Len. Tom was determined to find employment in a share broker's office but Len was uncertain as to his future other than a vague desire to travel. As it happened, after nearly two years in the club an event occurred which was to propel the two young men into the world and towards their separate destinies.

A group of eight elderly retired city gentlemen met at the Palmerston each Wednesday for lunch. The two young employees despised them as it was this group's practice to later retire to the billiard room to drink and smoke cigars throughout the afternoon, loudly barking orders periodically at the two lads for more whisky and the club's cigar box.

One evening walking home the two stopped outside a magic shop. Centrepiece in the window was a box of authentic-looking cigars with a card bearing the message, 'Surprise your friends with exploding cigars.' It was illustrated with a shocked, soot-blackened face with a freshly exploded, frayed cigar end dangling from its midst while other background faces were shown wreathed with laughter. The two lads bought a dozen.

The following Wednesday they placed these in the club's cigar box and in mid-afternoon when the group of sozzled elderly gentlemen lurched into the billiard room after lunch and the usual roar of, 'Boy!' was bellowed ungraciously, Len brought over the club's cigar box.

Each man took one while Tom recorded their drinks orders. The two watched from the doorway. Four cigars exploded simultaneously with a deafening thunderclap which brought the club manager, staff and other members present in the building rushing to the room. The shock caused a fatal heart attack to one member while the others, their faces blackened, were in a traumatised state.

Len and Tom were instantly dismissed and at the age of nineteen stepped out of the club but not, as events were to transpire, for the last time. Before them the whole wide world, unknown, uncertain, beckoned with all its promise and excitement.

3

A fortnight after Len lost his first and as it turned out, only ever employment, he embarked on his initial entrepreneurial venture in partnership with Tom.

His father's message to observe and look for the angles had been well installed and he applied these maxims based on his judgement of the Palmerston Club's explorers, geologists and other scientific members' vulnerable gullibility.

Classified advertisements were placed in the International Geologist Monthly, the Global Mining Engineers Journal, the International Scientist and four other similar publications, old copies of which he had taken from the Palmerston Club.

The message in each varied slightly but the essence was the same. 'Lonely young female Laboratory Assistant – aged 23 – said to be attractive – seeks penfriend – view to marriage' and the address, a post office box, the first of many Len was to rent in the years ahead.

The responses began arriving a month later. After a week the post office stopped placing letters in his box through lack of space and instead inserted a card instructing the box holder to pick up a red mail sack. By nature Len was a do-it-yourself, hands-on type whereas Tom's vision was more far-reaching. Tom employed a down-at-heel seventy-year-old retired schoolteacher, rented a one-room office above a Putney butcher shop and the school-teacher, a self-rolled cigarette drooping permanently from his mouth, sat at a desk writing love letters to the correspondents. Surrounding the desk were twelve filing cabinets Tom had purchased at an auction of redundant office furniture.

As the letters poured in from colonial outposts and Saudi Arabian mining camps, from the Arctic circle and African universities, a file was opened for each correspondent. The schoolteacher was given three draft letters, A, B and C as models, each composed by Tom. Usually by letter C the correspondent was in love.

Len and Tom were kept busy by this enterprise. Photos of models were sent to the correspondents while elderly crones throughout the East End were employed knitting socks to send to the smitten, these being referred to in letter B.

With few exceptions the response followed a generally prescribed pattern.

By letter C Cupid's arrow was firmly embedded and the correspondence turned to a meeting in Rome or Nairobi or Vancouver or whichever exotic location was nearest the besotted's lonely outpost.

The fallen one would arrange for return air tickets to be sent to his new love and in order to impress, many made them first-class and some sent a few hundred pounds as well for the future bride to purchase tropical clothing and for taxis and other disbursements. On receipt of the air tickets Tom gave these to a mate in a travel agency who paid him seventy per cent of their face value.

'The buggers will be too embarrassed to complain to the police,' Tom boasted, and he was right. Thus for almost a year the two enjoyed the high life with smart clothes, a fancy shared riverside flat and two matching sports cars.

Had they been more diligent this cottage industry might have survived longer than it did but the easy money led to management lassitude resulting in the schoolteacher inadvertently sending identical photographs to three correspondents in the same Libyan oil exploration camp. So the thriving enterprise came to an abrupt halt when late one day, while they were entertaining two city typists in their riverside apartment, the telephone rang.

It was the schoolteacher. 'There's three men here going through the files,' he told Tom. 'Well, don't ring me; ring the police,' Tom shouted. 'But they are the police,' the schoolteacher protested.

That night the two vacated their flat. The following morning they emptied their bank accounts, sold their cars and fled to Paris.

Drinking coffee at a Parisian sidewalk cafe in the early spring sunshine a few days later Tom said, 'We did a good job when you think about it. We taught these mugs about the wickedness of women. That will serve them well in the future and they'll be a hell of a lot more careful.'

But Len was not interested in philosophising. He had been reading the International Herald Tribune and an idea was germinating. He outlined his scheme to Tom who added a few embellishments and very soon they were back in business.

Over the subsequent week they followed up the many classified advertisements in the Herald Tribune offering luxury apartments for rent for the summer until they located the best on offer, paid three months' rental in advance and took possession. Then they too advertised the apartment in the Herald Tribune for a six-month occupancy at an attractive below-market rental, payable in full in advance. Over four weeks the two re-leased the apartment to forty-seven different Americans with possession to commence on the same day. Both were now affluent young men and they discussed their future, conscious of the need to leave Paris before the inevitable unpleasantness when the forty-seven different lessees arrived simultaneously to take occupancy.

Eager to put as much distance as possible between himself and the London and Parisian police, Len chose Australia and tried to persuade Tom to come with him. But Tom, always the more confident of the two, was unconcerned.

'It's two months now since we left London,' he said. 'You can't seriously believe the police are still interested in the love-letter lark. I'm going home. I'm getting speech lessons to learn to talk like a gent and then I'll get a job with a sharebroker. I want to find out how it all works. That's where the money is and I'm going for it.'

So the two shook hands and took their chosen paths. Forty years were to pass before they saw one another again.

4

Arriving in Sydney was like a spiritual homecoming for Len. It was a world tailored precisely to his taste. Unlike London's class rigidity a cavalier spirit pervaded with an openness towards all comers, unsurprising in a city bubbling with the influx of an all-continents migration. Len types abounded and were tolerated with humour and even sometimes admired for their imagination. The more outrageous their ventures, the more they were applauded for their entertainment value.

Ensconcing himself in an inner-city furnished flat, Len promptly created a head office in the form of an anonymous post office box for his still undetermined operations. A quick scan of the universal rogues' bible, the telephone book yellow pages, revealed the existence of the NSW Fire Service. Within a week Len possessed business cards as the Retail Premises Inspector, NSW Fire Board. Purchasing small portable fire extinguishers for $30 each, Len called on shopkeepers for three months.

'Good morning. Are you the proprietor? I'm the retail premises inspector for the NSW Fire Board, here to check on your shop's fire extinguisher.'

Revelation of the absence of same induced a shocked lifting of eyebrows, some tut-tutting and 'dear oh me' rebuking and then, 'Well, we better get you sorted out smartly' and the shopkeeper, now $75 lighter, found himself the relieved owner of a wall-fitted extinguisher.

It was marginally honest and arguably useful toil and three months plugging away lifted Len's capital sizeably. But the daily door-to-door tedium soon saw him seek less arduous activities. They were to be many in both number and diversity. There was the Chinese Registration Board, a creation which, like so many to come, followed a path beginning with a cash cascade culminating with criminal prosecution-avoiding heavy legal expenses, once, as invariably occurred, it was pushed too far.

Obtaining a list of Australia's Chinese ethnics Len sent each an account for $10 from his newly created, by dint of printed stationery, Chinese Registration Board. The cheques flowed back and a certificate formally confirming the payer's ethnicity was issued. Len was happy as were the Chinese he registered, many having their certificates framed and prominently displayed. An eighty per cent mailing success rate encouraged him to widen his scope whereas a more prudent approach might have seen contentment with this project as an annually renewable, solid little earner. But such conservatism is contrary to the entrepreneurial spirit and much capital was dissipated in postage and typing costs targeting Irish ethnics, most of whom wisely preferred non-disclosure of their origin (a less than ten per cent response and forty per cent of the cheques bouncing) and then a spectacular end-of-venture public brouhaha when attempting to certify Australia's Jews. The ever-sensitive Jewish lobby swung into well-practised aggrievement action with statements in Parliament, newspaper investigations, police inquiries, public meetings with much hysteria about fascism and newspaper correspondence with the routine 'I lost my entire family in Auschwitz because of this sort of thing' assertion, all of which festered away for some weeks.

'Why couldn't they simply decline payment and leave it at that?' Len protested to Detectives O'Reilly and Mahoney when passing over five thousand dollars, the then standard looking-the-other-way fee in Sydney for non-homicidal mishaps on the edge of the law.

But he followed their 'Best be on your bike, mate' advice and moved to New Zealand where, for fifteen years, he resided in Auckland, a city much to his liking for its more innocent passivity to his activities.

Once again facilitated by the essential post office box the cash flowed, initially from his tabloid newspapers classified advertising services. Winning horse-racing formulas, horoscopes, 'Keys To Instant Wealth' guides, ancient Celtic lucky charms, secret philosophy society memberships; the money streamed in, mostly without disruption although there was a minor outburst when some customers complained to newspapers after receiving a small pair of scissors in return for their twenty-five dollars in response to his 'Cut Your Electricity Bills In Half' advertisements. While supplying these diverse services provided Len with a comfortable man-about-town income, it fell far short of his ambitions.

For a time New Zealand provided rich pickings with the advent of franchising. Len travelled the country following pre-arranged advertising in provincial newspapers. Territorial rights to mow people's lawns under his Christian Services trade banner were sold for twenty thousand dollars. Scheme followed scheme. Len allocated regional agencies to sell potatoes on roadsides, recipients receiving large car-roof fitting signs for their twenty thousand dollars; to clean people's cars in their backyards, to shift their goods (a small enclosed, heavily sign-written car trailer costing two thousand dollars was exchanged for the twenty thousand dollar signing-on fee) and one glorious coup when more than thirty women across the land parted with ten thousand dollars each for regional rights, under the Christian Ironing Services banner, to solicit home ironing. Fascinated by the seemingly boundless public gullibility and driven more by a sense of humour than the pursuit of money, Len racked his mind to test the limits. At two thousand dollars a head he succeeded in selling regional dog-walking rights to seventeen people across the land.

There was a patterned response to each franchise enterprise. The first doubting letters would arrive about two months after payment.

'I've spent over three hundred dollars advertising but the business has been nothing like you said it would be,' was the common protest. Assurances that it took time to build a clientele would delay for about six months the never-answered inevitable provincial lawyers' letters to his post office box, demanding reimbursement. Ultimately each venture would culminate with advertisements in the same tabloid press calling for other aggrieved Christian Services lawnmowing, ironing or whatever franchisees, to write to a Proposed Action Committee Coordinator. Len monitored these campaigns by sending in a stooge who would attend the first, and invariably last, franchisees' protest action meeting.

The co-ordinator, usually a garrulous bearded schoolteacher accompanied by a dimmish provincial lawyer, would initially monopolise the meeting's discussion. These soon became unruly as speaker after speaker insisted on bitterly recounting their largely identical experiences. Eventually the lawyer would outline a programme of action. But once the need to create a fighting fund to pay him arose the atmosphere would darken and the meeting would break up angrily as unhappy franchisees abused the lawyer for his unwillingness to guarantee a favourable outcome. Three months later the now fiery but even less wise schoolteacher would join his local Labour Party branch and irritate members with his new-found misanthropic anti-business fervour.

By the late 1970s a new liberalism saw authorities look the other way to the advent of brothels, euphemistically described as massage parlours. Len established four Auckland locations and in an ambitious attempt at respectability, persuaded his rival operators to form an association. He became president, an office which led to some marginally pompous public utterances on behalf of 'the industry' following the fairly regular flow of firebombing of premises, irate clients running amok and similar such occurrences. As always there was a pattern in the customer behaviour which Len soon detected and exploited.

'A sore shoulder you say, sir,' he would soothingly assure the furtive client lurking hesitatingly in the dimly lit foyer. 'You've certainly done the sensible thing coming here,' and he would point to the noticeboard of 'services' for the customer's selection.

'A wise choice, the Cleopatra Special, sir. I'm sure it will fix the problem,' and an hour later, 'How's that shoulder now, sir?', this followed by, 'It's always best to have a course of treatments for these things.' Taking a deposit from the customer to secure the same 'therapist' at an appointed time two days later he would wait for the inevitable response.

'You know, she's a very intelligent girl, that Zola,' to which Len would soberly agree and there would follow a brief exchange layered with the excessively polite veneer coating all embarrassment.

The 'ladies' business proved an educational turning point in Len's commercial life. While it had much to commend it in a profitability sense, its corresponding nuisance component was tiresome. The hours were terrible, peak activity times being 8pm to 1am; his girlfriend's constant accusations of infidelity with his stable's prettier members were tiresome; while the 'ladies' brought with them troublesome baggage in the form of angry boyfriends, child-minding problems, squabbles among themselves, loan requests and a general unreliability.

A brief period of relief was achieved when, after complaining about the constant hassles at the association's annual meeting, a competitor offered advice. 'Change the stable, mate,' he advised while outlining the trouble-free virtues of running an all-Asian house. Helpfully he provided the name of a specialist 'ladies' importer who for two thousand dollars a head delivered girls for six-month stints. For a time peace reigned with a steady supply of Thai, Indonesian and Malaysian girls whose uncomplaining servicing capacity hugely exceeded their now ejected predecessors' in both quality and quantity.

But this happy situation was abruptly terminated following a series of raids from immigration authorities. They took a dim view of the girls' 'studies', all having entered the country on educational visas, and soon Len was back to the previous situation.

Complaining to his accountant about it one day he was startled by his suggestion to sell the businesses. This was a hitherto unconsidered concept, none of his previous enterprises having possessed a saleable character. Len's interest heightened when the accountant explained the standard sale price capitalisation formula for a going concern on an earnings basis. Tentatively he approached a real estate firm specialising in business sales and to his surprise, exactly as his accountant had indicated, the agents soberly accepted the enterprises as saleable entities.

Four months later he had two and a half million dollars safely banked with the bonus of being tax-free as a capital gain, another exciting new discovery; not that Len's past relationship with tax authorities could be described as other than fleeting and theoretical.

'What you must do,' the accountant advised Len over a celebratory lunch in the city, 'is deal in leveraged capital, not people. Money is reliable; people are not. Why not look at property?'

And so Len turned towards respectability, a metamorphosis he found disconcerting at first in a 'letting the team down' sense. Despite this infidelity the capital compounding machinations of the activity soon engrossed him.

His first venture was a neglected 80,000 square foot empty industrial building costing seven hundred and fifty thousand dollars. At an additional cost of a hundred and twenty thousand dollars he repainted and subdivided it into ten 8000 square foot units, described them as 8300 square foot areas as no one ever checked the measurements, then leased them at the then going annual rate of two dollars per foot. He strata-titled the units and sold them to small investors on a ten per cent return for a total of $1.66 million.

This exercise was carried out in the name of a company with fictitious shareholders and prior to the annual returns being filed, the shareholding was changed to another set of bogus shareholders to confuse the tax trails. The company then wallowed in a no man's land until eventually struck off by the registration authorities for failure to pay its trifling annual registration fee and so, being no longer in existence, was no longer a tax issue.

A repeat project saw sophisticated added-value refinements. Having agreed on the market rental with tenants, Len found most were agreeable to it being inflated thirty per cent by payment to them of the first three years' rental differential up-front in cash. The tenants had tax-free cash while deducting the higher rental payment from their taxable income. Everyone was happy but most of all Len who yielded even larger profits selling on a ten per cent return.

At the age of thirty-seven Len married. There had been many women in his life, mostly of the dolly-bird variety.

As a hobby Len undertook the management of a promising Samoan middleweight prizefighter, which brought him into the Auckland South Pacific Islands community life. At a wedding reception for his fighter he met his future wife, Selina. She was a university graduate schoolteacher and like many Islanders had a rich racial make-up.

Selina's mother was half Mongolian and half Rarotongan. Her father was half German and half Rarotongan. Such combinations of Polynesian, Oriental and European blood were common throughout the South Pacific although the Oriental lineage was usually Chinese.

Selina's Mongolian grandfather had been a political activist in Ulaanbaatar who had fought against the 1921 Chinese invasion.

Following the communist takeover in 1924 he was a hunted man and had fled south into China. Two years later he reached Shanghai and near starvation, willingly joined a labour recruitment ship destined for Fiji. A storm caused the ship to divert to the Cook Islands to shelter. Her grandfather had jumped ship and hidden in the hills until it departed, then settled into village life, acquiring first a wife and eventually a small trading store.

Selina's influence sobered Len. She polished his speech, encouraging him to have elocution lessons just as his friend Tom had astutely recognised as a desirable self-improvement necessity a quarter century earlier.

Two years after their marriage their daughter Claire was born and Len, by now a respected member of the commercial world, threw himself into a frenzy of commercial and community work. For a happy decade his life was full and satisfying.

It is a curiosity of sizeable wealth that its acquirers never have enough. Swiftly obtained money brings corresponding rapid life-style adjustments. Former luxuries become necessities, which behaviour leads possessors of sudden wealth to be always slightly in arrears.

In Len's case the acquisition of a large waterfront home, a Rolls-Royce replacing his Jaguar, a holiday home at a northern beach, a Sydney apartment, all at the time viewed as absolute essentials, and of plush Auckland and Sydney offices with pretty secretaries and an eighteen-level office tower bearing his name, ensured a constant pressure to maintain the momentum.

By late-1987 his total building asset position valued at nearly two hundred million dollars, against which was a bank debt of one hundred and forty million dollars. After debt servicing and other costs the ever-growing cash surplus was about five million dollars annually.

Tax avoidance was now more difficult adding to the pressure of his situation. Selina urged him to sell up, take the fifty million dollars equity and retire, but Len loved his buildings and the daily stimulation of their management. Selling was anathema.

But the death of his wife in a motor accident followed by the 1987 sharemarket crash brought a change of heart. The subsequent deep recession caused a collapse in commercial buildings' values and brought bank pressure over his reduced equity ratios.

So finally he sold and when all was squared up, his wealth was reduced to twelve million dollars.

When his daughter Claire won a music scholarship in London Len decided to join her. Although not on the scale of triumph he had envisaged a few years earlier, nevertheless in his mind he was still a returning hero of impressive proportion. Under his belt were nearly forty turbulent, amusing and stimulating years but now he had come full circle. It was time to go home.

5

Prior to returning to England with Claire, Len arranged through his travel agent for a six-month lease on a two-bedroom furnished apartment in Kensington. It would serve as a base while he sought out country homes and refamiliarised himself with London. Also it would be convenient for Claire being only two stops on the underground to the Music Academy.

Len was fifty-five years of age and it was exactly thirty-five years since he had left the city of his birth.

Aside from numerous trips between Australia and New Zealand and occasional winter holidays in various South Pacific islands, he had felt no great yearning to travel, unlike most Australians and New Zealanders. It had been a frequent topic of conversation with his daughter who had occasionally suggested trips to Asia, South America or Africa and while Len admitted to curiosity and held a vague expectation that one day he would make the effort, the years had passed and he had not. Contemplating this he concluded his inaction reflected a contentment with his life in the antipodes, particularly in his latter years when his commercial activities had totally preoccupied him.

He had always taken regular holidays but, winter south seas excursions excepted, these had been confined to skiing and trout-fishing in New Zealand. Now his working days were over and his immediate concern was to purchase and furnish a final home, invest the balance of his funds and establish a new life. He planned to join a golf club and perhaps a London club and begin building a new social circle.

Claire was not due to start at the academy for three weeks so he spent the first week with her on the London tourist route. Even though it was only April, well before the onset of the summer tourist hordes, the city was more crowded than he recalled but otherwise it remained the London of his memories and seemed to have changed very little over four decades. Only the East End was different; gone were the ramshackle slums of his youth and in their place, crisp new blocks of sterile flats.

Len spent the second week telephoning estate agents. His

specification was a large manor house and garden within sixty miles of the city costing up to two million pounds, in a village or on the outskirts of a small town. Len inspected fourteen seemingly suitable houses over the next three weeks, at the end of which he concluded the idea of returning home to England had been a huge mistake. Some he saw were broadly satisfactory. What was not was the dismaying ambience. Even in the smallest village uncouth, dead-eyed, loitering nose-ringed yobbos, fast food operators, the racket of bawling factory-hand pop singers and other coarse vulgarities were ubiquitous and tarnished the atmosphere. The reek of decay hung in the air. This was not the idealised image of England as his final destination he had privately savoured for so long.

One Sunday morning while reading one of the real estate supplements in the weekend newspapers, Len's attention was captured by the lead story. It included a photograph of a glorious stately home called Wyebury, the family seat of an aristocrat called Lord Melcup, which was about to go on the market. The article outlined the property in all its magnificent detail. Len realised it fitted precisely what was in his mind despite its more distant location and although no price was mentioned, the sheer scale of the property when compared with those he had already inspected made it obviously beyond his means. Nevertheless he could not resist the temptation and the following day he telephoned the estate agents named in the article as handling negotiations.

He spoke to a Mr Rutledge who did not hide his reservations. 'Lord Melcup is naturally anxious to avoid sightseers, sir,' Rutledge said, arousing Len's ire.

'This may be exactly what I'm looking for,' Len replied. 'If it is I can write a cheque for it now so you need have no concerns. I'll come and see you and you can tell me all about it to save the trouble of a journey in case there's something which disqualifies it.' It was unspoken but both knew this meant its price.

Len met Rutledge in his Bond Street office later that morning. He was well used to dealing with real estate agents and soon had the broker accepting his credentials and seriousness of intent. Rutledge told him the familiar story of the gap between the vendor's expectations and the market. But, he added, if Lord Melcup was a serious seller then he would have to accept the market figure which the agent indicated was circa six million pounds. Len had four million pounds and needed to keep at least half that for investment to provide an income. But something drove him on to take the next step and so an appointment was made to drive with Rutledge to Wyebury the following week.

Like everyone by late middle-age, Len assumed his die was cast but his discovery of Wybury was to render dramatic changes to his life he could never have anticipated.

6

Having accepted Lord Melcup's fishing invitation, Len drove for two hours across central England and arrived at Wyebury around mid-morning. To his relief, Melcup had not forgotten and actually seemed pleased to see him.

'We'll have morning tea then we'll tog you up and have a go at the midday rise,' he said. 'I sometimes think the salmon are rather like us. It's my observation they dine three times a day; dawn, dusk and midday, but you still strike the odd all-day feeder, just like people.'

After morning tea they repaired to a tackle room where Len chose waders and selected a rod from the stand. A ghillie stood by with a luncheon basket and in due course they strolled across the fields to the river.

Melcup invited Len to take the front position while he came in behind, half a mile back. For two hours, up to their waists in the water, the two cast their streamer flies across the current, allowed them to sink and swing round, retrieved them slowly, then in symmetry moved a pace or two downstream after each retrieve. Eventually, the ghillie called that lunch was served so Len wound in and strolled back to where a folding table and chairs had been set up on the river bank. Melcup and Len loosened their wader straps and sat down. The ghillie had laid out cold chicken, sliced beef, salad and freshly baked bread. A bottle of light Pinot Noir waited uncorked.

'There's plenty of fish in the river,' Melcup said. 'It's been getting better every year for the past decade. We have records of each year's catch going back to 1883. I rather expected we'd take one by now but we'll give it another couple of hours after lunch. They'll wait for us.'

And so they had; within ten minutes of entering the water after lunch Len felt the familiar exciting wrench and found himself playing a salmon. A half hour later he beached a fine 14lb fish which the ghillie carried back to show Melcup.

Not long after that Lord Melcup hooked into one. Len left the water and walked back to watch it being played. Eventually

Lord Melcup landed his salmon which, to his excited pleasure, weighed in at 21lbs.

They left the two fish with the ghillie to clean and returned to the house for a light early supper before Len's drive back to London.

It had been a splendid day. Plainly elated by the catch, Melcup was in high spirits. To Len's delight he discussed his future ownership of the property as if it were already the case.

'The thing you have to watch out for, Edwards,' he warned, 'is those damned National Trust lot. You know Wyebury is listed, of course. It's a damned outrage. They come down here once a year and inspect everything. Write for an appointment of course, but one can't stop them. Expect that sort of thing from a Labour government and the Tories quite rightly kicked up a hue and cry when it all began. But what do they do when they take back the reins? Nothing. It's an absolute disgrace. It's always the same,' he continued. 'They come in pairs. Different lot every time but they look the same. There's always a very plain female with spectacles; quite dreadful; never stops babbling, and a silent bearded fellow who says nothing and carries the files.

'Fixed them last year, though,' he continued. 'Made it all worthwhile. They wrote they wanted to inspect the monastery ruins in the back field. Load of rubbish, of course. Just a pile of old rocks. My chaps were going to use them for a wall. What a fuss they made about that. The day they came I had my men put the bull in the back field and lock it in the holding pen under the trees. I went upstairs and watched with binoculars. After they arrived my fellow opened the gate, stuck a stick in the bull's backside and off it shot. It was during the breeding season so it was damned fired up, I can tell you. Came out of the pen like a rocket, spotted the babbling woman and bearded chap and was at 'em like the charge of the Light Brigade. It was wonderful.

'The woman started shrieking while the bearded fellow climbed a tree. When the talking woman realised he wasn't going to save her, she ran to the river. Just made it too, the bull was almost on to her. She plunged in up to her waist while the bull pranced up and down the bank. I told my chaps to stay out of sight and we left them there all afternoon. Just before dusk one of my men slipped a few cows into the far side of the field and off the bull trotted. Never saw those two again. A wonderful day. Wonderful, wonderful,' Lord Melcup repeated dreamily.

Later he farewelled Len. 'Always remember, Edwards,' he said. 'Damned useful things, bulls. There's bearded fellows and ugly women wandering about everywhere these days making a nuisance of themselves. They think private property is immoral. Bulls are the answer. Don't ever forget it.'

Len assured him he wouldn't, thanked him for his hospitality and with a cleaned salmon wrapped on the back seat, drove back to London, more than ever determined to own Wyebury.

'Are you quite sure it's for me?' Philip, Lord Melcup's sole son and heir, queried the delivery man. 'I definitely didn't order this.' Leaning against the wall in his Paddington flat's entrance-way was a glistening new motorbike.

'I know nuffink, sir. I just delifer wot they say. There's a package wif it.' Philip tipped the deliveryman and after he had gone, opened the package. Inside was an envelope and he recognised his father's handwriting. The note was succinct.

Dear Philip,
As you know I disapprove of your choice of career. Indeed I disapprove of any career other than that of a gentleman, a path you have inexplicably chosen to reject. But I would not wish that disagreement to divide us and forward this gift as a gesture of goodwill. I gather these machines are much coveted by young men and trust you will find it useful.
Your loving father.

The old boy must be bonkers, Philip thought. Anyway, it will be no use to me in the Antarctic. I wonder what I can get for it.

For unbeknown to Lord Melcup, only the previous week his son had been selected for a six-month duration, United Nations-sponsored, Cambridge University scientific research team to the Antarctic to measure water temperatures and monitor the melting ice cap threat.

Len exchanged contracts for the purchase of Wyebury including all of its existing furnishings two weeks after returning from the salmon fishing visit.

The price was six million pounds. Len paid a five hundred thousand pound deposit with settlement set down for one year's time. When he proposed this, justifying the delay to allow time to allegedly tidy up his affairs in the antipodes, Lord Melcup willingly accepted saying it suited him also in allowing time to reorganise his life. Len had twelve months to find six million pounds or a minimum of five million pounds as the grander scale of life Wyebury represented required a much higher investment income than he had budgeted.

But how? In recent years he had been very much richer than his current four million pound capital but that had been dissipated in the 1990 global property collapse. He flirted with the thought of returning to Australia and undergoing a year of frenzied activity. But market conditions were unfavourable and the long-term nature of commercial property activity made achieving his goal in the time available unlikely. Nevertheless it became his fall-back position for he also knew that one king-hit deal, perhaps with a large empty industrial building or a near vacant office building, could achieve his goal. It could be tight for a couple of years and Wyebury might have to carry some debt and be closed while he completed such a transaction.

The thought of once more going to the well didn't please him. He had cut his ties with all of that. It would be totally contrary to the bigger plan; time was of the essence, not just financially but with his life and there had to be an easier and quicker way.

He avidly studied the financial and business press looking for an angle but nothing arose to stimulate an idea. It was while doing this he read an article on the economy quoting a prominent merchant banker with an accompanying photograph. Len recognised Tom whom he had not spoken to in forty years. The photo showed a plumpish silver-haired man but despite that Len immediately recognised his boyhood friend. He picked up the telephone book, looked up Tom's firm named in the article and called him. That night the two were reacquainted and over dinner were soon laughing together as they recalled their youthful days in London and Paris. Each outlined his history.

On returning from Paris Tom had landed a clerk's job with a small privately owned merchant bank. He had thrown himself at his work with gusto: behaviour, he told Len, which captured his seniors' attention as it was uncharacteristic of the predominantly Hooray Henry types then employed in the City. He had quickly risen through the ranks, experiencing all of the firm's activities from brokerage to investment advice and by the time he was thirty, was the bank's highest paid employee. Despite being married and offered a partnership he had plunged out on his own with capital provided by a wealthy client in return for twenty per cent equity.

'The foundation of this activity is bullshit and imagery,' Tom explained. 'No matter how good you are, if the image is not right you can't get off the ground, which is why I got rid of my accent with elocution lessons. That was absolutely essential.'

'That's all very well,' Len said. 'But how on earth did you build such a large organisation against all of the established competition?'

'First I bought from a liquidator, a 110-year-old Leeds drapery shop company which was about to be wound up,' Tom explained. 'I changed its name to Frederick La Font and Company to add a desirable Continental touch and paid a small fee to accounting firms in Zurich, Paris and Brussels to shove our name on their doors to give an international flavour on our letterhead. I rented ground floor premises in Dover Street and paid for naming rights for the whole building, then planted a pretty Dutch receptionist in the foyer to reinforce the Continental flavour and we were away laughing. At that stage it was basically a charade but it worked. You should have seen our stationery. We used a slightly old-fashioned typeface and under our name had 'Founded 1845' which, as far as the company structure was concerned, was literally true. Within three years to all intents we were part of the establishment.

'Shortly after we started I had a holiday in Paris. I was wandering through the flea market and for a few quid bought a large early nineteenth-century oil painting portrait of a dignified-looking grandee type; God knows who he was. I carted it back to London and had it fitted into a lavish gilt frame with a small brass plaque set in its base with the words, 'Our Founder, Frederick La Font – 1815-1892'. We hung it in the foyer and it completed the imagery nicely.'

'And everyone just accepted all of that?' Len quizzed.

'Oh absolutely. I'll give you an example. Over the years we've acquired lots of expensive antique furniture for the offices so recently Sotheby's valued everything for insurance purposes. They put thirty-five thousand pounds on the painting because, they said, it was the only known portrait of Frederick La Font in existence. That tells you how well established our name is now after thirty years in business.'

'It's a wonder a journalist has never sussed all of this out,' Len said.

Tom laughed. 'You must be kidding. Journalists when worked right are our biggest allies. Last year we celebrated the firm's 150th anniversary and the Financial Times ran a special four-page supplement with a biographic account of La Font which I made up, although they didn't know that of course. They had an artist sketch La Font from the flea-market painting and filled half the first page with it. We had a huge party with nearly two thousand guests and the Chancellor of the Exchequer, the Governor of the Bank of England and the French ambassador all gave speeches. I was killing myself with laughter remembering I was just an East End lad not too long ago and thinking, if they only knew the truth. Mind you, the truth's never a big issue with any of those types. You should have heard the French ambassador speak movingly about La Font's significance in nineteenth-century French banking history.'

'Did you make money from the start?' Len enquired. 'That's what really counts.'

'Absolutely. That was the most important thing about becoming part of the financial establishment. The other stuff, the name, the building and so on, that's just playing the game, showing you belong and know how to behave and won't embarrass anyone with the wrong tie or knife and fork. It's necessary to get started. But this business is different from any other. Everyone else in commerce becomes passionate about what they actually do, you know, making things or selling goods or providing some sort of service. But with merchant banking only one thing counts and that's money.

'Talk to sharemarket and finance people and you'll find they're big on recreation; skiing, tropical holidays, country homes with horses and all that showy stuff, but it's really just a facade. Their only real passion is money. Put two of them together anywhere and within five minutes their conversation will come round to that and stay there. So once we started to crack it no one cared much about anything else. We were in. We had money.'

'You make it sound almost easy,' Len said.

'Well, to begin with I took some sizeable clients with me and worked my butt off for a few years, which in the City at that time was fairly unusual. Also, we introduced a whole new employment approach for those days which sorted out the men from the boys. We were the first to reward dealers on a commission basis. With us in those days you ate what you killed and that certainly paid dividends although it's normal now. The funny thing is we still do it differently. We're now the only outfit that doesn't pay commissions.

'I've got a simple test for sorting out the real thinkers from the run-of-the-mill types. I get them talking and sit and listen. If they trot out garbage like "window of opportunity" instead of "opportunity" or "the bottom line" for "outcome", then we know they're basically humdrum, regardless of academic qualification. Anyway, it's all different now. These days finance attracts quality people but when I began the City competed with the army as a receptacle for drudges and dullards, just like the Irish used to put plain girls into nunneries, so the competition was non-existent.'

'My way was different,' Len interrupted. 'When I started employing executives I'd wangle a reason to have them drive me somewhere. If they were careful drivers, and these days most younger people are thanks to all the intimidation and excessive carry-on about road safety, then I didn't employ them. I wanted buggers with a bit of spark and get up and go; not mice.'

'Yes; I agree with that,' Tom said. 'Ultimately it's the quality of your people which your fate is riding on. It certainly was with us. Nowadays we never advertise for staff. We don't have to as we receive over three hundred unsolicited applications from graduates every year and we usually take on two.'

'Rather you than me having to sort through that number,' Len said.

'It's actually quite easy,' Tom said breezily. 'We simply draw a circle fifty miles around London and decline all applicants outside of it. That automatically cuts out the commerce degree types and the Kevins and other rubbish and we're left with about a dozen to interview.'

'So you had a straight run ahead all the way once you were up and running?' Len queried.

'Absolutely,' Tom said. 'Five years after starting we owned our own building and had about thirty staff plus genuine branch offices in New York and Zurich. After that it just grew and grew. I've thought about going public but then I ask myself, why bother? I don't need more money and I like the mystique of a private house without the pressure to constantly do better. That's the biggest weakness of the public company system. There are times in the market when the going is rough and it's smart to just roll with the punches and wait.

'Public companies rarely do that. They're performance-obsessed so in bad times they push against the flow and invariably get into trouble. The bank's been so successful it's completely changed from what it originally was. Now, effectively our biggest client is ourselves, just investing our own wealth. We confine ourselves to a few major clients but never get too involved and certainly never own anything. Bugger that. We just clip the ticket of anything good going past.'

'I certainly agree with you there,' Len said. 'I thought I had it made when I owned buildings all over the place but I've learned my lesson since about the virtues of liquidity and flexibility.'

'Dead right,' Tom said. 'And never more so than in today's rapidly changing world. Another thing I discovered,' he continued, 'is that when it comes to selling intangible services, always charge more than your competitors. You not only make more but the client thinks he's dealing with the very best and is immensely grateful to be even given the time of day. Human behaviour is certainly funny but to crack it big in the money sense, it's the most important thing to study.'

'I learned that early,' Len said. 'The problem was I stayed with petty schemes too long. I think it was their humour that captivated me but once I became big, I found nothing was different. Basically it still got down to dealing with people and success depended on how well you did that.'

Later in the evening Len told Tom about Wyebury.

Tom responded harshly. 'You're a silly bugger. I suspect you've just blown an eighth of your capital waving goodbye to your deposit. You're telling me that in one year in a country now foreign to you, you plan to make as much again as the result of a lifetime's work. Not very logical let alone likely, old man.'

'I want this place desperately,' Len said. 'There's got to be a way, even if it means risking my capital.'

'Crazy, crazy, crazy,' Tom snapped. 'Commerce isn't like that any more. It's much tougher in the new competitive global culture and no one outside of finance really makes serious money any more. It's all one hell of a struggle compared with the way it used to be. It's just too bloody competitive with nothing left in for the other fellow. There are no gaps anywhere to just do conventional things and prosper. To make big lumps of money quickly today you have to come up with radical new ideas and very few people do that.'

'If that's the case then that's what I shall do,' Len replied, but in his heart he knew his friend was right. Probably he had blown his deposit. Still, he had no intention of writing it off without having a go first. A few weeks of solid thinking, reading the newspapers, plotting and scheming, was his initial plan. Something would come up. It always had in the past and he had never had the motivation he felt so strongly now. Later the two men parted having agreed to keep in touch.

'Anything you dream up, run past me first,' Tom had said. 'I'll be surprised if we can't help you with it. In this game we deal with absolutely everything so go ahead and surprise me.'

Len returned to the apartment determined to do precisely that.

9

Frustrated, Len flung the business and finance section of the *Sunday Times* on the floor. He'd read every article in his search for an angle but nothing seemed right. Bullish accounts of individual sectors or particular companies' prospects would spark his interest only to collapse when the projections were spelt out for ten to twenty per cent growth over the year ahead. He needed to at least double his capital to buy Wyebury and have the necessary investment cash to furnish it and live in a manner appropriate to his new role as lord of the manor and he needed to do it quickly.

A twenty per cent price rise would be more than enough to double his funds if he leveraged the investment and bought futures but when he had raised this with Tom over dinner the previous day, he had been strongly cautioned about this strategy.

'If you work it out mathematically,' Tom had explained, 'you'll find levering to compound your wealth essentially requires risking all of that wealth. We can put a stop/loss on any exposure you gear up but it becomes pointless unless it allows some meaningful leeway. So, is this really a risk you want at this stage of your life? It might work, in which case you would be laughing. Conversely you could blow the lot if some other factor comes into play, which happens all too often.'

'But we're talking about blue-chip stocks,' Len protested. 'Surely their predictability is more assured.'

'Think who writes this bullish stuff,' Tom responded. 'They're either business reporters or sharebrokers. Show me a rich business journalist and then I'll take note of his financial advice. You know the old saying that if you can't do it you teach it. Well, there should be a second leg to that. If you can't do it you teach it and if you can't teach it you write about it.

'Basically what you're proposing amounts to gambling and with gambling, every winner has a matching loser. Don't delude yourself that if you take a positive position on a particular investment based on your rational view you're better informed than the person who sold to you. He's obviously taken a negative stance based on his information so ultimately it's just a toss-up and the luckiest wins. And as for sharebrokers, well they're just hucksters, even if sincere. Surely it was the same with real estate agents when you were big in property down in Australia, wasn't it?'

Len thought about it and conceded the truth of Tom's comments. He recalled in his heyday the daily deluge of commercial property proposals from real estate agents. They were always sincere but none understood the subtleties of the business. If they did they would be doing it themselves, not acting as brokers. Their primary value was as an information source. And their submissions were always too optimistic in terms of likely rental and capital growth. Why would sharebrokers be different?

Morosely he reached for the newspaper's magazine supplement. The cover did not dispel his gloom. It showed a penguin colony on the edge of the sea against the backdrop of a snow-covered mountain. The cover story's title was 'The Antarctic – The Last Frontier'. He turned the pages desultorily. Photos of bearded men, penguins, seals, maps, a shrine to Captain Scott; God it was boring.

A picture of a bleak room filled with laughing men held his attention and he read the caption. 'Every summer up to 3500 scientists drawn from all over the world spend up to six months at McMurdo base engaged in an astonishing range of scientific research activities,' it said. Len stared at the photograph, the nub of an idea forming. Around 3500 men, probably highly paid, nothing to spend money on, confined to the single location for six months. This was a heaven-sent opportunity. His mind raced, seeking ideas of how to mine this situation. Excited, he returned to the front of the magazine and read the article carefully.

He learnt that the Antarctic was a territorial no man's land, that an international treaty guaranteed access to scientists and researchers without impediment subject to results being shared, that ships could pull up right alongside the McMurdo American base for the six summer months after ice-breakers cleared access in early September, and that for half a year in the winter months the region was in total darkness.

He read of the growing number of tourist ships sailing into the bases and that no authority existed to stop or control them.

The legal issues particularly held his attention. Essentially the territory belonged to no one despite claims by some countries. The international agreement prohibited all mining but otherwise it was a no man's land, open to all. He read of the airstrip at McMurdo built by the Americans on which anyone could land and the nearby Scott base run by New Zealanders linked to McMurdo by a road at which a further several hundred scientists were ensconced over the summer months.

Len finished the article and made himself a cup of coffee, his mind churning. Something intuitively told him his quest was over. Now came the challenge. A lifetime's experience had taught him; if he looked for it, he always found an angle. Some 3500 highly paid men confined for six months in the one isolated location with no spending outlets represented massive potential. It was a golden crop just waiting to be harvested. Even taking only one hundred dollars a week per head off them over the duration represented eight million dollars. But how? Mostly they were Americans. Probably as scientists and professionals they received at least a hundred thousand dollar annual salaries and in many cases more, given the hardship posting. A hundred dollars a week was ridiculous. If he could find the right angle, especially with the single men, five hundred dollars per week per head was perfectly feasible. Over six months that was forty million dollars. And in the Antarctic, a no man's land, tax avoidance would be a piece of cake.

Suddenly the light dawned. What was it they would be missing most? The answer was obvious. He recalled his original love-letter venture forty years earlier with Tom. It was exactly the same market and while it was almost two decades since his involvement in the massage parlour business, the fundamentals could hardly have changed. He knew the ropes. He needed a ship but this was something outside of his experience. Len was due to have dinner with Tom that night. Tom would know the answer to this and other problems. For the first time since he had seen Wyebury a month earlier, Len's spirits soared.

When Claire returned to the apartment late that afternoon she was delighted to find her father in a highly excited state. Despite her protests he insisted on opening a bottle of wine to celebrate. 'We're going to have Wyebury, my girl. I've finally latched on to something.'

Claire had increasingly worried about her father in the time they had been in London. Her own life there was full of excitement with the music school, new friends and the joys of exploring London, all of which magnified her distress at her father's increasing melancholy.

'I think I've finally found the answer,' Len told his daughter as they sipped their wine. 'I'm having dinner with Tom tonight and he will know the solution to one or two of the fish-hooks. It's a rather unusual investment situation. I'll be away for about six months so you will be here on your own. I don't suppose you'll be too unhappy about that anyway. I'll have to go back to Sydney but it's a chance in a lifetime so I'll grab it.'

'But what is it, Dad? Tell me about it.'

'Well, it's a little complicated unless you want a lecture in finance and that sort of thing so rather than earbash you I suggest you just leave it to me. I'll make sure the flat rental is paid and leave you with plenty of money but if any problems arise you can always call Tom. Perhaps you should think about having one of your friends as a flatmate for company.'

'But why would I have to call Tom? Won't I be able to telephone you?'

'Probably. Possibly. I don't know yet. There's no danger or anything but the proposition will involve me in some fairly remote locations so I'm not sure.'

'Well I'm really, really pleased you're so happy, Dad, so I hope it all works out, but now I must get ready. We're all going out to a restaurant early and then on to a party so I'm being picked up in an hour. Even if you don't want to tell me about it just yet you know I'm interested. You never know, I might be able to make some suggestions,' Claire laughed as she left the room.

I bloody well hope not, Len thought to himself and he too left the room to change for dinner with Tom.

10

Life as a financier had immunised Tom to new venture promoters' optimism but such was Len's excitement as he recounted his idea, his friend's enthusiasm was contagious.

'You just might be on to something big here, mate. I glanced at the Antarctic article this morning but didn't bother reading it. The face value assessment certainly looks good if you're sure of your facts. Around 3500 mainly youngish men, probably highly paid, locked in the one spot and few if any women present. Right. I accept there's no questions or doubts there. A lovely market ripe for plucking. At two or three hundred dollars a pop they can afford it and should be good for two or three dips a week each. That's serious money over six months.

'The question is access. Can anyone stop you? If you can deliver the goods you could really clean up. I must say it's a novel ruse but why hasn't someone thought of it by now? There must be some special difficulty you haven't considered.'

'Come on, Tom. That's a bit weak. You could say that about anything. There has to be a first time for everything and I'm it for this just like we were all those years ago with the love-letters business. It's exactly the same market in principle. I've got about four months to organise everything before the ice-breakers go in at the beginning of September. As I see it, the big question is the ship. What special things might be required for the Antarctic? Will the cost be prohibitive outfitting it into bedrooms and bathrooms; that sort of thing. I know nothing about shipping.'

'Well I can tell you this,' Tom said. 'You'll have no trouble on that front. It's one industry we won't touch. Shipping has been stuffed since the advent of containerisation. Ships are just about given away today and can be hired for peanuts. They're probably the most oversupplied commodity in the modern world. A friend of mine, David Levy, is a shipping broker. I'll chat to him on Monday morning so come in for lunch on Tuesday and I'll let you know what he recommends. But what about the girls?'

'I'm not worried about that,' Len said. 'I'll make a few calls back home and find out who's active in the field then commission someone to broker the supply. The question is how many we need.'

After that the two had a raucous evening conjecturing such weighty topics as the number of girls required, their individual servicing capacity and just how much they could get away with charging for them.

11

On arrival at Tom's office the following Tuesday Len found him buzzing with enthusiasm.

'Bloody hell, Len. I think you've struck oil. Yesterday I had one of our analysts research the Antarctic situation. You're right about the number of men down there over the summer period and also the access issue. No one can stop you. Apparently the ice edge acts like a wharf and you can tie a ship up right alongside the base. But the best news is from Levy, the shipping broker I mentioned. I took the liberty of telling him in confidence what you wanted the ship for and straight away he put his finger on the solution. You're going to be bloody thrilled about this. Mind you, it should have occurred to us on Saturday night.

'What you need, he said, is a cruise ship. It's already outfitted into hundreds of bedrooms with all the facilities you want. You could just step into the operator's shoes with the ballrooms and bars and saunas and shopping arcades and nightclubs and restaurants and everything. It's tailor-made for this operation. I'm becoming really excited about it – 3500 highly paid and no doubt bloody bored men and no women is one hell of a market. Probably it's the equivalent of a city of 60,000 in spending capacity only you will be the sole shopkeeper. It's a dream situation. You could have restaurants and bookshops and all sorts of things over and above the girls, all earning heaps.'

'Of course,' Len exclaimed. 'A cruise ship. It's so obvious. Why didn't I think of that? I've already thought about some of those other ideas since Saturday,' Len continued. 'I'm certainly going to be busy organising things, which is the big problem. I've got to do it this coming southern summer and when I started a list of things to organise it seemed endless. I mean basically I've got to cover every contingency for a sizeable community for six months. Things like a doctor and sickbay and food and cooks and laundry; the list goes on and on the more I think about it. But the big thing is I have to do it this year if I'm to have Wyebury. It's going to be one hell of a circus, which is a pity in terms of exploiting its real potential but even so it should still be good enough to get me the amount I need. The cruise ship angle is terrific. The trouble is, where do I get one and how much will it cost? And maybe none are available.'

'That's the really good news I've got for you. Levy came up with a great idea. Apparently when the Russians were looking for new ways to earn foreign currency back in the early 1970s they latched on to the cruise ship market. The old Soviet Union's problem was that apart from raw materials they couldn't sell anything to the West because their manufactured stuff was so bloody awful. So they had a shot at the cruise market because even if their service wasn't up to scratch their arbitrary cost structures meant normal pricing went out the window and they could easily undercut Western competition. After all, the main thing with a cruise ship was the places it visited and those were accessible to everyone.

'According to Levy,' Tom continued, 'like everything else the Russians did it was a bungle and the result was they built dozens and dozens of different size cruise ships and apparently there're swags of them, in some cases never used, just lying idle in St Petersburg and other ports. Levy knows the fellow in charge of all their shipping and reckons you'll cut a fantastic deal. He says the Russians will be over the moon as they would never expect to see many of those ships operational again. He claims you'll get one for a song. All you have to do is to list what you want by way of services, write it into a specification and lay it before them for a price.

'The great thing is that apart from organising the girls there's nothing else you need do as you can subcontract the whole shooting box to the Russians. That's always the key to doing anything complicated, in my experience. The hands-on approach is crazy if you can subcontract everything out. That's how we operate here on behalf of clients. We use a small in-house team of analysts solely for our own purposes to ascertain areas of activities we should be in.'

'I'm really grateful for your help,' Len said. 'I must admit it would never have occurred to me but your way makes it all sound so simple. When can I meet Levy and go to St Petersburg?'

'Get stuck in. Use your imagination and try and think of every contingency. Just write it all out and bring the list in here and we'll tidy it up for you into contractual form. That shouldn't take long so I suggest we book to fly to St Petersburg late next week. I'll get Levy to organise flights and hotels and a meeting with the Russians. You can meet those costs but Levy will get his commission from the Russians. I'm coming with you for a laugh and I might be useful with a few thoughts along the way. I must say it's such a bloody amusing idea I want to help with the planning, which brings me to another point.

'You remember I told you about Andrew Potter, my chief executive? He will take over from me in a few years but he's chafing at the bit and I suspect is getting a little bored. I don't want to lose him but I think a break would do him a power of good. Also, doing something fairly wild and radical like this would be good experience for him. Like most young fellows in this industry he's had a fairly sheltered life so an earthy hands-on management experience would be a useful thing. And this exercise is about as earthy and offbeat as any imaginable. Also, he's not married so he's a free agent.'

'What are you proposing?' Len asked.

'It's entirely over to you but I think the scale of this exercise is too much for you alone,' Tom replied. 'Not just you but anyone. You need a right-hand man to help and talk through problems and take over if you get sick or God knows, whatever might arise. It's ridiculous trying to tackle this on your own. As I say it's your decision but if you're willing then I'm prepared to loan you Potter for a few months. I've sounded him out and he's a starter. He thinks it's an enormous hoot. You can cover his normal salary and of course any expenses.'

Len needed no convincing of the logic of this suggestion. Indeed, as Tom was speaking he felt a burden lift from his shoulders. He hadn't met Potter but if Tom recommended him then that was good enough and he readily accepted his friend's offer.

There are two principal categories of merchant banking employees. One is the East End barrow boy smarty possessing an innate cunning and a natural feel for trading. Selling fifty million pounds of Polish government debt securities or a truckload of stolen video recorders requires essentially the same animal intuitive cunning. The City, which once confined its employees to the upper social strata's rejects, had now in the new free market environment discovered the value of street-smart, Cockney wide boys. They received monstrously high incomes, occupied a common trading room and were kept well out of sight, or more particularly earshot, to prevent their appalling assault on the language offending the bank's clientele's sensibilities.

The top category of employee was more in line with the City's traditions. These were sophisticated and refined Oxbridge graduates, necessary for dealing with corporate chairmen and treasurers who provided an elegant intellectual dimension to the bank's strategies. The preferred choice were those with classics degrees although a point could be stretched to the broader humanities, notably history. It was considered, correctly, that such a choice of academic pursuit demonstrated an enquiring mind. These senior executives occupied large, antique-furnished, individual, computerless office suites. Even their rarely used telephones were out of sight.

The City did employ redbrick university graduates of the cell-phone carrying category, possessing commerce and accounting degrees. These pony-tailed and earringed clones, gazing at computers in a basement room, were easily replaceable fodder and were confined to mundane backroom management and buying and selling order-taking activities that stretched the limits of their capabilities. They rated slightly beneath the more attractive secretaries in the bank's highly stratified status pecking order. The always out-of-touch press referred to them enviously as yuppies, blithely ignorant of their insignificance.

Andrew slotted firmly into the top category. At Oxford he had read classics and medieval church history, an experience that transformed him from a passive agnostic to a militant atheist. He was the eldest son of a bookish public school history master and had grown up in relative affluence thanks to his mother, the daughter of a wealthy city stockbroker who had brought to the marriage a financial wherewithal rarely enjoyed by schoolmasters.

Tom called Andrew into his office and introduced him. He was a tall, good-looking, fair-haired young man in his early thirties and Len felt a rapport with him at first sight.

'It will take me a day to tidy things up then I'm entirely yours,' Andrew said. 'I suggest we use my office to work out the specification and what we have to do ourselves. The trick will be to pass as much as possible on to the Russians and reduce our role to over-seeing the operation.'

After two days the two had everything complete. They decided it would be wise, for language reasons, to employ their own doctor and Andrew advised the name of a medical placement centre in London. They deferred dealing with this until after the St Petersburg trip to ensure it was all go before making any commitment.

'It seems to me it would be desirable to cut a deal with a private flight contractor,' Andrew said one morning. 'Almost certainly we'll overlook things or need to bring in stuff. Also, with a hundred or so girls things are bound to go awry with some of them and replacements will be needed. I had our researchers on to it and apparently there are plenty of operators in Australia or New Zealand who could supply regular flights. It will be a question of cost so I've drafted a tender document and faxed this through to six of them. We should have their prices within twenty-four hours.'

The successful tenderer was a Sydney private flight operator called Bruce Harding. Len spoke to him by telephone.

'I don't own a suitable plane for this myself,' he said, 'but I can access one we can use on a flight time charge basis. There's a surplus of the bloody things right now so it won't be a problem.'

The two agreed to meet in Sydney and thrash out final details when Len and Andrew arrived in early September.

Andrew had another idea. 'I've been thinking about how the fellows are going to pay,' he said. 'Chances are they carry no cash down there; after all, why should they? But they'll all have credit cards and even if they haven't got them with them, so long as they can give us the details we can function.

'But lots will have wives so we need to be careful what name we use. I've come up with a few such as Scientific Book Supplies and also the High Risk Venture Fund so they'll be able to explain away the expenditures if they have to. I'll get our back-room boys to organise accounts with all the major credit card companies. Also, Tom's opening a dozen interest-earning bank accounts in different tax havens for you into which the credit card companies can transfer the funds regularly.

'As I see it everything is pretty much in hand. We'll keep our fingers crossed all goes okay in St Petersburg next week and if so, then all you have to do is organise the girls. You've got four months for that. I don't think the bank can be much help on that score,' he laughed.

'I've already made some enquiries,' Len said. 'I telephoned a fellow I used to know in this business in Auckland. He's retired now but he put me on to someone who gave me the name of a character in Sydney called Rippin. I've spoken to him and he's undertaken to rustle up a hundred or so good-lookers but says it will take him about three months for that many so I'll call him next week, all going well with the Russians, and give him the go-ahead.'

'It's a funny thing,' Andrew said. 'If you told me when I came up from Oxford that I was going to end up organising a floating brothel I would have been outraged. Yet somehow it seems like a career high-point and a culmination of all my training, including studying the classics. It sounds absurd but I'm really excited about this project. It's so damned basic in meeting a human need. So much of what we do here seems esoteric and removed from the everyday realities. And I have a gut feeling there'll be a lot of laughs along the way.'

'Oh you can rely on that,' Len replied. 'Believe me, I know. I suppose all sorts of management problems will arise and have to be dealt with but as for the basic activity, well, you can forget about rationality. This is a business about behaviour and emotions. You'll get your fill of laughs, my friend. Too bloody many, in fact; you'll see.'

'I don't know about too many,' Potter said. 'There's not a lot of gaiety in banking. As far as I'm concerned, let the laughter begin.'

The day before they left for Russia Tom popped his head around the door.

'I've been speaking to Levy,' he said. 'We're being picked up on the tarmac in St Petersburg so scrub the wheelchairs.'

'Good show,' Andrew replied.

'What was that all about?' Len asked after Tom had gone.

Andrew rose and opened a cupboard from which he pulled out a flat portable contraption of wheels and metallic limbs. He unfolded it into a wheelchair.

'We usually take one of these with us to places like the Middle East or eastern Europe,' he said. 'They're absolutely essential. When we get off the plane Tom climbs in and I push him. We get through immigration and customs ahead of everyone else. It can save a highly frustrating hour or two. Sometimes we use them here with rugby internationals if we have lousy seats. That way we get placed on the ground at the halfway mark.'

'My God,' Len exclaimed. 'You buggers think of everything.'

Andrew reached up to a ledge in the cupboard and pulled down a stubby white stick. He pushed a button and it telescoped into a white cane.

'This is a variation for the developed world,' he said. 'We use these with dark glasses when we go to places like New York. That way we go through in about ten minutes flat. Much more convenient to cart about than the portable wheelchair but it only works in the civilised world. There's not much sympathy for the blind in the Middle East. Tom tried it once in Amman and it was no use at all. Instead everyone tried to pick his pocket and steal his bags.'

'You'd look bloody silly if anyone ever sussed you,' Len said.

'No we wouldn't. What could they do about it? If we want to get about in a wheelchair or carry a white stick, that's our business. Actually, everyone benefits. It makes people feel good making way for us so we're happy and they're happy. Now what more could you ask than that?'

12

Len, Tom, Andrew and Levy were shown into the State Shipping Director's office. Mr Zirovsky, porcine and perspiring, rose from behind an enormous desk and advanced on them, arms extended, gold teeth glinting and effusively bearhugged Levy, who was obviously an old acquaintance. After introductions to the others he waved them to the late-Stalin-era sofas.

'Velcome, velcome to St Pedersburg, gendlemen,' and he called through the open door for coffee. For a few minutes the group pattered politely about St Petersburg, a city only Levy among the visitors was familiar with. Eventually Zirovsky terminated this innocuous chatter.

'Enuff, gendlemen. Ve vill show you our great city. I haf some very nice young ladies for you as interpreters and guides.' And he added pointedly, 'Zey are very intelligent young ladies. You will find them very helpful. But now, let us perhaps do some business.'

From his briefcase Len produced a copy of his specification and handed it to the director. For a few minutes the room was silent while Zirovsky read through the dozen pages. Finally he looked up and beamed.

'Dere are no problems. We haf many nice ships for you. Tomorrow night I haf a price. But first I must know. Vere is this ship to go?'

'Nowhere,' said Len quickly, then, correcting himself he added, 'that is nowhere once it's got there. It will be permanently anchored in the Antarctic for six months. The specifications require a minimum 140 insulated single three-quarter bedded cabins, each with its own bathroom and shower and continuous heating but if there are more rooms, it doesn't matter.'

'Ve haf many suitable boats,' Mr Zirovsky assured them and for an hour the group discussed the requirements, each item eliciting a 'No problem' from the director. One detail not mentioned in the specification remained.

'Mr Zirovsky,' Len said, 'there's a final vital matter. All the crew must speak English and be fairies.'

'English is no problem. We haf such crews now. But vairies. Vot iz vairies?'

Levy intervened. 'Homosexuals,' he said forcefully, adding, 'It is most important.'

'Ah,' boomed the director. 'Vairies. Now I understand,' and extending a limp wrist he wriggled his monstrous bulk grotesquely in his seat, fluttered his eyelashes and winked playfully.

'Vairies are no problem. We haf za vairies stewards. Russia is a modern nation, gendlemen,' he added by way of explanation. Then his face clouded. 'But za engine-room crew. Perhaps is a problem. Regrettably there are still some shortages in our new Russia. Za vairy stewards, yes. But perhaps ve haf difficulties with engine-room crew and also za captain.'

Twenty minutes' discussion yielded a compromise. All the stewards and non-engineering crew would be guaranteed homosexuals. Additionally, the State Shipping Department would use its best endeavours to provide a full homosexual ship's complement.

Len emphasised the importance of the specification. 'You see, Mr Zirovsky, all our passengers will be young ladies. We want no interference to them in their work.'

'Ah,' cried the director triumphantly. 'Za mystery is explained. You haf a floating universidy, gendlemen. Ve Russians, ve luf the study. Next only to our great Russian music this ve respect most. I understand now. Za young ladies must not be distracted from dere studies. I shall delifer za vairies.'

As arranged, Zirovsky arrived at the party's hotel the following evening. He brought along three breathtaking young women who took Len, Andrew and Tom off to show them some of the city's attractions and who, despite shortcomings in English, proved to be as promised, very intelligent young ladies indeed.

Levy and Zirovsky spent the evening negotiating and by midnight all was resolved.

Seven days from signing the contract Len would deposit half a million American dollars to the credit of the State Shipping Department's Zurich bank account. A further instalment of a half million American dollars would be paid on the ship's arrival in Sydney on 6 September and thereafter, for the duration of the hire, half a million each month. On arrival in the Antarctic an additional one million American was to be paid to a Cyprus law firm's account, this latter proviso being a gentlemen's understanding as it would not arise in the contract. Len would receive an annually renewable option for a further ten years on identical terms.

The total all-up cost would be four and a half million dollars against which Len hoped to gross nearly fifty million over the six-month period. The girls would receive ten million and he had budgeted approximately two million for the aeroplane and other ancillary expenses. The chosen vessel was the Olga Buskova, named after a thirteenth-century Russian heroine who had persuaded the women of her village to a mass suicide rather than endure violation by the rumoured oncoming Mongol hordes. As it transpired the Mongols had by-passed her village, a fact which apparently added special lustre to her sacrifice and legendary purity in the eyes of storytellers.

After a brief and unsuccessful life as a Black Sea cruise ship, the Olga Buskova had been transferred to St Petersburg where it had been laid up for eight years. Farewelling the group at the airport, Zirovsky promised the ship would arrive in Sydney in mint condition on 6 September to take aboard its passengers.

'You vill be very happy, gendlemen. And the crew,' whereupon the director affected a startlingly lewd mincing writhing, 'I promise you. Zey will be za vairies.'

13

Len attended an appointment in London with Mr Rose, of Rose, Rose & Sons, Medical Placement Services (est. 1910) in a dingy Soho first-floor office.

Mr Rose listened patiently while Len outlined his requirement. When he was finished Rose clasped his hands together and launched into a mournful monologue.

'Oh dear me. A hardship posting. They so often end in tears. One's tempted to decline supplying them altogether. Sometimes I think things would be much happier in these cases if there were no doctor present. You see, Mr Edwards, your requirement isn't unusual. We get them all the time. Saudi Arabian oil bases, Siberian forestry schemes, Brazilian mining camps; but it always ends up with complaints and sometimes litigation. Unfortunately the only candidates for foreign hardship postings are those gentlemen prevented through some slight mishap from practising here. No one else wants to go.'

'Well, can you get me someone?' Len asked anxiously.

Mr Rose shook his head, a worried look crossing his face.

'Hardship postings are such a problem. There are only two categories of doctors available for them and they're the newly graduated or the disgraced. We have a policy here not to place the newly graduated. Goodness me, the legal fees; it's a wonder we're still here. No. It's far better for graduates to go north. Bradford, Newcastle, those sort of places. Practise on the lower orders and the unemployed. Nobody minds losing a few of them while they learn. The working classes are always unhappy and expect the worst from life. And if someone dies they never blame the doctor. It's a curious thing but they think all doctors are brilliant.'

'Disgraced for what?' Len enquired anxiously.

'Oh, nothing serious, Mr Edwards. Generally there are three categories. There's the malpractice chaps, the sexual molesters and the disorderly. That's usually drunkenness or bankruptcy; as I say, nothing serious. Right now we have four sexual molesters available but to be honest we have no trouble placing them. We send them to East Africa and never have any complaints so long as they're Christian countries.'

'Well, I don't think one of those would be at all suitable, Mr Rose,' Len said, 'and I don't like the sound of the malpractice lot.'

'I wouldn't rush to judgement on that, Mr Edwards,' Rose responded. 'Often they're the very best doctors. They do tend to be a little forgetful, leaving instruments in people after operations; that sort of thing. And they can sometimes be weak on diagnosis. Otherwise they're perfectly satisfactory, particularly for hardship postings.'

'No,' said Len firmly.

'Well, if you're quite certain,' Mr Rose continued. 'Actually, we have no problems placing them either. They go to Africa as well. In fact,' he added brightening, 'we've got one of them right now running Tanzania's largest hospital, another is chief surgeon in Kampala and another professor of medicine in Zambia. I don't know what we'd do without Africa.

'Anyway, that leaves the disorderly. Now let me see,' and humming quietly to himself, he pulled out an ancient card drawer and began thumbing through it.

Once he looked up and asked lightly, 'You wouldn't object to a murderer, I presume?' and before Len could reply, he added hastily 'It wasn't a patient, only his wife.'

'Yes,' Len said. 'That is, I would object.'

'Oh dear, he is proving rather difficult to place. A quiet appointment like yours so far away from things and in the cold seems eminently suitable.'

'Can't you send him to Africa?' Len asked helpfully.

'Oh, the Africans wouldn't mind. After the Nigerian business we adopted a policy of full disclosure to clients. As a matter of fact, the East Africans are quite puzzled about chaps being struck off for sexual offences and drunkenness. They don't see the point. That is the Christians of course. The other lot, the Muslims, well...' Mr Rose paused and lowered his voice conspiratorially. 'In many respects they're still savages, the Muslims. They come in here in smart suits and putting on airs but their civilised trappings are a very thin veneer indeed, I can tell you. Complaining because a chap's gone off the rails once. No. Give me your Christian black every time. A much more reasonable lot, believe me.'

'So what's the problem with the murderer in Africa?' Len urged.

'Oh, I quite forgot. Raise the subject of the Muslims and I do get carried away. As I said the East Africans would grab him. I offered him a post in Lusaka but the poor chap can't stand the tropics. That's why I thought the Antarctic would be perfect.'

Len pressed on. 'Who else have you got?'

Rose continued shuffling the cards then pulled one out triumphantly. 'Ah! The very chap. Only been on our books two months. Dr Peter Isaac,' Rose read from the card. 'Aged seventy-three, um,' he paused and looked up. 'You don't mind an Irish degree?'

'Should I?' Len queried.

'No, of course not,' Rose responded quickly. 'Just like to cover these things,' and he read on, reciting Dr Isaac's career credentials.

Dr Isaac, it seemed, had enjoyed a constantly changing career. Northern hospitals, country nursing homes, numerous remotely located private practices, prison doctor positions; nothing, it seemed, lasted longer than eighteen months. There was a three-year gap which went unexplained.

'What's wrong with him?' Len asked sharply.

'Why, nothing at all. I have no reason to question his competence. And consider his extensive experience. You can't put a price on that. Now you may be thinking he's a little old but how else can you build credentials like that without putting in the years? I understand Dr Isaac is rather fond of a drink from time to time which has sometimes led to difficulties. People can be awfully prudish about the medical profession and we must acknowledge that, which is why Isaac is in the disorderly category. But I do believe he's your man. Best of all he's not married, which usually cuts out most candidates for hardship postings. Yes, he's your man. I think you will be very happy.'

A week later Len had lunch with Isaac in a West-End hotel. The candidate wore an old-style, frayed tweed suit with an unsuitable tie. He was portly, florid, cheerful and familiar.

'Sounds a bit of a lark, old man,' he said after Len had cautiously outlined the six-month trip. 'Girls on the game, are they?'

Len shuffled nervously. 'Well, as I said, the fundamental exercise is a broad range of entertainment in which all contingencies are covered.'

'Will they be pretty girls?' Isaac asked, ignoring Len's floundering.

'Yes'.

'Excellent. Pretty girls are young girls. Young girls are healthy girls. So long as they're not old slags. I'm not up to a hundred of them. They imagine problems medicine's never heard of. And they talk. My God, how they talk,' Isaac shuddered and shook his head slowly, contemplating this horror.

And so Isaac was appointed. He was given a thousand pounds to outfit a basic medical chest and a return air ticket to Sydney where he was to join the ship in September.

Part Two

And Away

1

Two weeks before the Olga Buskova's scheduled arrival in Sydney Len and Andrew flew in via a stopover in Singapore. Before leaving London Len telephoned Zirovsky in St Petersburg. The Russian assured him the ship was on schedule and that he had been in communication with it only an hour earlier as it was passing through the Timor Sea.

'A beaudiful ship in beaudiful condition vich I personally inspect. Your students, zey vill be very happy.'

Sydney's familiar cavalier spirit prevailed unchanged. The newspapers were filled with stories about scams and politicians' bad behaviour, the sun shone, the harbour glistened; it was all wonderful and exactly as he had left it.

One afternoon Len and Andrew took a taxi to Rose Bay, hired a catamaran and for three hours scudded about the harbour dodging the ferries. That night, in nostalgic mood over dinner, Len said to Potter, 'This is where it all began for me.'

'Good God. Why did you ever leave?' Potter asked. 'I must say, if I crack it in the next few years I'd be tempted to shift out here. There's a wonderful sense of optimism in the air. You can feel it in the people and even when we were out on the water it seems to be there.'

'Warda, mate,' Len laughed. 'If you want to be understood here then it means abandoning some standards. Like the letter T, for example. You won't believe it when you hear seemingly civilised people going on about pardy for party and warda for water. It's quite dreadful. The free spirit also leads to awful sloppiness.

'Still you're right: Aussies do have a bright outlook. Wait till you see them in nationalistic mood singing their national anthem. I reckon it's one of the world's great spectacles watching rows of geriatrics croaking out 'We are young and free.' They belt it out at the drop of a hat. One of the lines refers to our land girt by sea. No one seems in the slightest embarrassed. They've even invented their own football game, which is typically Australian. It's called Australian Rules and has the unique feature, as far as I can ascertain, of having no rules.

'But it's not all vigour and exuberance. Like everywhere they've still got a whining welfare-sated underclass and you haven't seen that side yet. You wouldn't believe how they're widely referred to, and I can assure you no one's taking the piss. They really mean it. They call them Aussie battlers when of course the truth as always with these types is they've never battled for anything in their miserable hand-out lives. There are lots of speech curiosities like that here. For example, all redheads are called Blue but I could never find anyone who knew why. But it's still a great place and I owe it everything. It got me off the ground and that would never have happened if I'd stayed in England.'

Len told Potter his story. He had struck a rapport with Andrew from their first meeting and the succession of hilarious scams and schemes he recounted quickly cemented a bond between the two.

The following day they met Bruce Harding, the private aviation operator. They sat in an outdoor restaurant in Double Bay in the warm spring sunshine. Harding was a typical laconic Aussie so Len made no bones about the purpose of the exercise, which amused the pilot greatly.

'Sounds like a hell of a lot of fun,' he said. 'I reckon I'm gunna really enjoy this operation, mate.'

Harding had flown private planes all over the world. He amused his two companions with a series of extraordinary stories of flying in Africa, Asia, the Middle East and the Caribbean.

He had done his homework and outlined the type of plane needed.

'The bastards can't stop us landing down there but if they don't like what you buggers are up to they could make things bloody difficult if they wanted to. I need a plane which can carry enough fuel for a return voyage in case of bad weather should they refuse to co-operate with radio information, and that's a hell of a lot more costly than should be necessary.'

'Why not load up the ship with aviation fuel and use us as your radio contact?' Len suggested.

Harding thought a while. 'Yeah, mate,' he said after a pause. 'Thadud be practical. But I'd have to train you what to look for weatherwise. You'll need a snow-cat to transport fuel and the supplies I'm bringing in from the airstrip to the ship. I've checked it out. The airfield is some distance from McMurdo base. I know a joker who can organise that and I'll get right on to it.'

'Are you very busy?' Len asked.

'We're never busy in this game, mate,' Harding replied. 'But I came home with enough cash to buy a couple of small planes debt-free so I only need one or two jobs each week to keep the cat fed.'

'How would you like to be our agent?' Len proposed. 'We need someone here to deal with supplies and any contingencies which arise. You could keep a notebook of your time at, say, fifty dollars an hour.'

And so Harding became the operation's Sydney agent and over the next few days accompanied the two men as they set about meeting suppliers.

They met Rippin in his office to interview the accounting and bar staff he had organised. Len had instructed him to advertise for eight female bar staff for the six-month tour of duty and to ensure they were all young, pretty and personable.

'It winds the fellows up,' he explained to Andrew. 'If the bar girl is pretty they buy lots of drinks and try and charm her and the next step of booking a girl becomes inevitable.'

From Rippin's pool of fifteen candidates they selected eight. As well, Rippin had organised an accounts girl for the back-room work, two girls to operate the shops and a chirpy forty-year-old redhead called Pauline to manage the girls' booking office.

'She used to be on the game herself so she knows the ropes,' Rippin explained.

Pauline would operate the office on a conventional eight-hour opening period each day. If Len's projections proved correct they would be booked up days ahead so there was no need of a twenty-four-hour access booking system. The customers would prepay and be given a chit showing their booking time and the room number.

On the Olga Buskova's scheduled day of arrival they break-fasted in the hotel rooftop restaurant with its full harbour view and watched the ship, glistening with its new white paint, slide up the harbour and berth.

This is it, Len thought. It's now or never. I've already spent over a million quid getting to this stage. By God, I'm going to make it work, he vowed to himself.

The two men packed their bags, paid the hotel and took a taxi to the ship.

On board they met the captain, Boris, who as specified spoke English. He was a gruff, down-to-earth character and he showed them around the ship.

Zirovsky had been true to his word. The cabins were excellent, their former double bunks replaced by fixed three-quarter-size beds. The nightclub just off the main lounge had a regrettable, Russian, dated ambience but would pass with the lights dimmed. On the other hand the Chinese restaurant decor was right on the button, exactly as prescribed. The shops were neat and the office was wired with a fax machine and internet computer as ordered. Len and Andrew had two adjacent luxury suites. And plainly Zirovsky had delivered with the crew who fluttered and flounced about their tasks.

The Olga Buskova was scheduled to head south in three days' time. Over the next two days they were flat out organising and checking off lists as the holds were loaded with fruit, vegetables, meat and other foodstuffs and supplies.

The Chinese restaurant operator Rippin had organised arrived with his wife and three waitress daughters who, after taking possession of their cabins, noisily supervised the loading and frozen storage of their foodstuffs.

Andrew and Bruce found a discount bookseller and cut a deal. They purchased 2000 hardcovers at a twenty per cent discount on a sale or return basis. It was proposed to monitor sales and fax Bruce prior to each flight with the required fresh order.

Then they struck a discount deal with a florist to supply fresh cut flowers for the flower shop prior to each flight and established a similar arrangement with a liquor wholesaler.

The bookshop's magazines and paperbacks arrived and were dumped in the shop to be set out on the shelves during the voyage.

Two trucks pulled up with Harding in the cabin of one; a snow-mobile and a dozen large containers of aviation fuel were craned over the side and stored in a hold. Later, Len wrote Harding a cheque on his Sydney account for the snowmobile and to cover the costs of his first flight down, scheduled for a fortnight after their arrival at McMurdo.

After unloading his things in his cabin Potter went ashore to inspect the stable. For two days he and Harding sat in Rippin's office as one by one girls of several dozen different nationalities trooped in.

It had been left to last for as Rippin had said when they spoke to him on arrival in Sydney, 'These girls are unreliable. They'll agree to come and then something will happen and they won't think to let us know. They'll just not turn up. Leave it to the last minute and the drop-out rate will be much less.'

Eight of the girls were rejected as too fat, plain or old but anticipating this, plus the need for back-up, revitalisation and periodic replacements, Rippin had arranged for 120 to come in. Potter questioned them, covering their experience, their realisation that it was a six-month tour of duty, their state of health, and made a quick assessment of their attitude and spirit. Finally they had their 100, plus four reserves to cover non-appearances. The chosen girls were given a facts sheet detailing what they should bring and were instructed to board the ship by midday on the day of departure.

'It's a much more diverse crop than I expected,' Andrew later reported. 'I thought they'd all be Aussies but only about half are. We've got every nationality under the sun and a terrific mix of physical types: tall, medium, short; blondes, brunettes, redheads – I cut out any whose English wasn't up to scratch. A funny thing, though. All the Australians seemed to have these appalling names ending with "ene". At first I thought they were pulling my leg but a lot turned up with passports thinking they would need them and the names were absolutely true. There were Ralenes and Jolenes and Darlenes and Sharlenes and Marlenes and so on; I got quite dizzy at times. And those who were the exception had names like Kylie and Hayley and Trixie and Pixie. You don't think it will put the chaps off do you?' he asked pensively.

Len laughed. 'They'll put up with it so long as they're pretty and deliver the goods. Like I told you the other day, Australia's the easiest-going place in the world, which is one of its most appealing features. But the price is a pervading crassness and no one seems to care much. Remember there's a very strong Irish Catholic component here. Anyway, you'll find it's the same in most places. Look at America with their Candys and Rustys and Mandys and Randies and Brandys and Misties; the same cringe-making stuff. It's just a working class thing.

'But don't underestimate Aussie girls. They're the best in the world, especially the middle-class city girls. They don't speak with the appalling accents of this lot. They're pretty, they're feminine, but they're also fairly street-smart and they'll go fishing or play golf or tennis and half the time whack you. There was no need for women's lib and feminism here. The Australian woman was already on an equal footing. Maybe it's something to do with the tough pioneering background. But we're not exactly dealing with the creme de la creme of Australian womanhood with a boatload of tarts so you're being a bit unreasonable.'

'Well, I'll tell you another odd thing,' Andrew said. 'I've been worrying about the girls getting bored. After all, apart from being shafted from dawn to dusk there's nothing for them to do. So I asked them about their interests, thinking we might be able to cater for them in some way. But they all seemed astonishingly vacuous. Mostly they looked puzzled and when I pressed them about seventy per cent said astrology. It's bloody extraordinary.'

'Don't worry about them getting bored,' Len replied. 'Remember, I've done this before. Their lives on the ship will be the same as here in Sydney; being ravished, eating, sleeping, watching videos and sitting around drinking and talking rubbish to one another. They'll be quite happy.

'I know about the astrology foolishness too. You remember I told you that when I first went to New Zealand I ran a mail-order business for a year or so selling nonsense to punters. The more nonsensical the better it went and the best of all was my astrology service. I had over a thousand women customers across the land. They'd pay for a six-month mailing service for a weekly horoscope. It was great fun for a while. I was Dr Primakov in the advertisements which I ran with a photo of a dark Errol Flynn-looking type. To legally cover myself I actually bought a doctorate in the name of Primakov from one of those bogus mail-box American universities. They wanted five thousand dollars, I offered them five hundred and we settled at seven hundred and fifty.

'On Sunday nights I would compose a dozen different messages for the week; one for each sign. I soon got the hang of it by reading what the newspapers and magazines were running. You know; mumbo-jumbo about the different star signs passing into the influence of one another. Monday morning my secretary would type it all up and send it out to the clients.

'After a while I started to get bored and made their week's instructions more and more outlandish. Don't wear knickers on Wednesday, don't eat cheese for a week, don't under any circumstances have any contact with horses. It all went very well but eventually I realised the basic theme I was flogging was negative with all of these prohibitions so I decided the clientele might be happier if I adopted a more positive note and I was right. They lapped it up as the increased subscription renewal rate showed. Once I told the whole bloody lot of them to go to a small town in the South Island the following Friday, carry a red handbag and they'd meet the love of their lives. After three days out of curiosity I telephoned the airline and pretended I wanted to book a flight there. Can't do it, they said. There must be a conference on. We've been deluged with bookings from across the land. God knows what the locals made of hundreds of deranged women carrying red handbags bowling up and down the main street and gazing intensely at every male who walked past.'

'Didn't they complain?' Andrew asked.

'Complain! I've never known anything like it with anything else I've done and most of the things I did in those days were characterised by customer complaint. But not over the advice. I suspect they attributed the lack of results to their own fault. Carrying the handbag in the wrong hand or the wrong shade of red or whatever.

'No, the complaints came when I got fed up with it all and gave it away. It was actually quite tricky thinking up new things to tell them and I began feeling a bit of a charlatan when my week's instructions were vague or uninspiring so one day I wrote to them all saying Dr Primakov was returning to Bulgaria to lecture in astrology at Sofia University and the service would stop when their current subscriptions expired.

'You wouldn't believe the distress. Bloody mailbags of distraught letters saying they couldn't continue living without the weekly advice. Don't ask me to explain female irrationality but I'm certainly not surprised by the girls telling you what they did. I'm almost tempted to start a service on the boat if it will keep them happy but we don't have to go that far. Tell Harding to bring in twenty copies of each of the Aussie women's magazines on each flight. They're full of this astrology claptrap. That will keep them engrossed.'

On the day of departure Rippin and Potter sat in deckchairs at the head of the gangway checking the arrivals. As the girls drove up in taxis and came on board with their suitcases they were greeted with a glass of champagne, a layout map of the boat and a copy of their employment conditions. The crew members escorted them to their cabins and soon they were buzzing about the ship locating the gymnasium and sauna, the restaurant and other facilities.

In early afternoon Isaac arrived direct from the airport in a taxi, plainly very drunk. 'I say old man,' he bellowed to Potter. 'Do you mind fixing up the cab? I've got no Australian currency.' He staggered on board and disappeared to his cabin where he remained for the next two days.

Finally 101 girls were duly ensconced on board and Potter, Harding and Rippin met in Len's cabin. They had a celebratory drink to toast the enterprise's success. Len wrote Rippin a cheque drawn on the Sydney bank account.

The fee was three thousand dollars per girl. The cheque, however, was for two hundred and fifty thousand dollars with fifty thousand withheld as agreed to cover replacements as might prove necessary over the duration. On the voyage's completion, all going to plan, Rippin would receive the balance.

At 5pm they sailed, the girls and the crew lining the deck as they shimmied up the harbour.

Once through the heads and into open sea Len announced over the ship's intercom that there would be a welcoming banquet in the ballroom at 7pm.

Later, when all were seated, Len rose to speak. He announced that once in the Antarctic there would be a regular Sunday morning assembly for approximately one hour. Morning tea would be served while productivity and any problems would be discussed. During the six-day voyage south there would be a daily two-hour assembly to cover routines and systems.

'Finally and most important of all, ladies,' Len concluded,

'we have a dual aim with this expedition. We want to enjoy ourselves and we want to make lots of money for everyone.' An unladylike roar of approval greeted this last pronouncement. 'The objective,' Len continued, 'is that at the end of the voyage you will each receive a cheque for at least ninety thousand dollars. And if you don't feel inclined to mention it to the tax authorities then you can be assured we won't.'

And so the good ship Olga Buskova plunged its way south through the southern ocean, its inhabitants, as with all in pursuit of El Dorado and the unknown down through the ages, filled with optimism and some trepidation.

2

Lunging with the gaff Philip caught and yanked float twenty-three towards him. He drew up the weighted line hanging beneath it, read the attached thermometer and after recording the temperature into his dictaphone, tossed the gear back into the sea. Climbing back on to his snowmobile to move to the next checkpoint half a mile further along the coast he heard a faint snatch of music.

I'm going crazy, he thought, and for half a minute sat in the snowmobile gloomily contemplating his situation. His father had been right, even if for the wrong reasons.

When the Cambridge University Antarctic expedition had been first mooted it sounded tremendously exciting. Professor McLean, the expedition leader, had lectured the chosen three in London in briefing sessions prior to their departure.

'It is probably the most important environmental issue facing mankind today. The Antarctic is the front line of the coming battle for survival and the research you will be doing is of the utmost significance. Your role is akin to the miner's canary detecting the unseen threat ahead.' The professor had listed a number of countries, mainly small island states, which on current projections would be totally submerged by rising sea temperatures through the melting polar ice cap within the next thirty years.

'We cannot take this lightly,' the professor had warned. 'One of the most severely affected countries is Bangladesh which as you know is a Commonwealth nation. At least thirty million people there will be landless and will need to be resettled in an already overcrowded region. But also there are additionally at least fifty other nations which will be severely affected. Many of them may be unknown to you but they exist and have their own histories and cultures every bit as much as Denmark, Canada or indeed England.'

He had shown the team a video on Tuvalu, a small Pacific island state lying south of the equator which, he said, was almost certain to disappear on current rising sea level projections.

'Before it was independent Tuvalu was a British colony called the Ellice Islands. In that sense it's part of our heritage as Englishmen and I mention that to emphasise that this problem, directly or indirectly, touches us all.'

The United Nations-funded three-month expedition was to monitor Antarctic water temperatures covering thirty miles of coast-line. In England it had sounded wonderful and Philip had spent the month prior to departure reading the huge Antarctic bibliography in the Scott Polar Research Institute at Cambridge. The books were largely adventurous in tone and soon he was familiar with the exploits of those who had preceded him and the great dramas of the failed Shackleton and Scott expeditions.

He had particularly enjoyed the occasions when his friends had mentioned forthcoming winter holidays skiing in Europe or heading south to sunnier climes.

'Unfortunately I have to work,' he would drop into the conversation and, affecting an outward gloom, would joyously recount his forthcoming Antarctic adventure. But within days of arrival at the McMurdo base Philip's work proved excruciatingly boring.

The base camp personnel comprised a small American military engineering unit, there to aid in the base's maintenance but who seemed to do nothing but drink beer and noisily play snooker and ping-pong, plus more than eighty other scientific teams drawn mainly from North American universities. The scientists' diverse esoteric activities frequently bordered on the ludicrous. Additionally there were airstrip personnel, base administrators, a Catholic priest, cooks and other menials; in total, more than 3000 souls there for the six months' summer duration. In the evenings the men gathered for a plain fare dinner in large communal dining rooms. Afterwards they drank beer and frequently became raucous. There were card games and table tennis competitions and darts matches and chess tournaments, initially organised by Father O'Hearn, the New York Catholic priest who had unofficially attempted the role of base entertainment officer.

A tetchy atmosphere lingered permanently about the base and fisticuffs and arguments were daily events.

Conversation at the base was either mundane or in the case of the more earnest scientists, confined to their work. Sometimes after-dinner discussions evolved into drunken arguments. Also present were eighteen female scientists, all of whom were fat, plain, bespectacled and enthusiastically wooed. McMurdo was beyond question a plain girl's heaven.

The Cambridge water temperature team had been treated like pariahs following the unpleasantness over Professor McLean's refusal to participate in the international dwarf-throwing tournament.

Professor McLean was 4ft 10in tall. He had inadvertently learned of his role in the dwarf-throwing contest when confronted by a Marseilles University volcanologist who had insisted in broken English the professor provide a written undertaking as to his consistent still-body movement in flight, so as to provide no advantage for the English team.

When Professor McLean finally got to the bottom of the matter and discovered he had been allocated the missile role in the forthcoming event he had protested indignantly, whereupon a great deal of unpleasantness had followed. It transpired over twenty thousand dollars in bets had been laid on the outcome and the bettors and delegated team throwers all individually complained to the professor at his lack of co-operation.

The last straw had been the appeal by an Edinburgh University jellyfish translucency variation researcher who had argued that the professor's withdrawal was un-British and not playing the game.

In response to McLean's outraged complaint that far from withdrawing, he had never agreed in the first place, the Scot had countered that philosophically speaking the professor's consent was irrelevant given the widespread assumption of his involvement, which therefore made the professor's participation a reality. However, the Scot had added, in the interest of maintaining goodwill, all forty-two national sides entered in the competition had agreed to reduce their team sizes from four to two, thus the professor would now only be airborne on eighty-four occasions. In desperation Professor McLean had suggested the event be transformed to a dead penguin-throwing tournament, a proposal received with horror by the Scot.

'Are you mad?' he had bellowed. 'Imagine if word reached the outside world. All hell would break loose if people found we had treated an animal in this derisory fashion.'

But McLean had remained stalwart in his non-co-operation and his team members had all borne the brunt of the base's disapproval.

Philip sat on the snowmobile contemplating how he could possibly survive five more months when again he thought he detected the sound of music. Slowly it dawned on him that it was music; inexplicable, given that he was twenty miles from the base. Curious, he started the engine and driving round the promontory jutting into the bay, he saw a white cruise ship gliding towards the base. To the thumping beat of a public address system about thirty naked young girls swayed and frolicked and on seeing Philip, thrust their breasts and pelvises suggestively. Philip waved and they waved back. To hell with the temperatures, he thought; they're always the same each day. I'll fill them in later, and he opened the throttle and sped back to the base.

By the time he arrived the ship was already tied up. There were now nearly 100 naked girls dancing erotically along the ship's deck. Drawn by the music a crowd of some 300 men had gathered at the water's edge and were shouting to the girls who were responding lewdly with obscene gestures.

Abruptly the music stopped. A public address system began crackling and then Potter's amplified voice blared at jet engine decibel level: 'Greetings from Penguins nightclub, gentlemen. We will be opening in two hours' time so it's a big, big welcome to you all. Bring cash or credit cards. We've got a sauna and a bookshop, we have top international cabaret acts with no cover charges and a wonderful Chinese restaurant. And best of all, gentlemen, we have lots of lovely young ladies who will be very pleased to see you.'

The lovely young ladies were now beginning to turn blue in the chilly air and in a maul of breasts and buttocks they turned, packing and pushing in their anxiety to get back inside to the warmth. Two hours later the gangplank was lowered. More than 400 eager beards stormed aboard where they were greeted by a welcoming committee of bare-breasted girls. Soon the ship was roaring with laughter and noise and after initial hesitant enquiries, the men began disappearing into the cabins from where they later emerged very happy indeed.

Andrew and Len rushed frenziedly about the boat, monitoring activities and solving problems.

The sixty-seat Chinese restaurant was full within an hour of opening. The bookshop was jammed with customers snapping up the week-old magazines and Sunday newspapers and browsing among the bookshelves. Twelve beards reclined in the sauna, lured by the bait of two naked girls who were first on the roster sheet of an hour at a time sauna duty.

The sultry Russian nightclub singer had completed her hour-long show and the three-girl Russian band comprising a guitarist, drummer and clarinettist was in full swing.

Four hours after opening Potter sought Len and pulled him into a booth where he called to one of the waitresses for coffee. Potter was in a state of high excitement. 'It's bloody phenomenal,' he cried. 'As we say in the financial world, the trend's your friend and believe me, the trend is very healthy indeed.'

Potter had been monitoring the booking booth. 'We reached 100 per cent cabin occupancy forty minutes after opening and it's been a full house ever since,' he said. 'The best news is after two hours we had a three-hour service delay and it's rising fast. Ten minutes ago the booking delay went through the five-hour mark. It's bloody wonderful. At this rate we'll put 1000 through over the next eight hours. The chaps are so excited they're going through in less than half an hour which is quicker than we calculated.'

'That will change,' Len said. 'They'll soon cool down, mark my word. We won't know the true position for at least a fortnight. A slower pattern will have developed by then.'

The booking office had been instructed to make no appointments from two in the morning that night for a five-hour period, then the roster programme began to maintain a continuous seventy-girl complement on duty twenty-four hours daily.

As more and more beards streamed aboard the noise rose to a deafening crescendo. Soon the ship was packed tight.

'Jesus, we never anticipated this,' Andrew said excitedly. 'The ship can't take them all. We need additional management staff. You'd better come and help.' Len and Andrew fought through the crowd to the top of the gangway.

'I'll go on duty for an hour, then you can relieve me,' Andrew shouted above the noise. As more scientists loomed on the scene he stood in the gangway and stopped them. 'Sorry, gentlemen. It's a full house. Come back in an hour and we should have some space.'

Later Len and Andrew met again. 'Christ, Len. This is far bigger than we thought. The problem is that with no night-time down here this lot don't recognise normal sleeping times. We're going to have to control access and we haven't got the staff. We may have to use some of the Russian stewards so we'll get the captain to provide us a chain for the gangway. The place is packed to the gunwales and there's at least 1000 standing in the snow bitching about not being allowed on board. We need more girls and half a dozen assistants.'

'It will settle down,' Len said. 'It may take a week but I know this industry. There's over 3000 men ashore. Possibly up to a tenth of them won't be starters. The rest will be content with access at two or three day intervals.'

'But that still leaves a huge overlap,' Andrew cried. 'We need another 100 girls. You'll have to contact Rippin and get them shipped in. We've got the rooms.'

The ship did not simmer down. Things got increasingly out of hand so that by the second day a long queue of angry men wound its way from the gangplank back to the base.

Len telephoned Rippin to send in the reserve team Tom had interviewed in Sydney. Rippin's response was discouraging. 'They're not bloody pints of milk. I can't just produce thirty girls at a moment's notice. It took three months hard yakka to get the original batch together.'

'The arrangement was you were to have a thirty-girl back-up team. That's why we held back fifty thousand dollars. Tom interviewed the reserves so send them in,' Len replied angrily.

'That wasn't the deal,' Rippin insisted. 'The agreement was to supply a minimum of thirty girls on a drip-feed basis over six months, to cover any problems with the original stable. I can do that but I can't bloody well deliver them in one job lot. These girls come and go all over the place. I'll chase up the reserves but we'll be doing bloody well if there's still ten of them around.'

By the fourth day the ship's operation had descended to unrelenting chaos. Len and Tom had almost no sleep as they rushed from crisis to crisis trying to establish some order. When Tom reported that one of the girls had refused all customers since arrival it was the last straw. Len lost his temper and ordered her brought to his office.

As it turned out, this development was to be the turning point in not only the operation's successful functioning but also Len's future.

3

The recalcitrant girl, Claudia, entered the office and at Len's beckoning, sat in an armchair. She was an attractive mid-twenties brunette and slightly disarmed Len with her cool composure. There was something different about her from the others; the way she sat elegantly, her steady neutral gaze and obvious self-control but strangest of all, the fact that she was wearing a smart pinstripe suit.

'Look here,' Len spluttered, 'we're up to our necks with demand. The booking office says you're refusing any clients. What the hell's going on?'

Claudia hesitated then said, 'I'm afraid I owe you an apology. I suppose I've cost you something with food and whatnot so I'm happy to pay for that but I'll take the next flight out and I'll pay the cost of that as well.'

'But why? What's the problem?' Len asked.

The girl gathered her thoughts. After a time she said, 'I made a mistake. I shouldn't have come.'

'But what's wrong?' Len persisted. 'Why have you changed your mind?'

Again Claudia paused and then she explained. 'I don't wish to sound precious but I'm a bit different from the other girls. I was with Ascot Escorts in Sydney. They're in the yellow pages and your man Rippin mistakenly sent them a brochure about this Antarctic trip. I was about to resign and when the brochure came in the whole office was sitting around laughing about it but I looked at it and thought it sounded interesting so I telephoned and…' she hesitated and then continued: 'Well, it doesn't really matter but here I am.'

'But what's the problem?' Len pressed.

Again the girl paused, gathering her thoughts. Finally she said, 'The problem is that I'm not, as they say, on the game. It was really foolish of me and I'm dreadfully sorry I've messed you about. I honestly can't think what on earth made me come; that is, taking everything into consideration. I mean the idea of seeing the Antarctic obviously appealed and I suppose I was silly just ignoring the other business but one thing led to another; anyway, it doesn't matter now. I'll pay whatever I owe and go home.'

'But hang on a minute,' Len persisted. 'If you were with Ascot Escorts whoever they are then you must have been turning it up.'

'Actually not,' Claudia said somewhat stiffly. 'Ascot Escorts is a well-established temporary staff firm. They often get mixed up with the other thing. What they do is employ highly versatile and capable people who for whatever reason are only seeking part-time work which is better paid than the usual part-time stuff, waitressing and that sort of thing. Most of their staff are people like young artists or university graduates doing doctorates who need a base income. That was my situation. I was doing a doctorate.'

Len listened to Claudia's explanation with astonishment. 'What sort of work did you do then?' he asked.

'Not escort work in the way it's now known. Ascot pre-dated all of that and then found the escort word evolve into another meaning. They talk about changing their name now, even though it's well established.'

'But what did you do?' Len pressed.

'Mostly trade work usually relating to highly expensive commodities,' Claudia said. 'For example, I once accompanied an armaments firm to a military base where they showed off a new mortar. I'd dish out the information material and be a general assistant. Apparently, smartly dressed young women are seen as a helpful selling tool. Our standard uniform for most jobs was a pin-stripe suit. Mind you,' she added brightening, 'one could be called up for a rich variety of things. Once a flu epidemic laid waste to the Australian Opera's chorus. Three of us were called in for spear-carrying type roles. It was nervy stuff and we just mimed along with the chorus. Fortunately they were doing Aida so we pretty much were buried in the crowd on stage.'

Len stared at the girl, fascinated by what he was hearing. After a while he said, 'So you're a university graduate?'

'Oh yes,' Claudia replied. 'I have a masters degree in economics. I majored in monetary policy.'

'Well how in the name of God did all that lead to here?' Len asked.

'I suppose looking back I was a bit naive,' Claudia said. 'I come from Naribi. It's a small country town out west on the New South Wales border with South Australia. I won a scholarship to Sydney University and after I graduated I got a job in a bank's economic research department. They gave me silly childish things to do so I decided to chuck it and do my doctorate. My particular interest is the behavioural element of human nature and its conflict with current monetary policy and other economic beliefs that make rational sense but fly in the face of human nature. My professor accepted this as my thesis subject but the problem was I couldn't afford to do it. One day I ran across an old university friend and we had coffee and anyway, after a while she told me she was with Ascot Escorts while she was doing her doctorate and she explained it all. So I tossed in the bank and started with them about a month ago, which is when this came up. And here I am. I'm sorry I've put you to this trouble. It was really thoughtless of me.'

Len stared at Claudia. 'What do you mean about behavioural conflicts?' he asked.

'Oh that's quite interesting,' Claudia said, brightening. 'When I was in my third year it suddenly struck me that the lecturers were talking tripe. They just trotted out the standard line, whatever the current received thinking was. Then I'd read the newspapers' financial writers and the same thing was happening. It was all a bit of a shock at first. I mean, I was only twenty-two at the time and at that age you sort of assume everyone older is sensible and honest and knows what they're talking about, especially at a university. One day it all dawned on me that they didn't and were just peeling it off rote-like because it was the fashionable thinking.'

'Why, what happened?' Len asked, his curiosity aroused.

'We had this lecturer. He was a bit of a smarty-pants. Very cocky and assertive. He used to go on about the virtues of the market and simultaneously preach about the desirability of price stability. So one day I asked him in front of the class which prices he wanted stable; cabbages, shares, houses – what? And I went on and asked him how he reconciled that with his free market beliefs, which is all about price instability. You know, ever-changing price signals reflecting fluctuating supply and demand. Anyway, he waffled on and on and of course he couldn't possibly reconcile the two propositions. But that didn't matter. It just got me very interested in the whole behavioural thing, the finger in the wind stuff, the way everyone jumps on bandwagons to unthinkingly back illogical propositions just because they're fashionable. So I decided to do my doctoral thesis on that subject.'

'Well, that's all very interesting, my girl,' Len said. 'But it still doesn't make sense you coming down here. The bottom line is you knew what it was all about and even if you put your hand up on an impulse, you had a few days to come to your senses before the ship left Sydney.'

There was a lengthy silence. Finally Claudia spoke.

'I haven't told you the whole story. To be honest I was in a terrible emotional turmoil. Just before I went into Ascot to hand in my notice; that's when I saw your brochure as I said; I was a mental mess. I had just come from a specialist. I don't want to go into the details but I'd had a problem and the upshot was the specialist told me I could never have children. It had never occurred to me to actually want children, after all, I was only twenty-five and pre-occupied with thinking about my doctorate, but being told that, well, I suddenly felt empty and nothing seemed to count any more and I just sort of lost all rationality and well; here I am.

'I'm sorry. It seems silly now but I just acted on an impulse. I couldn't carry on with Ascot as the abrupt nature of the jobs, being called up suddenly that is, was making my thesis research impossible. That's the funny thing about it. The money was terrible waitressing and doing other usual mundane part-time things but at least it left the mind clear for studying. But Ascot's jobs were often terribly interesting and turning back on again to research writing was simply impossible. I was in a confused state and when I saw the brochure it seemed just the answer. I saw it as an Antarctic holiday away from everything and just sort of thought I'd come along for the ride and stay clear of everyone and then go home after a week. I was shocked by the reality; you know, the whole factory approach.'

Listening to all of this made Len warm to the girl. He got up, walked to the cabinet, opened a bottle of red wine and poured out two glasses.

'I'm sorry to hear about that,' he said, 'but you still need a kick in the backside for giving us this problem and taking up a space.'

Claudia laughed. 'That's the least of your problems. You and your sidekick; what's his name? The smooth one?'

'Andrew,' Len said helpfully.

'Yes, Andrew. You two think you have it all worked out. I listened to you in those dreadful assembly sessions coming down. Goodness, you have some problems ahead.'

'What do you mean?' Len asked alarmed.

Claudia laughed again. 'Well, I listened to you talking about the productivity programme. At first I was outraged and then just astonished at the cold-bloodedness of your attitude. Of course, it wouldn't occur to most of the girls. They're not used to lectures and just turned off through all of your sessions. I was watching them and could tell. But have you thought about menstruation? It didn't sound like it. It varies of course, but with this number of girls there will be some unavailable for up to five days or so each month. And there's heaps of other things like that as well.'

'Jesus,' Len exploded, slapping his head. 'That's so bloody obvious. How did we forget that?' Then after a pause, 'What other things?'

'Oh, all sorts,' Claudia replied. 'They're people you know, not robots. Sure they're here willingly but women are different from men. They'll tell you they're happy and then suddenly explode. And that's about to happen. I can see the signs.'

'What signs?'

'Oh, just stress. Make-up, for instance. Some of the girls are beginning to pile it on, I've noticed. That's the first sign of unhappiness with women. It may pass, of course. Perhaps it's just the new environment and its confinement. Most of these girls have had fairly humdrum lives and are not used to dramatic changes.'

The two sat silently for a while. After a while Len said, 'I say. Would you consider taking on a management role? A sort of intermediary post between us and the girls. We could give you a title; something like operations manager.'

Noticing Claudia hesitate Len pressed on.

'I'll tell you what. We'll pay you a thousand dollars a week free of tax for the first two or three weeks. If you're happy and we're happy at the end of that time we can discuss doubling it.'

So Claudia became operations manager and very soon things began running smoothly.

4

On her third day as operations manager Claudia approached Len with a proposal.

'I've chatted to lots of the girls about the stress issue. Most of them come from parlours where they're on duty for eight or ten hours each day. From what they say there are days when there are almost no customers. So when they talk about ten different clients in a day they're only thinking of the money because it almost never happens. But here it does, every day. They're getting worn out and if it wasn't for the money we'd have had a strike by now. But they won't last much longer.'

'That's disastrous,' Len protested. 'They've only been on the job a week. We did our homework and were told they'd manage ten a day. All our projections are based on those assumptions.'

'Physically they can,' Claudia continued. 'That's not the problem. It's psychological. But I may have the solution. What we need is a private lounge for when they're off duty and where there's not a male figure in sight, at least not one rampant and naked.

'We need comfortable furniture, coffee, tea, drinks and nibbles on tap, soft music, lots of women's magazines, two television corners with videos of movies; all of that and I think you'll find everything will be okay then. One of the Russians can wait on them. Preferably one who's really camp, lots of fluttering and squealing and raised eyebrows and mini-scenes over trifles; that sort of stuff. The girls relate to it for some reason. I think they find refreshing a male presence which is undemanding.'

'You really think it would work?' Len appealed anxiously.

'It will certainly improve the situation, but yes, I think it will and we've got the perfect room. We're only using half the ship's facilities. The first class lounge is available and it's just the right size and already set up with some ghastly but still comfortable Russian soft furniture.

'If you're happy about it I'll select three of the most suitable Russian nancy-boys for a twenty-four hour roster. One waiter at any time is enough so it shouldn't disturb the other operations.

But we've got to lay it on. Really nice food, free drinks, hot savouries, cakes and so on. I want flowers from the florist shop and I'd like some pets for the girls to play with.'

'I'll have Andrew capture a couple of penguins at once,' Len said sarcastically.

Claudia ignored Len's jibe. 'I want the pilot to bring in a large goldfish tank, some packets of goldfish food and a dozen fish in a plastic bag. I need two kittens and two reasonably large birdcages. And I want a parrot for one of them and four budgies for the other. They'll make the girls feel at home.'

So Len did as Claudia bid.

The ladies' lounge was a great success with rarely fewer than thirty inhabitants and the crisis passed. Only the parrot was a failure. Its repertoire of foul language, which Harding had assumed would go down a treat and for which he paid a sizeable parrot premium, jarred with the ambience Claudia was seeking. 'It's totally abrasive and like having a man in the room, which is exactly what I want to avoid,' she complained.

So the parrot was transferred to the main lounge entrance-way where it found parrot heaven, continuously insulting the passing beards and being abused in return. Encouraged by the beards it acquired a taste for red wine and became the first perpetually pissed parrot in ornithological history. It was frequently to be found drunk, lying on its back on the cage floor with its legs in the air.

Claudia complained bitterly about the bird's corruption so eventually Len intervened and issued a prohibition order on the beards buying the parrot drinks. Thereafter it was limited each day to a single thimbleful of its favourite tipple, a South Australian cabernet sauvignon, and as with the girls in their lounge retreat, balance was restored.

5

Under Claudia's management the ship soon settled into an orderly commerce. The average daily servicing target was maintained despite periodic tantrum-related fluctuations. Best of all, demand in the form of advance bookings remained a steady three days ahead of supply.

But not everyone was content. A steady flow of complaints and mini-crises occupied Len's time. Some of the girls displayed a curious prudishness as to acceptable behaviour, notably in respect of the stewards.

'Lorene to see you,' Potter announced and in came a plainly disgruntled girl.

'It's bloody well indecent, Mr Edwards. Also it's upsetting the clients. We want something done about it.'

Lorene's protest produced the first of what were to be many unanticipated consequences of Len's homosexual staffing insurance strategy. Two of the stewards were taking daily walks along her corridor, one crawling on all fours wearing only a pink G string being led by the other on the end of a chain linked to a leather studded collar round the crawler's neck. Potter was dispatched to have them confine their activities to their own quarters.

On another occasion Potter reported he had encountered one of the base personnel coming out of a steward's cabin. The fellow had ducked his head on being spotted and quickly scuttled off, ignoring Andrew's shouts to stop. 'There was something familiar about him,' Potter said. 'Can't quite place it but I'll remember if I see him again. I never got a good look at his face.'

'I suppose with over 3000 blokes at the base we can assume they'll have their share of ponces,' Len replied amiably.

'Damn it all, we can't have this, Len,' Potter complained. 'It's an outrage. We're effectively feeding and housing these windjammers while inadvertently supplying the bloody base's perverts with free sex.'

'Well, what do you suggest we do?' Len asked. 'Charge them corkage?'

Nevertheless the captain was instructed to tell the stewards visitors were strictly forbidden, following which some could periodically be seen slipping ashore in their free time.

Marlene, a particularly belligerent girl Potter had been monitoring with a view to shipping home had her clientele not uniformly spoken well of her performances, bitterly claimed a particular steward had stolen a favourite pair of lace panties. This led to a virtual court martial with the captain present as interpreter. The steward volubly protested his innocence and eventually the inquiry collapsed when he broke down in tearful hysterics.

'I think he does not panties haf,' the captain solemnly pronounced.

This unresolved matter festered away and periodically boiled over into unseemly screeching disturbances for another week. Len called Marlene in and offered financial recompense for the missing garment.

'It's not the bloody money. It's the principle,' the girl retorted angrily, echoing the litigant's cry which more than any other down through the ages had gladdened lawyers' hearts.

Once, returning from a particularly pleasant lunch Len found Sharlene, a somewhat boisterous Australian blonde, waiting for him. She purported to represent a number of the girls.

'It's about the food, Mr Edwards,' she whined uncharacteristically. 'It's not a fair whack. We were promised real beaut food if we signed on. We're gunna get sick if somethink's not done about it. Some of the girls are bloody near starving cos of this crap these Russian poofters are dishing up.'

Len was taken aback. Three months earlier in the State Shipping Department's office in St Petersburg, he had hammered Zirovsky on the subject of food quality. Diets and menus had been agreed and the jet regularly brought in fresh vegetables and fruit. He had meticulously inspected the daily menu since their arrival and noted the satisfactory tour ship standard fare being served.

'But the food is excellent, Sharlene. I check it myself every day.'

Sharlene's eyes narrowed with doubt and suspicion. 'Well we're bloody well not eating it. We want proper food. What we want is hamburgers and chips, not all this vegetable and salad muck and chicken kevin rubbish.'

'Every day?' Len queried weakly.

'Of course every day. Wotcher think we are? You think we wanna eat only twice a bloody week?'

'But what about some variety?' Len quizzed.

Sharlene screwed up her face and squinted at the ceiling above Len's head while she tackled this intellectual poser.

'Well, yeah; we can mix it up now and again. Waddaboud some baked beans and some bread and budda?'

Peace and the stable's Australian faction's health were soon restored as the jet added cartons of frozen hamburger patties, cases of baked beans and boxes of sliced white bread loaves to its cargo.

Then there was the black market scandal, which outraged Potter when he discovered that Wilson, one of the base's administration officials, had partially cornered the market by continuously block-booking forty girls then on-selling access rights for twenty-five dollars a head. Potter promptly served Wilson with a banning order from the ship.

Through an intermediary Wilson secured an appointment with Len.

'I have a degree in economics, sir,' he protested. 'It's a fundamental economic principle that market makers add value. We act as commercial underwriters by guaranteeing sales for suppliers.' For ten minutes he rattled on in this manner outlining the virtues of his activities.

Len heard him patiently. In the month since the ship's arrival he had become aware of an increasing deference and respect from the girls, the ship's crew and the base's personnel. His position on the ship, which had become centre stage at the base and his absolute authority over everything pertaining to it, induced a sense of responsibility and power manifested by an exaggerated politeness. As Australians say of their senior politicians who begin to believe in their own importance as statesmen, he had un-wittingly been duchessed.

'I shall defer my decision for twenty-four hours,' he announced rather grandly and the following day had Potter deliver to Wilson a written response. It read:

'I have fully considered your arguments and while accepting

the economic principles you advance (although I note you ignore our unregulated monopolistic position) I am obliged to weigh some wider considerations.

'Currently, demand exceeds supply for the ship's services. We anticipate this situation continuing until relief can be achieved through an increase in staffing numbers. Consequently there is only one economic outcome from your activities, namely to increase the cost to our consumers for no ancillary benefit other than to yourself. Pending restoration of a satisfactory balance between supply and demand your underwriting function is redundant. In these circumstances the effect of your role is to create a privileged position for the financially advantaged consumer which is contrary to the democratic spirit of our enterprise.

'However, conditional on your agreement to cease all secondary market activities, the prohibition on your access to our services is forthwith lifted, subject to your future purchasing being confined to personal consumption.'

To the draft of this message, which in fact had been written by Claudia, he added a pompous footnote, 'There will be no right of appeal.'

One surprise overture came from the Chinese restaurant proprietor's daughters. Having learned that the girls were averaging five hundred dollars daily earnings they requested permission to join the stable.

The Chinese restaurant had proven a popular success so Len quickly rejected their request with a warning against any side activities and a promise they could join the team on the following year's tour of duty.

On another occasion Len received a disgruntled four-man New Zealand delegation from Scott base. Their spokesman, a huge bearded ornithologist researching skua beak lengths, implored Len for a Scott base quota allocation claiming the Americans through their proximity advantage were hogging the ship's services. He pulled from his pocket some computer spreadsheets and placed them before Len.

These contained an extensive analysis of all Scott base personnel's waiting times, concluding that they averaged six days while the anecdotal evidence suggested the Americans endured a mere two-day delay between bookings. Taking a leaf from

Wilson's book Len extended to the New Zealanders a two-weeks block-booking privilege up to a maximum of sixty servicings in any twenty-four hour period and the delegation left in good humour.

Some problems were more worrying.

One afternoon while studying Potter's productivity reports Len was interrupted by the arrival of the captain. Len poured him a whisky.

'Ve haf big problem,' the captain declared and went on to advise the ship would have to return to a port to discharge its effluent holding tanks. Len exploded, pointing out that the hire contract guaranteed six months' adequacy in respect of the tanks.

The captain retorted that the tanks' capacity allowed for eight months but something was going wrong. They were mysteriously clogging up and a serious health issue threatened.

Len discussed this crisis with Potter who quickly produced a solution. Unfolding a map of the southern ocean, Andrew drew attention to a strong eastwards current running forty miles offshore. 'No one will know if we discharge into this,' he claimed, arguing that the current would soon dissipate the sewage which would eventually sink.

A few days later notices appeared throughout the ship advising that for engine-testing purposes it would be sailing away for a half day. All bookings were set back six hours. A Chinese banquet followed by a bingo session would be arranged for the girls, an announcement received with childlike glee.

At the scheduled time the ship departed and after two hours reached its destination. While the festivities were underway in the ballroom, Len and Potter joined the captain on the bridge. The three watched horror-struck at the appalling discoloration in their wake following the tanks' discharge. 'Zere is problem,' the captain cried pointing, for bobbing in the stew behind were thousands of condoms which had resisted the tanks' chemical system.

Len did a quick calculation. They had been anchored for six weeks during which the 1000 daily sales goal had been achieved. As the sewage gradually sank behind them, a great shoal of more than 40,000 condoms remained afloat, glistening and sparkling in the ship's wash.

On another occasion Len received Colonel Harris, the senior McMurdo base US military officer, who burst in to the office in a state of high indignation.

A much anticipated evening had been ruined, he protested. It transpired the colonel had booked a girl, this to be followed by dinner in the Chinese restaurant with a colleague and then afterwards the two had had reservations for the new nightclub act.

His girl, he said, had been sulky and refused to smile. 'It was God-damn necrophilia, I tell you,' the colonel protested. The colonel's lament was received sympathetically.

Almost from the first day of the ship's arrival at McMurdo Len had struck up a cordial rapport with Colonel Harris. The American had not enjoyed his Antarctic stint which contrasted dramatically with his previous posting in North Vietnam as the USA Army's Casualty Resolution Special Joint Task Force Accounting Deputy Chief Executive Officer, to give him his full title.

He had sought a transfer without revealing the real reason. That was his realisation that when Vietnamese villagers had periodically claimed recollection of captured US airmen having been buried in various difficult farming terrains, his teams had ploughed up acres of hillside without ever discovering any POW remains. One evening it had suddenly dawned on Harris that the Vietnamese were exacting a cunning revenge on the US misleading them into difficult land cultivation, following which they had moved in and planted their crops. Colonel Harris had mulled the situation over and ultimately concluded he would say nothing and that this outcome amounted to a minor redressing of a major debt. So he had sought a fresh posting which had resulted in his Antarctic stewardship but had been uncomfortable from the outset with the beards whose diverse activities largely struck him as unmanly and pointless.

Len opened a bottle of wine and the two settled into an enjoyable duet of empathetic complaining about the younger generation's shortcomings, their lack of any sense of service or duty, their general irresponsibility and selfishness; exactly, Len recalled, as he had engaged in with Lord Melcup six months earlier. Eventually the colonel left, happily rebooked for a two-girl performance on the house the following day.

Meanwhile, Potter was instructed to arrange for the offending girl to return home on the next plane. Len was acutely conscious that this venture was his 'last hurrah' and he was determined to milk it to the maximum. The key to success lay in superior service and to that end, following the colonel's complaint, Potter agreed to diplomatically sound out customers at random so as to root out any other miscreants.

By and large the eclectic mix of mini-dramas and problems were dealt with as they arose. But there was one problem which had arisen with increasing frequency since their arrival and for which Len had no answer and Potter's 'tell them to get stuffed' advice seemed unsatisfactory.

The first occurrence arose a week after their arrival. A bespectacled young geologist called Moriarty presented himself nervously in Len's office.

'It's about Kylie, sir. She's a very intelligent girl.'

'Yes; I know that, son,' Len replied warily.

'The thing is, Mr Edwards,' Moriarty continued, fidgeting furiously as he spoke, 'if you don't mind me saying so, she doesn't really belong here.'

My God, Len thought, he's in love.

'She came ashore this afternoon and I showed her my rocks. She's incredibly bright, sir. She picked it all up immediately. I mean, what I'd like to do, that is, how do I organise it if she could sort of leave the ship because I don't think she sees anyone else, or at least there may just have been one, or possibly two when she didn't realise the implications and I'd sort of like to take her back Stateside, so what do I do?' his voice rising plaintively with this cri de coeur.

'How does Kylie feel about this?' Len enquired gently.

'Well, sir, I'm certain she feels the same but I thought I'd discuss it with you first.'

Later, Len joined Potter in the lounge for a drink. Coincidentally, Kylie was sitting in the adjacent booth with two other off-duty girls, complaining bitterly.

'Fucking rocks; can you believe it? I thought at least I'd see nice little penguins and things. Just bloody rocks. And not only that; the little prick came over all mushy and started going on

93

about Seattle and talking about houses and schools and stuff. I think he wants to marry me. Christ; can you imagine it?'

This little saga soon became a regular occurrence. Len attempted various love-negating strategies but nothing he tried produced a satisfactory outcome. From time to time fracas broke out as smitten beards, lurking about the corridors, launched assaults on their loved ones' clientele.

Finally he raised the matter at the weekly Sunday morning ball-room assembly.

'Now, ladies. I want to address a problem which is occurring. It's been reported some customers are falling in love.'

An angry murmuring broke out, the bad language rule temporarily going out the window.

'We need you to report promptly to Andrew when the beards fall in love,' he continued. 'If, of course, any of you should reciprocate such feelings,' at which point the ballroom filled with derisory laughter, 'then we are happy to facilitate your return with your betrothed to wherever.'

'And,' he suggested mischievously, encouraged by the mirth, 'I'm quite sure, should you so desire, Father O'Hearn would be delighted to conduct a full shipboard wedding.' Rising to his subject Len added, 'Why, we could even fly in wedding dresses, bridesmaids' gowns; the whole regalia.'

A sudden mood change came over the room and an excited buzz broke out as the assembly's previous cynicism was substituted by a detectable feminine mushiness.

Potter, sitting beside Len, quickly rose from his seat and hissed, 'For Christ's sake Len; stop it. You're putting bloody stupid ideas in their heads.'

But it was too late; the damage was done and the meeting broke up in excited disarray.

Later, Len raised the matter during a management meeting with Potter and Claudia.

'I've been thinking about the falling in love problem. Does it really matter? Let's face it. These girls are never going to stray for the usual curiosity reason. They've already seen it all. The blokes are all bloody wet to tidal wave proportions. They couldn't hope to pull lookers like these when they return home. They could be bloody good wives too, with real scarcity value today because they'll be quite happy to stay at home and look after kids and what not. I tell you; these are marriages made in heaven. And they don't affect us as there's no problem topping up the stable with fresh faces, which in itself is a good thing.'

Potter stared at Len askance.

'You're missing the bloody point,' he barked. 'Of course there's no problem on the supply side. But for Christ's sake, mate. It's the demand side I'm bothered about. That's pretty well fixed. We can't have our market steadily downsizing just because the bastards fall in love. We've got to put a stop to it. You've got the girls all airy-headed talking about weddings. Females achieve their peak irrationality at the merest sniff of a full-scale wedding. Everyone knows that. It's an absolutely taboo subject.'

'Oh,' said Len thoughtfully. 'Well of course I was only joking.'

Claudia intruded. 'Look, I'm pretty much on top of things now. Why not let me handle this? I think the men might be more comfortable talking to a woman anyway.'

Thereafter Len and Andrew diverted the infatuated to Claudia who, by a process of trial and error, eventually resolved the problem.

6

Father O'Hearn called the meeting to order.
For the first time since his arrival in the Antarctic he felt purposeful. After four years' training in a seminary his teaching order had offered him the choice of Botswana or Jamaica, where they were already established. As an afterthought they had mentioned the Antarctic, which was a pioneering role. He had seized the chance knowing that Africa, the Caribbean and other places would remain open in the future, but his choice had not been a success. Most of the scientists were atheists, many of them aggressively so, and he had felt alien trying to be one of them and organising competitions rather than any religious or counselling role for which he was trained.

The competitions had all ended disastrously. First he had organised a soccer tournament between nations. The men had greeted this enthusiastically but with little provocation, each match had been called off early through the inevitable outbreak of fisticuffs. There was a constant abrasive atmosphere at the base, the men were all permanently edgy and arguments and altercations were frequent, particularly among the multitude of penguin researchers who seemed to be continuously at loggerheads. When a Tel Aviv University penguin kleptomania team angrily accused a Tokyo University penguin waddling speed group of denying opportunity for kleptomaniac behaviour by provoking the penguins into constant movement, the priest recognised the same vibes of violence in the air that had permeated his former boxing days.

Only one small group remained good-humoured. These were the men who had secured the favours of the few females present. In a form of collective security this faction detached itself from the others, ate and socialised together, the men guarding their prizes zealously, sensitive to their good fortune and the ever-present danger of invading predators.

They had cause to be vigilant for only a week earlier, one of their number, a Minnesota geologist, had fallen prey to outside invasion. In a momentary judgement lapse he had left the base for twelve hours to inspect a new quartz discovery thirty miles along the coast. On his return he discovered his booty, an overweight bespectacled Toronto poetess, possessor of a one-month grant from the Canadian Arts Council to create a poetic vision of the Antarctic, had been stolen by the swiftly pouncing Doctor Brockie, a New Zealand jellyfish anorexia expert.

In fact Dr Brockie's good fortune, while primarily attributable to negligence by the geologist, rested as is so often the case on chance rather than calculation. He had encountered the poetess walking alone when he was on his way over from Scott base to borrow a new weighing machine from an American jellyfish obesity research group. Like all of the men at both bases he was acutely aware of every detail pertaining to the few females present and casting his mind back to his schooldays had greeted her with: 'Wandering lonely as a cloud, I see.'

The poetess had clasped two fat paws to her cheek. 'Oh, you're a poetry lover,' she oozed.

Encouraged, Brockie again scoured his memory. La Boheme came to his aid. He reached out and took her fat, warm mitten-encased hand. 'Your tiny hand is frozen,' he said sadly.

'Ooh,' the poetess cried.

Brockie moved in for the kill and adopted what he hoped was an appropriately forlorn voice. 'Poetry is my whole life,' he said sadly. 'In fact, it's the real reason I'm here.'

'No,' exclaimed the poetess. 'So am I.'

'Yes, but in my case I was sent by my psychiatrist to escape poetry. I'd become so obsessed it was necessary to go cold turkey. Now I'm suffering from withdrawal symptoms. I'm desperate to hear a poem recited. Just one surely couldn't harm me. A simple sonnet would quench my need.'

After that the coup de grace was easy and the Canadian poetess was now safely ensconced at Scott base assisting Dr Brockie weigh his jellyfish and confined through Brockie's obsession-problem restraint-necessity to only two tortuous poetic recitations daily.

Back at McMurdo the constant brooding presence of the geologist who now mooched glumly about the fringe of the female-favoured group, reluctant to accept his new dispossessed status and conscious of his unspoken, growing 'outsider' treatment by his former colleagues, sent shivers of fear through the remaining fat-girl possessors. 'There but for the grace of God...' they worried and intensified their surveillance.

Following the soccer debacle O'Hearn had resorted to a less physical entertainment and had organised a debate.

The first of these, which as it transpired was also the last, had ended even more violently than the soccer tournament fiasco as the men, now uninhibited by their bulky outdoor clothing, had inflicted much physical damage on each other and for some days following the base hospital was busy attending to the injuries.

O'Hearn had chosen what he had considered a safe yet interesting topic for a large, multinational group of scientifically educated men; namely, 'That racism has no underlying scientific basis.'

To the priest's dismay the debaters demonstrated no intellectuality in their advocacies; instead, to a man they tendered clumsy evidence of their own liberal outlook by the uniform qualification as to whom they wouldn't object to their sister marrying.

The second speaker, an Australian plankton hysteria expert, launched the descent into anarchy with his comment that he 'wouldn't object to his sister marrying an Indian except for the fact that bloody Indians never stop picking their noses'. This was greeted with an approving roar by most present and a bitter protest from a Madras University albatross schizophrenia research group.

Thereafter speaker after speaker, each applying the sisterly marriage test, drew increasingly offensive attention to other nationalities' alleged shortcomings, inducing angry responses from those targeted.

Nevertheless, repetition of this sisterly marriage theme soon diluted its impact necessitating elevation of the offensiveness assertions to a higher plane. Thereafter addresses began with, 'As my father always said, when it comes to Italians...' and, 'Once I visited Cairo and...' and, 'When I was only twelve we had this Chinese family shift next door...' and, 'At university there was this student from Nigeria...' This second phase raised the level of complaint to shouting, threats and spasmodic punching exchanges but it was the lifting of the advocacy style to its third and highest plane that saw the debate end and an all-out brawl substituted.

Abandoning racial abuse generality the speakers now targeted the specific base personnel. Addresses began with, 'I sat down to breakfast the other day and those Japanese iceberg analysts over there...' the speaker pointing to the offenders at this juncture, 'you wouldn't believe what the dirty bastards...' and, 'In our block we have to share the toilets with those bloody Arab zoologists...' pointing 'and I tell you...' and, 'I was in the laundry the other day and in came those bloody Belfast university seal...'

Suddenly the room erupted into an explosion of whirling limbs, crashing furniture, shouts and tumbling bodies.

Dismayed, Father O'Hearn surveyed the scene. Most of the men retreated back along the walls cheering on the forty or more wildly punching brawlers in the centre of the room.

Overcome with revulsion and disinclined to intervene, the priest suddenly realised his distaste lay more with the ineffectual crudity of the punching than the fact of the brawl. His thoughts flashed back to boyhood viewing of Western movies in which the hero single-handedly overcame a bar room of villains and he quickly assessed the melee in terms of his own capabilities. Three minutes, he concluded. Three minutes and I could stand alone, centre stage, probably with damaged hands but with forty or so bodies stretched out around me.

Temptation briefly flared, then flickered and was extinguished. His entire training, both in the boxing ring and the seminary, was bound up in restraint, in self-control and in calculated resistance to impulse. Unnoticed he left the room.

There had been times recently when Father O'Hearn had questioned his career choice. As the former New Jersey amateur middleweight champion, he had sometimes wondered whether his life might have been better had he turned professional while simultaneously studying at university. The unexpected arrival of the Olga Buskova had reinvigorated him and he had called the meeting to protest against this development.

Expressing disappointment at the small turnout, Father O'Hearn congratulated the good and decent souls who were present.

'It's been my observation that temptation is the devil's greatest asset. Sadly we have seen that brought home to us in recent weeks. It behoves all of us to restore this once noble facility's dignity and decency which was previously its hallmark and to destroy this evil which has arisen in our midst.'

Before him sat the base's eighteen plain female scientists, uniformly enraged. Additionally there was a smattering of very short bearded men while at the head table alongside Father O'Hearn sat an unctuous New Zealand administration official, Stan Twigg, a man whose busybody wetness was a source of awe to even the base's dullest scientists and who was unnecessarily recording the meeting's proceedings. Within days of his arrival two months earlier, Twigg had earned widespread contempt for his failed attempt to introduce traffic lights at the base to avoid possible snowmobile collisions.

Father O'Hearn concluded, 'I shall throw the meeting over to the floor for suggestions as to how best we can combat this cancer,' and he sat down.

The ensuing discussion was not fruitful. Several fat girls rose but their contributions were confined to bitter protest. In just three days they had achieved invisibility as once-admiring pursuers now barely acknowledged them.

Eventually, when the discussion lapsed, Twigg looked up from his writing and spoke.

'One thing they've miscalculated,' he crowed. 'Over half of the base personnel are married men so we can discount them. I bet they never thought about that,' and he sat down smirking.

Eventually Father O'Hearn broke the perplexed lull that followed Twigg's pronouncement.

'Are you trying to take the mickey?' he barked. Twigg blinked furiously behind his spectacles, plainly uncomprehending.

The Canadian poetess, now back at McMurdo and restored to her conventional alone-and-unwanted Toronto status, suggested Father O'Hearn approach the base military commander to order the ship's departure.

'I've already discussed the matter with Colonel Harris,' O'Hearn replied. 'I was disappointed with his attitude for to be frank, he seemed totally unconcerned. I pointed out his own men were being affected and he said he knew that and would have a mutiny on his hands if he prohibited them from the ship. I threatened to go over his head to the Pentagon but he said it would make no difference. He claims the military has no jurisdiction in the Antarctic and he could do nothing. I'm afraid he's quite correct.'

At that, a fat girl who had been intensely wooed for two glorious weeks by one of the military officers but who had not spoken to her since the ship's arrival, burst into noisy sobbing. Plainly the meeting was making little progress.

'Pending any other suggestions there's one ray of hope we should all focus our prayers on,' Father O'Hearn said. 'In a week's time Senator Fulton flies in. I have no doubt he will share our concerns. As a senator he is very influential and I'm sure will rescue us from this satanic cloud which has been cast over us. In the interim I propose we picket the ship. It may be that our presence will turn some erring souls back before they descend into the hands of the devil.'

A twenty-four hour daily roster was established. In groups of four, fat girls and tiny beards stood beside the gangway holding signs with the single message SHAME.

At first the men streaming past ducked their heads and averted their faces. After a few days they stopped caring and eventually they became abusive. One by one the picketers dropped out so that a week before Senator Fulton's arrival, only Twigg and Father O'Hearn maintained the vigil.

7

Problem with the doctor,' Potter announced entering the office. Len looked up from the interest-bearing balances schedules Tom faxed daily.

'I've been expecting this,' he said glumly. 'What's the old bugger done?'

'The girls complain he's always pissed. They're worried he's giving them the wrong injections and pills and stuff.'

Dr Isaac was brought before them, dishevelled and bleary-eyed.

'Now listen, Peter,' Len began. 'The girls aren't happy with you. Claim you're drunk all the time and don't know what you're doing. You know I had reservations about you coming and I told you frankly I thought you were too old. We're sending you home on the jet. We can't afford cock-ups.'

Isaac snorted derisorily. 'Christ, Len. You'd be pissed all the time too, doing my job. I mean, I've seen the bloody penguins, I've seen the seals; the scientists are the most boring bunch of bastards on earth. I get a better conversation from the parrot than from most of them. What else is there but drink?'

'But hang on a minute,' Len protested. 'We've got a hundred girls and twenty-five crew. What about medical matters?'

Isaac chortled. 'Lenny boy. We're in the healthiest place in the world. There are no infections here, no viruses, no bugs, no accidents. These would be the fittest bunch of females on earth. They do nothing but lie on their backs all day and have hourly bursts of exercise. It's totally stress-free and believe me, son, that's the most vital element in health. If I were to prescribe a recipe for longevity, I'd describe these girls' lives.'

'But,' Len protested weakly, 'they've been coming to see you. There must be something wrong with them.'

'Let me tell you about medicine, son,' Isaac said resignedly. 'Ninety per cent of it's bullshit. We're the only profession which tolerates charlatans and racketeering. Look at Harley Street. The biggest bunch of gangsters in existence, taking advantage of gullible self-centred women with too much money and time.

Colonic irrigation, magic pill courses at outrageous cost to delude forty-year-olds they can be twenty again; oh the list is endless. I suppose it occupies empty lives. Gives 'em hope; something to do. That's probably therapeutic in itself. But believe me, a good boot in the bum and let nature take its course would be the most honest treatment a GP could deliver most patients. Most illnesses are imaginary and nearly all the rest will fix themselves.'

'Well what the hell are the girls coming to you for?' Potter muttered.

'Like I said, it's all imaginary. Women like visiting doctors and talking about themselves. If there's nothing wrong with them, and there's usually not, at least not physically, then they make it up. You must remember they're all a bit mad and our role's to humour them. I'll show you my records if you don't believe me. Sixty per cent of the girls are on placebos; the rest get bogus injections. At the beginning I injected saline water and they went away quite happily. But I ran out so now I just stick a needle in their backsides so they can't see, hold it there a few seconds then pull it out. Off they trot; cured.

'Actually I've been meaning to talk to you about the placebo pills. I'm running out as we're going through more than I anticipated. The trick is a prescription. Back home they go away quite happily if they've got a prescription. The important thing is good records. I dish out two large pink pills to be taken before sleep each night. Six months later they're back again so I check my records to make the treatment different. Next time it's a small white pill, three times a day before meals.

'But down here I can't dish out prescriptions without pharmacies. I have to hand out the bloody pills myself. It reduces credibility when they can't trot off to pharmacists and generally go to a bit of trouble. I've been thinking about it though and I've got the answer. I'm making the instructions more complicated to compensate. One pill at precisely 9am with a glass of water, the next at midday swallowed dry; that sort of nonsense. You've got to get them involved.'

'Jesus,' Len exploded. 'What if someone gets appendicitis or something?'

'Appendicitis; appendicitis,' Isaac exclaimed wearily, lifting his eyes ceilingwards. 'My dear boy. I could train a motor mechanic in thirty minutes to take out an appendix. When it comes to medicine the bullshit about surgery is the worst of all. Most of it's pretty basic.

'Look. I'll tell you what the real key is with medicine. It's diagnosis. Like I said, ninety per cent of complaints are either imaginary or will cure themselves. Now even if I say so myself, I've always been good at diagnosis. That's because I know it's the only thing that counts and I've made the effort. But being good at it doesn't get you far in this game. There's no money or honour in medicine with honesty. Sometimes I think I've been a bloody mug when I look at the chaps I went through medical college with; what with their country houses and foreign holidays and fancy cars.

'Take old Jeremy Aston-Walker. He was my best mate at med school. Wouldn't know a femur from a fishbone. Made a fortune in Harley Street with rejuvenation courses. Had mad Princess bloody Diana as a client. Twisted her round his finger and had her organise him a knighthood. Now he's an ambassador in South America.

'No, don't you worry about the girls. In the unlikely event one of them really gets something wrong, I'll know. And I'll tell you this. I might have a bit aboard at the time but I'll know quicker and more accurately than any bugger you're likely to replace me with. The young 'uns all know nothing and most of the older fellows give up caring after about ten years on the job.'

Len recalled the interview with Mr Rose. Isaac had him over a barrel. Probably he was as good as could be hoped for. Finally, Len spoke.

'I'll tell you what I'll do. But that's subject to you co-operating. Aside from real emergencies – broken bones, that sort of thing – I want you to set precise office hours. Let's say four hours a day. I want them established on a regular basis and I want your undertaking you will be sober and tidy. Patronise them a bit. Make an effort; you know, bedside manner stuff.'

'That's a deal,' Isaac said. 'Rely on me, sunshine. There won't be any more whining. I'll give 'em a bit more of the old stethoscope and all that rigmarole. That will keep them happy. I know the ropes.'

Isaac rose to leave. At the door he turned and spoke again.

'I say. While I'm here there's something I've been meaning to raise. Do you know Nadia?'

Len thought awhile and eventually recalled. Nadia, a quietish girl, had come to them almost directly from a convent. She had particularly striking features and he recalled reading her background notes; claimed a passion for poetry.

'Yes, of course,' Len said quizzically.

'Oh, I was just wondering,' Isaac said airily. 'I was thinking it might be a good thing if she went on a salary and became my nurse. She's a very intelligent girl, you know.'

'Piss off,' Len shouted and Isaac closed the door.

8

Problem with the beauty salon,' Potter chanted as he entered the room with a grin on his face.

'You think it's bloody well funny, don't you? I'm beginning to believe you enjoy these difficulties,' Len complained.

'Actually it's not quite like that this time, I'm pleased to say. We're on to a real winner here,' Potter announced triumphantly.

Len raised his eyebrows, questioningly. Potter explained. 'Do you remember back in London discussing the ancillary services; the flower shop, the restaurant, the bookshop, the sauna, the nightclub and what not, and I said to you then I was concerned about the overheads and you arguing the benefits were intangible but real. You'll recall I accused you of rationalising and told you how in the bank we monitored public companies which, as soon as they were on to something big and making lots of money, lost the plot with endless bullshit to justify self-serving indulgence; fancy head offices, corporate jets, management conferences in the Bahamas; all that sort of stuff. Tom has a great nose for this and always knew when to bail out of these companies. He says trying to talk to them about it is invariably a waste of time.'

Len recalled the discussion only too well. It had become heated and was the only time in his relationship with Potter in which any disagreement had developed.

Andrew continued. 'I've got to say I was being quite honest with you. I was angry at the thought you were going to mess up a fabulous idea by unnecessary expenditure. Well, I've done an analysis. We're absolutely creaming it with the lot; the restaurant, the nightclub, the florist, the bookshop. But the biggest winner by miles is the beauty salon, which, I might add is currently closed.'

'What?' Len exclaimed. 'What the hell's happened?'

'Raelene's gone on strike. Says she's heading for a nervous breakdown with everyone pressuring for appointments. We got it all wrong,' he continued. 'We pitched the beauty salon with a single operator to handle the girls and you'll remember we thought that was pushing it. But guess what? The girls are bitching because they can't get a look-in. The bloody Russian nancy-boys are in there all the time having their bums powdered and whatnot. We never thought of that.

'But best of all the blokes from the base are the keenest. Raelene started an appointment book and within three days was booked up five weeks ahead and, I might add, working a ten-hour day. She's only on a salary, remember. Anyway, it seems the fellows ashore normally cut one another's hair but now with the presence of the girls, and swags of them falling in love, they're all wanting to be perfumed and powdered, if you get my drift. Two of them have even cut off their beards.'

'That's wonderful,' Len cried. 'I'll contact Harding and get him to rustle up two more hairdressers. He's due in next week with a batch of Asian girls to freshen up the stable. Tell the Russians to prepare two more cabins, oh, and tell Raelene her salary has just gone up twenty-five per cent but she's got to get back on the job right now.'

A minute later Potter was back. 'I say,' he said. 'I've been thinking. Let's raise beauty salon charges fifty per cent.'

'No way,' Len said. 'Look, you said it yourself. We're doing very nicely out of it now. Far better to bring in more hairdressers than lift the prices, which will only annoy the beards. Anyway, if they're only hammering the beauty salon to look good for the girls then surely that's an argument for lowering the prices if it keeps them coming.'

'You know,' said Andrew. 'When I was at Oxford we used to look down our noses at economics students as philistines. But working with Tom changed my attitude. Economics is fascinating. Like Claudia says, it's got nothing to do with simple numbers. It's all about human behaviour, and anticipating that correctly can be a real hornet's nest. Probably you're right about the beauty salon. I suppose we could extrapolate that line of thinking to cutting the price of drinks to even below cost just to lure the beards.'

'Ah. But luring them isn't a problem,' Len retorted. 'Do that and they might end up just drinking. But going to the beauty salon is directly connected to the girls. We're on to a bloody good thing here. Surely the only consideration is to sustain it. Lowering the beauty salon prices helps that. Free drinks might harm it.

Still, we should think about all of those propositions and throw them at Claudia for another opinion. One thing though. Tell Raelene to refuse the Russians until she's got more assistance. They can go to buggery if you'll excuse the pun.'

9

.

Dear Al,
I hope you are well.
Today I had a most disturbing conversation with the credit card company. This month's statement showed some peculiar debits so I called and queried these and the credit card people said they were charges from you at McMurdo. There was $2,700 to something called 'The High Risk Venture Fund' and $600 to Scientific Book Supplies and some smaller amounts to the Yangzse Restaurant.

I told them that obviously there was no Chinese restaurant in the Antarctic let alone a bookshop so they must be mistaken but they insisted it was your signature. They faxed me photocopies and it was. How is this possible and what are those other charges?

The children send their love and we all miss you. The camellia tree died so I have had it replaced. Tibs was sick for a few days but the vet said it was a fever and gave us some pills which fixed her but she's still a little subdued.

I hope the research is going okay. I still don't understand why the molecular structure of Antarctic snow is any different from here in Boise or even why it matters.

Love,
Emily

Dear Emily,
I'm sorry to hear about the camellia. I hope you found a similar-sized replacement as it is so slow growing.

I was intending to tell you about the credit card charges and the fact that I haven't is a reflection of just how busy we are down here. Not having any night-time tends to make us work much longer hours and there's absolutely nothing to do here but work anyway, so I've been a bit remiss in not writing.

The Chinese restaurant charges were on a tourist boat which came in. They sure must have mystified you. It's been our only treat in three months.

The Scientific Book Supplies is fairly expensive but I had to order these books and they couriered them in without me asking for that sort of delivery and that was responsible for $200 of the cost. Anyway, since when have you, a librarian, been against books?

The High Risk Venture Fund was a special opportunity which arose and I had to make a decision quickly. Nearly all the men participated so I felt you would have agreed if you had been here and I signed up.

It's a special fund in which we pay in $2,700 a month for five months and stand to get back over $70,000 by the end of the year – if it works. But as its name suggests, it's high risk. It's a bit complicated as it involves funding a mining venture in West Africa. The chances of it working are less than 30% but the returns if it does are tenfold so I felt the mathematical odds justified the risk and as I said, everyone down here is in as it was a special opportunity only available to the McMurdo personnel. We can afford to risk $13,000 for such a potential return but you must remember it may not work and I'll know before I return. I suggest you forget about it and we'll only mention it if it pays off but you will at least know what the charges are on the credit card statement in future.

I hope the cat is better now.

Al

P.S.   Love to you and the children.

10

Following a referral from Len, Claudia arranged for Tania and Dr Wysocki to meet in her office to discuss their matrimonial plans. Prior to their arrival she rearranged her visitors' armchairs so they faced one another, ten feet apart.

Dr Wysocki was with a University of New England scientific team studying penguin dietary habits. A small bespectacled, bearded man, about thirty years old, he perched nervously on the edge of his chair.

Tania arrived ten minutes late, heavily made up and wearing blue jeans and a lurid scarlet and white patterned wind jacket zipped to the throat. Ignoring her betrothed she slunk sullenly into her chair and turned her face to the wall.

'Now I want to make it clear we will do everything to assist you both,' Claudia began. 'But you do understand, Dr Wysocki, Tania is only nineteen and in our care so we must have this little discussion to ensure you are quite certain you want to spend the rest of your lives together.'

Wysocki nodded vigorously. Tania grimaced and slouched further into her armchair.

'Let's begin with you, Doctor. So Tania can appreciate your work, let's talk a little about that. I understand you're studying penguins' diet. Perhaps you could tell us exactly how you do that?' Claudia suggested.

'What I'm doing,' Wysocki said enthusiastically, in a high pitched squeaking voice, 'is gathering penguin faeces from different sampling points and analysing their content. That enables me to monitor their dietary composition.'

Noting Tania was still studying the wall Claudia politely elaborated. 'By faeces you meaning droppings,' she suggested, knowingly setting the ball rolling on a rapid downhill journey.

Tania slowly turned her head and stared at Wysocki.

'You collect penguin pooh?' she queried, her eyes widening.

'Yes. It's really exciting. Of course they're frozen so I have to melt them first before I can do any analysis. I've got over 600 samplings collected now,' Wysocki said proudly.

There was a lengthy pause. Finally, Tania said, 'Why?'

'Why what?' Wysocki repeated, uncomprehending.

'Yeah. Why? Why do you collect it?' the girl demanded.

'As I said, so we can study their food,' the scientist replied, plainly puzzled by Tania's tone.

'Why? Whadda they ead?'

'They eat fish.'

'What else?'

'There's nothing else but fish.'

Tania stared in astonishment at Wysocki. After a while she said, 'So when you come and see me you've been playing around all day cooking penguin shit?'

Detecting an attitudinal shift Wysocki began twitching nervously. 'But that's what I'm here for, darling.'

Tania snorted. After another long pause she said, 'Who pays you to cook penguin crap?'

'The expedition is being funded by the university,' Wysocki answered unhappily.

'Where do they get their money from?' Tania pressed, by now sitting erect, an undisguised look of fascinated disgust on her face.

Wysocki struggled. 'Well, the university has various sources of income although this research is being funded by a special federal grant,' he spluttered, visibly miserable at the tenor of Tania's enquiry.

'What's federal?'

'Why, that's the government, darling.'

'Why do these federal jokers give you money for this?'

'As I said, so we can study the penguins' food habits,' the scientist mumbled.

'Why do they care what penguins ead?'

'It's not a matter of them caring. It's highly unlikely they even know what we're doing.'

Tania's short life to date had not involved the state in its more diverse activities. If asked as to its meaning she would have struggled to extend beyond policemen and welfare agencies.

'Where do these federal pricks get their money from?' Tania persisted after another thoughtful lull.

'Why, darling, from the taxpayers, of course,' the scientist said, plainly surprised at the need for explanation.

'So buggers go to work and get taxed so you can fuck about cooking filthy bird shit. What does it matter what the bloody penguins ead? Who bloody cares and wotcher gunna do about it anyway?'

These were propositions Wysocki had hitherto never considered. In the world he inhabited the state's cornucopian role and the pursuit of esoteric knowledge were accepted unquestioningly. He attempted a long floundering explanation until cut off in mid-stream by Tania.

'I'll tell you what I think. I think you're a fucking pervert. I'd be bloody terrified to have a crap with you around,' and she rose and left without further ado, slamming the door behind her.

Claudia spoke softly to the distressed American. 'I'd like you to stay and have some coffee so we can talk about this,' and she picked up the telephone and ordered morning tea.

Gently but firmly she pointed out to Wysocki the importance of shared interests and backgrounds in a marriage. In response to the tormented scientist's complaint that Tania was a very intelligent girl and had never been like this before, and his hopeful suggestion that she was unwell, Claudia stuck to her fine line between brutal honesty and sensitive mothering. Eventually he left with the assurance that her office was always open to him to talk about the matter.

The Tania-Wysocki affair was her eighteenth such consultation since she had taken over the beards-falling-in-love problem and as she explained to Len and Andrew during a management meeting, she had the procedure down pat.

'You joked once that they're marriages made in heaven,' she said to Len. 'That's neither true nor a laughing matter. The truth is they're potentially marriages made in hell. I try and keep an open mind when they come and see me but as soon as I apply the test, they blow up every time.'

'What test?' Potter asked curiously.

'Essentially the test of truth, namely letting them see the real person,' she replied. 'These fellows come in to the girls' half-lit rooms, sometimes a little tiddly but even if sober, they're wound up and emotional. They roll around with a warm, soft and sexy naked young girl then it's back to the base with all its coarse male oafishness. Of course they fall in love. So, I take them away from that extreme to the other, namely letting them see one another as they really are. That's why I seat them opposite one another. Their previous contact has been totally naked and tactile, which is why my method works. In a funny sort of way they're only really naked in the sense of seeing the real person, when they have their clothes on and are facing one another. Once in my office it's conversation only but I've yet to see one break out.'

'You mean they don't speak at all?' Len asked.

Claudia laughed. 'There are plenty of words but they're not what you'd describe as a conversation. What I do is get the beard to talk about what he does. Nine times out of ten the girls have no real idea, which in itself shows how absurd their marriage proposition is. Once they hear they're always disgusted at what they perceive as the utter worthlessness of their loved one's occupation. It offends their common sense. They can't believe anyone will continue paying the beards to do these things so they feel insecure.'

'But don't the beards explain it?' Potter asked.

'That's always quite funny,' Claudia replied. 'You must remember they're mostly a bit soppy and naive. I'm convinced some of them are quite mad. I had one come in; a Hungarian crevasse-depth analyst. He hummed quite loudly throughout the interview so I did all the talking to ensure he wouldn't stop. I'm quite sure he was unaware he was doing it but the girl fled in terror and that was the end of him. Most of them are academics and have never thought about such mundane matters as the actual value of what they do, which is why they're so unsuitable for the girls. They have enormous difficulty when they try and justify their work.

'These girls are probably about as hard-headedly pragmatic as you can get. They're bewildered by the beards once they find out what they do and probably see them as parasites. What eventuates is a massive cultural clash. If you asked most of the girls to write a pecking order of desirable occupations for a husband, they'd reverse the normal rankings. Used-car dealing would probably top their list.'

'So it works every time?' Andrew asked.

'So far, yes, although I had one close shave. You know the

very goofy six-foot-six-ginger-bearded, Welsh marine biologist; what's his name?'

'Thomas,' Len said. 'I know the fellow. He's hard to miss.'

'Yes, that's right. Well, he fell in love with one of the Polish girls, Sonja. So I had them in and got him started on what he does and to my amazement Sonja pricked up her ears and seemed genuinely fascinated.'

'He's a seal chap, isn't he?' Len asked.

'Yes. He's recording what he calls seal music. He lowers waterproof microphones under the ice. He told me the sole purpose of this is to determine whether Antarctic seals have different sound patterns than seals anywhere else. I must say I have a reasonably generous tolerance for knowledge for knowledge's sake as a proposition, which I might say all the beards have as an article of faith, but I thought this was a bit rich.'

'So what happened with the Polish girl?' Len pressed.

'Well, as I said, she looked like being the first exception to the rule of contempt for the beards by the girls when they find out what they do. I had two different reactions to this unexpected interest. First I thought, well, if the two of them do get along outside the sack, then good show. We agreed on that, remember. You know; that we wouldn't stand in the way of any genuine romances.

'But my second reaction was that I couldn't believe Sonja's interest. It was so inconsistent with the normal response. So in the end I suggested Thomas go ashore and fetch some of his recordings and he was off in a flash. No one had ever been interested before.

'He came bounding back with a tape recorder and we sat there listening to the most ridiculous noises. That did the trick. Thomas sat back humming in accompaniment with his eyes closed and waving his arms like a conductor to what he claimed was a rhythm in the seal racket. That sort of behaviour looks particularly ludicrous in such a big man and after about ten minutes I could see Sonja was responding very negatively, and I don't blame her. So when it finally stopped I suggested he play it again and that was the end of him with the girl.

'Anyway, so far there's not been a single marriage proposition which has survived my preliminary meeting. The Thomas case just needed elaboration. The girls mostly won't have a bar of the beards afterwards and the men tend to mooch and mourn for a week or so but of course the ship offers the perfect solution. So usually after a couple of weeks the beards are over it. Some of them have even come and thanked me later.'

'It's bloody astonishing,' Potter exclaimed. 'They're supposed to be educated and intelligent men. It just makes no sense.'

'Love has absolutely nothing to do with intelligence or reason,' Claudia said. 'Why do you think more than fifty per cent of marriages fail? I've had one beard who's been through three falling-in-love-sessions with three different girls. Some men seem particularly susceptible yet in every other respect can be coldly rational.'

Claudia rose. 'I've got work to do.' At the door she turned and spoke again.

'For me the surprise of this state of affairs is that so many of the beards are zoologists and yet don't understand the fundamental biological factors at play here. It's not hard. Men fall in love slowly and take a long time to get over it when relationships end. Women are the opposite. They're quick to fall in love but once it's over, they terminate it coldly and unlike men, without any lingering sentiment or nostalgia.'

Len and Andrew stared at her as they contemplated this revelation. Claudia laughed at their puzzlement. 'Think about it. It's not hard to understand. As I said, it's biological. It's just another manifestation of Darwinian behaviour; men always pressing to get into girls' pants and girls totally committed once they succumb and bloody cold – hard-hearted in men's eyes – once they decide it's over. They have to be to survive.' Laughing again she closed the door.

11

Three weeks after the Asian girls arrived in the plane Potter confronted Len waving a bunch of computer spreadsheets. 'We've got a serious problem. We're at full capacity but the booking time lag's dropped to only a day and a half. I've analysed the situation and I think I've got to the bottom of it.' Andrew spread the data out before Len.

'Look at this,' he said. 'It's the bloody Asian girls. Their customers are rebooking at an average four-day interval but if you study their past records, this is a day and a half later than before. Something's bloody well going wrong. At first I thought the chaps must be unhappy with them but then look at this sheet,' and he spread a different set of names and figures on the desk.

'Every man jack of the Asian girls' clientele is rebooking them, so it can't be that. Come out to the lounge because I think I've detected the problem.'

The two men entered the lounge and called for coffee. Potter produced yet another sheet.

'Here's a photocopy of today's bookings,' Andrew said. 'Watch the doorway and I'll tell you what I think's going wrong, but first, let's see if you can spot it.'

As the beards emerged from the cabin's doorway, most lingered in the lounge for a beer or coffee before returning to shore.

'Look,' whispered Potter. 'Here's Thompson, the iceberg analyst. He's been with one of the Asians. Study his face. And here's Wilson. He's been with a non-Asian. Just watch as I call them and see if you can detect a pattern.'

For half an hour the two men sat studying the emerging beards. As each appeared Potter would glance at the bookings sheet and recite 'Asian' or 'non-Asian'.

After a time it became clear.

The non-Asian customers emerged jaunty and gregarious. They seemed on the whole to be perfectly happy as they joined their friends at the bar. But the Asian girls' customers behaved differently. To a man they bore a slightly glazed look and, avoiding company, instead sank into armchairs, called for coffee and sometimes dozed off.

'Christ; I see what you mean,' Len muttered.

'We can't have this. The little buggers are laying it on too thick,' Potter protested. 'These fellows are all sated. That's why they're taking extra days before they're back for more.'

The two discussed solutions. Len suggested they charge more for the Asians but realisation of the rumpus this would cause with the non-Asian girls soon put paid to that idea. They called for Mai-Chin to be brought before them as her English was the best. Len's attempt to explain the problem diplomatically was received with Oriental inscrutability. Clumsily Len concluded, 'So, Mai-Chin. We want you to tell the others to tone it down a bit.'

Finally Mai-Chin spoke. 'I don't understand.'

'Never the twain shall meet,' Andrew said, misinterpreting Kipling, after she had gone.

Two days later the jet arrived with its usual load of newspapers, fruit, flowers and stable replenishments. Harding joined Len and Andrew for lunch at the Chinese restaurant and the Asian girls booking problem arose in discussion.

'Let's have a look at 'em,' Harding said. 'I think I know what's wrong,' and between client servicing, one by one the Asian girls were brought briefly before them.

'A huge blunder, mate,' Harding said after the last had been inspected. 'They're all Chinese. Why do you think there's one and a half billion Chinese in the world? You can't get 'em to tone it down any more than you can get them to stop breathing. You've gotta ship 'em out and if you want Orientals then replace them with South-East Asians. You've got Malays, Thais, Vietnamese, Filipinas, Cambodians; heaps to choose from and they're all prettier than the Chinese but more restrained in the sack. Of course if you want to spice it up a bit it's no trouble for me to zip up to Africa or South America. They're both about the same distance from here.

'But basically, the issue has nothing to do with race. It's about variety. Racial differences provide that but I'll bet I could bring in a 300lb fat girl and all the beards would want to give her a serve at least once. It's simply a novelty issue.'

'That could be worth a try,' Len said thoughtfully.

'No,' Potter said. 'There's no need to provide more variety with this number of girls and a handful of Asians. The beards are perfectly happy. The problem is the Chinese girls have made some of them too happy. We've just got to fix that.'

And so over the next two plane trips the Chinese girls were protestingly replaced by a batch of Thais, Filipinas and Malays. Ten days later Potter happily reported that the full house advance booking buffer zone was back at the three-day level.

Nevertheless the subject arose again when Harding returned three weeks later.

'I've been thinking over our discussion about the Asian girls and variety,' he said. 'It seems to me you could achieve something very positive just by peppering up your entertainment.'

'We could achieve a lot more by ending it,' Andrew grumbled. 'That bloody Russian so-called singing group's low-life bawling and wailing is driving me mad and I'm damn sure most of the beards would agree.'

'They're part of the package,' Len protested. 'We've paid for them so might as well use them. Although I must admit they're beginning to irritate me as well. But what have you in mind, Bruce?'

'Right,' Bruce said. 'Here's the go. You know we only pay for the plane on flying hours clocked up. I could park here for up to a week and it wouldn't cost a penny more. So what I reckon is I contact a Sydney talent agency; one of those outfits which books club performers. We don't need top acts. The beards will think anything's great compared with the current situation of nothing. I book 'em on a performance basis for as little as possible and, considering they'll get a free Antarctic trip out of it, I reckon some will even come for nothing. You've got plenty of spare cabins so there's no accommodation cost. If the beards like the act we stay on for a few days and do several performances. If they don't then I bugger off as I would have done anyway. Seems fail-safe to me.'

'That's really a terrific idea,' Len enthused. 'Just don't go overboard on cost,' an unnecessary caution for as Harding had predicted, many came for nothing just to see the Antarctic.

Over the next six trips Harding brought in a rich variety of performers, all of whom yielded receptions from the beards totally contrary to Len and Andrew's pre-performance expectations.

A pert, cowboy-suited blonde country and western singer's repertoire of twangy sagas about dying dogs, fathers, mothers, horses and 'cheatin' larvas' was received coolly by all excepting the military personnel.

On the other hand a sexy Santo Domingo merengue singing group was a wild sensation. They joyfully delivered forty-minute frenetic performances six times daily, driving the beards into a frenzy and adding a further day to the booking office time lag during their stay.

A pretty Korean classical violinist was also well received and alone among the performers induced expressions of appreciation to Len and Andrew although without effect on the booking office.

By far the biggest disaster was an Australian comedian whose poor reception confined him to a single performance. He was well received by the small Australian, English and New Zealand faction on board but greeted with stony silence by the predominantly American scientists. Initially Len and Andrew were puzzled as they both found the comedian very funny. He had delivered a series of crass jokes centred around his presumably imaginary, paraplegic, wheelchair-bound older brother's life, which all resulted in even worse misfortunes.

Afterwards Andrew offered an explanation. 'It's a significant cultural difference between the English and Americans,' he asserted. 'Because Americans are basically polite their humour is self-deprecatory; on the other hand English humour, which the Aussies have inherited, targets others, particularly the innocently afflicted such as cripples or the blind or very fat or short people or whatever. That offends Americans' sense of propriety. They see it as cruel and callous but my view is it's the opposite. It's actually generous in involving unfortunates by drawing attention to them through their peculiarity rather than the American deceit of pretending they're normal but in practice ignoring them.'

The biggest and most astonishing success was an illusionist magician. Each trick yielded thunderous applause. Following the performances many of the beards queued to be photographed with the magician.

Andrew and Len were perplexed until all was revealed during a discussion with an American behavioural researcher, Dr Tullett. 'Scientific research is all about speculative guesswork and mystery,' he explained. 'Scientists frequently produce outcomes for which they have no explanations. If that wasn't the case we'd have a cure for cancer. The men don't just relate to the illusionist; they put him on a pedestal as a superior fellow-professional because they know he knows the answers to his mysteries which they spend their time seeking.'

Eventually the situation evolved whereby the sight of Harding's plane coming in to land caused chaos at the base. Snowmobiles pounded back at full speed as the beards scrambled to be among the privileged 750 allowed on board before the full-house sign was hung at the gangway. The beards responded to the plane's arrival like children on Christmas morning as it brought in its booty of recent newspapers, the latest books, fresh flowers, stable replenishment and the new entertainer.

The booking time lag rose during some entertainers' visits to a record seven days but Andrew's elation at this triumph was short-lived when he discovered this was partly attributable to large numbers of the girls taking time off to watch the acts. A roster system was installed to ensure a full servicing capacity and order was restored.

12

Len organised a daily mid-morning management meeting with Claudia and Andrew to discuss the ship's activities. The few minor issues which arose were easily disposed off, thus the sessions soon evolved into lengthy and, to Len, immensely enjoyable conversations on life at large. Eventually Andrew ceased attending. Len learned of Claudia's background, grilled her with growing curiosity about her monetary policy studies and in turn, entertained her with anecdotal accounts of his past life. For both, the morning meetings which usually culminated in lunch together followed by a two-hour walk along the coast, became their daily highlight.

One morning these pleasantries were abruptly disrupted when Andrew, plainly agitated, burst in and shouted 'There's sludge aboard.'

'Oh my God,' Len cried, rising from his seat. 'I've always feared this. Bugger, bugger, bugger! I hoped we'd get a longer run but I might have bloody well known. It's been too good to be true.'

'We've got to do something to counter it', Andrew said. 'We can't just give up. We should've had a gameplan anyway as it was always inevitable.'

'If you thought that why haven't you raised it before?' Len snapped and sank back into his seat, his head in his hands.

Claudia looked from one to the other, the sense of crisis apparent but the nature of the problem a mystery. Sludge? Was this an engine-room difficulty affecting the all-important heating or a mystery disease hitting the girls? Had the food supplies become ruined by some peculiar refrigeration tainting?

'Sludge?' she enquired. 'What's that?'

'Reporters, journalists, the bloody press,' Andrew said wearily.

Len looked up. 'Are you absolutely sure? Is it a television crew or what?'

'No, there's just one reporter so that means a newspaper but it doesn't matter. We're still stuffed.'

'But why?' Claudia enquired. 'We're a million miles from anywhere. Why does it matter?'

Andrew explained. 'This fellow might only be from a small provincial newspaper but it's still a great story and a journalistic coup and within days will be cabled worldwide.'

'I still don't see how that affects us down here,' Claudia persisted.

'Affect us?' Len snapped. 'It will bloody well ruin us. Half the beards are married. If their wives don't directly read the story one thing you can absolutely gilt-edge guarantee is that one of their female friends will and will be hot on the phone to tell them about it. Women are like that. The next thing the chaps will be getting hammered by faxes from their wives and will be terrified to come on board.'

'But can't we introduce more cover-up expenditure disguises like the High Risk Fund and restaurant?' Claudia suggested.

'Not with this lot. We're pushing it now as it is,' Andrew replied. 'Remember they're basically suburban. They'll have joint bank accounts with their wives but most of all, being scientists, they're careful evaluating types not given to reckless or unplanned expenditure. It will be so contrary to their nature it won't be plausible and their wives will know it and the beards will know they will know it and won't take the chance.'

'Listen, Andrew,' Len asked. 'How certain are you? Has this bastard actually divulged anything? After all, he might just be a conventional Antarctic writer and for that matter, a potential customer.'

'I'm fairly certain all right,' Andrew said. 'I was having coffee with Helmut, the Frankfurt seal homosexuality research chap. He was earbashing me about East Germans' poor academic standards which had come to light since unification. Anyway, I looked up and saw the four Swedes from the Gothenburg University penguin sleep patterns research crew swigging beer at the bar and this little bastard was with them.'

'But how do you know he's sludge?' Len pressed.

'He's sludge all right, make no mistake,' Andrew retorted. 'He might just as well have carried a placard saying 'I'm a reporter'. You know what those Swedes are like. Ten foot tall, open healthy faces, guileless and honest and then in glaring contrast, this ratty little bugger, mid-thirtyish, furtive and weaselly, poor posture and sneaky body language and when he took his snow jacket off, a nasty cheap shirt and a bad-taste sweater.

'He was classic sludge and absolutely screamed of loser. I watched him for a while and the final proof was his evasive behaviour when it was his turn to buy a round so I shot in here to tell you.'

'Yes, that's a reporter all right,' Len said gloomily. 'But what can we do about it?'

'He must have come in on the Starlifter from Christchurch yesterday,' Andrew continued. 'Apart from scientists there was quite a swag of politicians and other civvy types on board. I always wander over and have a look to see who's arrived but I must have missed him. I got caught up arguing with the leader of a twelve-man Washington University animal sociology team who came in on the plane. They've received an eight million dollar grant from the Rockefeller Foundation to come down and study penguin racism. They reckon some penguins have darker beaks than others and they want to see if they're getting picked on. I had him on, asking how it could be racism when they're the same species. He claimed racism was a generic term and the same thing applied to people; that is, that black or white, we're all the same human species. I got interested as I'd never thought of it that way and because of this I must have missed the sludge sneaking in.'

'Why not lure him into having it off with one of the girls, then he'd look silly writing about it,' Claudia proposed.

'For God's sake, Claudia, be sensible,' Andrew snapped. 'He's a reporter, remember. You wouldn't get him to pay for coffee if he could avoid it and believe me, journalists are pretty adroit at dodging payment for anything. He'd certainly never pay for a girl even if he could afford it, and he can't. Remember we live in a market economy now and people are paid what they're worth to society. This bugger will be penniless. Still, maybe we could try and buy him off. That sometimes works. Problem is he could take the money then a few weeks later send one of his mates down for a collect as well. Dishonesty comes naturally to the press. Anyone in public life will tell you that.'

'Hang on, Andrew,' Len said. 'Claudia might be on to something. Payment doesn't matter. We could tee up a couple of the really pretty girls to come on to him. He'll be only too keen to talk to them. They could drop in to the conversation that the sauna is free and offer to take him to it. He'll want to see everything. We could set up cameras there and in one of the bedrooms. There's heaps of high-quality camera gear at the base we can borrow and the ship's engineers can rig it all up. Get a couple of the more assertive girls on the job and promise a big bonus if they get it away with him. You will know the best candidates. Believe me, give some of them sufficient incentive and they'd have the dress off a bishop.'

'But I don't see how any of this helps,' Claudia said. 'So okay, he tastes the goods but that doesn't kill his story.'

'Oh yes it does,' Andrew crowed. 'Reporters are cannibals. They're driven by envy but love nothing more than blowing one of their own out of the water. Show him a set of photographs and assure him prints and an explanatory caption will be dispatched to the news media worldwide if he so much as utters a peep. Most reporters are married. It's the only way they get any sex, so there's the wife bit as well. Oh I love it; this is going to be a very great pleasure. Maybe we could pay some of the Russian nancy-boys to gang-rape him as well. He wouldn't be too thrilled about photos of that going home.

'I'll tell you about reporters. When you're back in London, Len, I'll show you a study about the press Tom commissioned years ago. Apparently when the bank started to become prominent Tom employed a psychologist to study journalists' behaviour so as to know how best to handle them. It's bloody interesting.

'The psychologist claimed journalists had amazing parallels with homosexuals insofar as after an initial flush of exuberance they descend into misanthropy through suppressed self-loathing and disgust. It all makes sense when you think about it but, according to the psychologist, what particularly enrages them is any sign of success or happiness in others.

'He claimed they try and compensate for their sense of inferiority by endlessly issuing themselves awards and prizes, which is why every reporter always describes him or her self as an award-winning journalist. They're like Indian students; everyone gets a prize; in their case a degree and the reporters, an award. Of course no one else takes any notice of either. Anyway, understanding the enemy is the first rule of warfare, which is why I'm confident about nailing this little bastard.'

'But what if he doesn't return?' Claudia questioned.

Andrew laughed mockingly. 'Don't be ridiculous, girl. That's what he's down here for. He'll turn up, you can be sure about that.'

The three swung into action with Len in control determining tasks and responsibilities. Their efforts took on the atmosphere of a high-risk military commando raid on an enemy fortress and for the first time in some weeks the three became excited and purposeful. Being well planned the exercise went perfectly, the reporter taking the bait at its first presentation.

Later that night as he was leaving the ship he was seized by two burly Russian crew members and frogmarched protestingly into Len's office. Across Len's desk lay a freshly printed set of large blown-up photos clearly showing him in embarrassingly compromising situations.

'Take a look at these, lad,' Andrew barked aggressively. 'Make no bloody mistake, every newspaper and television station in the world will have a full set within a week. You've chosen to mess with us and now we're going to destroy you, sunshine.'

The reporter slumped into a chair and for a fleeting moment appeared close to tears.

'I'm terribly sorry,' he whimpered. 'I just don't know what came over me. I can only assure you I've always been faithful and will never stray again. I beg you for mercy. I'm a family man,' he pleaded.

'Mercy? Jesus, you've got a cheek,' Andrew shouted. 'You're quite happy to sneak down here to ruin us and now you cry for mercy. You wanted a fight, chum, and you've got it. Believe me, we're going to do you. Now; spit it out. Who do you write for?'

The reporter looked at Andrew, puzzled. 'But I don't write for anyone,' he bleated.

A silence fell on the room. After a while Len broke the impasse.

'Why exactly are you down here?' he asked quietly.

'It was a prize,' the little man squeaked. 'I won it, or at least three of us did at last year's science teachers' national conference. All the delegates were automatically in the running. Look, I'll show you,' and he fished frenziedly in his jacket, pulled out a sheet of paper and handed it to Len.

It was addressed to Mr Cecil Scott, Science Master, Ambrose High School and headed 'Itinerary, Three Days Antarctic Trip'. Flight times, accommodation and expedition details were set out on the sheet.

Mr Scott's first day in the Antarctic had been the most eventful of his bleak thirty-five year existence to date and for the remaining two days, in a semi-traumatised state, he faithfully accompanied his two teacher colleagues to penguin colonies and listened attentively and took lengthy notes at lectures on albatross flight patterns, seal life-expectancy variations and the changing technology of sub-zero temperature clothing. And he kept well clear of the ship where he had been originally invited by the Swedes who had been his designated hosts for his first day.

Later that night Len and Andrew sat back with a bottle of wine open between them.

'A valuable exercise, old man,' Andrew said contentedly. 'It went swimmingly from go to whoa, no matter that it was a false alarm. And as a bonus we brightened that little bastard's life.'

'And terrorised mine for a day,' Len added. 'I'll let you tell Claudia.'

13

'I must say everything seems to be running along rather nicely,' Len said contentedly as he met with Claudia and Andrew for their routine morning coffee discussion.

'Well, sort of,' Claudia said tentatively. 'There is one thing I want to raise which is making the girls a bit fidgety.'

The two men looked at her, puzzled. 'Bloody hell, Claudia,' Andrew exclaimed. 'What next? I thought they were all happy now we have the private lounge set up for them.'

Claudia looked uncomfortable. Finally she blurted: 'The girls need to shop. They need to buy things.'

The two men looked at her, dumbstruck.

'What things?' Len asked after a short silence.

'Just things. It's something they like to do.'

'For Christ's sake, Claudia,' Andrew exploded. 'They signed on for a six-month tour of duty. They knew where they were going. There are no bloody shopping malls here. I've never heard such nonsense. What do you want now? We're not setting up bloody shops. Anyway, there are two here already. Let them buy books and flowers.'

'Look. I don't want to argue about this or put up with smart alec remarks,' Claudia said testily. 'You've employed me to make sure the girls are happy so I'm just doing my job telling you about this. Anyway, you're usually in one of their rooms every day, Andrew, so you know damn well all of them already do buy flowers. And they buy books too, even though they don't read them. They have to because that's all there is to buy.'

'This is extraordinary,' Len said.

Claudia ignored him. Flushed slightly with obvious embarrassment she pressed on. 'I'm not suggesting you set up a shop. I've thought it all through and what I want is Bruce to bring in about thirty copies of tabloid newspapers on each trip. They carry lots of advertising from Sydney shops. And I've a list of larger stores in Sydney that put out catalogues. I want Bruce to get a couple of dozen copies from each of them. Then I want to knock up order forms which the girls can fill out and which will list their purchases for Bruce to arrange for someone to buy and bring down on each flight. The costs can be debited from their weekly earnings credit notes. Bruce might be able to get his wife to do the shopping and fill the orders as each item has to be individually wrapped with the girl's name on it. So maybe you'll have to throw whoever does it say a thousand dollars a trip but it will be a good investment as it will keep them happy.'

'This is extraordinary,' Len repeated.

'Let me get this clear,' Andrew said. 'Am I to understand that what you're basically saying is the girls are suffering from some sort of shopping withdrawal syndrome?'

'You could put it that way,' Claudia said tersely.

'And am I also to understand that they have no particular things they need to buy but instead just need to buy anything at all; the purchase itself is irrelevant?'

'I'm only telling you the way it is if you want a happy ship,' Claudia snapped.

'This is extraordinary,' Len said again.

'Let me ask you this,' Andrew persisted, emphasising each word. 'Tell me the honest truth. If we had only one shop here; no flowers, no bookshop, nothing – and if the girls were stuck here for six months – and if we opened a shop selling nothing but crowbars – are you telling me they'd buy them?'

Claudia shifted uncomfortably. After a time she spoke very quietly. 'Yes. Not necessarily straight away but once they knew that was it for six months, eventually most of them would probably buy one.'

'This is bloody extraordinary,' Len muttered again.

'Would any buy two?' Andrew continued.

'Some would. Some might even buy more over six months.'

'Would they know what they are?' Andrew pressed on.

'Probably not,' Claudia replied coldly.

'So, if say after three weeks or so we brought out some coloured ones, they'd all buy another, would they?' Andrew demanded.

'Probably.'

'And a few weeks after that if we produced some children's models; they'd be in again would they?'

'Probably.'

'And then say striped crowbars; they'd be in yet again, would they?' Claudia sat in silence.

'Christ. We could then have a sale,' Len enthused. 'We'd get 'em on a fifth or sixth one each. We could start a second-hand shop, buy them all back and recycle them.'

'And tell me, Claudia,' Andrew persevered. 'If instead of crowbars the shop just sold bulldozer axles, would they all buy one?'

'I'm not putting up with this any more,' Claudia protested, plainly close to tears. 'You've asked me to do a very difficult and sensitive job. I try and do it and you both sit there and ridicule me. I don't want an argument and I don't want to listen to you two mocking and sneering. I'm not going to debate it or explain it or justify it or anything. I'm just simply telling you how it is. Rightly or wrongly, women like to shop. If you want a happy ship then I've told you what to do.' At that she got up and stormed out.

So it came to pass and on the next flight it was arranged with Bruce.

'Mate; the missus will be rapt,' he said over lunch prior to his return flight. 'She'll be in a bloody pigs' heaven.'

He scanned through the screeds of order sheets.

'Honestly, mate. She'd probably pay for the pleasure of doing all this shopping but to be able to do it and get a grand as well, I tell you, I'm gunna be gettin' the royal treatment.'

'It's bloody extraordinary,' Len said.

14

I'm sorry to interrupt, Mr Edwards. Could I have a quick word with you?'

Len looked up, annoyed at the intrusion by the wispy-bearded, bespectacled young man standing anxiously beside his table. He was in the Yangzse with Claudia, regaling her with accounts of his Doctor Primakov astrology business thirty years earlier and she was responding with encouraging gales of laughter. Not another bloody love-struck beard, he thought.

'What is it, son? I'm rather busy at the moment,' he said tersely.

'My name is Adam Templeton, sir. Professor Paviour-West sent me,' the young man replied nervously in a high-pitched voice. 'He was wondering if he could see you today at 4pm.'

'Paviour-West?' Len frowned as he tried to put a face to the name.

'Seals,' Claudia offered helpfully.

'Leopard seals actually,' the young man corrected her.

'What does he want?' Len asked irritably.

'I'm not sure, sir. I'm with his Durham University team and he sent me over to seek an appointment.'

Len curtly agreed and Templeton mumbled his thanks and fled.

At the appointed time there was a furious banging on Len's door and Professor Paviour-West strode in trailed by two beards.

The professor, a short, pencil-moustached man in his mid-sixties, affected an exaggerated brisk military manner acquired during fifteen years with the navy following completion of his doctorate. That service, at the height of the cold war, had been devoted to attempts to utilise seals for various electronic spying strategies. None had succeeded and considerable embarrassment threatened when an entire experimental seal colony in Scotland had simultaneously exploded while being viewed by a party of boy scouts on a nature ramble. To the scouts' delight their intensely disliked scout master had been swiftly decapitated by a flying seal flipper but their pleasure was short-lived when, like sharks drawn by the whiff of blood, they were descended upon by hordes of slavering grief counsellors from across Britain. These contemporary versions of the equally ghoulish professional mourners of an earlier age succeeded after two days of persistent counselling in achieving a satisfactorily distressed state in the scouts.

Fortune had intervened when the police arrested two Dublin theology students holiday hiking five miles away. Their subsequent release for lack of evidence four months later had incited a great furore in the tabloid press and a ministerial inquiry into police incompetence. Nevertheless, a navy scandal had been averted but in disgrace, Professor Paviour-West had been obliged to retreat to academia.

The professor introduced his two companions as Doctor Basham of Seattle University and Professor Cortez from the University of Lisbon. Both headed seal research teams and both were clearly intimidated by Paviour-West. The professor wasted no time on formalities.

'We're here because we demand prompt action to fix a problem,' he barked.

Len's mind raced. Who from the ship's entourage could have caused trouble and even more puzzling, what on earth could it be?

Paviour-West continued. 'Australians,' he exclaimed, as if that were self-explanatory when the subject of problems arose. 'It can't carry on. You have the power to end this outrage. We insist on immediate action.'

'Which Australians?' Len queried, fearing revelation of what his stable's Sydney faction could possibly have done. Soon it became clear as Paviour-West recounted his concerns, at times spluttering almost incoherently with indignation.

It transpired that three weeks earlier an eight-man Queensland University leopard seal weight-recording team had flown in with a large portable weighing platform of their own design but had overlooked any methodology for inducing the leopard seals on to it.

Not discouraged by this oversight and to the great disgust of the other scientists, they had wheeled their weighing platform to the leopard seal colony, surrounded the targeted snarling beast, then hurled themselves at it in a vain effort to wrestle it on to the platform. After a collective toll of four broken ribs, a fractured leg and a dislocated shoulder, the now depleted Queensland researchers had retreated to devise a fresh and, as it eventuated, more successful tactic. Specifically, they had replaced wrestling's brutishness with boxing's science.

Their leader, Dr Owen Jensen, was a former Australian universities heavyweight boxing champion. Slowly he would approach each animal, throw a few tentative left jabs to find a length and as the snapping and roaring leopard seal lifted its head, knock it unconscious with a neatly executed right uppercut to its jaw. The remaining team members would then rush in, shove the stunned beast on to the platform, weigh and tag it.

All of this, Paviour-West claimed, was not only highly unscientific and grossly undignified but appeals to the Australians to desist had been greeted first with jocular disdain and then ultimately abuse.

'But I don't see what any of this has to do with me,' Len protested when Paviour-West had finished.

'We want the Queenslanders banned from the boat,' the professor barked. 'That'll bring them to their senses and end this disgrace.'

Len was reluctant to become involved in the scientists' quarrel. 'Doesn't anyone have any authority?' he asked. 'Isn't there some sort of organisation or international body or code of conduct that controls you chaps?'

'Oh, don't you worry about that,' Paviour-West bellowed. 'I've already drafted a complaint for *Seal Monthly* but we can't wait for that to appear. We want action now and only you can do it.'

'*Seal Monthly*?' Len said quizzically.

'Augustus has been on the cover five times,' Doctor Basham said sycophantically.

'He's the uncrowned leopard-seal king,' the Portuguese added.

'There's a seal magazine?' Len queried.

The three scientists stared at him, plainly puzzled. Finally Paviour-West spoke.

'Of course there are seal magazines,' he said, scornful of Len's ignorance. 'I prefer not to be nationalistic but regardless of my cover appearances, *Seal Monthly*'s high quality photography makes one favour it over *The Seal, Seal Bulletin* and the others. Anyway, enough of that. Now look here, Edwards,' Paviour-West continued. 'You have a vested interest in this base. If we weren't here nor would you be. These Australians are interfering in everyone's work. This year's the penultimate one for my project. We've secured a government grant to fund a twenty-man team, complete everything next year in one fell swoop and eliminate the Finns. These uncouth, these...' and the professor struggled as he searched for and eventually found a word conveying sufficient odium to describe the offenders, 'these... these... Australians,' he hissed contemptuously, 'they're jeopardising all of that.'

'I didn't know seals had fins,' Len said.

There was a brief silence.

'What on earth are you going on about?' Paviour-West demanded.

'No, no,' the American intruded. 'The professor meant Finns as in Finland.'

'Oh, I see,' Len said. 'But how do they come into it?'

Professor Paviour-West explained angrily.

'I've spent twelve years researching leopard-seal yawning. My team has filmed more than one thousand hours yawning over that period. We're determined to be first to find out why they do it but the race is on. We've a two-year head start over Helsinki University but this summer they haven't turned up. There's British prestige at stake here damn it and those Finns are up to something; I can sense it.

'Now we've got these, these...' and again he spat out the word contemptuously, 'Australians. They're interfering. How can we film seals yawning when these barbarians are knocking them unconscious? Answer that, Edwards!' he demanded and without waiting for a reply he continued afresh. 'Now look here. You're an Englishman. This is your chance to do something for your country. How will you feel if the Finns get there first and you're responsible? You'd never live it down.'

'Let me get this straight,' Len said. 'You're researching why seals yawn. Is that right?'

'Leopard seals, not just seals,' Paviour-West snapped.

'And the Finns are doing so too?' Len continued.

'They've not arrived this summer. Something's up and time is of the essence. For all I know they've made a breakthrough. This is a crisis. Surely you can see that. Now will you help or not?' the professor demanded.

'And you gentlemen are doing the same?' Len asked, addressing the other two.

'Certainly not,' Paviour-West snapped. 'Yawning is my speciality.'

Doctor Basham explained. 'We're all affected though,' he said. 'My team is researching leopard-seal magnetic-impulse properties.'

'They have magnetic properties?' Len enquired, wide-eyed.

'That's what we're trying to ascertain but the evidence seems fairly compelling. Nearly all face towards the South Magnetic Pole when they come ashore so we're on the verge of quite an exciting discovery. We've put four years into it so hopefully a breakthrough will come soon.'

'I'm a leopard-seal census taker,' Professor Cortez piped up. 'My team have counted the colony twice a day for the last two months.'

'For God's sake, why?' Len exclaimed.

Paviour-West leapt in. 'It's extremely important work. The Portuguese are doing a damn fine job. How else will we know if the colony number varies?'

'Does it?' Len asked.

'Not so far,' Professor Cortez said. 'But if it does we will know.' Professor Paviour-West indicated his approval with vigorous nodding.

'Don't you see the point, Edwards?' Paviour-West glowered. 'We all pull together. Couldn't operate otherwise.'

'Quite right,' said Professor Cortez. 'Augustus wrote an introduction to my book, *Peculiarities of The Leopard-Seal Spinal System*.'

'Peculiarities?' Len exclaimed. 'What peculiarities?'

'That was the point of the book,' Professor Cortez explained. 'They don't have any. I proved that beyond doubt,' he added proudly.

Len stared at the three scientists and briefly wondered if they were taking the mickey. No, he concluded. Two months at

McMurdo had immunised him to this sort of endeavour.

'Who buys such a book?' he enquired after a lengthy pause. The three scientists looked dumbstruck, plainly puzzled by his enquiry.

'What do you mean, who buys?' Paviour-West snapped.

'Well, who reads this sort of thing?'

'Damn it all, man,' Paviour-West cried. 'It's not meant to be read. We're not entertainers, damn it, we're scientists. The important point is that the research is done. It's immensely valuable. Adds to the broad body of knowledge. Frankly, Edwards, you seem sadly lacking in any comprehension of the scientific world.'

'I'm learning, Professor. I'm learning,' Len said quietly.

He thought quickly. Eventually he said he'd have a word with the Australians first before acting precipitously.

Professor Paviour-West glared at him. 'I hope you won't let England down, Edwards,' and without further ado he rose and marched out, followed by the others.

Len called Andrew and told him what had occurred.

'I know Jensen,' Andrew said. 'He's okay. He's here most nights so I'll pull him in for a chat. Paviour-West's a nasty bugger; runs a reign of terror with his crew. They're an insipid lot and dead scared of him. Paviour-West has the same Estonian girl booked every Wednesday and Saturday night.'

Later that night Andrew brought Jensen in and Len poured him a drink.

The Australian, a large bluff character, listened while Len recounted, without mentioning names, that complaints had been registered against his methods.

'That'll be that Paviour-West bastard,' he said when Len had finished. 'Listen, mate. We're not harming the seals. I'm laying them out cleanly with uppercuts. I'm careful about that; you know, no left hooks. Hooks could break their jaws hitting them on the side. It's probably a bloody sight less physically intrusive than a stun gun, not that it matters 'cause we haven't got one.'

'I just don't see why we have to be involved,' Len grumbled, but he knew as he said it his protest was in vain. His simple service-provider role at the base had quickly evolved into a far greater status. He controlled the commodity the beards most required next to food and shelter and was treated with almost royalty-like respect by the scientists as a result. Over the past two months he had been called upon to adjudicate in numerous disputes, despite his efforts to distance himself from the beards' quarrels.

'I tell ya, mate,' Jensen said. 'It's got nothing to do with me knocking the bloody seals out. Bloody Paviour-West just hates Aussies. He spent eight years researching leopard-seal blinking patterns before he started on yawning and he got all sorts of awards for it. Then an Adelaide University team proved his blinking findings were rubbish and he's never forgiven Australia. It's as simple as that.'

The following day Len sent Andrew ashore to fetch Paviour-West. When the professor arrived Len offered him a drink. The professor, plainly suspicious, declined. Len got to the point.

'I'm sorry, professor. I'm simply not prepared to get involved,' he said. 'It's not our role and it invites all sorts of potential problems if we delve into issues beyond our particular discipline.'

Paviour-West eyed Len menacingly. 'You're not fooling me, Edwards,' he said. 'I'm not the idiot you've obviously taken me for. I've put two and two together, make no mistake about that.'

'I'm sorry, Professor. You've lost me. We're simply here to provide a service,' Len found himself almost grovelling.

'Oh yes,' the professor shouted. 'I've no doubt about that. But service to whom? That's the question. The pieces in the jigsaw are starting to come together. There'll be consequences, make no mistake about that.'

Len stared at Paviour-West with open disbelief.

'You must take me for a simpleton, Edwards,' Paviour-West bellowed. 'Where's this ship from? St Petersburg; right? Helsinki; just across the water; right? Long history of trade and cultural affiliation; right? Olga the Estonian girl; always enquiring about my work; right? Estonia; a stone's throw from Helsinki, right? Jensen the saboteur; that name's Scandinavian; right? I see it all now. You're all in this together. What a subterfuge this operation is! You've fooled some, Edwards, but not me,' he spat out accusingly. At that he rose, marched to the door then turned to Len again. 'You know, Edwards, under British law technically you can still be hanged for treason.' He paused, his face contorted with rage as he boomed, 'Philby,' then after a pause, 'or, should I say Quisling? That's more accurate,' he shouted accusingly.

'He was Norwegian,' Len said.

'Well, you'd know all about that,' the Professor bellowed and slamming the door he was gone.

Later that night, still smarting from Paviour-West's tirade, Len sat in the lounge complaining to Andrew. Then he noticed a small group at the bar including Adam Templeton, the young scientist who had made the appointment for the professor, and an idea brewed in his mind. Len caught Templeton's eye and beckoned him over.

'I'd like a chat with you in private,' and he rose and led Templeton to his office.

Once there he poured two glasses of wine and studied the young man. His mind flashed back thirty years. Had he retained his intuitive art of picking them? If he was reading it right, Templeton appeared to be classic king-hit fodder, precisely the sort of rare category of wetness he once fitted into dog-walking franchise rights. He decided to test the water first.

'So how did you get into this business, son?' he enquired casually.

'It was a toss-up,' the young man squeaked. 'After I graduated I was offered a place on the professor's Antarctic team. It was that or touring India and Nepal with a friend.'

Eureka, Len thought excitedly. I can still pick 'em. India and Nepal. The suction pump for the West's dimmest caste. Sociology degrees, alternative theatre attending, necklaces of dried seeds, brass rings in one ear, blue jeans uniformly torn at the knees, backpacks, marvelling at the beauty of ubiquitous squalor, cross-legged in rows before near-naked conmen fakirs; bespectacled, earnest sari-wearing plain girls, chanting sessions and gurus, grave-faced, sandal-wearing, bearded and ponytailed wimpy males, seekers of truth; wettest of the wet, saturated.

Again Len recalled his earlier scams period. Activist or passive he asked himself? This simple test had been a useful tool in his franchising period. In the course of conversation he would endeavour to mentally picture his targeted victim maypole dancing. If they danced with a frenzied and exhibitionist high-kicking intensity they were categorised as activists and slotted into dog-walking and lawn-mowing type territorial rights. On the other hand if the image was of a more subdued stumbling round the maypole then roadside selling passive pursuits were allocated. No doubt about it, Templeton would be a restrained dancer, carefully maintaining his distance from the whirling skirts of the fat girl in front of him. The passives could be sold anything. Len decided to have some fun.

'Are you aware of your professor's charges against us?' he enquired gently.

Templeton shuffled uncomfortably. 'Professor Paviour-West can be a little difficult. But you must understand. He's put twelve years into this research. He's become quite obsessed about the Finns getting there first.'

Len stared intensely at the young man, paused, then mumbled hesitatingly, 'I'm afraid the game's up. It's a fair cop. He's a very clever man is your boss. He's certainly tumbled to what's going on.'

Templeton gazed wide-eyed at Len.

'I know it's no excuse,' Len continued. 'But they got me at a particularly vulnerable stage. I'd just lost everything in a business deal. When the Finns offered to fund this ship interest-free in return for my sabotaging your research I grabbed at it without thinking through the implications. But the professor's made me feel very guilty. To be honest I never thought of it in loyalty terms. I simply didn't realise the importance of your work when it was first put to me but damn it all, I'm only a small cog in the wheel.'

'Gosh,' muttered Templeton.

'Everyone's involved,' Len continued. 'The Americans are behind it, needless to say. Why do you think those so-called military personnel are here? Of course they're not really military. You must have noticed that by their behaviour. CIA the lot of them; all spying on your research.'

'Gosh,' Templeton said again.

'The Americans have spared no expense. They funded the Queensland team and planted a special operator among them; that's Jensen; he's Danish but the Scandinavians are working together on this one; anyway, he was sent here to slow you down.'

'He's certainly done that,' Templeton squeaked.

'And of course Oxford and Cambridge Universities are into

it up to their necks,' Len continued, warming to his task.

'But why?' Templeton bleated. 'They're on our side.'

'They've never been that,' Len said. 'Both have long histories of producing traitors to Britain. As I understand it, they're concerned about Durham University. Apparently they see its growing reputation as a threat to their elitist position. It's bad enough having to share the top shelf with one another but they don't want it split three ways if they can prevent it. Discrediting Durham is the best way to shove you back to red-brick ranking so they were happy to join in.'

'I'm really appalled by all of this,' Templeton gasped.

'And you must have noticed the girls,' Len continued. 'Been particularly nice to you, have they?'

'Yes, yes,' Templeton agreed eagerly.

'Discussed your work with you. You noticed that?' Len asked, conscious of Claudia's reporting the stable's constant complaining about the beards always talking about their activities.

'I'm beginning to see it all now,' Templeton muttered, ashen-faced.

'Trained to grill your team, they are,' Len continued. 'They're all on bonuses for anything they find out. Mind you,' he added, 'I can't see the point. The Finns have already solved the problem. Basically, they sent us down to ensure your team was kept happy and stayed here through summer. But they're going to blow you out of the water in February. Next February's Seal Bulletin is doing a huge issue, glossy pages, lots of colour photography, graphs; big press conference in Washington; the works. They're announcing the Finnish victory and of course with this coup they hope to sink Seal Monthly. The Americans are behind that as well.

'But look here. I'm not prepared to be a traitor to Britain. I'd never thought of it that way until Paviour-West made me think clearly. I feel deeply ashamed for what I've done. As I see it my only honourable course is to be a double agent, which is why I invited you here. I know the Finns' discovery. I'm going to give it to you but I can't be seen to be involved. My life could be in danger.'

'I had no idea, sir,' Templeton muttered. 'This is awful.'

'It can be ugly out there, son. There've been too many deaths already,' Len continued, now thoroughly enjoying himself. 'Three since the submarine came two days ago. It's got to stop.'

Templeton's jaw dropped.

'Doubtless you've noticed a few new faces at the base in recent days,' Len continued, knowing that with more than 3500 personnel most of them would not know one another. 'US Navy. They landed from a sub two miles up the coast two days ago and six spies came ashore to monitor your lot. Unfortunately they were seen by a couple of scientists when landing. Iceberg chaps I believe,' he explained, screwing up his face and shaking his head sorrowfully. 'Of course they had to be taken out. Their bodies are now lying on the ocean floor 6000 foot down, I'm told.'

'That's dreadful,' Templeton cried. 'But why are the Americans doing this?'

'The usual,' Len said wearily. 'Power politics. It's just another negative consequence of the cold war ending. In the old days when Russia and America spied on one another it was accepted behaviour and upfront and honest. Now they have to pretend they don't do it any more but of course they do so it's all much more complicated and they try and camouflage it with this sort of thing. America needs to curry favour with Finland to watch things happening next door in Russia. So it's a trade-off. You scratch my back, I scratch yours. They can't buy the Finns as Finland is a rich country. But they can help them in other ways such as scientific prestige. Finland doesn't have submarines or trained killers to take out you chaps. The Americans do. They paid the Queenslanders and sent Jensen in to lead them. Anyway, I've had enough. Too many innocent people are getting hurt. I'll do my duty and tell you what the Finns have discovered and then get out and just hope they don't come after me. The onus is on you not to spill the beans on me, otherwise I'm done for.'

'I promise you,' the young man said solemnly. 'You have my absolute assurance. I was a boy scout,' he added by way of reassurance.

'You can claim it as your own, son, and good luck to you,' Len said warmly.

'That's extraordinarily generous of you, sir,' the young man said. 'What is it? I can't wait.'

'The leopard seals are tired when they come ashore. That's

why they yawn.'

'My goodness,'Templeton gasped, clasping a hand to his forehead. 'That's absolutely brilliant.'

'I agree,' Len said. 'You have to hand it to the Finns. A very talented race. They got there first. Still, a man's country must come first, so here's your chance to nip them in the bud. It's all yours, son. I've done my duty. Just promise me again you'll never tell a soul about me disclosing everything. I'm a dead man otherwise. You can be absolutely sure of that.'

'Yes, yes, I promise. You can rely on me. And if I may say so, sir, I think you're behaving in a very honourable and noble manner. You're a true Englishman, sir.'

Len hung his head. 'That's very kind of you but I'm not sure I can ever truly redeem myself. Look, there's one other thing,' he added. 'You can tip off Doctor Basham as well. The Finns have also solved the magnetic puzzle.'

'No!' the young man exclaimed.

'The thing is, the Antarctic coastline generally runs latitudinally. What they discovered is the leopard seals come ashore head first which means pointing south and once on land they're too heavy to move about much. No magnetic properties, I'm afraid. It's quite simple really.'

'It's ingenious,' Templeton gasped.

Four days later the Durham University team flew out secretly and two months later the January issue of *Seal Monthly* once more bore a cover photograph of Paviour-West and the bold lettering message, 'Another Triumph for British Science'. The entire issue was devoted to the yawning breakthrough. 'A team effort,' the professor was quoted magnanimously.

Unwittingly Len had indeed executed a patriotic duty in saving the ever-suffering British taxpayer the cost of the now unnecessary twenty-man leopard-seal yawning expedition scheduled for the following summer.

15

A recent national poll declared Senator Samuel Fulton to be the third best known public figure in America. The same polling organisation recorded the firebrand senator commanding twenty-three per cent endorsement as America's most respected politician and fifty-one per cent as its most despised. It is an American oddity that even though Fulton stereotypes emerge from the bible belt every fifteen years or so, their appearance persistently ignites a news media and public frenzy.

Born into poverty in the Mississippi delta, physically large and strikingly handsome and a former national football star until a back injury which was to dog him for the rest of his days ended his career, Fulton was destined for a cardboard cut-out role as a hellfire and damnation demagogue. At the age of thirty he was elected to Congress in a landslide and seven years later was a popular choice to fill a Senate vacancy when it arose. His theme was the standard package of economic and political isolationism and an unspoken but well understood racial segregationism.

Additionally, the senator was an outspoken opponent of liberalism, free trade, the sexual revolution, foreign aid, homosexuality, fluoridation in the water supply, Wall Street, the United Nations, reverse discrimination, the World Bank, welfarism, the International Monetary Fund, feminism, environmentalists, banks, atheism and Hispanic, Arabic, Jewish, African, Asian and Southern European immigration.

He was in favour of the family, religion in schools, the bomb, tobacco and the right to bear arms.

All of these positions secured him an unswerving core support from poor whites, elderly ladies, trade unionists, and a sometimes bitter animosity from everyone else. Nevertheless his followers were sufficient in number for him to capture twenty-two per cent of the votes in the last presidential election and in the process consolidate his position on the national stage. He ran on his own created party ticket, 'America First' with the slogan 'People Before Profits' having realised that he could never capture a main party nomination through eastern states' antagonism towards him.

The senator understood the political process only too well and without cynicism recognised that maintaining his support necessitated constant repetition of his multitude of messages. Conversely, he also understood that sustaining news-media interest required ever-new messages which, in his case, took the form of a constant revelation of new enemies of society.

Fulton came to terms with this dichotomy early in his career following his call for a nuclear attack on Nicaragua when he discovered his supporters' enthusiasm for this proposal rested more in a general pleasure at the prospect of blasting non-Americans into oblivion than in any animosity towards, or for that matter, knowledge of Nicaragua.

Thereafter for a decade and despite its formulaic nature, the senator satisfied both his supporters' and foes' prejudices alike by, at approximately nine-month intervals, urging an immediate nuclear attack on respectively Iran, Libya, Vietnam, Cambodia, North Korea, Iraq, Mozambique, Cuba, Ethiopia, Syria, Somalia, Columbia and, following a misunderstood briefing from an aide who had referred to the Congo as the Belgium Congo, an all-out nuclear blitz on Belgium. The aftermath of each call, with the exception of the Belgians, was a methodical one per cent rise in his popular support. The senator was acutely sensitive to his self-serving fulcrum role in the persistent balance of mutual loathing between his poor southern conservative support base and the affluent northern liberal establishment.

The Belgium blunder initially concerned him as the sub-sequent furore tilted the previous balance, culminating in a potentially damaging presidential apology to the bewildered Belgians. For the first time his political ledger failed to be credited with the usual one per cent polling dividend and he became perceived as an eccentric gadfly rather than a serious political contender for high office. He dealt with this difficulty by refusing to comment, conscious that despite the hubris in the liberal press, his rescue would eventually come from the predictable quarter.

For Senator Fulton's rise in the national psyche had not relied on chance. Like all highly successful politicians he possessed an acute understanding of human behaviour and knew that any contrary outburst invariably flushed forth an attention-seeking exhibitionist academic who would advance an oblique and often incomprehensible revisionist argument opposing whatever the received thinking was.

Experience had taught Fulton in such circumstances to stay aloofly silent above the debate so that when the verbal battle finally waned and the bloodied sideline protagonists retreated, he somehow prevailed, having acquired a fresh respect as a man of firm but honest view and dignified manner. But he learned his lesson well from the Belgium debacle, noting the necessity of future nuclear attack calls being confined to non-white races.

When a further year passed and the need to stir the publicity pot arose, he decided to pepper his brew with a new approach and become a man of peace. The senator delivered a well-publicised speech calling for a cut in defence spending so that America's poor could enjoy a peace dividend. The outcome with his supporters was confusion but unable to retract and with the need to reinforce his supporters' faith, he quickly recognised the flaw in this revised tactic. His peace dividend message lacked the vital ingredient of an enemy of society.

For a disturbing six weeks he wallowed in the ambitious politician's distressing wasteland of being targetless. In desperation he abandoned his previously reliable intuition for the high-risk strategy of reading newspapers, a policy which quickly struck oil when he discovered environmentalism.

Noting the rich potential in newspaper photographs of environmentalists in action, comprising the magic unloveable ingredients of bearded, bespectacled, earringed males and beaded, nose-ringed plain women opposing ordinary job-threatened Joes, the senator knew he would soon be back on track. And so it came to pass.

For a glorious high-polling year he received a hero's welcome from miners and foresters, fishermen and developers, dam builders and industrialists as he railed against environmentalists. The death of his wife through cancer yielded a further sympathy polling boost and now alone, he compensated with a new vigour which revitalised his career.

When one of his researchers advised of the untold mineral riches in the Antarctic and of the international Antarctic non-mining treaty and its United Nations Organisation endorsement, the senator's ecstasy reached new heights.

For a month he dominated television talk shows with savage attacks on airy-fairy environmentalists, the uncaring government and the evil United Nations. His theme, which he pounded repeatedly, was always the same. 'There is only one loser from this situation. That is the ordinary, decent, salt of the earth American working man.'

During one such televised debate while in the process of hammering a stuttering, bearded, academic environmentalist, the out-bellowed pedagogue had spluttered: 'You've never endeavoured to experience the Antarctic's pristine beauty to understand its importance,' he quashed him with: 'As with everything you've said so far, you don't know what you're talking about. I'm scheduled to visit the Antarctic in a fortnight.'

The following morning he instructed an aide and by midday arrangements had been confirmed for him to ride aboard an airforce supply plane heading for the McMurdo Antarctic base from Christchurch, New Zealand, in ten days' time.

16

The flight south from Christchurch to McMurdo began badly for Senator Fulton when he discovered a fifteen-man Toronto University polar bear research team accompanying him. 'Forgive me, doctor,' he enquired of the rotund, heavily bearded team leader after introductions, 'I thought polar bears were only in the Arctic.'

'That's the point of our expedition,' Doctor Piacun had replied. 'We're researching the reason for that. We'll be studying the various geological, climatic and other points of difference between the two polar regions.'

'For Christ's sake, why?' Fulton had snapped. 'What the hell does it matter?' and the startled fifteen-man team visibly recoiled at the ferocity of his response. For the next hour they huddled together at the rear of the cabin in a simian-like, muttering group, peering at Fulton with open concern and distaste. When one of their number rose to use the toilet Fulton grabbed his arm as he passed. 'So what's your line then?' he barked.

The Canadian pulled free and shrank backwards, gazing at Fulton with genuine terror.

'You should be aware, Senator,' he squeaked. 'I'm a fully trained member of the Edmonton neighbourhood watch organisation,' and he fled to the bathroom.

Disgusted and bewildered, Fulton rose, walked to the front of the plane, knocked on the cabin door and entered.

He was greeted effusively and respectfully by the clean-shaven, neatly uniformed air-force personnel and an hour later, under the guidance of the chief officer, was in the pilot's seat handling the controls as the plane bucked through the southern ocean gales towards its destination. These were real men, much more to the senator's taste, and he began to relax and enjoy himself.

On arrival Fulton shook hands with each of the flight crew then descended the aircraft stairway and was greeted by Colonel Harris and an eight-man full dress marine honour guard.

'Welcome to McMurdo base, Senator,' Harris said. 'We're

deeply honoured to have you with us, sir. I'm afraid the accommodation is a little spartan.'

'If it's good enough for American boys,' Senator Fulton said, shaking Harris's hand vigorously, 'then I'm damn sure it will be good enough for me.' As he inspected the guard he noted with distaste a priest lurking in the background. O'Hearn darted forward and Harris introduced him.

'We're very pleased you have come, Senator,' O'Hearn said. 'There's an extremely serious problem here and we need your help.'

'Later, father, later. I have three days so there's plenty of time.'

But Father O'Hearn proved persistent. Two hours later, as Fulton sat in the mess and accepted his fifth whisky while surrounded by admiring marines and in full anecdotal flight, the ghastly priest re-appeared.

'I wonder if I could have five minutes, Senator,' he appealed.

Fulton turned to Harris with whom he was getting along splendidly. The colonel raised his eyebrows. 'Father O'Hearn is rather agitated about a development here, Senator. You might like to use my office.'

Unhappily Fulton rose although to ensure the bloody Papist understood his attitude he boomed, 'I'll be back in a few minutes, men. Stick around.'

In Harris's office O'Hearn recounted the arrival and activities of the Olga Buskova. The senator listened with growing curiosity but exploded anachronistically at mention of the ship's name.

'That's a God damn Russian ship. Coming down here corrupting and exploiting our American boys. By the bowels of Christ I'll have those Commie bastards bum-rushed out of here. We'll get the navy in.'

He was interrupted in this diatribe by O'Hearn's naive correction.

'I'm afraid it's a charter ship, Senator. It's really got nothing to do with Russia. The operators are Englishmen.'

Fulton pondered this fresh information. After a while he spoke. 'First thing tomorrow I'll visit the ship personally. Organise a meeting with whoever's in charge. I'll give them a shot across the bows warning and by Christ if they're not out of American territory in two days I'll send the navy in, mark my word.'

'With respect, sir, McMurdo is not American territory in a jurisdiction sense,' the priest said.

'I'll decide what's American territory, Father. No God damn Limey will come at that crap with me. Just organise the meeting,' and at that he rose and returned to his waiting audience.

17

W ith some trepidation and no little curiosity Father O'Hearn climbed the Olga Buskova's gangway and hesitantly entered the ship's foyer. 'Fuck off you bastard,' a voice shrieked in his ear. Startled, he turned to find a parrot glaring malevolently at him. His mind awhirl he was unprepared for the near-naked, bare-breasted young girl who loomed up suddenly and pressed a glass of red wine into his hand.

'Miss, Miss,' he spluttered. 'I would like to see the manager.'

'Follow me, darling,' the girl instructed. Scarlet-faced and unable to avert his eyes from her mincing G-stringed buttocks, he stumbled after her absurdly high-heeled prancing figure into the crowded lounge. Humiliated, he tried manfully to ignore the roar from the milling beards that greeted his entry, but their ribald taunts only compounded his confusion and disarray.

The girl led him through the lounge and down a corridor until they came to a door. She knocked and entered. 'A bloke to see you, Mr Edwards,' she announced, then holding the door open, stood in its entrance-way inviting O'Hearn's entry. Staring rigidly ahead the priest tried and failed to avoid brushing her pert breasts as he entered the room.

Inside, a pleasantly open-faced, middle-aged man looked up from behind his paper-strewn desk.

'My name is Father O'Hearn,' the priest stuttered. 'I'm the base Catholic priest. I'd like a word with you.'

Len rose and extended his hand.

'Len Edwards,' he said. 'I see you're enjoying our very good wine, Father,' and he ushered O'Hearn to a seat. 'If you don't mind I'll join you,' and he turned, opened a cabinet behind his desk, pulled out a bottle and drew its cork. Bringing the open bottle and another glass with him, he sat down in an armchair opposite O'Hearn.

In the parlance of the street, Len had been around the block. Indeed, he had traversed the route many times and with long accustomed skill he resorted to his greatest attributes when dealing with unexpected potential problems: charm and setting the agenda.

'I'm really delighted to meet you, Father. As a matter of fact it's been remiss of me but it's been my intention to come ashore and speak to you since we arrived. Unfortunately we've had a series of engine-room problems and I've been flat out dealing with those.'

Father O'Hearn made sympathetic noises.

'Drink up, Father. You'll make me feel guilty,' Len said. O'Hearn took a sip, then another and, enjoying and desperately needing the wine's salvation, yet another. Len rose and topped up his glass. 'We have a sizeable personnel on board, Father,' he continued, 'what with the engine crew and cooks and singers and hairdresser and shop assistants and stewards, and we try and run a happy ship. But there's one thing missing, which is why I was intending to come and see you in the next day or so, so I'm really appreciative of your visit. The thing is, quite a lot of our personnel are Catholics and I know they would very much like contact with you.

'Personally I'm not of your faith but I know how important it is to our Catholic folk and was hoping you might be prepared to come aboard and conduct some services and hear confessions. The crew would certainly be enormously grateful,' he added, topping up O'Hearn's glass again.

O'Hearn, entering into the spirit of his reception, heard himself as if in an echo chamber saying he would be very happy to do as Len bid. With some difficulty he pulled himself together.

'Mr Edwards,' be began, only to be interrupted.

'Len, please. Calling me Mr Edwards makes me feel old. Well, I am old and don't wish to be reminded,' he laughed.

'Len,' the priest began again hesitantly. 'You may not be aware but a famous American senator, Samuel Fulton, has arrived at the base. He has expressed a desire to meet you, which is why I'm here.'

'I will be delighted to meet him,' Len responded quickly. 'Any time which suits the senator will be satisfactory with me.'

Having agreed on that and following yet another topping up of the priest's glass, Len searched for a common ground. Eventually they found it in boxing and for two hours, during which a great deal more wine was consumed, they engaged in reminiscence and debate on the respective merits of various champions.

Finally O'Hearn rose to go. He was a little tiddly but still determined.

'It's been a pleasure meeting you, Len. I must say our discussion has not gone as I intended but I must also be honest and say I've really enjoyed this evening. I can't talk boxing with the scientists. I've tried but they become very disapproving. I would very much like to come again and continue our chat. But I must also tell you I'm not happy with this ship's activity. I'd like to discuss that with you.'

'By all means, Father,' Len said. 'But let me assure you it's not a one-way path. I've really enjoyed tonight as well. You know we have a plane call regularly. It's due tomorrow so I'll fax them to bring in a set of boxing videos. We can watch some fights together. It's no fun alone. You have to discuss a bout while it's underway to really enjoy it and I've got the same problem as you. There's absolutely no one here who understands it.'

'I'll certainly look forward to that,' the priest said. 'But you must stop calling me Father. You're not of our faith so the name's Danny.'

'Okay, Danny,' Len said jocularly. 'Tee up a time with the senator. Let me know tomorrow and come and have some breakfast with me here. I'll wager we can do a better job of it than on the base. You might like to read some recent newspapers as well. We get them in regularly.'

The visit had turned out totally different than planned. Father O'Hearn returned through the crowded lounge and again ran the gauntlet of the beards' lewd taunts. But this time, to his puzzlement he found himself actually enjoying the good humour and he responded with some wisecracks. Perplexed by all that had occurred, he went to bed.

18

Senator Fulton trudged across the snow to his mid-afternoon appointment Father O'Hearn had arranged with Len. He was in an ugly mood. The Antarctic idea he now realised had been a foolish mistake, all for the sake of a quick points-scoring over an idiotic environmentalist. Everyone watching the television broadcast would have forgotten it by now. Still, he had said it and he could be damned sure those environmentalist bastards would drum-beat had he not come down. He should have issued a statement postponing the trip, he thought ruefully. Pressing Senate business would sound plausible. But it was too late now and the prospect of three more days filled him with dread.

It had begun promisingly enough with Harris and the marines until the awful priest had stuck his head up. Worse was the thought of the next three days with a full itinerary of field trips his people had arranged. He'd spent the morning meeting the scientists who were to accompany him and a more boring bunch he couldn't imagine.

The cold was playing havoc with his old football back and knee injuries and he felt the spasms that always signalled a week's pain ahead erupt.

Approaching the ship, Fulton turned his mind to a strategy. The God damn priest had wanted to accompany him but he had insisted on going alone, not the least through a degree of curiosity. Who knew, there might be a few laughs in it. It certainly sounded like fun. Contrary to his public utterances the senator was no Calvinist and after the dreariness of the earnest scientists he was in a carnival-seeking mood. Anyway, what the hell was the difference between this whorehouse and those back in civilisation? They were everywhere and especially around military bases. Certainly Harris had been strangely reticent when he had raised the subject with him so there was obviously no complaint from that quarter.

Fulton's political modus operandi was practised by few politicians. Driven by a compulsion to avoid making enemies they always sought the middle ground of compromise. The senator's success rested on his recognition of this weak-kneed behaviour's futility and the vacuum it left. From the beginning he had uncompromisingly sought out foes and in so doing built a sizeable electorate from those similarly ill-disposed towards his multitude of targets. In politics you should never try and win your enemies, he was fond of saying. You never can, no matter how much you compromise, but you will certainly lose your supporters.

As he hefted his throbbing and now stiff leg up the gangway the senator weighed the options. Even if he could eject the ship and word got home of his triumph, he would simply have reaffirmed both his support and his opposition for a neutral outcome. And why? To please a God damn Papist. Stuff the priest, he thought.

To his surprise he was greeted at the gangway by an attractive young woman dressed in a smart pinstriped business suit. 'Good afternoon, Senator,' she said in a carefully modulated English accent. 'I'm Claudia Waite, the ship's administration manager. Mr Edwards and Mr Potter are looking forward to meeting you.' She led him down the entrance arcade, stopping outside each shop to describe its activities. In each, conservatively dressed young shop assistants with their hair pulled back tight and without make-up could be seen quietly assisting browsers and customers.

They entered the foyer where groups of scientists sat chatting quietly or reading newspapers. One or two had beer or wine glasses but most had silver service coffee or tea sets before them. Waitresses dressed in long white uniforms and, like the shop girls, with their hair tied back and without make-up, moved solemnly about serving the customers.

'This is our principal entertainment area, Senator,' Claudia said. 'The men like to escape the noise of the base and use our dining and reading facilities. One yearns for some peace and quiet when surrounded by several thousand men. We fly in the latest newspapers on a regular basis.'

Senator Fulton was stunned and not a little disappointed. That God damned priest had painted a Hogarthian picture of debauchery which bore no resemblance to this. He had been promised an orgy and delivered a gentlemen's club.

They entered Len's office. Claudia's economics textbooks,

mixed with scientific books borrowed from co-operative beards, were carefully placed about the room to effect a studious look while a side table displayed some labelled rock samples borrowed from another beard. Others had contributed framed photographs of their children. Len and Andrew wore conservative suits and spoke quietly. Fulton felt disadvantaged. He was aware his heavy-duty, padded Antarctic clothing made him a coarse misfit in this picture of refinement.

'I can't tell you what a pleasure it is to meet you, Senator,' Len began. 'I'm afraid the Antarctic is not the usual stamping ground for the celebrated and famous. It really is quite an honour,' and he motioned Fulton towards an armchair. The senator gingerly lowered himself and groaned as he sat down.

'My God damn leg's playing up. So's my back. Football injuries. Always strikes in the cold. I tell you, it might sound un-American but I warn every young man to stick with basketball or golf.'

'I quite agree with you, sir,' Len said soothingly. 'When we're young no one cautions about the consequences. I've seen it time and again.'

'Can we offer you afternoon tea, sir?' Potter said, only to be interrupted by Len. 'I rather think the senator would be more comfortable with something a little stronger. I can offer you some decent Southern Comfort to take your mind off the leg, sir.'

'Sounds good to me,' the senator replied.

For ten minutes they discussed the senator's Antarctic mission. Len, Andrew and Claudia were agreeable, charming and encouraging and warmed by a fourth whisky Fulton was soon in full flight recounting gossipy anecdotes about the Oval Office. Suddenly he twitched violently again, this time grabbing his back.

Entirely on her own initiative and to the scarcely suppressed astonishment of Len and Andrew, Claudia abandoned the pre-arranged script which so far had gone far better than any of them could have expected.

'Senator, I think we can help your problem. We have a very pleasant sauna on board. I'm sure you will find the heat helpful. Also, I'm a fully trained physiotherapist and would be very happy to treat your back. I'll just go and arrange things,' and she left the room.

Outside she picked up a telephone and barked instructions

for the sauna to be vacated and everyone to stay out of sight. Returning, she walked over to Fulton and reached for his hand. 'Everything's ready, Senator, come with me.'

Two hours later Fulton returned to Len's office.

'I'd just like to thank you for your hospitality. As far as I'm concerned you're doing a damn fine job down here for our American boys so far from home. I'll look forward to seeing you tomorrow. Claudia has recommended further treatment sessions. You know,' he paused, 'she's a damned intelligent girl.'

For three consecutive days the senator enjoyed additional therapy while the ship's activities slipped back to normal. Fulton made no comment about the dramatically changed newly raucous atmosphere although he was puzzled by the appearance of a birdcage in the foyer entrance with an apparently dead parrot lying on the bottom with its feet in the air. The crisis was over. But a new and entirely unexpected one arose.

On the day of Fulton's departure Claudia came into the office. She had a distant manner.

'Len, I have something to tell you. I'm leaving the ship. Sam has offered me a job as a permanent assistant.'

'For Christ's sake, Claudia, you can't do this,' Len exploded. 'We need you here.'

'You'll get by. I've got everything running smoothly now. You don't require me any more. Besides, I've been here twelve weeks. It's been lots of fun and rather interesting but not exactly the sort of career I planned. If you want me to recommend one of the girls to take over my job then I can. But I don't think it's necessary.'

Three hours later she flew out with Fulton and twenty thousand dollars Len had pressed on her.

19

Following Claudia's departure Len became depressed. Leaving the ship's management to Andrew his days fell into a routine of meals, a two-mile walk alone along the coastline and then sitting in his office armchair reading the books Claudia had instructed Harding to bring in for him. He was not the only one. Despairing at his failure with Fulton, Father O'Hearn became a regular visitor in the evenings. The two would sit together watching and commenting on the fight videos which now arrived on each flight. Despite their pleasure from this their conversation invariably turned to the ship's activities. The debates led nowhere, largely due to being conducted on different planes. O'Hearn talked of exploitation, Len countered with free choice and willing buyers and sellers; the priest argued moral duty, Len responded with respect for individual determination; O'Hearn proffered the sanctity of the sexual relationship, Len the biological needs of men and women. Round and round they went with diminishing enthusiasm each time. Usually the discussions petered out and they sat in morose companionship while slowly descending into a heavy-headed, wine-induced lethargy.

During one of these sessions Andrew entered the room in what transpired to be a turning point in Father O'Hearn's future. Andrew was in a no-nonsense mood. Following Claudia's departure they had inherited a number of problems she had handled with aplomb. The most frustrating was the beards falling in love nuisance. Attempts to emulate Claudia's methodology had been unsuccessful, verging on disaster when Andrew had resorted to abusing the smitten for their poor judgement. Two girls had been dispatched to America to await the return of their betrothed. They were easily replaced but what angered Andrew was the loss of the two love-struck beards who no longer came on board.

A slight anarchy had settled over the ship with occasional brawling between besotted beards and their loved ones' clientele. On two occasions the prohibition on buying the parrot drinks had been breached, once almost fatally following which the parrot had spent twelve hours on its back with its feet in the air, drying out on Len's desk.

On the positive side productivity had risen thanks to the addition of the two Russian nightclub singers to the stable. Shortly after Claudia's departure they had asked to join the stable having learned of the girls' daily earnings, which contrasted impressively with their twenty-five dollars paid by the Russian State Shipping office. Len's immediate impulse to decline as he had done with the Chinese waitresses was overridden by Andrew's vigorous endorsement of the idea.

'It's not a comparable situation,' he had said. 'The restaurant is a real winner and an asset to the operation. But this factory-hand bawling so-called music is a serious misjudgement. It might be par for the course with cruise ship vacuous clientele but the beards are educated men. They come here for sex, conversation, a few laughs and to get away from the base. The acts Harding brings in periodically provide the men with sufficient entertainment. Chances are the beards don't want any background music but if they did, believe it or not they'd probably prefer Mozart or Rossini string sonatas, very quietly in the background. We can provide that with CDs. The only chaps who pay attention to this racket are the American military personnel and they're mostly brain-dead and would find the opening of an envelope an exciting social event.'

To confirm his assessment Andrew sounded out several dozen beards and received a uniform response. All were delighted at the prospect of an end to the Russian racket. They were even more ecstatic at the prospect of the two singers joining the stable.

'At first I couldn't understand it,' Andrew explained. 'There was a tremendous sense of excitement and a couple of the beards even offered me bribes for early bookings. I mean, the two Russian girls are pretty, but so what? So's the existing stable. Then I worked it out. They only ever saw the Russian girls with clothes on so they alone among the younger women on the boat still preserved a sense of mystique. You can imagine how they must have been secretly slavering over Claudia.'

When Andrew had entered Len's room he desperately needed a drink having just come from listening to a tiresome tirade from a Canadian beard, Dr McGowan, who had protested bitterly at his inability to secure a booking with one of the Russian singers. McGowan and Andrew did not get along having crossed swords a few weeks back when Andrew had ridiculed the Canadian's sub-terranean plant fossil research.

'What's up with you miserable sods?' Andrew remarked, noting O'Hearn and Len's melancholy.

The priest sighed. 'Oh, we're just thinking. Nothing to get alarmed about.'

'Danny's bothered by the girls,' Len explained. 'Says we're rotters exploiting them and corrupting the beards.'

'Does he now,' Andrew said as he poured himself a glass of wine. 'Well, let me tell you, if you knew what you were talking about that's the last thing you'd say. When it comes to exploitation in these relationships it's a one-way path and that's the girls exploiting the men. It's a voluntary act by both parties, only one side does the paying,' and he sank into an armchair. 'If you really thought deeply about this exercise,' he continued addressing O'Hearn, 'then it would give you hope. In many respects it epitomises the very pinnacle of civilisation.'

O'Hearn cackled. 'That's a good one. I'll enjoy hearing you justify that.'

'Look at it this way,' Andrew said. 'What was it Hobbes said about man's natural state? Poor, nasty, brutish and short. And it wasn't just Hobbes. Most of the great philosophers took a starting point that without imposed rules and authority man would naturally descend into anarchy. So they argued human relationships from the assumption of a need for authority. Well, down here there are no rules. This is the only truly free society in existence. And what do you see? Lots of happiness and laughter as everybody does exactly what they want while still maintaining order and respect for the other fellow. It just may well be that this ship, which at any given time has about 700 people on board, is the happiest place in the world. Now that puts the lie to the age-old belief that life would become a jungle unless we accept being bossed about and told what to do.

'That's why I say it's the pinnacle of civilisation. Everyone gets along beautifully with no one telling them what to do. And consider it another way. Look at the mix. We've got thirty or more different races, different skin colours, different religions, different ages. We've got professors and tarts, mechanics and academics, Italian scientists and poofter Russian waiters; we've got the whole human gambit and as I've said, with no rules, instead just a few understood and accepted systems, the result is an atmosphere of contentment, co-operation and happiness.'

'What about the girls?' O'Hearn fired back.

'Why don't you talk to them?' Andrew said. 'I'll bet if you gathered up 100 girls at random from London or Nairobi or Toronto or anywhere, you wouldn't find any as happy as this lot. Soon most of them will be back home with nearly a hundred thousand dollars Australian each in their hands. Some of them may waste it but most will use it to buy an apartment. It's their main topic of conversation. And mark my words, they'll fight to come again next year. So what would you prefer for them? Sitting all day at a checkout counter for eight dollars an hour being bored witless and eventually a miserable marriage to a pot-bellied, beer-sotted panel beater? Because that's their fate otherwise, at least with ninety per cent of them.

'The problem with you, Danny, is the same as with all purveyors of religion. You've personally bought a bill of goods, which is your business, but under the guise of caring for others, regardless of the fact that those others neither seek nor need your intervention, you want everyone to adopt your taste, which is why you're such a misfit down here. By that I don't mean just the line you're flogging, the God stuff and all that. You're a misfit because as I said, down here is the ultimate free society with everyone doing precisely what they want and you and you alone, wanting to stop them and make them do what you want. Well, I'll tell you this, chum. By pushing tyranny in a truly free society, just maybe the freest ever in history, you're pissing in the wind.'

'Not entirely,' the priest said quietly. 'I'm quite sure my influence has acted as a deterrent on some of the men.'

Andrew did not hide his anger. 'Too damn right it has. And the key word is deterrent which is a euphemism for force. When I said this was the happiest place on earth I should have excluded your little flock. But mark my words, I'll wager they're sobbing themselves to sleep every night with their hands on their groins. Try buggering off and see how long before they're here on board making up for lost time.

'If the measure of your success relies on coercion or intimi-dation, and it bloody well does, then it's not got much going for it. The net outcome of your presence has been to produce the only pocket of misery down here, which is a pretty poor advertisement for your so-called good work.'

Len intruded. 'Lay off, Andrew. Danny means well. If that's what makes him happy then that's his business.'

But Andrew was in no mood to lay off. 'He doesn't look too bloody happy to me. I'll say this,' he continued. 'When I agreed to come down here I did so knowing I could get out when I wanted with the plane coming in regularly. Well, the fact is I've stayed the distance and I've done so of my own free choice. And why? Because I've never been so exhilarated. I've felt good about bringing so much laughter and pleasure. That's something I never anticipated. We've made a lot of money. I've just about been through the entire stable. I've had time to read the sort of books I always intended to but never actually did. All sorts of interesting issues have arisen which have kept me stimulated. The company's interesting. Oh I know many of the beards are bloody wet but some of them are doing fascinating things and I've enjoyed discussing them and being shown what they're up to. Honestly; I'm quite sad about going home again. If there was a golf course and a tennis court and no winter dark months I reckon I'd be happy to stay here for ever. But aside from all the pleasure, the best bit is a sense of doing something useful and the measure of that is being deluged by customers of their own free will, and that my friend,' he said, emphasising each word, 'is the exact opposite of what you have done here.'

At that Andrew rose, picked up the wine bottle and topped everyone's glass up.

Silence fell on the room, the three men deep in thought.

Finally O'Hearn spoke. 'You've given me something to think about, Andrew. I appreciate it,' and he got up and left.

A few days later he came back on board and bailed up Len and Andrew in the office.

'I've come to say goodbye. I'm throwing in the towel. I thought about what you said, Andrew, and you got me most on one key point. If people come through the door of their own volition then that's the test of one's usefulness. I'm tired of constantly pushing adult people to do things they plainly don't want to do. Basically I'm treating them like children and you're right; it's sheer arrogance to imply I know best even if I don't approve of their behaviour. In the final analysis it's their business. I'd only have a role if they sought my advice and to be frank, they don't and I suspect never will. Most of all I can't deny the unpleasant abrasiveness at the base has ended since your boat arrived.'

'Good God, I've made a conversion,' Andrew teased.

'In one sense you have,' O'Hearn replied. 'You know, there was a time when the clergy sought piety through practical good works. In the twelfth century, for example, they helped travellers by building and maintaining roads and bridges but it didn't last long and soon the church descended to simply mendicant priests leeching off the poor. Chaucer had it right about that. Ever since then it's been a downhill ride no matter how well intentioned, of bullying people through fear. For me, the moralising is over.'

'Jesus, Danny, don't be too hasty,' Len said, plainly concerned. 'I mean, what will you do?'

'I'll do exactly what I've always wanted to do,' O'Hearn said. 'I'm going back to New York to open a boxing gym. I know a wealthy fight aficionado who'll back me. And best of all, if fighters want me to train them then they will walk in the door of their own free will. I want you both to know I've enjoyed meeting you enormously. I hope I'll see you again. If you're ever in New York, look me up. Telephone any newspaper and ask to talk to their boxing writer. He'll know how to contact me.'

He shook hands with the two and left. As he walked back through the lounge it occurred to him that, aside from an occasional genial greeting, the beards now accepted his presence on the ship. And for the first time, the parrot, which happened to be sober, did not abuse him but instead screeched a friendly 'Gidday'. An unaccustomed sense of pleasure washed over him as he wallowed in the joy of feeling normal and whole.

20

With O'Hearn and Fulton gone Twigg found himself battling alone with his morals campaign. Zealotry brings its own satisfaction and unhappy is the crusader whose cause is won. Such was the case with Twigg who, unperturbed by his now solo mission, continued campaigning with heightened fervour.

Twigg-created notices appeared pinned on the barracks walls warning of AIDS, sexual diseases with horrendous consequences, the virtues of chastity, monogamy and the family unit. As quickly as they appeared they were converted to darts which flew about the barracks in an atypical display of frivolity by the beards.

It was then Twigg resorted to his ultimate weapon; blackmail.

Erecting a small tent on the water's edge alongside the ship's gangway Twigg sat for seventeen hours daily on a deckchair, ostentatiously writing into a notebook the name of each beard going aboard. And to ensure his presence was never lost on the ship's clientele, for the other seven hours he slept in the tent.

The beards were by nature mostly passive souls but this implied threat caused alarm among the married men in particular and eventually a counter-attack was planned. Twigg was monitored and, when the news came that he had retired inside the tent to sleep and after allowing a half hour for him to doze off, the reprisal assault began.

A guard was posted on the ship's toilets. Drinkers and diners arriving for relief were redirected to the Twigg tent, thus in the following seven hours a total of 2890 beer and wine filled bladders were discharged over the tent.

When Twigg woke he found himself encased in a two-inch thick, frozen urine fishbowl. In vain he endeavoured to break the opaque sheeting with his fist. Quickly tiring from his exertions he became conscious of an increasing difficulty breathing, for his prison was in fact airtight.

The prospect of Twigg dying through suffocation had not crossed anyone's mind. In fairness, had it done so, at least some of the urinators, although few of the married beards, might have hesitated. But it now crossed Twigg's mind and he began to panic.

He made a futile attempt to scrape under the tent's side but the snow was only three inches deep and beneath it lay solid rock. The hot urine had cut through the snow thus the lemony sheeting extended down to the base.

Strengthened through fear he coiled spring-like at one end of the tent and despite the space limitations, hurled himself in a crazed panic at the other end with such velocity as to not only crash through the glazing but onwards into the frozen sea. This new crisis was lost on him for the sub-zero-temperature water instantly rendered him unconscious.

As it transpired this was not the end of Twigg for a steward leaning against the rail and gazing vacantly at the tent while painting his nails witnessed the spectacular breakout and subsequent splash. Shriekingly he raised the alarm and two minutes later the unconscious and now dark blue Twigg form lay stretched on the lounge floor having been fished from the sea by some freshly serviced beards.

Len was summoned. He took one look and instructed the growing audience to strip Twigg's wet upper clothing and rub his limbs and body vigorously, a task the stewards set about with enthusiasm. Isaac was sent for and he duly stumbled inebriated into the room, took a swaying hazy glance at Twigg and declared him a goner.

In an inspirational flash Len shouted to Potter, who had arrived on the scene, to fetch Big Bertha. Big Bertha was in the stable to accommodate a particular taste, her peculiarity resting on possession of a forty-eight-inch bust.

Potter burst into her cabin, wrenched an astonished mounted beard to the floor and ordered her to come quickly. Big Bertha rose from the bed, pulled a very large and loose T-shirt over her massive breasts and searched around for further attire. 'Don't worry about that,' Potter bellowed and leaving the bewildered dislodged beard spluttering indignantly, the two rushed to the lounge.

'Give him the treatment, Bertha,' Len shouted.

The girl knelt beside Twigg and raised him to a sitting position. Lifting her T-shirt she pulled it down over his head to his waist, enveloped him in 400 cubic inches of warm breasts and pulling the bottom of the shirt tight about her and Twigg's waists, she rocked back and forth crooning softly.

A minute passed then to a triumphant roar from the assembly, the Twigg limbs began to shudder.

A hazy consciousness flickered, faded then fanned into focus in the Twigg mind. Vague memories of a green glass prison, of suffocation, of a penetrating coldness and of wetness swirled confusingly in his head, a jumble of thoughts now overwhelmed by a beautiful floating-in-warm-oil sensation. As he began to drift off again into a pleasant delirium, a sharp pain from his frozen feet brought him back to semi-consciousness and he felt his legs twitch.

The victorious cry this movement prompted from the two dozen spectators brought him to semi consciousness. He heard Len's voice shout to remove his wet clothes and felt hands tugging at his shoes and belt and then at his pants.

Twigg had had an unusual boyhood, unique in that he had never once engaged in a fight with another boy. Observers of the scene which followed would be disbelieving of that for Twigg, his mind now clear, began to fight. He fought with a frenzied ferocity for freedom from his fleshy embrace. Opening his mouth to shout, he was temporarily disabled when a huge breast filled it. Choking, he kicked and struggled and eventually, disgorging the breast, he fought for his very life. But in vain. Subdued by a dozen firm hands he was stripped then deshrouded from the embracing T-shirt and eventually he lay almost naked, twitching tearfully like a flopping fish before a now-silent audience. But not for long.

A shriek penetrated the silence. 'The filthy bastard,' screeched Marlene for exposed before the gathering lay Twigg's awful secret. He was wearing the missing, much coveted lace panties. It was then Potter remembered who he had seen furtively escaping from a steward's cabin a month earlier.

Three days later Twigg shipped out and the Olga Buskova settled into a routine of undisturbed peace, pleasure and prosperity.

21

Christmas arrived and the Olga Buskova was closed for the day. By mid-morning a melancholic atmosphere descended like a dark fog upon the ship and McMurdo base as thoughts turned to home, families and conventionality.

Len was reminded of Claudia and became nostalgic. Prior to her departure she had organised a Christmas Day dinner with the galley and arranged for Harding to purchase gifts she had chosen and personally wrapped for everyone on board and also, to bring in a Christmas tree and decorations. Len's gift was a powder-blue cashmere sweater and a copy of *Catch 22*. For Andrew she had procured a Cossack fur hat and a recent biography of Flaubert.

Over the past month the snow had melted, exposing a drab surface of sharp pebbles and brown rock across which an unseasonal blizzard now swirled and whistled and continued to do so throughout the day. The leaden sky pressed down and even the sea, now whipped into waves that snapped and crashed at the shore, had turned an unwelcoming dark grey. Both the base and the ship seemed to shrink as if nature was venting its fury at their intrusive presence.

Just before midday a group of drunken choristers stumbled across to the ship and huddled together at the bottom of the gang-plank, vainly attempting to bellow out a bevy of carols against the roar of the wind before eventually capitulating and retreating to the base.

At 1pm all the ship's occupants except the catering staff gathered in the ballroom for Christmas dinner. They arrived singly and almost begrudgingly and were greeted by Len dressed in a Santa Claus suit and white fluffy beard which on Claudia's instruction had been brought in by Harding. Their pleasure on receiving their unexpected gifts, aided by the free-flowing champagne, soon saw spirits lifted on board.

Paper hats were donned, Christmas crackers pulled and many of the girls exchanged gifts with one another. Huge plates of roast turkey with all the traditional trimmings were consumed along with copious quantities of wine, and the laughter and gaiety rose to such heights that occasionally it could be faintly heard at the base when the gale periodically abated.

Following Christmas pudding Andrew rose and delivered a muddled address, initially on the spirit of Christmas but which tapered out to an advocacy of the mutual rewards of maintaining servicing productivity over the remaining months.

The captain responded in broken English with a largely unintelligible but fortunately short speech, apparently on the subject of international friendship.

Inspired by these offerings and wine-induced courage, three Scots girls took the stage and sang a Christmas carol. The quality of their rendition was unremarkable but the tumultuous applause gave courage to others.

A tiny Irish girl, who until a year earlier had lived almost her entire life in a convent, stepped up and with soulful eyes fluttering heavenwards, as she had done on fourteen previous Christmas days, recited a syrupy poem of the genre beloved by simple Irish nuns on the birth of 'dear baby Jesus'. Its saving grace was its brevity and she was accorded generous applause.

Next up was Heidi from Munich. 'I gif you traditional German Christmas song,' she announced. Stepping to the edge of the stage she slowly spread her arms, lifted her head and sang. Her voice was stunning. It filled the ballroom with a crystal-like clarity, with a beauty that touched every breast. The audience sat frozen, bathed in the unexpected melodic brilliance. From the galley the Russian staff emerged and stood quietly at the rear. Soon tears of joy ran down their broad Slavic features, for Heidi was on the boat after failing entry to the Bavarian Opera. 'Your voice is beautiful,' the examiners had said, 'but alas, it is not sufficiently strong for the opera.'

Heidi was accorded a tumultuous standing ovation and cries of 'more' produced two further equally acclaimed renditions before she was allowed, flushed with triumph, to run a gauntlet of hugs and kisses and return to her seat.

Five Australian girls now lined up on the stage. 'Here's an Aussie show,' their leader Sharlene bawled. On her command they simultaneously stood on their heads, their tumbled skirts revealing three without knickers before they crashed into a heap of whirling limbs.

This performance was also well received, only the Asian girls lowering their heads and covering their mouths to hide their muffled bell-like tinkling laughter.

By mid-afternoon everyone, by now happily contented, had retired to their cabins to sleep off the festivity's excesses.

On shore the atmosphere was less benign. Shortly before midday an ugly brawl broke out between a Prague University penguin neurosis team and the Queensland University leopard seal weight recording group. The Czechs were hugely offended when the Queenslanders, maintaining their Australian Christmas barbecue tradition, captured, killed and roasted a penguin beneath a canopy adjacent the Czech quarters.

Following the barbecued-penguin fracas an unhappy friction hung in the air and many of the base's planned Christmas celebrations were abandoned. The remainder were conducted in a steely cold atmosphere, the beards confining themselves to their national or particular research groups before retreating to their cabins for solitude where they lay on their bunks, deep in self-pity and remorse at their choice of careers.

Late in the day the blizzard began to fade and eventually it died entirely. The sea became still, the clouds faded away and the dark mood ashore slowly lifted.

When at 8pm Andrew lowered the gangplank and the men eagerly surged aboard, everything was quickly back to its surrealistic normality. Laughter, joy and warmth prevailed as Christmas's recriminatory reminder of the outside world's more restrained existence was forgotten.

22

The Olga Buskova was due to depart for Sydney in two weeks. Len and Andrew sat in the office discussing the accounts. 'Here's the latest figures, up to date as of yesterday,' Andrew said. 'So far we've taken forty-one million dollars with the girls which should net about thirty million after paying them. Food and drinks, book sales and other ancillaries will produce between two and three million more when everything's paid. Currently there's forty-six million sitting in bank accounts earning interest all over the world. We've got two more weeks to put some cream on the cake. Nearly half the beards have already left with winter approaching and they're flying out at about 100 a day. The waiting time for servicing is down to two hours. Still, it's worth hanging on and milking the last penny from it.'

'I'm a bit worried about that,' Len muttered. 'There's bloody icebergs floating around everywhere. I think we should have a chat to the captain. We'd look bloody silly having achieved all of this if we end up doing a Titanic.'

As it turned out there was no need to call the captain because at that moment there was a knock on the door and he came in.

'We haf again problem with tanks,' he pronounced solemnly.

'Bloody hell,' Andrew cried. 'We can't afford to forfeit a day to empty them again.'

'I'm not too averse to returning early,' Len said. 'Tell me, Boris. Is there any danger with the icebergs?'

'I watch icebergs. Is no problem. When we sail we go at daybreak so we see icebergs. We haf eighteen hours daylight and will go 400 kilometres before dark into Ross Sea where are no icebergs. I haf problem with tanks but also haf answer if you wish.'

'We wish, Boris', Andrew said. 'What are you suggesting?'

'Is only solution for two, maybe three weeks. That is why I suggest. If engineers shift water pipes and we tip hot water into sea, tanks will freeze. When frozen is no health problem. Tanks will unfreeze in time for Sydney. Maybe problem for a day before Sydney.'

'Brilliant thinking, Boris my boy,' Potter cried. 'Go to it, mate.' So the engineers diverted the plumbing. For its remaining two weeks at the base the ship daily discharged the water from nearly 5000 hot showers and the continuously functioning laundry and galley through a single out-of-sight pipe on the seaward side.

The steaming water was sucked into the light current running along the shore line for about ten miles. Within two days the current's fish population departed as they left for more amenable climes. With the fish gone the penguins too disappeared in search of food. The remaining scientists whose work related to this fauna didn't noticed as they were finished for the season and preparing for their departure.

As anticipated the holding tanks, lacking the continuous hot showers supply, soon froze into a solid block of waste. All was well.

23

Professor McLean came into the meeting room where his three-man team sprawled about awaiting him. He braced himself as he had done a thousand times before when entering lecture halls back in London and dolefully recalled the wonderful three-month lectureship exchange he had once enjoyed with the University of Singapore. Out there in the civilised East he had been treated with near reverence by his students.

The tiresome familiar chanting began. 'Stand up, stand up, stand up, stand up. We can't see you. Stand up.'

'Okay, settle down, men,' he said after allowing the requisite twenty seconds insult period, which long practice had taught him was the minimum before the chanting faded.

'I've an exciting announcement to make, which you are going to be rather thrilled about. Or at least all bar one of you, regrettably. As you know, we return to London in eight days' time. This expedition has served its purpose having confirmed that for the moment, at least, the melting polar ice cap crisis has diminished. Our six months' sea temperature recordings have revealed an improving trend from a year ago with a 0.3 per cent cooler average reading. Yesterday I received advice from the United Nations that the Secretary-General personally, no less, has convened a special general assembly meeting in two weeks' time to report this expedition's good news.

'The work you have done has, I know, been uneventful and at times boring, as is so often the case with such scientific research. So as a reward I have a little surprise. Tomorrow Colonel Harris is leading a twelve-man motorised marine team on an expedition to the South Pole. Helicopters will pick us up at the halfway point and bring the expedition back. The journey has no other purpose than adventure and he has very decently accepted my request for our team to join him.'

An excited buzz broke out. Professor McLean held up his hands for silence.

'Before I continue is there anyone not particularly interested in going?' he asked lightly. 'Oh dear. I feared as much,' he continued. 'I'm afraid one of you must stay behind. Our contract with the United Nations doesn't expire for three more days. It's vital we continue recording the temperature over that period and then, of course, all the floats and gear must be brought back to base and packed away.'

Professor McLean opened his briefcase and produced a folded pillowslip. He shook it out.

'Inside this I have three playing cards. One is an ace. You can each reach in and take a card and the chap who draws the ace stays behind. I can't be fairer than that. There's no advantage in going first or last,' he assured them.

The first man stepped forward and tentatively drew a card then shouted joyously as he examined it. Then it was Philip's turn. He reached in and pulled out a card, hesitated for a second then glanced at it. It hit him like a punch in the nose. It was the ace.

Later, sunk in despair in Professor McLean's office, he traversed the procedures.

'I know it's dreadfully disappointing for you,' the professor said. 'It's ridiculous of course, but telling people you've been to the Antarctic always produces the same query as to whether one went to the South Pole. People associate the two. It's not as if there's anything there. Just more snow. And it won't be a comfortable trip, either. It's my bet that after a couple of days roughing it the chaps will wish they'd volunteered to stay behind. You may well conclude the ace was the lucky card after all.'

Philip was unconvinced. He'd offered five hundred pounds to each of his colleagues to change places and been scoffed at in return.

'What's vitally important,' the professor continued, 'is that you continue to fax the results through to New York each afternoon at 3pm. They're in constant contact with me so don't think we can simply pull stumps a few days early. I don't say they read everything but the important point is the Comments section on the bottom of the form. All you have to do is write 'normal temperatures' each day.'

The following morning Philip glumly watched the expedition depart, the men whooping and shouting as two dozen snow-mobiles snaked their way south in a roar of engines.

He went indoors, gathered his bag with his dictaphone and set out to read the temperatures.

172

24

Fleetingly Philip contemplated filling the temperature records form without checking the thermometers. They'd been almost the same for six months. Why waste time? Then he recalled that with the onset of winter the last few weeks had recorded marginally decreasing readings. The sea was beginning to ice up and almost half the scientific teams had left the base.

The recollection of this exodus cheered him. He'd finish the readings as quickly as possible, fax through the results, tidy up and spend the day on the Olga Buskova. It was due to sail in six days and was cutting it pretty fine. Large icebergs had appeared out in the bay and for the past three weeks there had been darkness which had increased in duration every night.

Still, with the McMurdo base's personnel halved, Philip contemplated, he would have a better prospect of scoring one of the Asian girls or possibly the spectacular redhead he had seen in the lounge occasionally when she was off duty. McLean was right. All the expedition would see was snow. He began to feel happier about remaining behind.

After ten minutes in the snowmobile he reached the first float. Philip switched off the engine, reached with the grappling hook and hauled in the first of the sixty thermometers to be checked.

Curses, he thought when he read the measurement. It must be broken. The reading was almost a tepid water temperature. But hang on. How could it break? They never broke. Anyway, if they did there would be spare thermometers and he couldn't recall seeing any in the expedition's equipment boxes.

He decided to ignore the sampling. He would scout about back at the base for another thermometer and if he found one, he'd attach it tomorrow. Tossing the gear back into the sea he remounted the snowmobile and moved to the next float, 200 metres along the coast.

He pulled in the line and read the temperature. I'm going crazy, he thought. Again it showed a tepid water reading. Two couldn't possibly be broken. Baffled, he dropped the gear back into the water and sped to the next float. The temperature was the same.

For the first time Philip pulled out his dictaphone and recorded all three readings. He sat on the snowmobile for a minute and thought. The implications were horrendous. He decided to apply the standard scientific methodology when in doubt; subjective measurement. Philip dismounted, knelt at the water's edge, tugged off his glove in the freezing air and tentatively submerged the tip of his finger. After a few seconds he pushed it in further until ultimately his hand was immersed. My God, he thought the water is tepid. You could almost swim in it. For half an hour he sat deep in thought on the water's edge, appalled at his discovery.

Back at the base, Philip filled in the temperature sheets and in the Comments section wrote, 'Refer attached sheet.'

On the blank paper he wrote, 'Professor McLean is temporarily indisposed and I am in charge of the research. The temperatures shown are accurate and have been double-checked. Extrapolating them suggests an imminent major global crisis with sea levels rising between twenty-five and thirty feet. The implications are catastrophic. Urge you monitor any current Arctic circle research. Will advise temperatures tomorrow following routine checks. Dr Philip Melcup, Cambridge University Antarctic Oceanographic Survey Team.'

He faxed the sheets to New York and began to wonder if anyone else had noticed the change. Philip showered then strolled across to the Olga Buskova. In the Chinese restaurant he observed Professor James, leader of the National Geographic Society penguin distemper team, eating with a book propped before him on the table.

'Sorry to disturb you, Professor. I was wondering about the penguins. They're behaving oddly and I was curious why.'

'What bloody penguins?' the professor snapped. 'There are no bloody penguins. They've all buggered off and we don't know why. Where did you see any?' Philip thought quickly. The professor was right, come to think of it. He'd not noticed any penguins during his temperature monitoring that morning but plainly the professor was ignorant of the water temperature change.

'Oh, I was thirty miles down the coast this morning,' Philip bluffed. 'I saw a batch gambolling about and just wondered. Sorry to bother you,' and he rose quickly and left the American to his meal.

The following morning's readings reaffirmed the previous day's.

Later in his report he advised of the disappearing penguins, advancing the supposition they had fled in pursuit of cold water. He had spent the previous night researching and now advised that if the present temperatures remained for another month, the entire ice cap would melt down. At least twenty per cent of the earth's surface would be submerged within two months he predicted. It was imperative appropriate action be taken to warn the world. All low-lying countries, and he listed those he could recall from the team's discussion sessions: Holland, Bangladesh, the Mekong Delta; the list extended to an entire page, on which he estimated circa 2.5 billion people resided, would be submerged. Most coastal cities would be affected he wrote.

He received a fax back within an hour. It was from the United Nations Secretary-General's office and signed by the Secretary-General personally. The Secretary-General congratulated Philip, asked him to continue monitoring and advising the readings, urged confidentiality and assured him appropriate action would be taken.

Five days later, with his colleagues back from the South Pole, Philip informed Professor McLean of what had occurred and showed him the faxes and temperature records. He assured him he had told no one at the base and the professor instructed him to maintain the secrecy. 'This devastating information belongs to the United Nations to act on,' he said. 'Do not even tell the others. I see no reason to spoil the poor lads' last night.'

Philip urged McLean to come down to the water's edge. He persuaded the reluctant professor to remove his glove and test the temperature. McLean withdrew his hand and re-gloved it. He turned to Philip and plainly struggling with emotion said, 'We're too late, my boy. The outcome of this is too horrible to contemplate. The world as we know it is finished.' As events transpired, this was a very accurate comment indeed.

That night the Olga Buskova held a riotous farewell party. The girls accommodated all comers on the house. Food and drinks were also gratis and for the first time in two months the parrot was given free rein and went on a blinder. After an hour it was on its back drunk, its feet in the air.

Philip and Professor McLean sat silently in a corner watching the festivities. After a while the professor spoke.

'You're still young, Philip. You should join in and enjoy yourself. You may never do so again,' which as it transpired, was a very inaccurate comment indeed.

The following morning the Cambridge team flew out. As the plane dipped and wheeled round northwards, Philip saw below him, like a tiny toy boat, the Olga Buskova plunging through the McMurdo Sound white-caps as it headed for Sydney.

A week later silence descended on the base as the five unfortunate marines selected to hold the fort over winter settled into a six-month hibernation.

25

Twelve days after Philip's discovery he flew from London to New York where he was picked up in a limousine and taken to the United Nations Secretary-General's office.

The Secretary-General welcomed Philip gravely, congratulated him at length and advised he would be the special guest of honour at the world's biggest ever press conference to be held in one week's time at Madison Square Garden. 'Our scientists are still compiling a complete impact and strategy report,' he informed Philip, pledging him to secrecy in the interim.

The following day Philip flew to Washington for a White House meeting with the President. Again, he was warmly congratulated. The President discussed the implications of Philip's findings, describing them as the gravest threat to mankind in history.

'I've had no more than two hours sleep each night for the past week,' he said. 'I'm afraid there's no good news. The political and economic consequences are horrifying. We can only pray that with generosity of spirit from all mankind we can somehow first save and then rebuild the world. It's certainly going to be a very different world. My advisers tell me we are destined to lose at least forty years of development progress.'

Five days later Philip was taken to Madison Square Garden. The building was surrounded by more than 2000 armed marines. The adjacent streets were closed off by armoured cars and patrolled by a special US army corp with sub-machine guns in hand.

In the stadium 106 world leaders, whose presence had been solicited by the United Nations Secretary-General telephoning them personally to advise of the gravity of the crisis, were seated on the stage. Before them were 6000 people comprising newspaper editors, journalists, television crews and senior military, economic, scientific, engineering, planning and other officials drawn from almost 200 nations, all having been forewarned of an announcement of unprecedented gravity.

The proceedings were broadcast worldwide and watched by

the greatest television audience in history totalling more than three billion people and translated into 122 languages.

The Secretary-General rose.

'It is my sad duty to inform the peoples of the world of a development that will gravely affect us all.

'Recently a United Nations-sponsored scientific team from Cambridge University has discovered that the Antarctic ice cap has commenced melting at a velocity far in excess of any anticipated rate. You will all be aware of the warnings in recent years of the dangers arising through human-instigated release of carbon dioxide, methane and other greenhouse gases and the possible catastrophic consequences of global warming.

'It is my sad duty to inform you that the worst fears have eventuated. Over the past week, with the goodwill of the world's leaders gathered here today, we have combined mankind's best scientific minds to ascertain the impact. It is anticipated that within twelve months the global sea level will rise by eight to twelve metres. A minimum area of one-fifth of the globe's land mass will be submerged, which will directly affect approximately one-third of the world's population.

'It is the collective wish of the leaders gathered here today that we should fully and honestly inform you about this situation. Having said that we wish to emphasise that with goodwill and co-operation there is no need for panic.'

Within ten minutes the Dow Jones plunged eighty-three per cent in its largest and fastest fall in history and shortly afterwards all the other world's bourses followed suit.

'On behalf of all nations,' the Secretary-General continued, 'we have declared a special state of emergency and agreed that until this problem is accommodated, all nations will suspend civil liberties.

'I repeat; no one should panic. We are working on evacuation plans for people directly affected. Over the next few weeks we will be constantly announcing our programmes of action. The world will be kept fully informed.'

In preparing this address the Secretary-General's advisers had recommended a dual approach of full disclosure mixed with optimism. Unfortunately there were no grounds for optimism. Finally it was resolved that in lieu of optimism a positive focal point must be presented and after a great deal more discussion, the advisers had settled on Philip as discoverer of the crisis.

'I want to say on behalf of the people of all nations that we are grateful and admiring of a young British scientist whose brilliant research has detected this problem. His name is Dr Philip Melcup of Cambridge University. We should remind ourselves that it is the human genius epitomised by Dr Melcup in which lies hope for our ultimate salvation,' and at that he left his microphone, walked across to Philip, took his hand and drew him back to the podium. 'This is your saviour,' the Secretary-General said.

'Finally, I repeat and shall continue emphasising; although this is a gravely serious problem, it presents a magnificent challenge to us all. Humankind has repeatedly demonstrated its ability to overcome problems. With your goodwill we will do so again.'

Over the following three weeks Philip appeared on more than sixty magazine covers across the globe and next only to the Secretary General, his face became the best known in the world.

26

The Secretary-General's address created an all-time record. Never in history had so many people ignored a single piece of advice; in this case, not to panic. After their initial dramatic collapse the world's stock exchanges continued to fade, reaching a base seventy per cent below their previous levels. But when analysts weighed the situation, some stocks soared. Civil engineers, armament manufacturers, transport, construction, forest, boat-building and tinned food companies were among those which boomed in the new doomsday environment.

The gold price doubled in a week, then following a well-publicised Hong Kong broker's report arguing that in the chaos ahead, gold would be the most useless of commodities, it promptly collapsed.

Churches, mosques and synagogues were packed tight and in three weeks pocketed a year's normal takings.

Despite waterfront and coastal real estate plummeting, this deflation was offset by inland cities' values climbing to all-time record prices. Even the most remote locations such as the Honduran capital Tegucigalpa, lying in a valley high in the Central American mountains, forgotten for 300 years and blacklisted by the World Bank for two decades, were inundated with clamouring land buyers and began a new era of prosperity.

On watch at 2am during a full moon, a Chilean naval officer on board a frigate in the eastern Pacific reported a massive shoal of squid further south than ever before sighted. In fact, this was the condom flotilla destined ultimately for Peruvian beaches but the report added to the worldwide panic as evidence of the ocean's warming. Korean and Japanese fishing company shares climbed in anticipation of this promising new bonanza.

Jesus appeared in a vision before an Italian shepherd high in the Dolomite mountains and engaged him in five minutes' dialogue, the contents of which, so the peasant insisted, Jesus had forbidden him to divulge. Within a week more than 10,000 pilgrims descended on the peasant's village and great prosperity ensued. Reports of this phenomenon apparently induced Jesus to reappear over the next four days before impoverished village inhabitants in nine other locations across Europe and the pilgrimage fervour was soon diluted in line with its diminishing scarcity value.

Across the globe many thousands of impending-doomsday depressed souls committed suicide rather than face the coming holocaust. The undertaking industry enjoyed an unprecedented boom.

Throughout all of this turmoil the Secretary-General issued daily reports. His first and most important was that international agreement had been unanimously reached on fossil-burning fuel consumption, which would be rationed forthwith. Effective from one week's time, total usage would halve. Private cars could be used only on every alternate day and all vehicles would be issued with large red or blue plates signifying the specified days.

'If this policy is adhered to,' the Secretary-General said, 'it may well be that we can rapidly alleviate the situation.' In the wake of that announcement nuclear power shares hit an all-time high.

Following the Madison Square Garden press conference Philip was confined for two days to a luxury Manhattan hotel suite pending his scheduled all-continents whirlwind tour with the Secretary-General. Philip's role had been explained to him as that of an inspirational hero figure representing hope and salvation.

After breakfast on his first morning he turned on the television.

A spindly, pencil-moustached, dark-suited black man, the Reverend Otis Juvenius Smith, filled the screen, prancing up and down a stage waving a large Bible. Behind hung a banner inscribed The Caribbean Church of International Brotherhood while before him, his congregation of mainly middle-aged and elderly black ladies clutched their Bibles and leaned forward eagerly.

Abruptly the preacher stopped, spun on his heels to face his audience and shot his right, Bible-bearing arm skyward.

'Who drive de cars and cause de problem?' he bellowed bulb-eyed and then, after a ten-second ceiling-gazing pause, he hissed: 'De white man.'

'Hallelujah,' the congregation shrieked.

'Who do de suffering?' and following another theatrical

pause: 'De black man.'

Hallelujahs again resounded through the auditorium.

'What colour de Antarctic?'

Philip changed channels.

A small female wearing dark glasses, her face barely visible among her unruly mop of hair, was being interviewed. Philip recognised a popular Irish ballad singer, much given to anguished and toneless songs about the world's wrongs, attributable always to the ubiquitous conspiratorial 'they'.

'It's like disastrous,' she droned nasally. 'Like the people should be told what they, like are doing, like…'

Philip again changed channels.

The chairman of the New York Stock Exchange, his anxiety apparent, was appealing to investors to return. 'The fundamentals remain fundamentally intact and…'

Philip turned the set off and wondered how he would fill the next two days. In the event the problem took care of itself as the telephone rang. It was the Secretary-General's office advising him he would be picked up in thirty minutes for two days of non-stop photography and press interviews.

Philip spoke solemnly to the assembled journalists about the impending catastrophe, but, as instructed, optimistically about the possibilities for relief. Few were convinced.

In the Bangladeshi delta a vast migration of thirty million people decided not to chance such optimism and began walking towards India. They were bombarded from the air daily by food packages from the world's relief agencies and explosives from the Indian airforce. Still the survivors marched on.

The Secretary-General publicly implored India to allow them access. The Indian Prime Minister demanded the burden be shared by the world, an announcement greeted by an eerie silence. In one twelve-hour period three million hungry Bangladeshis crossed the border into India, like a great locust plague, razing crops as they passed while behind marched millions more. The Indian army blazed away, mowing them over in their tens of thousands but on they came.

It was then the crisis reached its height. The Indian airforce dropped a nuclear bomb on upper Bangladesh, wiping out three quarters of a million refugees and farmers. Two hours later

Pakistan, in the name of Muslim brotherhood, dropped a nuclear bomb on Amritsar and in response India dropped one on Peshawar. Both were carefully chosen targets, each side aware that outraged public utterances notwithstanding, the other would be privately pleased, as indeed was the case. For India, the total destruction of Amritsar ended for ever the Sikh problem. So too with Peshawar, which for long had been a hot-bed for protest and a permanent thorn in the Pakistan government's side.

This unspoken understanding regrettably did not extend to the two protagonists' allies. Following the destruction of Amritsar, Russia hinted it would enter the fray and nuke Pakistan. Within hours China threatened India, citing a long-forgotten military pact with Pakistan. The world stood on the brink of obliteration as Russia and China drew lines in the sand and made menacing noises towards each other. When the Kashmiri Parliament seized the opportunity to declare independence, Pakistan and China immediately recognised it and announced they were ready for war to defend its integrity.

In vain the United Nations Secretary-General and other world leaders appealed for peace. The United States President called in his strategists. First they discussed the Pentagon's enthusiastic advocacy of allowing the Chinese and Russians to wipe each other out. But the military was overruled by the President's technical advisers who argued that an all-out nuclear war between China and Russia would have a devastating environmental impact on the United States. So the President became a peacemaker instead.

He telephoned the Russian and Chinese presidents and obtained their agreement for a week's grace to solve the dispute. Then he called the Prime Ministers of India and Pakistan. The world breathed again when it was announced that following the President's initiative they had agreed to meet in Geneva in three days' time, for if truth be known, behind their public bravado the two Prime Ministers were now very frightened men indeed.

Conscious of the eyes of the world on them, the respective sub-continent Prime Ministers engaged in a frenzied behind-the-scenes diplomatic exchange. The outcome was an agreement that the United States President would not personally mediate but would send a prominent citizen instead to fill the role. They were both aware this was to be their greatest moment of glory and the last thing either wanted was the President stealing their place in the sun.

A frantic White House meeting considered who to send. The President's first proposal was rejected by his advisers. He's one of ours, they said. If the talks fail then sending a Democrat will lead to condemnation for risking world peace for political gain.

'Well, I'm damned if I'm sending any Republican to capture the glory,' the President responded angrily.

So Senator Samuel Fulton was appointed the mediator.

27

S tultified with fright at the impending doomsday, billions of people across the globe sat petrified before their televisions awaiting their fate. All eyes were on Geneva where more than 4000 journalists, radio and television crews crowded and spilled over into nearby cities' hotels.

Senator Fulton arrived in the Presidential jet with a token thirty-strong advisory party whom he had no intention of consulting and an hour later gave a platitudinous address to a jammed press conference. A similar exercise was repeated separately by the two Prime Ministers after they flew in.

The following morning the three factions met for a joint photographic session then, as arranged, Fulton and the two Prime Ministers entered a top floor suite in the city's leading hotel. The world held its breath and waited. Outside a crowd of 15,000 packed the plaza and neighbouring streets, gazing silently upwards at the curtain-drawn windows. Numerous clerics and priests led hymn-singing groups, nuns mumbled prayers and fingered their rosary beads while earnest bearded schoolteacher types with soulful staring eyes, holding up placards bearing the single word PEACE, were scattered among the dense crowd. Gypsy pick-pockets darted throughout enjoying the richest pickings in their experience.

Television cameras panned the crowd, periodically switching to the hotel's top floor where the future of the world hung in balance. Commentators describing the scene in several dozen different languages spoke in funereal tones.

Once in the suite Fulton locked the door, put the key in his pocket and turned to the two Prime Ministers.

The Indian Prime Minister, a tiny ascetic man who modelled himself on Ghandi, sat haughtily bird-like on the edge of his armchair.

The Pakistani Prime Minister was obese and smug. The two leaders waited for Fulton to speak, each averting their eyes from the other.

Fulton placed his briefcase on a table and opened it. He drew out some papers and waved them before him. 'Gentlemen, these are from the President,' he said. As Fulton had anticipated both showed sparks of recognition at the glimpse of the letterheads' presidential coat of arms. Following a hunch the senator had checked a few days earlier with the American ambassadors in New Delhi and Islamabad. They had confirmed both leaders had framed congratulatory letters on their office walls from the President following their ascent to their prime ministerial offices. Fulton reached back into his briefcase and pulled out a small pistol which he pointed in the direction of the two.

'This heah is a Pakistan gun,' he said, affecting a menacingly exaggerated Southerner's lingo. In fact it was a Taiwan-manu-factured plastic toy revolver Claudia had purchased in a New York children's shop three days earlier but he gambled neither would know the difference. The Prime Ministers stared at him wide-eyed and began to splutter, demanding explanations.

He picked up one of the presidential letters and read it.

'"Confidential presidential instruction to Senator Fulton,"' he recited.

'"This letter authorises you in the interests of world peace, to forthwith terminate the Prime Ministers of India and Pakistan should they refuse to sign the peace and disarmament agreement.

'"Signed, President of the United States of America."

'Have a look-see for yourself, gentlemen,' and he passed the letter to the Indian while pointing the gun at the Pakistani. When the plainly shocked Indian had read it Fulton gave it to the Pakistani and redirected the gun at the Indian.

'This is an outrage,' the Indian shrieked. 'Absolutely. Quite disgraceful,' added the Pakistani.

'Well, in five minutes' time you won't be worrying about that because you'll both be dead. Now I ain't gonna beat about the bush. I can't tell you just how much pleasure it would give me to shoot you pair of black bastards and by the bowels of Christ, make no mistake, I intend to.'

The Indian began whimpering. The Pakistani gurgled, 'You'll never get away with this.'

'Oh yes I will,' Fulton boomed. 'That's why it's a Pakistani gun. We'll be telling the world you pulled it and shot this goose and then turned it on yourself. I'll be the only witness. Your name will be mud for ever after, which won't matter to you because you'll be dead. I've already seen the draft of the Swiss coroner's report on your murder-suicide deaths. We have your deputies standing by and primed to step into your shoes.'

Both Prime Ministers stared at the senator wide-eyed and speechless. This was not at all how they had envisaged proceedings would occur.

'Now lookee heah gentlemen,' Fulton continued, waving a sheet of paper. 'Before you start snivelling your God damn prayers, I got heah one more option. This heah is a peace agreement. It's real sweet and simple. It agrees on total nuclear disarmament and a halving of your armed forces, all to commence forthwith under permanent United Nations supervision. You can sign that and live, or,' Fulton paused melodramatically, 'refuse and die. Don't seem like too tricky a choice to me.'

Both Prime Ministers began remonstrating. Fulton held up his hands. 'There's one more letter I ain't read so shut up and listen or I'll change my mind and send you on your way right now.' They shut up. Ensuring the two noted the presidential letterhead he read:

'"Confidential presidential advice to the Prime Ministers of Pakistan and India.

'"I herewith undertake that subject to you both signing the peace agreement I will facilitate,

1) That you jointly receive this year's Nobel Peace Prize, and,

2) That the grand foyer of the United Nations headquarters be permanently renamed the Singh-Ali Commemorative Peace Foyer.

'"Signed President, United States of America."

'Now. Make up your minds real quick now because I wanna take a leak. What's it gonna be. Life or death?'

The two signed.

Fulton went to the window and with a flourish pulled back the drapes and the sliding full-length windows.

'Over here, gentlemen,' he said and he drew the dumbstruck Prime Ministers out on to the balcony where earlier he had arranged a microphone and loudspeaker.

Standing between the two bewildered Prime Ministers he

took a hand of each and held them up over their heads. A gigantic roar rose from the masses below and for some minutes the three basked in the weeping, laughing, shouting and applauding adulation. Eventually the senator lowered their hands and gestured for silence.

'Good people of the world,' he bellowed into the microphone. 'I bring you great tidings. We have peace.'

Across the world jubilation broke out. The Dow Jones index rose twenty-eight per cent setting an all-time record ten-minute rise. Churches filled with spontaneous thanksgiving services. Two condemned murderers in Texas walked happily to the gas chamber, their lawyers having obtained a three-hour stay of execution so they could know the outcome of the Geneva showdown before their execution. In a thousand cities bells rang out and continued to peal throughout the day. Congratulatory letters to the respective Prime Ministers and Fulton poured in by fax from hundreds of world leaders. Many countries immediately declared a public holiday and the streets of great cities were thronged with merrymakers while on the hills above Cape Town celebratory bonfires were lighted. Before the day was over five third-world nations had announced their intention to produce commemorative postage stamps bearing the portraits of the two Prime Ministers.

Twenty minutes after leaving the balcony Fulton and the still dazed Prime Ministers sat on a stage surrounded by beaming officials. Before them several thousand journalists pushed and shoved in a blinding pyrotechnic explosion of camera flashlights.

Fulton rose, went to the microphone and held up his hands. The room fell silent.

'Today I feel very, very humble,' he said. 'Today I have had the enormous honour and privilege to be in the presence of two remarkable statesmen. I have been deeply moved by their extraordinary dignity, their individual courage and their determination to bring peace to the world.' At that point Fulton lowered his head, his large frame shaking a little as he muffled a sob.

'Jesus, Sam. You're laying it on with a trowel. They'll see through you if you don't tone it down,' Claudia muttered to herself as she watched Fulton from the side of the room. But Fulton was enjoying himself. He took a handkerchief from his pocket and with his head still lowered, dabbed at his eyes. Most of the women journalists and a considerable number of the males in the assembled throng sobbed a little, overcome with emotion. Tens of millions of television viewers across the world wept along in unison.

The senator looked up, turned his head slowly to the Indian Prime Minister and gazing at him, his voice choking, he said quietly but audibly, 'From the peoples of the world and from the bottom of our hearts, thank you Prime Minister.'

He repeated this performance with the Pakistani Prime Minister, then stood silent for about ten seconds, his head again lowered, dabbed once more at his eyes with his handkerchief and then abruptly sat down. There was a deathly silence. Then from the body of the hall someone began to clap. Soon everyone was on their feet in a stupendous and deafening applause. On and on it went until finally Fulton rose again and held up his hands for silence.

'Let us honour the real heroes,' he shouted and repeating the balcony exercise he walked to the two Prime Ministers, brought them forward and held their hands high again. Once again tumultuous applause broke out. When it finally died the two politicians each gave overly lengthy addresses about their love of peace and the prosperous new age ahead for their nations through the defence expenditure savings, both insisting this was the culmination of lifelong personal quests.

Late that night Fulton and Claudia sat alone in their suite picking at a supper and drinking champagne.

'Jesus, Sam, you play it rough,' Claudia said. 'While you were in the meeting with the Prime Ministers I thought I would die of suspense. I can't believe they bought it just like that.'

'People are the same the world over, my dear,' Fulton replied. 'Fear and ego; that's what I got 'em on and that's what you'll get anyone on if you handle it right. I haven't the time or inclination to piss about with this effete diplomacy crap. It's results I'm interested in.'

'Imagine if anyone discovered. Just think if the President found out,' Claudia said, shuddering at the prospect.

'Find out what?' the senator laughed, pointing to the ornate fireplace. 'You don't think those pair of poseurs will spill the beans.

They'd look God damn foolish and would wish I had shot them after all.' For lying on the grille lay a smouldering pile of cinders. These were the remains of the presidential letters Fulton had produced in the Prime Ministers' meeting. Using the hotel's business centre, Claudia had typed them the previous night, having first created presidential letterheads on blank sheets from Fulton's letter of appointment.

28

Following his Geneva triumph Senator Fulton arrived back to a hero's ticker-tape parade in New York. The two Prime Ministers returned to their respective homes to flower rather than paper strewn adulation and the world rejoiced along with them. In New Delhi, the Parliament, in recess for the emergency, was hastily reconvened and unanimously approved the construction of a sixty-metre-high archway modelled on the Arc de Triomphe, to be known as the Singh Peace arch.

Not to be outdone, the following day Pakistan released hurriedly drawn sketches of a 150-metre-high column to be known as the Ali Victory monument. India retaliated three days later with a set of twelve postage stamps depicting various stages of the Prime Minister's life and Pakistan responded by renaming a north-western region Alistan.

While all this was occurring Philip Melcup was winging his way across the Pacific to New Zealand on a US military plane with a team of ten handpicked scientists under his command. In Christchurch they were transferred by security guards to an airport hotel and early the following morning they returned to the airport and boarded for their secret United Nations return trip to the Antarctic. It was a high-risk mission in the extreme winter conditions but with the world's future at stake, Philip's team had volunteered willingly despite the danger.

Shortly before midday in the leaden half twilight of winter the plane bucked through a raging blizzard across McMurdo Sound, slid down the snow-covered runway on its ski landing gear and after the men had descended, refuelled, turned and immediately took off again for Christchurch.

Philip's team's task was to monitor the temperatures over three days, aided by the base's wintering marines, and to ascertain whether the position had deteriorated or improved. Immediately on arrival they unpacked the floats and set out on snowmobiles. Soon they were back again. The air temperature was minus 30 degrees Celsius and the bay was frozen solid. By 3pm it was totally dark.

Philip discussed the problem with the marine's commanding officer. 'We have equipment which can smash holes in the ice,' the officer said, so at first light the following morning about 11am they set out again. Scarcely able to stand in the 80mph gale the marines carved large holes in the ice, dropped in their floats and returned to the base.

On the second morning they endeavoured to check the temperatures but had to return to the base to fetch the marines again as the holes had iced over. The marines smashed through the ice and they read the temperatures. All were sub-zero and normal. Philip noticed the penguins had returned. Was the world saved? Plainly the United Nations emergency measures had succeeded beyond their wildest dreams.

The next day as arranged, the plane returned and lurched across the snow, skidding to a halt with engines roaring. They flew back to Christchurch and three days later, with Philip standing beside him, the Secretary-General gave a televised address to the world, advising of the wonderful news. He had three principal messages.

'Human fallibility has been exposed by the terrifying experience we have endured,' he intoned gravely. 'Our misjudgements brought us to the brink of disaster and remind us we are mere guardians of the globe and its life-forces. For the sake of future generations we must never forget that. But conversely, it has been the great virtue of our willingness to co-operate which has seen us rescue the situation. As citizens of the world we must learn from this experience and recognise that with goodwill between nations we can achieve extraordinary things.'

At that he turned to Philip and placed his arm around his shoulders. 'And finally, we can rejoice in the individual genius, epitomised by this brilliant young scientist to whom we are all so very much indebted.'

Over the following three months the world's bourses gradually restored and soon people forgot the alarm which had filled their lives for five dread-filled weeks. In total, 1,847,231 lives had been lost through the crisis; mainly Bangladeshis, Indians and Pakistanis from the nuclear attacks so nobody minded terribly, but also a sizeable contribution from suicides and heart attacks in other nations.

Three months later the Nobel Prize committee announced Philip as that year's science prize recipient and Fulton as the peace prize winner. They were popular choices and congratulatory letters flowed in from world leaders with the conspicuous exception of the Indian and Pakistani Prime Ministers.

29

In the months following Philip's dramatic ascension to international fame his life became a turmoil. Uncomfortable with celebrity's excesses and obliged to work fourteen-hour days dealing with the avalanche of mail which descended on him, he became reclusive and rarely left his flat.

Each morning Royal Mail vans unloaded sacks of correspondence redirected from Cambridge University to his London home. A secretary arrived at 9am and spent her first two hours opening the letters and placing them in the approximately dozen categories the correspondence largely comprised.

These included begging letters seeking part of his Nobel Prize money; anonymous and frequently illiterate, abusive letters written in large childish print on lined paper; autographed-photo seekers; oblique diatribes illustrated with graphs and charts from nutters and academics offering turgid explanations for the water temperature mystery; invitations to participate in television panel discussions on a rich kaleidoscope of subjects from baby care to international politics with other equally unqualified celebrities; speech requests from every quarter of the globe; book-writing solicitations from publishers; conspiracy theorists seeking an appointment to show Philip the 'evidence'; marriage proposals; radio, magazine and newspaper interview requests; invitations to lead scientific expeditions; and numerous investment offers, all of a dubious nature, even to a naif like Philip. By far the largest category consisted of congratulatory letters from strangers all over the world.

Initially the secretary replied with a printed form letter designed for each category but after a few weeks, such was the volume, Philip acknowledged only those the secretary concluded deserved his attention. One such was a letter from Professor McLean. Philip read it with some trepidation.

There had been many moments since his return from the Antarctic, usually at night in bed, when Philip had felt guilt-ridden by the deluge of tributes accorded him for he remained acutely conscious of the reality of his perfunctory role in the water temperature discovery.

To his relief the professor's letter was warm and without hint of castigation.

'It has been remiss of me not communicating earlier,' Professor McLean wrote. 'Nevertheless I do so now with my warmest congratulations for your Nobel Prize. The ace card certainly came up trumps for you and it is to your credit that you responded diligently and responsibly.

'I must also thank you for your generosity. I have been inundated with publisher requests for imminent disaster articles and books and as all mentioned they first approached you, I greatly appreciate your referring them to me. It was kind and thoughtful of you and as a result I have signed a number of contracts and taken early retirement from Cambridge. I cannot tell you how happy I am. It is a matter of personal regret that I chose an academic teaching career for which I too late realised I was eminently unsuited.

'I suppose with your hectic lifestyle you are unlikely to pass this way but should chance bring you to these parts then I would be delighted to see you.

'Again, my heartfelt congratulations and best wishes.'

The letter contained a rural West Country address. Philip reread it and a twinge of guilt hit him again. He had not referred anyone to Professor McLean.

But Philip's anguish was misplaced for as McLean had written, he had never been so happy.

Many years earlier the professor had woken from a particularly joyous dream which he had vividly recalled and mentally returned to throughout that day.

Inexplicably jungle-exploring alone in his dream, the professor had stumbled across an unknown pygmy tribe, the Wogadoos, not one of whom exceeded 4ft 6in in height. The tribe was neither negroid nor Asiatic but golden brown, well formed and attractively featured.

For the first time in his life McLean found himself a giant among men and he had been greeted with a mixture of awe, fear and ultimately affection by the tribespeople when within minutes of his arrival he had felled with a bevy of blows a gang of tribesmen who had been conducting a bullying reign of terror in the community. Within the space of a minute he had stood triumphant among a pile of bleeding, unconscious bodies and then been hailed by the community as a conquering saviour.

Over subsequent years the professor had retired each night with enthusiasm, alone with only his imagination for company. Lying awake in the dark he would joyously play out his ever evolving central role as a much-loved benevolent ruler, fantasising his supreme authority in a perfect world cast to his own design.

As the years passed he further developed the scenario, every previous detail firmly retained in his mind. He had applied his Western-culture organisational aptitude to the grateful and admiring tribespeople by gradually introducing more productive systems of agriculture, fishing, hut and canoe construction. He had guided the tribesmen in the construction of his palace, notable primarily for its enormous size. It opened to a large central hall with his elevated throne at its end, behind which lay his sleeping quarters. Around the exterior were fixed elaborately carved frieze panels which graphically portrayed his arrival among the Woga-doos and his multitude of subsequent years' feats. His every whim was served by a bevy of bare-breasted devoted maidens who jealously vied for his attention.

As king, a title he somehow slipped into, he embraced such elements of Wogadoo culture as his judgement deemed desirable. He routinely carried out his royal deflowering of virgins obligation, presided with much admired wisdom over disputes, gave his royal assent to marriages, rendered funeral orations and on one glorious occasion, played out over two months of richly imaginative nights lying alone in his bed, he led the village warriors in a tactically brilliant attack on a neighbouring tribe and thereby extended his monarchical status into an emperor's, the defeated readily accepting his benevolent rule. Over subsequent years he had extended his empire to incorporate eight more vanquished tribes. After each conquest he had personally selected three of the subdued tribe's most attractive and nubile maidens to join his household and thereby reinforce the imperial linkage.

But always in the past his nightly imaginative world's pleasure succumbed each morning to the cruel jolt of reality and the harsh absurdity of his lilliputian insignificance.

Now, blissfully ensconced in his cottage and free of all human contact, the professor worked on his commissioned apocalyptic articles and books for six hours daily before resorting to his primary existence, unimpeded by any reality intervention, as Emperor of the Wogadoos. Never again would he suffer the indignities of the outside world. Now he was a truly free man.

The professor had commemorated that new-found liberty by shaving off his beard, which he had grown twenty-five years earlier after being handed a child's colouring-in book and crayons by a newspaper-dispensing air hostess on a flight to address a Paris climatology conference. The professor's joy had carried into the night manifesting itself in a rejuvenated procreative burst increasing his already sizeable Wogadoo issue by a further nine. Professor McLean was very happy indeed.

But not everyone was.

Philip's two graduate colleagues on the Antarctic tour of duty bitterly resented his fame and grumbled among themselves at the unfairness of it all. Finally they announced a press conference in a London hotel which attracted only two jaded newspaper reporters and a pop music radio station advertising salesman who uplifted all such invitations in the hope, wrongly on this occasion, of free food and drinks. The two angrily recounted their protest to the motley gathering.

The ocean-warming discovery had been a team effort; no appropriate recognition of that had been made; it was unfair that the honour should be Philip's alone and each took pains to emphasise that while they personally could live with this outcome, conscience dictated they speak up on their colleagues behalf.

The reporters duly recorded their comments but said nothing and the meeting eventually broke up with a vague feeling of dissatisfaction in the air.

Only one newspaper commented on the press conference in a brief second leader. It read;

'Periodically a gloomy shadow descends upon these islands and we lapse into second-rate status. For many of us, viewing the recent years' demise of British industry, the failures of our politicians and the humiliations to our cricket team, such an eclipse has marked the recent past.

'But there exists a curious quality in the British character which, in our darkest moments, yields up a Drake, a Nelson, a

Churchill, a Thatcher and now, a Melcup, who through their deeds inspire us to a new vigour and restores the 'Great' in Great Britain.

'Regrettably, always accompanying such glorious times of national triumph there emerge the inevitable killjoys, or, in this newspaper's opinion in respect of the most recent episode, it is not too strong to say, Judases.

'This newspaper deplores the ignoble attempt by Philip Melcup's Antarctic expedition bystanding lackeys, whose names will not be allowed to sully these pages, to capture an undeserved attention and devalue an extraordinary solo achievement.

'We say this is not the British way and these nonentities should be cast, if unfortunately not from our shores as once was within authority's scope, at least from our minds.'

In the event this indeed was the last ever heard from Philip's colleagues whose pre-press-conference unity had been instantly shattered by bitter acrimony when the hotel had presented its function room hire bill. Within a month both had secured science schoolmaster positions and faded into obscurity.

Also unhappy were many of the beards, or at least the married ones, who had returned home to prolonged wifely denunciation for their irresponsible Antarctic spending. Most lapsed into a sullen ruefulness as they fondly recalled the Olga Buskova's stable, which memories contrasted harshly with their homecoming experiences.

One American beard profited greatly from the saga. A seaweed-mite expert, he promptly registered with a speakers' agency and was rewarded with over three hundred thousand dollars inside six months from a nation-wide universities lecture tour, his topic being: 'My role in the Antarctic temperature crisis.'

The Poet Laureate enjoyed a rare time in the normally poetry-despising British limelight after producing a composition 'Ode to the Antarctic' in which he praised Philip in a mumbo-jumbo of fashionably oblique, unrhyming staccato lines.

Big Bertha was happy. In the absence of Claudia's cautionary counsel she had been wooed and won by a tiny Florida Oceano-graphic Institute beard who had proudly borne his prize home, conscious of her outstanding credentials for successful Miami residency.

Stan Twigg was happy. On his return he had been snapped up for a, to him, dream job as Tasmanian Boy Scouts assistant commissioner on the basis of his Antarctic credentials of rugged, outdoors, manly, adventurous imagery.

In St Petersburg Mr Zirovsky was elated on being informed of the Olga Buskova's option exercising and a further million dollars being credited to his personal Cypriot bank account.

Dr Isaac was happy. After being dismissed on the Olga Buskova's arrival in Sydney and flown home to London, he was promptly offered and accepted a senior position in West Africa, by Mr Rose.

Also very happy were the stable, most of whom on arrival in Sydney headed to northern Queensland beach resorts where for a fortnight they lay in the sun reading trashy magazines and the works of Mr Jeffrey Archer before rejoining the ship for a further tour of duty, this time in the Arctic circle.

Further disembarkees in Sydney, albeit illegal, included four stewards who quickly found live-in lovers and employment in the city's homosexual area as restaurant and wine-bar waiters. They were very happy indeed.

Several movie studios commissioned writers to produce film scripts about the drama although none were ultimately made. Liberia and Tonga profitably issued commemorative postage stamps bearing portraits of Philip, not one of which ever adorned an actual posted letter but which sold well to collectors worldwide.

A book written by a bad-tempered revisionist Guardian journalist alleging the whole affair was a hoax was widely ridiculed and eventually pulped, at great expense to the publisher.

A public petition for Philip to be knighted enjoyed a fleeting momentum but waned when it was pointed out that in the course of time he would inherit his father's title and become Lord Melcup.

The regular advent of life's ever-arising dramas soon saw the Antarctic crisis fade and become forgotten and tentatively at first, Philip re-emerged into the streets of London and to a normal life.

Part Three

Full Circle

1

Well, old chap, you're going to come out very prettily indeed,' Tom said, swaying back in his heavily padded seat, hands clasped across his equally padded stomach.

'I bloody well hope so,' Len replied tersely. 'I went on the line, pulled it off, came back with eleven million quid and you promptly rip it off me and dump it into some questionable Canadian outfit.'

Tom laughed. 'Was questionable, lad. "Was" is the operative word. Now it's a winner and don't worry, you own ninety-seven per cent of the stock so you effectively control your money. Just give us a few weeks to tidy things up.'

Tom outlined what he had done. Through a Canadian associate, M.K. Maddox & Partners, he had acquired all but three per cent of the shares in Pontiac Resources, a listed but non-trading Vancouver mining company. Pontiac Resources had an eventful history. Following its initial listing three years earlier its share price had soared over 2000 per cent within three months, driven by some remarkable luck with the company's exploration activities based on the samplings sent in for analysis. For a glorious four hours one day Pontiac shares were the fastest rising in the world. Two years later, the chief executive and head geologist were in prison while arrest warrants remained outstanding for other key company personnel whose disappearance suggested a disinclination to help the police with their inquiries. The company had lain in hibernation up until a month ago when through a share exchange it had acquired Len's Cayman Islands-based Antarctic venture holding company and its cash resources.

'But I'm giving away three per cent of my money by not owning the lot,' Len protested. 'Damn it all, that's a third of a million quid.'

'Two points there, Lenny lad,' Tom said smugly, rocking back and forward. 'One; it's necessary to have a minimum number of shareholders to maintain the listing and if past experience is any guide, most of them will have disappeared so your de facto ownership position is probably nearer ninety-nine per cent. Two;

it wouldn't matter if your eleven million was represented by only half the company's shares. You'd still be better off. You're overlooking the leverage factor we'll achieve transferring the ship's operation to a public company. This, as you will see, is a modern version of the loaves and fishes story.'

'So what's next?' Len asked sceptically.

'On Wednesday Pontiac will make the financial pages,' Tom replied. 'It will be quite a story. First will be announced a change of name to Global Services Ltd; second, a new chairman and board. I must say old MadDog Maddox has done us proud on that score. He's called MadDog because he's a mousy little fellow. But that's his strength, the fact he looks and sounds pathetic. A lot of the best brokers are like that. It gives confidence to people when you're investing their money. Anyway, MadDog has procured a former Canadian Governor-General, Sir James Beadle, as chairman. Actually, he's a bit sleazy but they don't know that over here, of course. And MadDog has put together quite a nice little board as well. Got an ex-Ernst & Young regional director down on his luck plus a couple of main-chance old buggers. One's a retired judge and the other's a former banker. Also there's a token female director. A good catch there. She's an ex-Cabinet minister. The whole package shapes up nicely for the London market.

'I must say it never ceases to amaze me how these pathetic buggers clamour to be directors of public companies. It's the most bogus job. Absolutely no one takes any notice of them or even pretends to. The key executives always call the shots. In my experience most directors know that yet still they carry on for cat's-meat money and a self-delusion of prestige.

'I'll tell you this. I've never met a non-executive director who has any bloody idea what their company's up to. That's certainly true in this case. MadDog made sure of that with lots of blather to them about what Global's not doing, in particular exploration which frightens the hell out of people, rather than what it is. That's where MadDog's so good. He can be excruciatingly boring when it's necessary and go on and on and on saying absolutely nothing. After a while they stop caring what he's talking about and just want him to stop and the only way he will is when they agree with what he wants. He's a first-rate financial professional, up to the very best in London. Anyway, enough of that. We need a board so we should be grateful for these poor boobies' existence.'

'I don't understand how that helps me,' Len protested.

'The best part of the announcement,' Tom continued, ignoring Len's interruption, 'is the company's change of activities and profit report. Sir James will be advising Global has abandoned direct mining and is now an international conglomerate. He will additionally report that having embarked on this new direction, the company has made a profit of thirty-one million dollars for the year; that's your Antarctic profits, of course, which I might add will certainly impress given that this outfit has never made a bean in its history and has accumulated losses of over sixty million dollars Canadian. They will be very nice to offset against future profits, tax-wise. And finally, he will announce some very bullish forecasts which actually may not prove too silly when you consider Andrew's plans. I rather think my man Potter will make this thing hum a bit for a year or two. It was generous of you letting him take the show over.'

'Well, that's all very well,' Len said. 'But where do I come in? I want my money,' he added firmly.

Tom laughed. 'You keep forgetting, my dear fellow, you own ninety-seven per cent of Global stock. So you still have your money. And you will have it in cash very soon. Now if I know my business, those shares will be worth somewhere between eighty and a hundred million pounds by the end of next week.'

'Cut the crap, Tom,' Len said angrily. 'Just tell me how I unload. I want to cash up. I'm not interested in carrying on with the girls business or this public company blarney. It sounds bloody fishy to me. Also, I've contracted to complete the settlement of Wyebury in three weeks from today.'

'Quite so; quite so,' Tom replied complacently. 'Be assured everything's in hand. All going well you will be out within a fortnight. As I said, we're only running a small public offering in Canada to set a price and MadDog will do that solely through placements. I have the perfect buyer for your stock. But quite frankly I'm obliged to tell you my professional advice is to stay in for another year. You could sell a small parcel to pay Melcup and also for some walking around money, but when I look at what Andrew has planned now he's Global's chief executive, I honestly think the shares will at least double again in a year's time.'

'No,' Len said firmly. 'I did this to buy Wyebury. It's no reflection on Andrew but I don't want these bloody shares.'

'You know Andrew now has the ship contracted full-time from the Ruskies,' Tom continued. 'He's planning to work it in the Arctic circle over the northern summer. A lot more similar bases up there, he says. He's looking at ways of using smaller transport units to access these. Apparently there's oodles of bearded wets all over the bloody globe, buggering about with geology and science nonsense of one sort or another like you found in the Antarctic and they're all highly paid with nothing to spend their money on and all needing servicing. Andrew claims his total stable will exceed 200 girls within three months. They're impressive figures, Len. You should think responsibly about this. At four dollars a share I'm pricing them at a PE of less than nine. Two years' consistent profit growth will see a PE of twice that. I can see these shares at over twelve dollars each and conceivably more, inside a year.'

'Good luck to him then,' Len said coldly. 'He's welcome to it and I hope you're right. He did a good job for me and I appreciate it but I'm not staying in.'

'One thing I'll say about Potter,' Tom continued blithely, ignoring Len's protestations. 'He certainly knows how to structure a deal. He turned down a salary and instead took an option at a dollar a share for three million shares, exercisable at any time in the next three years. I reckon he could come out with at least twenty million quid. That's why I think you should stay in. You've got inside information. Should anything go astray, we'll know and be first out.'

'No,' Len said firmly. 'I just want my money and as soon as possible. If it's more than my eleven million pounds then well and good. But I want it now so how do I get it?'

'Okay. I've exercised my fiduciary duty and I want to emphasise that but in the final analysis, it's your choice. I need two, maybe three weeks, then we'll see how it's going and of course MadDog will prod it along a bit should it be necessary. At best there's probably only one per cent of stock freely available. We will be sitting tight on our ninety-seven per cent. We could easily drive it up to twenty dollars a share if we wanted. But when it's that contrived it's fools' gold. You try and jump ship and the price just as quickly drops back again.

'Now there are fifty million shares on issue and you've got nearly all of them. This year's earnings represents fifty-eight cents Canadian a share. If we sell the story right then we should be able to justify five to six dollars a share which will be nearly a hundred million quid for you, tax free as well. We'll slug you a fee of two per cent to cover everything. Actually, it's fortunate this is just a bullshit token public offering which we can control. The markets are still devastated after the India-Pakistan nuclear war scare and the melting ice cap crisis and in the normal course of events it would be impossible to get away a public float in this panicky climate. Amazing coincidence when you think about it with Melcup's son discovering the situation. He's obviously a brilliant mind. Did you meet him down there?'

'I don't know,' Len replied. 'If I did I can't recall, although the newspapers say he was at McMurdo where the ship was. But with 3500 or so scientists all looking much the same, beards and that, very few stood out. You must remember they're mostly boring buggers and screamingly bloody wet so after a while they all sort of blended together.'

'Strange, that,' Tom mused. 'One always thinks of scientists as being incredibly bright. How wet are they?'

'It varied,' Len said. 'Some were okay but mostly they were a bit soppy and naive. They'd fall in love with the girls. But how wet?' Len pondered.

'Mostly they're sort of morris-dancing wet,' he continued after a pause. 'They've got beards and I can picture them back here driving small cars with "Baby on Board" signs; that sort of wetness. As to how wet. Well, in fairness they weren't bad chaps. Andrew got on with them. They were more at the damp end of the wetness spectrum. A puddle or at worst a babbling brook rather than the Nile in flood degree of wetness.'

'What the hell are they all doing down there?' Tom asked quizzically.

'Ha! If I told you, you wouldn't believe me. Unbelievable stuff. Grown men playing about with rocks or penguin egg sizes and lots of that sort of rubbish.'

Tom thought a while. After a time he said, 'You know

205

something? I don't believe I've ever met a scientist. I thought in my game we covered the field but of course these buggers aren't trying to make a profit, which removes them from normal human activity. But who on earth funds all of this?'

'The usual. Directly or indirectly, taxpayers. We used to talk to them but eventually I lost interest although, as I said, Andrew found some of them and what they were doing, quite interesting.'

'Exactly why I'm not a taxpayer,' Tom snapped. 'It's a bloody disgrace. I don't wish to sound altruistic but I really do get angry about the abuse of taxpayers' money. Anyway, enough of that. We've more important things to discuss such as the relaunching of Global on the Vancouver exchange and then we'll organise a buyer for your stock based on the price we establish which, as I said, should tot up to damn near a hundred million quid.'

'For Christ's sake, Tom,' Len exclaimed. 'Who's got that sort of money and yet is dumb enough to give it to me for this bullshit?'

'Well, that's the point I have tried and failed to make to you,' Tom said somewhat hurt. 'It's not bullshit. Inadvertently you have discovered a virgin industry of very considerable virtue. And to answer your question, we will be placing the parcel with a client of ours, the Church Commissioners. Well, seventy per cent of the share-holding anyway. If you're quite sure you want out now then I trust you won't mind if we pick up the other twenty-seven per cent for our house account.'

'You mean the Church of England?' Len asked, his eyes widening. 'But how do you know they'll want them?'

'It's not what they want, old man. It's what we tell 'em,' Tom replied. 'They wouldn't buck our advice, not with their history and our track record with them.'

He lowered his voice to a conspiratorial near-whisper. 'Between you and me, old man, the Church nearly hit the wall back in the '89-'91 property crash. Blew away two-thirds of five centuries' accumulated wealth in just two years, so they called us in. The Archbishop of Canterbury was in quite a state at the time. I've never heard such bad language. The usual story with all lay types. He'd bought the line about property as the ultimate security. Anyway, the only thing the Church Commissioners were interested in was to restore their wealth. They didn't much care how and I don't blame them because it was pretty much touch and go at the time.

'I told them if we ran their affairs then it had to be on our terms. We wanted the whole operation thoroughly analysed. His Grace and the Church Commissioners blew their tops when they heard what it would cost but eventually we got our way and called in the consultants. They went over the whole shooting box and a worse-run outfit you've never seen. The consultants' report was as condemnatory as any I've seen and I've seen some beauties.'

'Funny, that', Len said. 'I've never had much to do with churches; actually nothing come to think of it. But they always seem so rock solid. What was wrong?'

'For a start, their cash-flow situation was woeful. They had thousands of retired clergymen dotted across the land soaking up the Church's dividend income with their bloody pensions. The problem was they'd had such soft, stress-free lives; just a weekly burst of praying and singing and in between, nothing but cups of tea with old ladies. According to the consultants they were denying all normal demographics and living too long.

'The consultants came up with some first-rate innovations to alleviate that but persuading the Archbishop and Commissioners to run with them was damned difficult. The problem was it meant more cash outlay and when it came to cheque-writing the Church was a bit gun-shy at the time, after the property debacle. I got so annoyed I threatened to resign so in the end his Grace gave me the go-ahead on a trial basis. Let results be your future guide, I said to him, although I must say he was not particularly gracious. Anyway, as it turned out the schemes worked like a dream and eventually we cut the numbers of pensioned parsons on the take by half. I was the Archbishop's golden-haired boy, I can tell you. I went from pariah to messiah in his eyes inside three months. If they'd been Catholics they'd have made me a bloody saint.'

Len briefly forgot his money-access worries, his curiosity aroused. 'How did you do it, for God's sake?'

'Well, the most successful scheme was the Amazon organised tour. Most of the old buggers had never even been to France so the Church circulated the clergymen with the offer of a free Amazon trip as a reward for their lifetime service. The consultants were spot-on with their projections on that one. The first party we sent out totalled thirty and twelve were dead in Manaus within a week of arrival, which was a damned good start. The bugs and viruses out there are pretty ferocious apparently, although I doubt if they had ever encountered as easy pickings as this lot. And we saved the Church any costs of coffins and returning bodies to England too. We had them tell the relatives that with tropical diseases, cremation was necessary within an hour of death. A personal letter of condolence from the Archbishop kept them happy so they didn't complain when we later billed them for hospitalisation and cremation services. We turned a small profit on that.

'After the success of that first trip we made an effort to put the lot through the Amazon exercise inside a year. The problem was not all the old buggers wanted to go. Talk about looking a gift horse in the mouth; you wouldn't believe the ingratitude. I suppose it tells you what self-indulgent lives they'd had. Mind you, we nailed them eventually.'

'So what on earth did you do next?' Len asked, his curiosity now fully aroused.

'Well, after the travel exercise we found we'd scored an overall strike rate of thirty-four per cent. But the target was to cut the numbers on the take by half. We knew a fair number of the remaining pool were reasonably hardy because they'd survived the Amazon. So that only left accidents. With the chaos in Russia after the collapse of communism, all sorts of low-cost opportunities were opening up as you personally know only too well. One of the consultants popped across to the Ukraine and bought four container loads of dud household electrical goods. After the Amazon success we had no trouble getting the Church to write a cheque for this leg of the exercise, not that it cost much.

'We shipped the goods back and in *Pew News* offered them at an absolute song under the name of The Retired Clergymen's Discount Mail Service and a post office box address. The old gents snapped the stuff up, especially the bar heaters, which was fortuitous as they turned out to be the most effective of all. Most of the success rate came from instant electrocution but we scored well with heart attacks from the explosions when they plugged in the gear. Overall it was a very tidy operation and after that we had the Commissioners eating out of our hands.'

Tom became pensive. 'It's a very sad thing when you think about it. People are always making fun of consultants and yet here was a classic case of how valuable they can be to society. I don't say they're perfect; for example, we had a bit of unanticipated trouble from coroners with the accident exercise but fortunately no one could trace The Retired Clergymen's Discount Service so they wrote off the electrocutions as Acts of God. Sure, the consultants slugged the Church for a quarter of a million pounds in fees but overall you can't say it wasn't value for money.'

'What? A quarter of a million just for coming up with the Amazon and accident ideas?' Len exclaimed, horror-struck. 'It sounds bloody rich to me. I'd have thought up that sort of stuff for them for a helluva lot less.'

'Good Lord no,' Tom said. 'They did a lot more than that. That was only their work on the expenditure side. They carried out a thorough evaluation on the Church's income operation as well, excluding, of course, the investment component. That was our baby.

'No; they produced a first-rate study of church attendance, how much was going in the plate and who was putting it there. In a nutshell they found that Sunday attendances were falling rapidly and that seventy per cent of worshippers were elderly women of whom eighty-five per cent had hearing aids. Of that lot nearly ninety per cent were turning them off when the service started. Worse still, the old girls were bloody tight and putting bugger all in the plates when they came round.

'So they surveyed non-church-attending parishioners as to why they weren't turning out on Sundays. Apparently the problem was the sermons. Nearly all of the absentees blamed the bloody parsons rabbiting on about God. Basically they couldn't stand anything touching on the supernatural. Found it embarrassing and I quite see their point as it would be off-putting. So we had the Archbishop issue an edict to clergymen to cut all the supernatural stuff out of sermons. No mentioning of God or walking on water or any of that sort of carry-on. The Church appointed a piety inspector who travelled about listening to sermons and monitoring them for religious guff. As the Archbishop said, it's all very well parsons having religious beliefs so long as they're in moderation and they basically keep them to themselves. Too much of it leads to them constantly upbraiding their congregation and attendances fall off. It's perfectly understandable; after all, who wants to pay to spend one's Sunday morning copping a bollocking from some pious nutter inflicted with a mild form of insanity? Anyway, the results have been very encouraging although naturally these things take time. After three years we've lifted church attendances by twenty-two per cent and collections in the plate by forty-four per cent. My own view is the Church has a great future if we can stamp out religion from it.'

'But, hang on a minute,' Len intruded. 'Isn't that what it's all about?'

'Certainly not,' Tom snapped. 'The very essence of Protestantism is making it up as you go along. No, we changed the whole approach to try and drag in the customers. Told the clergymen to liven things up; no religion, no moralising; go for entertainment.

'We left it to the parsons to tailor their approach to suit their own taste. Most lacked imagination and went for rock bands and guitars and that sort of rubbish, to show they were with it. There's no doubt about it; the days of the pipe-smoking, polo-necked, captain of the village cricket team type parson downing ales in the local are definitely over.'

'As always with these things some overdid it. Dressing up was popular; delivering sermons in clowns' outfits and gorilla suits and that sort of thing. One actually turned out in a pink tutu. We put a stop to that as he had a moustache and therefore looked ridiculous.

'Another appeared in the nude. Claimed he was celebrating God's glorious design. He packed them in but the Archbishop put his foot down. Argued it was inflaming the lady parishioners although personally, I thought His Grace was a bit quick off the mark there. After all the fellow was fifty-eight and a weedy little bloke but he was certainly pulling the punters.'

'So where did you come in?' Len enquired.

'Well, while all that was going on we swung into action with what they had left. We've done a damn good job too, I can tell you. Got 'em back to where they were before the office buildings holocaust.

'First we bought up big in armament stocks and they ran

along nicely for about nine months. Then came a terrible disaster with the end of the Cold War. I began to think the Church was jinxed. You get clients like that. Everything you do for them turns out to be the kiss of death. As it happened we managed to bail out while still miles ahead. I was at a loss for a while but as so often's the case, a nice little opportunity arose. We received an approach to fund a Brazilian logging venture. It was a bloody massive exercise costing nearly half a billion pounds. That's including bribes to the Brazilian politicians and they don't come cheap. It's always a problem there, I can tell you. They're not reliable like your African who you can take out in a day for a couple of million quid to get a monopoly. It's all that Latin macho rubbish. It totally frustrates efficient commerce in Latin America, having to constantly haggle over bribes.

'Anyway, I cut a bloody good deal for the Church. They funded the whole exercise at fifteen per cent interest plus a half equity share and they really fell on their feet with this one. About the time we went in the greenies started kicking up a fuss about logging rainforests, which was a stroke of luck because suddenly there was a shortage. So our original profit projections were way too low. I had the Church donate half a million quid to Greenpeace specifically to agitate on this issue and a damn fine investment it proved as it drove exotic log prices up by sixty per cent.

'Then there was a change of government in Brazil, which was another unexpected windfall as the best deals are always done with new administrations. That's because they're broke after buying their way into office and don't know anything. For a lousy twenty million dollars, mostly to the president, we got the original logging licence turned into a land sale and instead of just ripping the trees out, we burned the whole bloody show down and turned it into cattle land. It was pretty impressive. I actually flew out with two of the Commissioners to have a look and I don't mind telling you, I felt bloody proud when I saw it in the flesh. We'd cleared over 400 square miles of useless rainforest. In this job you can easily get detached sitting here organising things so it gave me quite a charge to see the tangible benefits from our efforts. All those cattle hanging around among burnt stumps where previously there was nothing. It makes me feel quite humble, if you know what I mean.

'We did another good thing too. When we burned the forest out popped an unknown Indian tribe. There were nearly 300 of them running about naked, just fishing and hunting. Completely primitive they were. The cheeky buggers killed two of our bulldozer drivers with poisoned darts. Anyway, we put clothes on them, shipped them to Recife and got them jobs in a factory. According to one of the Commissioners we leapt about 25,000 years of normal human development time in a week. It was one of those heart-warming by-products that sometimes flow quite unexpectedly from progressive developments. I've often wondered how they're getting on.

'Overall, the returns on the whole exercise were terrific although we've since jumped ship. Sold our land interest to a Boston investment fund. They're incredibly boring buggers in Boston and they know it so they're always starters for grandiose adventurous-sounding schemes. You wouldn't believe it but apparently all the cattle walking about with their weight on four pinpoint hooves, actually destroys the soil. Don't you find that interesting?

'Of course, we kept the mining ventures as they're real money-spinners but the overall outcome was pretty much to restore the Church's original capital and when you remember that we've cut their pension pay-out in half and lifted church attendances, well, as you can imagine they're really rather pleased with us.

'Right now they're heavy in cash exposure, which isn't very satisfactory, so Global Services couldn't be more timely. It's exactly what they're looking for. The Archbishop's been on my back for a while now so he will be very pleased when I tell him about this, even if it's only a hundred million.'

A week later the *Financial Times* gave Global's announcement four columns including a sizeable part of Sir James Beadle's chairman's address written by Andrew. Sir James spoke glowingly of the success of the company's Scientific Book subsidiary and High Risk Financial Advisory Services. He reported a projected minimum doubling of profits for the forthcoming year. Prompted by payments from MadDog, a number of North American financial journalists wrote bullish reports in their respective newspapers.

The shares climbed steadily to eight dollars. On Tom's

instructions MadDog recorded transactions bringing them down to six dollars.

A week later Tom transferred them to his nominee company's account and handed Len a cheque for eighty-one million pounds.

Everyone was very happy.

2

After the sale of his Global Services shares Len spent two days with Tom planning an investment strategy for his eighty-one million pounds, currently on interest-bearing deposit in Hong Kong through a series of nominees. Tax lawyers established companies in the Cayman Islands with anonymous directors and cross-shareholdings with other companies in Mauritius, Belize and Liechtenstein.

'Well, that takes care of the tax issue,' Tom remarked blithely, adding, 'Of course, a chap might not mind weighing in a bit if the buggers didn't waste it. But they do so we won't,' and with that philosophic, legal and moral issue considered and disposed off, they turned to investment.

'First we must establish a strategy,' Tom said. 'What are your goals and expectations?' and without waiting for a response, he continued: 'With this much money at your time of life, the principal concern must be capital security. We can spread it about a bit; a base global mix of quality government fixed interest securities and about eighty per cent in blue chip infrastructure equities which altogether will yield about half a million pounds a month tax-free. That will keep the cat fed nicely. Mind you, I don't have any doubt that the value of your portfolio will be nearer a hundred and fifty million within a year. The stock markets have still not recovered from the nuclear war crisis so it's a wonderful entry time. On my assessment you will be buying in at around sixty per cent of a proper price level based on fundamentals so there should be a substantial capital increment in the next two years. After that, over any period of time this type of portfolio will produce about a ten per cent annual capital growth so your surplus income will grow by a like amount each year. It's a conservative approach but appropriate for you.'

And so it came to pass and for ever after Len received a weekly report from Tom's firm detailing his securities. From time to time some of the investments were changed, as were the income flows, which fluctuated slightly through exchange rate and dividend variations. Len's pleasure in poring over these schedules after they arrived each week never diminished.

While they were discussing this strategy Len received a message that Lord Melcup would like to see him prior to the settlement on Wyebury. He was coming to London the following week so a luncheon appointment was made, amusingly as it transpired in the Palmerston Club for Lord Melcup was not only a long-established member but the current president.

Once again Len entered the club from which he had been abruptly ejected nearly half a century earlier. In the foyer he was greeted with hushed respect by the butler who escorted him into the familiar reading room where Lord Melcup was waiting for him. The passing of more than four decades showed little change. He recognised the bust of Lord Palmerston, the portraits of past presidents, the gloomy pastoral scene oil paintings and the same old black and white photographs of past committees and First World War battleships.

'Nice to see you again,' Lord Melcup said shaking Len's hand. 'Tidied everything up down under satisfactorily?'

'Very satisfactorily, I'm pleased to say. I'm back for good now.'

'Never really understood trade or the City,' Melcup continued. 'Never had to, mind you. Same lot have handled our affairs since last century. Seem to know what they're doing.'

'I must offer my congratulations on your son, sir. You must be enormously proud. The world is certainly indebted to him.'

Lord Melcup's face clouded. 'Yes. Well thank you. Frankly I'm somewhat bewildered by it all. I don't say the lad's a buffoon but all this saving the world and Nobel Prize and genius palaver, well, I mean to say, it just doesn't make sense; I'm his father, damn it. I know the lad and they can say what they like but when they start on about him being a genius then I know something's up.'

'I think you have every reason to be proud, sir,' Len said respectfully. 'Probably he's a late bloomer but there can't be any question about his achievement.'

'Yes, of course. I don't wish to sound mealy-mouthed about it. Mind you, it wasn't very pleasant at Wyebury. We had a crowd of the most appalling low-life types turn up and lurk about. Dreadful down-at-heel, seedy-looking creatures. I telephoned the police and said there seemed to be some sort of tramps' conference or a gypsy gathering going on in my driveway. To be quite frank, while I was waiting for the police I was worried about my safety until I noticed how indolent they all were.

'The police turned up, drove 'em all away and reported to me they were journalists. So you can understand my scepticism about Philip once I saw the flotsam who had been writing this guff about him.'

After lunch they discussed fishing and then Lord Melcup talked for some time about farming. From this he carried on to the estate's traditional community obligations. These involved an annual hunt, a Christmas concert in the ballroom for the villagers and an Easter fete organised by the local vicar for church funds. The estate included fifteen cottages which housed the present staff and some elderly former employees, with one set aside for a retired clergyman.

'That's been a tradition with Wyebury for at least a century – providing a cottage for the village parson when he retires,' Melcup said. 'Mind you, right now it's empty. The vicar had a most unfortunate accident with a bar heater which electrocuted him. It was rather a puzzle as only a month earlier all the cottages had been rewired to modern safety standards. They're in tip-top condition so you don't have to concern yourself about that.'

'Of course,' Lord Melcup continued, 'when Wyebury is yours I cannot tell you what to do but these little traditions mean a great deal in the county and the village. It would be a damn shame if they weren't carried on. It's no trouble. The estate manager handles all the arrangements.'

Len assured Melcup he would do so.

'I'm pleased to hear that, Mr Edwards, which brings me to the reason I've asked you here. The thing is, Wyebury and its traditions represents something durable and important to the local community. Perhaps it's hard for a city person to understand but down there it's a totally self-contained world. Oh, they watch television and all of that but I rather think they see the outside world as some sort of entertainment spectacle which has nothing to do with them. Can't say I blame them, either. Most of them never vote, you know, and I doubt if many of them have ever been to London, let alone anywhere else.

'But what I really wanted to say is that it's not just Wyebury that's an anchor for them. It's more than that. It's the presence of someone occupying it who they can look up to, someone they feel is masterly and superior. People wouldn't understand it here but it gives them great comfort to doff their caps, if you know what I mean, to someone they see as way above their station.'

Lord Melcup shuffled uncomfortably.

'Look here, what I mean to say is that it would be helpful if you had a title. I hope you don't misunderstand but well, the villagers are going to feel insecure if there's a plain Mister in Wyebury. It's for their sake I'm raising the matter. I would really appreciate it,' he added pleadingly.

'But, sir, the fact is I don't have one.' Then the light dawned on Len. 'Do you mean I should buy one of those lord of the manor things that crop up now and again?'

'Good God no,' Melcup startled. 'That wouldn't do at all. But look here, I mean, I take it you've made a bit of money.' Len nodded. 'As I said,' Melcup continued, 'I don't understand trade but if you've made a bit as you say, then you must have done something useful. That's usually good enough and of course to make sure of it, well if you don't mind and can manage it, some help to charities would put a cap on things, if you know what I mean.'

'Well, if you think it's important,' Len replied.

'Excellent,' Lord Melcup said happily, rubbing his hands, and he beckoned a waiter and called for a bottle of champagne.

'Can't say I much like this stuff,' he said cheerfully as the waiter uncorked the bottle, 'but this does call for a celebratory drink and anything else doesn't seem right. I really am very pleased you've taken it like that.'

'You mean that's it? Just like that; it's fixed up?'

'My dear chap, we have a way to go yet; must go through the motions and all that. What I'd like you to do is to meet my solicitor. He will tidy everything up.'

When they were on their third glass Lord Melcup, now in ebullient mood, said: 'I say. I suppose what with you being abroad all these years you don't have a club?' Len confirmed he did not.

'Well, I've never done it before, pulled rank that is as the club president, but the fact is we have a five-year waiting list at the Palmerston. Still, leave it to me.'

So Len's name went to the top of the list and a month later

was posted on the foyer's noticeboard with Lord Melcup as his nominator. Shortly after Len became a member of the Palmerston Club.

A few days after the meeting with Melcup Len was again taken to lunch in the Palmerston Club, only this time by Mr Postlewaite, the senior partner in Lord Melcup's law firm. After lunch they got down to business.

'I have a nicely balanced list here of suitable names who will nominate and endorse you,' Postlewaite said. 'We've a city mayor, southern England of course, anywhere else would be detrimental, a sitting Cabinet Minister, a lord, a bishop, a former English cricket captain and an industrialist. We will handle the financial side and bill you for advice in the customary manner.

'I trust that's in order. The cost of advice for those names will be five thousand pounds each. Manage that all right? Splendid, splendid,' he added when Len nodded. 'And of course,' he continued, 'you understand twenty-five thousand pounds needs to reach the Conservative Party. We look after that as well. Under the current disclosure laws we need to obfuscate the source, but you may be assured that the information regarding the amount and the donor reaches those who need to know.

'Now', Mr Postlewaite continued, 'I do believe very strongly in writing in an insurance policy with these matters. It doesn't come cheaply but I think you will find it a very good investment. I suggest fifty thousand pounds to any three charities on this list. Have a look and tell me if any particularly appeal,' and he produced from his inside pocket a typewritten list of thirty old-established charities.

Len studied the sheet. There were animal welfare groups, retired military officers' organisations, medical research institutes, heritage preservation societies, orphanages and many others. All noted various members of royalty as their patrons.

One took Len's fancy. He looked up.

'Do you think it would be in order if I gave the lot to just one?'

'Oh dear,' the lawyer replied. 'It's really a question of strategy, you see. Frankly, we always favour spreading it around a bit. I suppose it depends on the charity. Which did you have in mind?'

'Well, I've always taken an interest in young women. The

YWCA appeals to me.'

Postlewaite pondered this suggestion. After a while he said, 'Mmm... a hundred and fifty thousand pounds to the YWCA. An interesting proposition. I rather think that could get you a joint patronage with Her Royal Highness. It's not our usual procedure. We normally do these things with a degree of what might be described as calculated refinement. What you are proposing is rather captivating; a sort of king-hit approach.'

'Tell me, Mr Postlewaite,' Len said, changing the subject, 'Do you do this sort of thing often? I mean, it's not exactly a legal issue.'

'My dear fellow,' Postlewaite exclaimed. 'There's only one measure of success in the professions. A chap knows he's finally reached the top when everything he does has nothing to do with what he's trained for. I don't believe I've considered a legal matter for over ten years now. The same goes with all the professions. That's why everything is such an appalling mess. The only chaps practising law or medicine, or architecture or journalism or whatever, are either mistake-prone new chums or proven failures.

'Mind you, it's not a bad thing. If everyone did what they were supposed to do in a competent manner we'd have half the country unemployed. I have no doubt that at least eighty per cent of all professional and management work relates directly or indirectly to fixing someone's cock-up somewhere along the line. It's certainly true of law and I believe it's equally so with everything else.'

In the New Year's Honours list Len became Sir Lennard and in due course, with Claire proudly beside him in the back of the Rolls, they drove to Buckingham Palace. As a relative of a major awardee Claire received a front seat in the crowded hall while Len was taken to a rear room and the forthcoming ceremony explained. After the anointment of two dames his name was announced and as instructed, Len climbed the steps to the stage and walked towards the Queen. He bowed slightly and dropped to one knee. Her Majesty lowered the sword to his shoulder and in her familiar high-pitched voice said, 'Rise, Sir Lennard.' It was her three thousand two hundred and twenty-second knighthood and as Len approached she glanced with well-practised familiarity at the brief information sheet before her.

When he rose, a knight of the realm, the Queen placed around his neck the beribboned medal and murmured: 'This gives me very great pleasure, Sir Lennard. Your wonderful work with young women is so deeply appreciated.'

'Thank you, ma'am,' Len mumbled. Recalling his instructions he took two steps back, turned and in a befuddled state, stumbled from the stage and took the seat kept vacant for him beside his daughter.

Claire reached across furtively and squeezed his hand.

'I'm ever so proud of you, Dad. I do wish Mum could have seen this.'

3

Shortly after his knighthood investiture Len received a letter from Andrew. It had been posted in Sydney and addressed care of Tom who had forwarded it on.

Olga Buskova
McMurdo Sound
ANTARCTIC
6th October

Dear Len,
I'm sorry not to have written earlier but I can honestly say I've never been so busy. It's literally been eighteen hours a day, seven days a week since I took over the ship in Sydney and then headed up to the Arctic.

Basically it's gone extremely well and I'll tell you all about it when I'm next in London but now I'm back down here for the southern summer season and am writing this for Harding to post in Sydney.

I know you did phenomenally well out of Tom's Global float but I'm still puzzled why you walked away from it all and can only assume you must have had pangs of conscience about the operation. Okay; so you'll never get a knighthood for services to young women but in my view if making the girls happy and everyone else, for that matter, is any measure, then you should certainly have no regrets about it all.

There's been plenty of amusing incidents since I arrived, one of which will certainly interest you.

Last Thursday Harding was due here to pick me up and return to Sydney to take care of Global's affairs. Three days before his arrival who should come on the boat but that wet little tosser Templeton who you spun the leopard-seal yawning story to. He spotted me and came over and I thought, here's trouble, after all, you recall they shot off after you gave them your 'scientific' solution and they must have looked bloody silly when they woke up. Not so, however.

In fact Templeton greeted me like a long-lost friend and immediately asked if you were here so I facetiously replied that you'd been murdered by the CIA for spilling the beans about the yawning. Naturally I expected him to storm off or abuse me for carrying on with the prank but instead he literally burst into tears and between sobbing, described you as a great and honourable Englishman – courageous and much more of this guff.

Well, it turned out they not only bought your yawning explanation but had it published and Paviour-West received all sorts of accolades for it. Now on the back of that the Ministry of Science has given them £4 million for their new research and the awful Paviour-West is back with a twenty-four man team with Templeton second in charge. Thank God I'm not a taxpayer although I shouldn't complain as they're all good customers on the boat.

Anyway, I took the opportunity once Templeton had stopped his blubbing, to find out what they're up to.

Turns out they're investigating whether leopard seals are like humans and have a natural bias to their right-hand side. They've been busy building four shelters spaced around the leopard-seal colony, each about half a mile away so as not to disturb the leopard seals and influence their movements. In each they intend rotating two-man crews for eight hour shifts, filming day and night with long-range cameras, every movement the leopard seals make. The whole lot is to be collated into a computer when they get back to Durham University and will supposedly reveal any left or right bias. Needless to say I haven't bothered to ask them why the hell it matters. We've been down that road too many times before.

Templeton told me the crew has Sundays off as it's unlikely the leopard seals would behave differently one day out of seven. After he'd gone I began thinking and decided to play a prank on them. I couldn't pull off your sort of thing as I'd burst out laughing if I tried to keep a straight face. Then I had an idea.

Harding was due in about four days' time so I faxed him instructions to bring two small weatherproof electronic beepers which would be controlled by a remote with a range of two miles. I had him arrange the remote to have a timer so one could set the beepers individually to emit a sound every minute or half hour or whatever one wished. That was a fairly simple mechanism to make and Harding duly brought it all in last Saturday.

The following day when I knew Paviour-West's lot weren't on the job, Bruce and I bowled down to the leopard-seal colony and buried the beepers in a pile of rocks, one on each side of the colony. Bruce shot back to the boat for a trial run and I stayed behind to monitor the situation. As I'd instructed he first set the remote to issue a beep on the left-hand side at one minute intervals for fifteen minutes and sure enough, suddenly all the leopard seals turned their heads sharply left and repeated this each subsequent minute.

A quarter of an hour later Bruce alternated left and right at thirty-second intervals. It was like watching a tennis match audience as all the leopard seals turned their heads back and forth in unison.

Back at the boat I set the remote to solely a left-hand side beep at one minute intervals and left it that way for Paviour-West's team's first day.

That night Paviour-West came on board, spotted me and came over which in itself was a surprise. He could scarcely contain his excitement. He made a few derisory remarks about you which was his way of being nice to me so I offered him a drink and he accepted.

'So how was your first day, Prof?' I asked him and out it all came. He spoke very slowly at first, measuring his words to emphasise their importance.

'Potter,' he said. 'You are present at one of the most astonishing zoological discoveries in the last hundred years.'

'No,' I said. 'On your first day, Professor.'

The old fool looked searchingly at the ceiling then said, 'It's not just natural talent, Potter. I've come to the conclusion forty years in the leopard seal business has given me an innate feel for it all which is unavailable to others. There's no such thing as luck, Potter,' he said solemnly. 'So-called luck is how lesser mortals describe the combination of genius and experience.'

'Are you able to tell me what you've discovered, Professor?' I asked.

By this time he's on to his second whisky and I suspect that combined with his pent-up excitement made him let it all out.

'Potter,' he said, 'Brace yourself,' so I tried to look wide-eyed and expectant.

He stared at me intensely for about twenty seconds; it was bloody embarrassing and I was on the verge of exploding with laughter and had pulled my handkerchief out to cover my face and pretend I was sneezing when he said very slowly, 'Leopard seals are left-handed.'

That was that. The laughter was uncontrollable and just welled up like vomiting. I fell to the floor covering my face with the handkerchief trying to pretend I was sneezing and choking, then I got up and spluttered, 'Need water' and rushed to my suite and thrashed about on the bed. I laughed so much I thought I was going to die.

Ten minutes later I went out to the lounge again. Paviour-West was waiting and he said, 'I can see you're deeply moved by the discovery Potter. You should be. It is the most significant zoological finding in Antarctic history.' Out comes the bloody handkerchief and I'm back on the bed again.

Anyway, I kept the seals left-handed until Thursday then I switched them to the right. That night in comes Paviour-West again. This time he's ashen-faced. 'A drink on the house, Professor,' I call to him merrily but he just ignored me and carried on through to an armchair and slumped into it so I left him alone.

I'll leave them right-handed a few more days then we'll have a run with the tennis-match scenario.

One thing's certain. It's enormously brightened up the leopard seal business here and I'm working on a few ideas to excite the penguin industry now I've got the bit between my teeth. It's made me feel quite creative.

I hope everything is going well for you. I imagine you must be pretty busy with Wyebury and investing your capital. Tom's your man for that.

All the best until I see you in London.

Andrew

4

The snow, which an hour earlier had been wafting down prettily, now began to swirl so that the entrance to the Palmerston Club became barely discernible. Some members, bent over in the wind, shuffled up the street towards the club while others dismounted from cars and ruddy-faced and rubbing their hands, entered the warm foyer and handed their coats and brollies to the doorman.

At the sitting room entrance Lord Melcup as club president greeted the members then introduced them to Len who as instructed, lurked to one side slightly behind his Lordship. Eventually more than eighty members were inside conversing noisily for this was the Palmerston Club's pre-annual general meeting cocktail party. Most in attendance were elderly although standing nervously alone along the walls and in corners with drink in hand and furtive expressions, were some younger bearded men. These were members from the club's scientific and exploration division back from abroad on leave. For most this was the social highlight on their London calendar. There were no younger City gentlemen present.

Lord Melcup moved about the room reintroducing Len to the members. He did so with generous praise about him couched in such meaningless generalities it would be impossible for anyone even a minute later to recount exactly what he had said.

In due course they moved upstairs to a seat-filled lecture room. The members took their seats and Lord Melcup, the club's secretary and the treasurer sat behind a table facing the assembly.

Lord Melcup rose and gave a short welcoming address. This was followed by the secretary reading the minutes of the previous meeting. Lord Melcup enquired whether there was any discussion arising from the minutes. There was. It was confined to the most elderly members who proffered garrulous and confused addresses, without exception based on misunderstanding. The young bearded scientists listened, enthralled by the speakers' eloquence, and said nothing.

Then the treasurer read his report which was followed by

more confused offerings from the same elderly gentlemen whereupon the meeting turned to the other items on the agenda.

There were only two being, 1) 'An announcement of importance by the president' and, 2) 'General'. As the club elected its committee for five-year terms there was no election of officers that year.

Lord Melcup rose.

'Gentlemen. I have served as president for the past four years and have been deeply honoured to have so done. It has been a personally rewarding experience and I trust I have executed my office in a manner satisfactory to my fellow members.

'However, many of you will be aware I have recently left Wyebury as it is my intention to henceforth live in London. But before doing so I wish to travel abroad for a period of one year and in two weeks' time leave for the first leg of a worldwide salmon fishing expedition. In those circumstances it is appropriate that I should resign as your president. I am delighted to tell you however, that subject to your approval, Sir Lennard Edwards has agreed to fill the role up until the next AGM.

'He is a man of very considerable accomplishment as evidenced by his recent recognition by her Majesty and I believe he would bring great honour to our club. I am personally indebted to him for his willingness to step into my shoes on such short notice, a sentiment I sincerely hope you will share. Accordingly I hereby move that Sir Lennard becomes the acting club president.'

After being seconded by a blushingly embarrassed beard who for months after would many times mentally relive his brief moment of glory, Len was duly elected. By an extraordinary coincidence this event occurred on the exact day of the fortieth anniversary of his ejection as the club's boy.

Over the following week Len lunched daily at the Palmerston, enjoying the attention of the members. From time to time he inspected aspects of the club's operation and although satisfied with all he observed, long experience in people management had taught him the merits of a gentle hint of discontent through minor modifying suggestions.

There was only one disharmonious matter. The club's boy, a gangling seventeen-year-old, disturbed him. There was something in the lad's manner; a certain glint in the eye, a jaunty cockiness, which made Len uneasy. The lout's conduct was strangely familiar but although Len thought hard, he could not connect it.

One day, having a pre-luncheon drink with Tom in the lounge, he called to the boy for the luncheon menus. 'Wait,' he instructed him. 'You can take our orders to the kitchen.'

Tom examined the menu then asked the lad whether the chicken was fresh or frozen.

'Personally hand-strangled this morning, sir,' the young man replied staring straight ahead. Later, Len instructed the club manager to dismiss the boy. 'I will not tolerate impertinence from staff,' he said officiously and felt his unease lift as if somehow a threat, the nature of which he was unable to discern, had been safely removed.

5

M r Whiting opened the file with distaste and groaned inwardly at the thought of the annual mystery-list meeting with Lord Eggington and Miss Pope. So much for the information age, he sniffed as he studied the stark lists of names.

Mr Whiting was chief co-ordinating officer for the Conservative Party's fund-raising division. He did not enjoy his job but had been wooed to the party by the incentive of double his previous salary. His reputation as king of the hill in the fund-raising industry rested largely on his thirty years' experience with a wide range of charities, all of which had taught him one golden rule, namely that the British public was generous when the cause was animals and parsimonious if on behalf of people.

Despite his discontentment Mr Whiting had been a great success in the five years he had held the position. His major innovation had been the creation of a highly successful strike force in the form of Lord Eggington and Miss Pope, whose engagement followed his initial survey of the party's traditional donors. He had employed consultants for this task and they had divided the donors into various categories with particular emphasis on their motives.

Neither Miss Pope nor Lord Eggington appeared on the party's employment record, each instead opting for the cover of consultancy companies with ownership disappearing into the vapour of foreign tax havens. They were rewarded with ten per cent of all monies they raised and as a result both enjoyed tax-free incomes more than five times that of the Prime Minister.

Miss Pope had been born Verushka Papp of Hungarian refugee parents and once of age had wisely changed her name to Veronica Pope. Her credentials of stunning beauty and a completed three-year drama course were ideal for targeting captains of industry and prosperous city financiers. Her methodology was simple: to make appointments late in the day when the victims' morning misanthropy had worn off and the impact of her appearance justified the resistance-destroying, earlier-than-usual opening of the drinks cabinet. Her thespian talents enabled her to affect a fragile vulnerability and appear on the verge of tears for fear of refusal. Although untrained, Lord Eggington also relied on thespian skills, adopting the role of the crusty aristocrat as perceived by the middle classes. This necessitated the wearing of tweed, which he detested, affecting a slight stammer, name-dropping references to the royal family whom he disliked almost as much as wearing tweed suits and protests at the declining standards of butlers of whom in fact he employed none. His targets were socially ambitious wealthy widows and nouveau riche wide-boy entrepreneurs, naively eager for the approving acknowledgement from the ineffectual aristocracy.

Lord Eggington had mastered the art of conversational in-clusivity, conveying to his willing victims the impression that they had leapt several divisions to the top of the English caste system, for which privilege they paid dearly.

Miss Pope and Lord Eggington arrived, each barely acknow-ledging their rival, and after tea was served, began the business of allocating the mystery list.

This comprised about fifty names who had made substantial unsolicited donations over the previous year and of whom little was known. Eventually they came to Len's name.

'Never heard of him,' Lord Eggington grunted.

Mr Whiting reached for the 'Who's Who'. It was unhelpful. No entry appeared. He picked up his telephone and called in his assistant Mr Wilson, who knew everything.

'Edwards, Edwards, Edwards,' Wilson mused, gazing at the ceiling. 'Twenty-five thousand pounds you say,' and then after a pause, 'Yes. Got it. We gave him a gong last year.'

'What,' Mr Whiting exclaimed, visibly outraged. 'A knight-hood for twenty-five thousand pounds? That's preposterous. See what you can find out.'

A few minutes later Wilson popped his head through the door. 'Edwards,' he said, 'One hundred and fifty thousand to the YWCA,' and he withdrew.

Mr Whiting whistled. 'One hundred and fifty thousand. That's serious money. We'd better go after him.'

'Hardly my territory, darling,' said Miss Pope. 'I know the type. He'll be a puritan of the very worst sort.'

Mr Whiting nodded reluctantly and looked appealingly at

Lord Eggington.

'No good looking at me, Cedric,' Lord Eggington snapped. 'I know his sort only too well. I will not tolerate being hectored about declining moral standards as if I'm personally responsible or can do anything about it.'

Later that day when alone again Mr Whiting unhappily telephoned the Prime Minister's secretary. 'Another name for Downing Street,' he said.

'Oh Christ,' the secretary exclaimed. 'The PM will go bananas. That's the fifth this month. Won't the chancellor do?' he pleaded.

Mr Whiting decided on firmness. 'Certainly not,' he snapped. 'The chancellor's far too busy. The PM has nothing to do and it's time he pulled his weight without this constant whining.'

So Len's name was placed on the Downing Street dinner party list.

6

Len's delight on receiving an invitation to a black-tie dinner party at 10 Downing Street was understandable. The past year had seen invitations and accolades rained upon him but this, he felt, was different.

His knighthood, palace garden parties, commemorative banquets, prestige charitable boards, the Palmerston Club's presidency; they represented the frothy end of the system. To him this invitation went to the very heart of establishment authority so for the first time, despite his rapidly accumulating trappings, Len felt he had truly arrived.

He returned his acceptance note and a week later a letter arrived from the Prime Minister's office listing his fellow guests.

The party comprised the American ambassador and his wife, a Scottish lord, an elderly, much honoured ballerina, the Archbishop of Canterbury, an eminent Oxford scholar, a lady Cabinet Minister, an acclaimed novelist, Philip Melcup and the editor of *The Times* newspaper and his wife. Philip's name bothered him at first. It was almost a year since Len had returned from the Antarctic. He could not recall seeing Philip when he was there; indeed, had it not been for Philip's sudden fame he would never have known he had been. Eventually Len concluded the lad could not harm him.

Arriving at Downing Street precisely at 7pm Len stepped from the rear of his Rolls, was saluted by the duty policeman, bowed to by a butler and warmly greeted in the hall by the Prime Minister. The two exchanged platitudinous pleasantries, each pretending a familiarity, then the Prime Minister introduced his wife.

'It's lovely you could spare us your time, Sir Lennard,' she oozed. 'We are all so appreciative of your wonderful work for young women.'

The Prime Minister piped up. 'There's one change to our guest list, Sir Lennard. Unfortunately the American ambassador is unwell. But there's always a silver lining,' he burbled. 'The renowned Senator Fulton is in London and I'm delighted to tell you, has agreed to stand in for the ambassador.'

Panic-stricken, Len was led into a drawing room. Numbly he took a glass of champagne and was introduced by the Prime Minister to the guests already present. Fulton could hardly fail to recognise him. What if he burst out accusingly and exposed him? It had all been too good to be true and now surely the most appalling humiliation awaited. He contemplated a dramatic collapse and escape.

Len edged to a corner occupied by the Oxford don to plan a strategy. But the academic, who had accomplished the rare achievement of appearing dowdy in a dinner suit, promptly began babbling with exaggerated affectation and clearly enjoying his own eloquence, seemed content with Len's silent audience.

But hang on, he thought. Fulton had been quite happy to have a few dips himself and then had stolen Claudia. I've got the bastard, he reassured himself. If he takes me down then he's bloody well going with me. Len began to relax. Excusing himself he moved away from the don, who seemed oblivious to his departure, and very soon he was discussing salmon fishing with the Scottish lord.

A noisy disturbance at the doorway heralded Fulton's arrival. Len glanced across. Good Christ almighty, the American had Claudia with him.

The Prime Minister moved round the room gushingly introducing the new arrivals to the other guests. Finally it was Len's turn.

'One of our leading captains of industry, Sir Lennard Edwards; Senator Fulton and his economics adviser Miss Claudia Waite,' the Prime Minister recited.

Len looked hard at Fulton as he shook hands. 'I'm honoured to meet you, Sir Lennard,' the senator boomed, showing no sign of recognition. Claudia looked sensational. She briefly shook his hand, murmured something, a slight flutter of alarm crossing her features, and then they moved on to *The Times* editor who began a loud braying about their previous meeting at a Washington party.

In the dining room Len was seated between the lady Cabinet Minister and the Archbishop. The minister chattered incessantly about Len's excellent work with young women so after a time Len concentrated his attention on the Archbishop and they talked about investments. 'The Church has had the midas touch in recent years,' his Grace said. 'We've been showered with the Lord's blessing. I can't help feeling there's a divine hand guiding our decisions.'

Across the table Claudia was seated alongside the Prime Minister who, ignoring the Oxford don on his other side, talked relentlessly at the subdued girl in what Len observed was pretty much a one-way conversation.

When the last course was cleared away the Prime Minister, beaming around the room, tapped the side of his wineglass with a spoon. Conversation waned with the exception of the don who, despite a lifetime of passively dumbstruck audiences, eventually sensed a mood change and tapered to a stop. The Prime Minister rose to his feet.

'Honoured guests. It would be inappropriate for me to allow such an auspicious occasion, such an outstanding gathering as is present tonight, an assembly which as I look about me, represents the pillars not only of all that is strong and noble about our two great nations, the United States of America and Great Britain, but, dare I say it,' and at that he paused and adopting a brow-furrowing seriousness, glanced pointedly along the table avoiding only his wife who was gazing at him with a rigidly fixed smile, 'a gathering that reflects the very foundations of civilisation, to go unremarked upon.

'As I look around this room I feel humble. We are all deeply conscious that recently the human race came disastrously close to extinction. What an enormous honour it is therefore to host this brilliant gathering in which are present two momentous figures, two whose names will remain forever honoured, two of whom it can, indeed must be said, saved the world.'

He paused and smiled at Philip and then at Fulton.

'And how proud I am,' he continued, 'as a humble English-man, to think that one of those two should be a fellow Englishman. But that pride extends to a claim on Senator Fulton for I'm sure I speak for all of us when I say that the cement in the bonds binding America and Britain is based not on politics, not on trade, not on treaties, but, instead, on a very deep understanding which no other nation can ever comprehend. It is a relationship which reaches to our very souls. We are in truth one people. And so,

Senator,' and again he looked down at the American, who plainly was enjoying every word and who returned his stare with equal solemnity, 'we welcome you here tonight as one of us.'

At that *The Times* editor, who was angling for a knighthood, cried out, 'Hear, hear,' and broke into applause which the others obligatorily followed. Fulton gave a nod of acknowledgement and in an unaccustomed gesture of humility, studied his plate. Inspired by this response, the Prime Minister became expansive, labouring under the garrulous airline captain misconception that a captive audience is a willing one.

'As I look about me I see in this room men and women who symbolise the ultimate pinnacles of achievement. I see our glorious Church, our renowned halls of learning, I see our great news-papers, I see the arts in all of their splendour and I see,' and here he paused as he struggled for words on observing the Scottish lord, who having drunk more than his recommended quota was nodding off, 'I see our noble and historic families,' whereupon he looked up and down the table and his eyes settled on Len. Wound up with his own eloquence and three glasses of wine too many, the Prime Minister, seeking a speech-culminating novel angle, reached a crescendo.

He paused then lowered his voice melodramatically.

'But there is one among us who quietly and with a consistency in character and integrity, represents the real strength of our two societies. I refer of course to Sir Lennard, unsung, unheralded, but who in a lifetime of service has sought neither tribute nor reward. It is men and women of his ilk working quietly behind the scene who truly are the real backbone of our two great nations.'

The Prime Minister, whose climb to the top had relied on a first-rate sensitivity to the mood of an audience, detected a bewilderment among his guests. He was unsure of Len's back-ground other than a vague awareness of something commercial, probably one of those dreary City money-grubbers, he thought. But his antennae were twitching strongest with familiar angry vibes from his wife. Better wrap it up, he thought.

'And so my fellow guests, let us tonight pay tribute to the hidden steel in our social order.

'I give you a toast: "Sir Lennard Edwards".'

All but Len and the Scottish lord, who was now asleep in a

well practised upright posture, shuffled to their feet and with discernible puzzlement, raised their glasses to Len. Then they went into the library for coffee and liqueurs.

Len moved to a corner and as he hoped, Claudia quickly joined him.

'I nearly died when I saw you,' she said. 'But I had to laugh when the Prime Minister went on like that.'

'Do you think he's drunk?' Len asked, slightly shocked at his own suggestion.

Claudia laughed loudly. 'Goodness no. Honestly, they go on like that all the time. It was quite moderate compared to some I've heard. You should hear Sam in full flight. They believe it too, that is when they're saying it. Afterwards they forget quickly. It's a sort of embarrassment avoidance knack.'

'It was bloody embarrassing for me,' Len said, then changing the subject, 'You look terrific, Claudia. But what about bloody Fulton? Thank God he didn't recognise me.'

'Of course he recognised you,' Claudia said testily. 'He's no fool, you know. He's well used to handling these situations. He's a politician don't forget. I've learned a lot about politicians and believe me, they're the ultimate thespians. They've got to be to survive. Anyway, don't worry about him. He enjoys intrigues. Let's talk about you. Things seem to have worked out rather well. How on earth did you snare a knighthood? Services to young women I suppose,' she joked.

'Actually yes, in fact. But I can't talk about that now,' Len responded. 'Still, it looks as if things have not been too bad for you either. You seem to have landed on your feet.'

'Well, I suppose it's been okay. You know, I really am his economics adviser. Everyone assumes there's more to it but I don't care. I suppose mostly I'm a companion and general adviser. It was quite a lot of fun at first. All those cocktail parties in Washington, but,' and she hesitated, searching for the right words, 'I rather think it's sort of time to move on again. It was really interesting for a period. Lots of travel everywhere. I say, that reminds me. Do you remember the drunken doctor on the ship? What was his name?'

'Isaac,' Len said.

'Yes. That's right. Guess what? I ran across him on a state

visit to Gambia. He's running the main hospital there. He had one of the girls from the boat with him. I remembered her, a quiet one; always reading. She was his personal assistant and they seemed really happy. It was quite funny really. We walked through all the wards with the Gambian president and Isaac showing us everything and pretending he didn't know me. But he gave me a little wink when we left.'

'Did you ever go to the White House?' Len asked.

'Oh yes; several times actually. The President told me I was a very intelligent girl. He offered me a job as a special consultant. But I'm not interested in that. No "consulting" for me,' she laughed.

'But what about Fulton? He can't be much fun. I mean, does he carry on at home like that? You know, all that religious guff and economic fortress blather.'

'Don't be silly. He doesn't believe a word of it. He's actually rather sweet in private. Sam claims he fills a vital role. Gives the little people hope and makes them feel involved in the democratic process. He knows it's all nonsense but he genuinely believes he's doing good work. Being a touchstone for losers, that sort of thing. He's really tickled about the Nobel Prize.'

'That's disgraceful,' Len exploded.

'Not at all,' Claudia replied coolly. 'It's all quite consistent with the wider adversarial system we live in. Look at lawyers. I'll bet probably fifty per cent of the time they don't believe in their clients' cases. And that includes commercial lawyers, not just courtroom advocates. Everyone accepts that as okay. And think about commerce. Advertising people go to bat for their clients claiming their products or services are the best. Well, they can't all be the best but it's just their job. Or what about salespeople? The same thing applies. So why should politicians behave differently? Sam's just another advocate pushing his clients' interests. He doesn't have to personally believe the story. It so happens these interests conflict with the trendy liberal set who for all their chatter are dreadfully intolerant and arrogant so they paint him as the Prince of Darkness. But he hasn't sold his soul pushing the little man's line. He's just providing what he calls music to the masses.'

'So you'll stick with him then?' Len queried.

Claudia bit her lip and suddenly looked vulnerable. After a while she said, 'Do you remember Father O'Hearn?'

'Of course,' Len replied. 'I've been following his career in the sports pages. It's Danny O'Hearn now though. He flagged the praying lark. Seems to be making quite a name for himself as a fight trainer. I gather he's got quite a stable of comers in New York.'

'A stable?' Claudia smiled. 'That's how you used to describe the girls, wasn't it?'

Noting Len's discomfort she continued, 'I don't mind. I suppose it was a fair description. The thing is, I've seen Danny. Actually quite a bit,' she added shyly. 'I've even been to Vegas with him for a fight. I wore a blonde wig. I know it sounds crazy but there's something awfully addictive about boxing. He really has got some promising fighters. I know lots about it now. I think he could make it with his Canadian heavyweight if he can just get him to work off the jab more. I know it's ridiculous, punching one another and all that, but it's actually much more complicated and there's something so basic and honest about it that doesn't seem to be so with everything else, especially in America. There it's all charm but then you wake up that it's really just smarm. It just seems as if everyone's pretending all the time, like tonight – don't you think?'

They were interrupted by a waiter with coffee. After he had gone Len said, 'So what happened with you and O'Hearn?'

Claudia thought for a while. 'We were in New York and Sam had gone away for a conference. Anyway, I read about Danny in the newspaper so I took a taxi down to his gym. I suppose we fell naturally together at the time because we were both a bit lost. He was very angry then. He talked a lot about suing the Catholic Church for stealing his youth and exploiting his vulnerability when young; that sort of carry-on. But after a while as things developed that all stopped. I think when you're really happy you don't think about the past whether it's good or bad. I think when you're happy you're bound up mostly with today and a bit with tomorrow.'

'So what are you going to do?' Len asked.

'I know this much. I want to finish with this political thing and I don't want to live in America. It doesn't matter who I'm talking to there, from shop assistants to the President, I always feel they don't mean what they're saying and I'm tired of all that. What I want to do is to finish my doctorate. I'm ready for that now. The trouble is I'm worried about leaving Sam. I don't know how he would cope. He's become awfully dependent on me.'

'Listen to me, Claudia,' Len said. 'Run for your life. Don't worry about bloody Fulton. Politicians are like fighters. Their lives are full of highs and lows. But they're tougher than fighters; they have to be to cope with all the abuse. That's why they're good actors. It helps smooth out the bumps. Believe me, Fulton will manage. Tell you what. Here's my card. Come down and stay for a few days at Wyebury and we can talk about it and reminisce about old times.'

At that moment the Prime Minister joined them. Claudia excused herself and moved across the room to Fulton.

'I must say, sir. Your remarks were very generous but of course totally unjustified. But thank you anyway,' Len said.

'Not at all, not at all. People sometimes think because we politicians talk for a living we're insensitive to what's going on but we have our ears to the ground.'

The Prime Minister had a wary look and seemed anxious to change the subject.

'I see you've been talking to Miss Waite. She's a very intelligent girl, you know.'

'I know,' Len replied resignedly.

7

Later that night as they undressed the Prime Minister's wife said, 'You certainly made a damn fool of yourself. What on earth came over you? That ridiculous rubbish about Edwards. Who is he anyway?'

'I don't think you understand, dear,' the Prime Minister said defensively. 'He's an extremely important man.' He decided to lie. 'There are certain people one knows little about publicly, my dear, but who pull all the strings. One doesn't dismiss them lightly. I can say no more but I certainly wouldn't underestimate Sir Lennard.'

The Prime Minister made a mental note to find out who Len was and then as quickly, decided to forget it. He must be important otherwise why would his people have him on the guest list? Mind you, it was a bit of a dregs list, what with that appalling Oxford bore and the old Scots sot and my God, the ballerina; totally gaga. Being Prime Minister certainly wasn't all it was cracked up to be. The Prime Minister's wife was not finished, however.

'As for that tart with the oafish American. I don't suppose you could consider my feelings. Slobbering all over her like that. I've never been so embarrassed. The Archbishop was quite shocked. I saw him watching you. You all but had her clothes off.'

The Prime Minister feigned amazement. 'My dear. Don't be ridiculous. She was sitting next to me. I was obliged to talk to her,' and he added the fatal words triggering a primeval female warning with his wife, 'I'll have you know she's a very intelligent girl.'

While this conversation was going on, *The Times* editor sat at his desk a few miles away in a Belgravia flat. He rarely wrote editorials personally but the night's experience seemed silly to waste. God knew, he'd invested enough favourable comment in that absurd twerp of a Prime Minister to the point where it was becoming embarrassingly obvious. Only two weeks ago he had been ribbed unmercifully at a Spectator luncheon about chasing a gong. His furious and spurious denials had simply induced more ridicule. Still, he would take his cue from the Prime Minister's prattle. Adopt the same florid style if that's what he liked, he thought. But by God, the little shit was on notice. If his name wasn't on the next awards list then he would start a 'time for a change at the helm' campaign and bring the bastard down.

'There are times in the affairs of state,' the editor wrote, 'when the natural order of authority is exposed with a clarity so pure, one can only but marvel that for some, it might ever have been even clouded.

'Such an occasion occurred at a recent Downing Street dinner party. It would be inappropriate to reveal the guests present other than to say they represented some of the most illustrious figures in the land. Yet also among them was Sir Lennard Edwards, a little-known businessman, and it befell to the Prime Minister, in a memorable and stirring after-dinner address which those fortunate enough to hear will long remember and which is already the talk of London, to detect that notwithstanding the sparkling company it was Sir Lennard and his quiet and unspoken achievements who was the true star of the galaxy.

'The Prime Minister's acute discernment revealed precisely why he holds the highest office and is a statesman of such formidable stature. In these oft-troubled times citizens can sleep well, knowing that the hand on the wheel of the great ship of State is firm and purposeful.

'This newspaper believes it is appropriate that the prime ministerial judgement be respected and Sir Lennard be elevated to the peerage. There can be little doubt he would be gratefully received in the House of Lords where his wisdom and experience would be invaluable.'

The editor read what he had written. Christ, it's a bit over the top, he thought. Better make it a second leader. But by God, that's the last stroking that fool gets. If he doesn't deliver bloody soon then next time it's the lash.

Two days later the Prime Minister's press secretary read the editorial aloud to him.

'Well, I must say,' the Prime Minister said, 'That's awfully decent of Charles. We really must look after him. We had better organise a peerage for Edwards if that's what Charles wants,' and he asked the press secretary for a copy of the editorial to show his wife. That will shut her up, he thought happily, little knowing he had just cast his political death sentence and in eight months' time would be at home writing his memoirs.

Across England many people started to read the editorial although few completed it. But in nursing homes and country cottages, in genteel boarding houses and small city flats, elderly schoolteachers, widows, retired parsons and army officers read every word and being *The Times*, did so unquestioningly. And as is the way with such people with nothing to do but direct the affairs of State from their armchairs, that very day they wrote to the Prime Minister aligning themselves with *The Times* and urging Sir Lennard's elevation to the peerage.

Contrary to these writers' beliefs, the Prime Minister did not personally read their letters, but a week later, the press secretary, whose unpleasant job it was to do so, said to his assistant, 'There's no doubt about the old boy; he certainly has his finger on the public pulse.'

And so Len became Lord Edwards of Wye.

'Life's a funny thing,' Len said to Tom as they sat in a fashionable restaurant celebrating his new status. 'You know, I really think I've got it worked out now. It's just a pity it's taken sixty years to do so.'

'Ha,' Tom exclaimed. 'Everyone says that.'

'Sometimes, I think it's a bit like a massive river with a narrow current running down the middle. You have to swim like hell to get through the slack water so most people don't bother and just frolic at the edge. Still, some have a go and a few drown trying to get to the fast stuff. Some overly ambitious types try and swim against the current and at first when they're fresh and strong they succeed and everyone applauds but ultimately the current always wins and the cheers turn to jeers. But if you do make it into the flow, you just have to move your hands and feet a little occasionally to stay afloat and on top of things. Everything becomes so easy once you've made it into the centre, just bobbing along with the current doing all the work and taking you further and further ahead.'

'Yes,' said Tom, 'but the problem is complacency. Once you're in the current it can become illusionary and you can forget to make those occasional little motions needed to stay afloat. And if you go under, well there's no return. Also, sometimes the river widens and the current fades and those who have just accepted the easy ride don't notice the change and bang; they're sunk. That's the history of money. It's hard work to make and easy work to keep but you can never totally stop working it or you're sunk. Never forget that, me old mate,' and Len never did. For the rest of his days he continued to bob along in the sunlight and enjoy the view, and keep moving a little, always with a cautionary eye for any change in the flow.

8

Claudia telephoned Len after the Downing Street dinner party and the following afternoon she came down by train.

Len guided her proudly through the great house. In each room Claudia made gentle decorative suggestions. The accumulative effect, despite her diplomacy, had Len viewing Wyebury in a new light as incomplete.

On their first morning Len taught Claudia to cast and in her second session in the river, both highly excited, she landed her first salmon after playing it for almost an hour. In return Claudia polished up Len's recently learnt riding techniques. After a few days they settled into a routine of breakfast in the sunroom with the newspapers brought up from the village, then a three-hour session in the river, a light lunch, then an afternoon period reading and sometimes snoozing. Late in the day they would ride across the estate for an hour or so and return at dusk to prepare for dinner.

On their tenth day they drove to Cheltenham where with Claudia's guidance Len made many purchases in antique shops and furnishing stores.

Once they drove to the bookshop town of Hay On Wye. They set out early and stopping only for lunch, engaged in a joyous frenzy of all-day book-buying like two children let loose in a gigantic toyshop.

No subject was too esoteric. Basics, such as Dickens, Thackeray, Proust and Shaw were mixed with complete sets of bound Punch magazines dating to 1880, long-forgotten travel sagas, biographies, memoirs, history and sports books, out-of-favour novels and fashionable contemporary works.

Arrangements were made for these to be freighted to Wyebury. 'By the time they're sorted into categories and placed in the library you will be surprised how small a dent they will make on those empty shelves,' Claudia warned. 'But they're a start and it will be another pleasure in the future adding to them and helping make this house complete.'

One morning Claudia abruptly announced her departure.

She needed to return to London to arrange her return to Sydney. Len did not hide his dismay. In the time Claudia had been there Wyebury had acquired a vibrancy and lightness. There was no need for her to go, he argued. She was perfectly capable of researching and writing her doctoral thesis at Wyebury. When she hesitated he added he would miss her dreadfully if she left and as well she was needed to help complete the furnishings.

So she agreed to stay a little longer and Len astutely maintained the weekly buying trips, sometimes to London and once to Dublin, scouring antique shops, art galleries, bookshops and furnishing stores. Gradually the great house took on a brighter, livelier ambience. A cat and then two Labrador dogs were added to the household. Even the farmhands became inspired as under Claudia's guidance a new orchard was laid out and flower gardens renewed. Suddenly the estate began to sparkle with a fresh purpose and vitality.

After two months Claudia's departure was no longer mentioned. She set up a desk in the library and most days spent about four hours on her work. When the weekly investment report arrived they discussed the portfolio and any new recommendations from Tom's office. It was a life of routine placidity, stimulation and contentment, precisely matching the world Len had dreamt about so often in recent years.

Increasingly Len found himself dependent on Claudia's advice. In particular, as his daily mail grew following his elevation to the peerage, speech requests, invitations to join boards and attend functions and a diverse range of requests flowed in from strangers. A word processor was purchased and twice weekly a part-time secretary came from the village to deal with the deluge.

Claudia constantly checked Len's impulse to agree to requests.

A letter arrived from India from the Calcutta City Council on behalf of its Mother Teresa Commemorative Award sub-committee. Would Len be agreeable to accepting that year's award, it enquired? The committee, Anglophiles all, had plainly been impressed by *The Times* editorial which had been reprinted in the *Times of India*.

Claudia was adamant in her opposition and for the first time they quarrelled. 'Enough is enough,' she protested. 'I don't care if you make a mockery out of the English but a line must be drawn somewhere. You're flying too close to the sun, Len, and I don't want to see you fall. This is beyond a joke.'

'Oh come on, Claudia,' Len protested. 'It could be fun to see India and if they want to give me an award, then so what? I never asked for it; they're offering it. What harm can come of that?'

'You're right,' Claudia said coldly. 'On reflection, in your case none. I don't understand why but with you I suspect nothing bad is ever going to happen. It's so damned unfair. Whatever you do seems to turn to gold. You just sail blithely along doing whatever you damn well please and the world stops to cast rose petals in your path. It's infuriating when I think what a struggle life is for everyone else. But I suggest it calls for some discretion and restraint on your part. I don't want you to accept this.'

Reluctantly Len did as he was bid. All further accolades for his 'work' for young women were declined and with the passing of time Len came to realise the wisdom of Claudia's cautionary counsel.

Only once did they ever refer to the Antarctic after Len tentatively broached the subject of her departure from the ship with Fulton.

'Men never understand what appeals to women,' she said. 'When you and Andrew tried to set him up the first time he came on the boat you were both so smugly certain you were charming him to death. But watching it all I quickly realised he could see through you both. He was all unkempt in his Antarctic clothing yet somehow he was in total control and seemed the real sophisticate among the three of you. Believe me, he had you both sussed and I sort of fell for him on the spot. He was just so masterly and such a super actor and in an odd way was being very kind to you both.'

'Were you in love with him?' Len queried.

'Don't be ridiculous,' Claudia snapped. 'It was never like that. I suppose it was more a sort of fascination. But ultimately I couldn't hack it; the endless charades and game-playing that his world revolved about. Sam found it all an amusing challenge but I suppose I'm a country girl at heart and prefer a straight and simple existence. At the end of the day, despite his worldliness he was still a man and that means basically childish. I discovered that very early in life. You know, my father was our town's mayor and as a little girl I was ever so proud of him. But then I began to notice the odd behaviour which I now know to be characteristic of all men but I didn't when I was only a teenager and initially it was quite disturbing.'

'What do you mean childish?' Len quizzed.

'Men behave as if they are victims of a massive conspiracy, only not from other people which if mad would at least be potentially plausible. Instead they rail away about inanimate objects; traffic lights and that sort of thing, as if they're a vast plot designed deliberately to inconvenience them personally. I once watched my father kicking our old car. He was hurting himself but that didn't matter to him as he cursed and carried on about teaching it a lesson.'

'You don't understand,' Len said. 'Carrying on like that makes us feel better.'

'It's still childish,' Claudia replied. 'Sam was exactly the same. He used to go on about things like the toaster taking too long and once I saw him fly into a rage and shout "I'll show you, you bastard" and he picked it up and smashed it on the floor and jumped on it. That's the difference between men and women. We see patience not so much as a virtue but as simply practical; men see it as a sign of weakness and become absolutely infantile when it's required.'

'And women lack a sense of humour,' Len retorted.

'We can laugh,' Claudia replied. 'But we don't like laughing at others, which men seem to have an endless appetite for and we certainly don't like laughing about infantile behaviour.'

'What about Danny O'Hearn?' Len asked after a pause.

'What about him?'

'Were you in love with him?'

Claudia laughed. 'Of course not. Our relationship was entirely platonic. We simply found each other in a moment of personal crisis. He was still working through the Catholic thing and I was in turmoil over the world I had inadvertently slipped into. It was terribly confusing. In the space of a year I had gone from being a Sydney post-graduate student to the absurdity of running a brothel with a pair of rogues in the Antarctic, then to functions at the White House and State visits on behalf of another country. I needed to stop and clear my head and Danny and his boxing scene's raw honesty helped me do that.

'But I've thought a lot about it since and I'm not sure it's the answer for Danny. That is, it's not sufficient a purge from the emotional saturation and escapism of the Church. They're too much alike.'

'What, boxing and witchcraft?' Len exclaimed. 'You must be mad.'

'They're almost identical, actually,' Claudia explained. 'Half the men in the gym, and I don't just mean the boxers, but the old fighters and hangers-on who were always there, were zealots. And just like the Church there were the lost and broken souls, despite their bravado. God knows how many ex-cons I encountered but in their defence they were armed-robbery types rather than purse-snatchers. For all of them the gym was a sanctuary from the real world, just like the Church. As with religion, accepting punching people required a suspension of one's rationality and in its place the narrowing of one's world so that only unquestioning devotion prevailed. For the obsessively religious faithful the world outside the Church is inconsequential and an irritating burden. I found exactly the same attitude in the boxing world.'

'I see what you're getting at now,' Len said. 'I can imagine it with religious obsessives and I've seen it everywhere in boxing. Still, doesn't success come from single-minded obsession?'

'It does,' Claudia said. 'But one can be single-minded about a particular goal without rejecting the rest of what life offers. That was the marvellous thing about politics with Sam. It embraced absolutely everything but also, there was the problem; we could only ever briefly touch the passing parade. There were so many times, especially towards the end, when I was just screaming to be able to pause a bit, to relax, to wallow in whatever it was we were doing. You know the old cliché about smelling the roses.'

'What you mean is achieving some balance,' Len proffered. 'I think I've done that,' he added after a pause.

Claudia laughed scornfully. 'For you it's easy, Len. That's because for you the world is comprehensible. I used to think you were fearless. Now I know it's not that; instead, your outlook on everything is simplistic. You basically see the world as just people and you view all people as essentially the same and when it gets down to fundamentals, of course in a sense you're right. So you just sail merrily along with the world well worked out and everything's a breeze. You're armour-plated by your detachment. Life's easy to deal with when you have that sort of perspective. I'm different. For me the world is insurmountably huge in all of its diversity so I don't cope as well. I get excited about the Acropolis or Machu Picchu. For you they're just a pile of old rocks. I get moved by ideas or worthy endeavour. To you it's all of no account. Everything will ultimately come out in the wash. You're right, of course, and maybe your way is smarter.'

'Well, that's refreshing to hear,' Len said. 'To be honest, I always felt you vaguely disapproved of me.'

'Vaguely?' Claudia shrieked. 'Are you kidding? At first I thought you and Andrew were despicable. It took a long time to adjust and come to terms with everything and eventually I began to see you and all that was going on in a different light, although I never really changed my view on Andrew.'

'Explain,' Len demanded.

'After a few weeks on the boat I tried to typecast you both; that is, to try and understand you better. Andrew was easy. His cold-blooded, single-minded mercenary outlook frightened me, particularly when I learned he was just doing a job and not taking any of the profits. I always mentally pictured him as a very smart, cold-blooded Gestapo officer. I still do, in fact. I don't think I could ever warm to him.'

'That's a bit rough,' Len said. 'And what about me?'

'You were really hard. Too many mixed messages. A sort of devil-may-care disregard for all conventions and a laid-back don't-give-a-damn nonchalance. And then overlying all of that, a confusing basic decency and kindness. It was quite perplexing and I used to struggle with it. After a while I decided you were a weird mixture of John Wayne and Noel Coward, so you can imagine my confusion.'

'Bloody hell,' Len exclaimed. 'That's ridiculous.'

'I agree,' Claudia said. 'I knew there was still something missing. Eventually I got it right.'

'Oh, so tell me,' Len demanded his curiosity aroused.

'I was right about John Wayne and I was right about Noel Coward. You display both at various times in your sentiments and values. But there was a missing bit and one day I worked it out. You are a mixture of Wayne, Coward and Ronnie Biggs.'

There was a long silence. After a while Len spoke.

'Are you happy now?' he enquired quietly.

'Blissfully. If there's heaven on earth then this is surely it. I just worry about what might go wrong. I'm not sure if I can trust you not to suddenly, out of the blue, be off on some new escapade. At least that's how I felt until recently. I'm starting to feel more secure about everything now.'

'Tell me, Claudia,' Len said. 'Why did you leave me on the boat? Things were developing with us and suddenly you were gone.'

Claudia paused and considered her reply.

'You say things were developing but I knew you were having it off with some of the girls. Okay; you weren't making a pig of yourself like Andrew but nor were you making any overtures to me. So what was my future; a madam? Is that what I'd spent seven years at university for? When Sam turned up he rescued me from what had mostly been a horrible year. Don't misunderstand me. I don't regret the Antarctic experience; after all, look where it's led. I'm not proud of it either. The whole thing was just so bizarre and frankly, so typical of you. As I said, that's the only thing that worries me now; the awful fear of some new outbreak of absurdity that seems to characterise your life. By comparison, working with Sam was a return to normality. Still, you might as well know what happened between us, which is nothing actually, at least in the sense you may have thought.

'Sam came on board three times. He'd have a sauna, which relieved his joint pain, then shower and join me in the girls' private lounge which was empty because the girls were all out of sight for his visits except the last day when we decided it was all going to be okay and he wasn't going to cause any trouble about the ship.'

'Well what the hell were you doing with him?' Len demanded.

'We just talked. And talked and talked and talked. He's a fascinating man. But I certainly jumped at what was a dream job when he offered it and I'll tell you this; it was hard work, too. But over-riding it was a sort of flimflam veneer and in the end I felt world-wearied by it all, which is ridiculous for someone my age.

I told you all about that when we met up again at the Downing Street dinner. Anyway, after that, just before I came down here, I sent Sam a long letter and explained everything. I think he filled in the gaps. He wrote a very nice reply and wished me luck and well, that was that.'

'And here you are,' Len said lightly.

'And here I am,' Claudia responded. 'It's funny really,' she continued. 'When I first came here I felt sorry for you. You were like a little boy with a toy you couldn't operate but were clinging to anyway. The vast empty house and you lost in it and unsure about it all and trying to live out some sort of absurd romantic vision. But I don't feel that way any more. Somehow now it all works. Everything seems snug and right and complete as if we belong here and anything else would be wrong.'

Eighteen months after Claudia's arrival they were married in a private ceremony at Wyebury. Tom offered the services of the Archbishop of Canterbury with an undertaking of no religious guff but they declined, opting for a brief civil ceremony with a marriage celebrant.

More than eighty guests were present including a Cabinet Minister, a minor royal and other people of prominence Len had befriended through the Palmerston Club. A surprise arrival was Philip Melcup who came with Claire. They had met at a London concert and had been seeing each other for some months, Len found out. After the ceremony Tom gave a rather solemn speech and then there was a rollicking party. Most of the guests stayed the night and when all the rooms were filled, others telephoned through hotel bookings to Cheltenham and Gloucester. The next morning Len and Claudia called on the estate's cottages with boxed pieces of wedding cake and a bottle of champagne for each of the occupants.

In fact, it was a double celebration for two weeks before the wedding Claudia received her doctorate. Len printed two sets of calling cards for her with Lady Edwards on one and Dr Claudia Edwards on the other. Being a wise woman, she mostly used the former.

9

Tom came down to Wyebury for a week's salmon fishing. One evening over pre-dinner drinks he said, 'I really must compliment you both on your financial discipline. Not once have you pushed for bigger capital gains investments. It's unique in my experience for new money to display such contentment with a low risk portfolio.'

'Why would we want more?' Len asked curiously. 'As it is we're having to make new investments every month from the dividend surpluses. The portfolio's grown to a capital value of nearly a quarter billion pounds after the stock market recovery. We were incredibly lucky getting in so cheaply, thanks to the Antarctic and nuclear war scares.'

'That's not the point,' Tom responded. 'Most people who make fortunes from scratch never stop wanting more. It may not be rational but that's the way it usually is.'

'I don't see that's so hard to understand,' Claudia intervened. 'After all, creating a fortune probably requires a great deal of passion and commitment, for whatever one's done. You can't turn passion off like a tap. Probably the money is just a by-product.'

'No. It's definitely a money lust,' Tom persisted. 'It must be because once it gets into our hands as investment advisers, which has nothing to do with its origins, the buggers never stop wanting higher returns. That means risk but they don't care. Enough's never enough. No, I can tell you from experience, it takes generations of wealth possession before people wake up that money only has meaning when it's being spent.'

'That's a bit unfair,' Claudia said. 'Surely the reason people go on wanting to build wealth is because of their children, and for that matter, subsequent generations in mind. Why scoff at that?'

Tom snorted derisorily. 'Maybe you're right about their motives but don't categorise it as altruism. It's actually self-aggrandisement. That sort of goal, the dynasty building thing, is totally egotistical. It's also illogical, which I point out when people start prattling on about looking after their future flesh and blood, because they've never actually worked it out. When I tell them they get quite upset by the reality of the illusion.'

'What illusion?' Len asked. 'Flesh and blood is hardly illusionary.'

'Look at it this way,' Tom said. 'You think of Claire as your flesh and blood. Well, she's not. She's half your flesh and blood and half her mother's. And her children will be quarter you and three-quarters strangers. And your great-grandchildren will be only one eighth you and seven-eighths God only knows who, but certainly not you. So leaving money to your future flesh and blood generations is an illusionary myth. Unless we start cloning people it's impossible to have future flesh and blood generations. It's just a fiction disguised by carrying on a family name.

'The same goes in reverse. Occasionally we encounter pompous asses who mention their family tree and ancestors. They're like stunned mullets when I bring them down to earth by explaining the mathematical illusion of it all. Had a fellow in once. When he mentioned for the third time in four hours that he was a direct descendent of William Pitt I pulled out some paper and had him acknowledge he was about the ninth post-Pitt generation, which he happily did. Then I showed him that meant he had less than one-five hundredth of Pitt's blood and 499/500ths of hundreds of other unknowns. That silenced him.'

'You've got me thinking,' Claudia said after a pause. 'Unless there's a flaw in your argument, basically genealogy is nonsense.'

'No, not entirely,' Tom said. 'It's meaningful if you're curious about your ancestors but the direct descendent claim is impossible and more important, the future-generation belief's a myth. I point this out to the super-rich and suggest they're better off covering their children adequately and leaving the rest to charities of their choice or creating something new in some activity of interest to them. It takes them time to think it through but usually about half then come to the party. They wake up that they might as well spend it now in some area of interest to them and derive some pleasure from that while they're here to see it and not some fairy-tale future generation that can never actually exist. As I said, dynasty creation is just egocentricity. They don't want to be forgotten, as if it possibly matters. Far better to be a live Joe Blow than a dead Shakespeare in my view.'

'You're making me feel guilty,' Claudia said. 'When your weekly investment reports arrive we're always very diligent in studying them and discussing everything. But I never think of it as money in a spending sense. Instead it's just our base security, which is ludicrous really, now it's so much. I suppose it would be fun and quite interesting to start doing things. We'll certainly think about it.'

'That's the funny thing about the Church of England,' Tom continued. 'Do you recall me telling you once how we restored their asset base? Now if ever there's a client which should have your type of portfolio, then it's the Church Commissioners. But not so. Having enjoyed a rapid wealth gain they've got the bit between their teeth and want more and more, regardless of risk. It's classic new wealth behaviour but somewhat peculiar coming from an old wealth institution.'

'I thought after the success with the consultants you had them sorted out,' Len said.

'Yes, we thought so too. But as the Church's advisers and after further analysis, we no longer shared the Commissioners' enthusiasm for those consultants. While in a cost-benefit sense their proposals were beneficial, we discovered the underlying problem remained. It's an interesting thing, competition,' Tom mused. 'No matter how good someone is, like sports champions, ultimately there's always another who can do it better. Recently we brought in specialist consultants and I can tell you their report was a revelation. They were right, too,' he added, noting Len's surprised look. 'The thing is,' he continued. 'We've learned with consultants that no matter how good they are, after a while it's always smart to bring in the consultancy consultants. They're the consultants who analyse other consultants and recommend new consultants if the original mob are falling down on the job. So this led to a new lot being engaged.

'Anyway, their analysis shows that the Amazon and electrocution schemes simply knocked off the older half of the retired clergymen. Apparently their average life expectancy was only about five years anyway, so all we achieved was to halve the Church's pay-out for about five years and then we were back with the same old problem.'

'I see what you mean,' Len said. 'It was like that with the

fairy stewards on the ship. What seemed a good idea at first produced heaps of problems we never anticipated. Still, that's management and you just have to deal with it. So, what are the new people suggesting?'

'There's the rub,' Tom said. 'So far they haven't come up with solutions, which is why I always say they earn their money. Answers are never as easy as people think. They just seem that way after someone else has thought them up. But as the new chaps say in their interim report, the first requirement is to accurately identify the problem, which is what they claim the previous lot failed to do. They argue the solution lies in targeting clergymen in their last five years on the job before they start on their pensions, which is an example of my point. It's only obvious when it's pointed out. They've flirted with a few ideas such as increasing the number of choirboys in the hope of ultimately luring lots of vicars into a prison cell, as one way of removing them from the pension merry-go-round. But that was no good. Further research showed their main interest lay in having it off with female parishioners so it would only work with the Catholics who seem to favour that sort of thing. I'd approach the Catholics and sell them the idea with the aim of taking over as their advisers but ethics prevent me; conflict of interest, you see. That's something people don't appreciate about the City. We set bloody high moral standards.'

'It's a hell of a problem,' Len agreed. 'It's really quite challenging though. Have they come up with any other ideas?'

'Yes, although not with the retired clergyman problem. This one is really interesting and demonstrates the merits of constantly bringing in fresh thinking. It's a pity more of our corporate clients aren't so proactive.

'One of the analysts argued the case for building grander cathedrals. The Archbishop was initially outraged but the analyst claimed it was a provable winner in a cost-benefit sense. The grander the cathedral, the more the parishioners left the Church money in their wills. The Church runs retirement and nursing homes across the country, which presented a wonderful opportunity as the consultants found that by lowering the temperature five degrees each night in winter they improved the mortality rate by forty per cent. The increment in the wills proceeds has been enough to pay for the cathedral building programme. It's an impeccable self-fulfilling exercise adding an intangible solidity to the underlying base.'

'I see what you mean about clever thinking,' Len said. 'It's all so tidy and obvious when you spell it out but I admit I'd never have thought of it. Still, you say the retired clergyman problem still has them stumped?'

'They're continuing researching,' Tom replied. 'Proper analysis is so important in these things. For example, they've discovered that sixty-eight per cent of parsons in their fifties are basically deranged. Unfortunately they're not barking mad in an asylum sense, which is a great pity as we could then get them certified and off the Church's books and into the taxpayers' hands. No, they're only what you might call dotty so they're looking at ways of utilising that knowledge. One of the problems we've uncovered is that when they retire, instead of taking up golf or whatever they often turn on the Church. Some become terribly intense and knock out pamphlets advocating Nestorianism and other heresies. One prepared a contingency plan for dealing with the second coming; riot control and all that sort of carry-on. It upsets the old ladies and they end up leaving their money to cats' homes and other such nonsense instead of the Church. Frankly we're at a bit of a loss how to handle it.'

'Why not issue them with motorbikes?' Len suggested.

'I say. That's bloody brilliant. How did you ever think of that? I'll pass it on smartly and get a few trial runs under way.'

'Best to wait a few months,' Len suggested. 'Middle-aged men learning to ride motorbikes in winter can't miss. They'd go over like ninepins on wet and icy roads.'

Claudia intervened. 'I'm not entirely certain what you're both alluding to but even so I'm fairly sure I don't like the sound of it,' she said coolly, and she rose and left to see how the chef was doing with dinner.

'Funny buggers, women,' Tom said after she was out of ear-shot. 'I mean, Claudia's typical. She's a sensible girl in every respect; far superior to most I've met. But she's still no exception. When it comes to some things women can be extraordinarily impractical. The Church would be dead in the water by now if it took that sort of line. It's all very well being a bit soft about these buggers but if there's one thing analysis shows, it's what a deadweight the bloody retired clergymen are and frankly, the same goes for the nursing home crop. They've had their innings and aren't playing the game lingering on in that fashion. Fortunately the Archbishop is a sensible chap. He quite sees the problem and has been very supportive with all of our proposals. And if I know my man, he'll be tremendously excited about the potential of your motorbike scheme.'

'Only too happy to help,' Len said. 'Sorry about Claudia though,' he continued. 'Normally she's amazingly practical. Thinks logically, just like a man. It was what attracted her to me in the first place. Unfortunately, every now and then there are these little give-away feminine lapses, like feeling sorry for the parsons.'

'That's because she doesn't understand the Church,' Tom said. 'If she did she'd realise we're doing the clergymen a huge favour by knocking them off at the end of their careers.'

'If that's the case, why not issue them with suicide kits?' Len asked. 'It would be the most efficient way to deal with the problem.'

'Good Lord no,' Tom exclaimed. 'We couldn't possibly be party to such a thing. It would be quite immoral and even if I didn't care about that I can assure you the Archbishop is a man of impeccable moral standards and would never sanction it. Let me explain,' he said noticing Len's quizzical look. 'The Church is totally bound up with the past rather than the future. That's probably why before we came along they'd been such poor investors. Investing requires one to focus entirely on the future and forget the past other than as a guideline. Consider what a clergyman's entire thinking and babbling is about. The past. Like creation, for instance, which to them is the absolute beginning point in time and you can't go further back than that. Mostly though they go on about alleged events in the Middle East 2000 years ago so by the time they're sixty they're absolutely programmed into a backward-looking mentality.

'Now think about Church history through their eyes. There's a steady pattern of martyrdom. More than anything else the Christian martyr is the only human Christian hero and remember, clergymen are like socialists; they're simple buggers with a dependency mentality and therefore readily prone to hero-worshipping. So from that perspective, committing suicide, even in the interest of the Church, is essentially self-serving. On the other hand, being knocked off by an extraneous party or event in the interest of the Church is an act of martyrdom so it puts a very nice crowning glory cap on their careers.'

'I see it all now,' Len said. 'But I certainly wouldn't try and explain it to a woman. They lack the subtlety to understand the practicalities of that sort of proposition.'

At that point unsubtle practicality intervened when Claudia called that dinner was ready and they rose and strolled into the dining room.

10

It was time for the Palmerston Club's annual general meeting. Len drove across to London, hosted the cocktail party, chaired the meeting, diplomatically handled the perennial inane comments from the elderly garrulous members and was unanimously re-elected as president for a new five-year term.

The following day he lunched with Tom at the club. Afterwards in the sitting room over coffee and brandies Len was fidgety and plainly had something on his mind. Eventually he spoke.

'I need a favour from you,' he said.

'Spit it out, old man,' Tom replied. 'If I can assist then I'll be delighted to do so.'

Len hesitated again then spoke. 'I've been thinking about your comments last week at Wyebury. You know, the stuff about using one's money now rather than hoarding it for future generations. There are a few things I've decided I'd like to do. The problem is I'm not sure how to go about it and I know you will know. But it's not exactly banking business so I want to pay for your staff's time if you'd handle it for me.'

'Let's not worry about any of that now,' Tom replied. 'What have you in mind?'

'Well, first I want to set up a fund with whatever amount's required, to provide top quality private schooling for a bunch of kids in Australia. And not just school fees, but the whole bit; you know, walking-around money, schooltrips, clothing and all of that.'

'Do you have any particular group of children in mind?' Tom asked solemnly, correctly judging by Len's awkwardness that a particular sensitivity applied.

'Yes I do,' Len said. 'You know, I reckon at least a third of the girls on the Olga Buskova were solo mums. I want to look after their kids and I want the very best; the top private schools, personal tutorage where necessary; absolutely everything and no expense spared. I want to pay for them all the way through to and including university. And I want each to have private tutorage for elocution.'

'Guilt money?' Tom queried quietly.

'Emphatically not,' Len said. 'In fact, the very opposite. Call it a gratitude payback if you like.'

Tom reflected for a while then spoke.

'It's not a straightforward issue, Len. For starters, who qualifies? For example, does a child whose mother may only have lasted a month on the boat? There'll be lots of considerations like that.'

'I've thought about that,' Len responded. 'I realise the difficulties but basically I don't see it matters. Good luck to the little bugger even if his mother was only a short-termer. What the hell; whatever it costs is peanuts in terms of my financial circumstances. And I want it backdated to include all the girls on the first trip. Look; it's very simple. As you said at Wyebury, spend it now on things you will enjoy. Well, I'll enjoy this. It will give me a real charge thinking of these kids being tarts' offspring and ending up as lawyers and doctors and even the Prime Minister. Why not? Anything's possible. I've got it running out of my ears so believe me, I'm doing it for myself most of all. It appeals to my sense of humour.'

'Okay,' Tom said. 'It's no great difficulty. We can set up an Australian trust and our Sydney associates can locate suitable trustees. We've got plenty of time to work out qualification criteria and anyway, they can always be modified as circumstances dictate. But it sounds like a sizeable exercise so we may need to set up a small office with perhaps a part-time secretary-manager. There are lots of worldly-wise capable middle-aged women marking time who would make a good fist of this. We'll get it right by trial and error so I'll have it under way and you can forget about fees. That can be my contribution. We've done bloody well out of the good ship Olga, at least indirectly, so we'll do the organising of this for gratis.'

'That's terrific,' Len said, sitting back in his armchair. 'I'm really grateful for your help, Tom, but, there's more.'

Tom looked at him quizzically.

Len looked away as he spoke.

'I want a separate fund large enough to produce a million a year for each of three countries: India, Pakistan and Bangladesh. The problem is I haven't worked out exactly where I want it to go other than that it reaches ordinary punters and helps in some educational or development way. What I do know is I want to do something directly; I don't mean with my name attached; in fact I want my involvement in both schemes to be confidential, but I don't want to deal through the established charities. I've thought of a name which can cover both funds. I want it called the Phoenix Trust.'

'I'm surprised you're interested in the subcontinent,' Tom queried. 'You haven't been there, have you? Personally, I can't stand the place. I went to New Delhi once to organise a government bond issue. They were all posturing incompetents so I withdrew from any involvement.'

'No, I've not been there,' Len said. 'But I have my reasons and I'd prefer not to go into them. There's one other thing,' he added. 'I don't want Claudia to know about any of this. Is that possible?'

Tom raised his eyebrows in surprise.

'Actually it's quite easy in your circumstances,' he said. 'We're talking about a sizeable capital sum, possibly as much as fifty million pounds. But it doesn't actually matter. When I created your investment structure I did it all through a series of tax haven trusts across the globe. What we send you each week is the current assets schedule for each of them and their share prices' performances, dividends and all that detail. As it stands you are the current beneficiary for each of them but it's a simple matter to change the beneficiary for the required amount and channel it to this Phoenix entity without that being evident on the schedules. But, if you don't mind me asking; why don't you want Claudia to know? I'd have thought she would be pleased about this.'

'Yes, she would,' Len replied. He hesitated and thought for a minute. 'I'm sorry, mate. I know why I don't want her to know in a feeling sense. I just don't think I can explain it. I would if I could. Let's leave it at that for the time being. Claudia's working on a list of ideas for innovative things to fund, but I want these two kept quiet as far as she's concerned.'

Detecting Len's intensity Tom said jokingly, 'So you're an old softie after all and you want your wife to keep thinking you're a steely-minded tough guy.'

'Not exactly,' Len replied quietly. 'Call it part-payment on a debt I suspect I might have; I'm not sure actually but if I have then I can't ever settle it; that is, the subcontinent bit. Anyway, enough of that. Let's go upstairs and I'll hand you a thrashing at billiards,' and the two picked up their brandies and headed for the door.

11

A letter from Tom arrived.

You recall when I was down a month ago you came up with the first-rate motorbike suggestion for the retired parson problem. You might be interested in the outcome as I passed your idea on to the consultants. They declared it sound in principle but with a critical fault we both overlooked.

The difficulty was the Church would have to offer it to everyone and their survey revealed the biggest response would be from young clergymen. In other words it had the same fatal flaw as the Amazon project only at the other end of the scale, that is it would be most effective with the wrong age bracket.

The Church invests heavily training their clergy so the optimum pay-off expectancy naturally rests with the new chaps.

Another danger was the possibility young clergymen would cope with the motorbikes, making the exercise self-defeating and a wasted capital outlay. Also, it would set a bad precedent if the Church gave them things. Apparently the new chaps are bound up in youthful enthusiasm allowing the Church to get away with paying them a pittance. They don't wake up until it's too late, when they're about forty. They're easy meat of course for as the consultants' evaluations have demonstrated, vicars have IQs three points below average.

Nevertheless your idea has not been wasted as the enclosed brochure shows. It's a variation on your scheme and the Archbishop is delighted and has given it his blessing.

As you can see it's only open to retired vicars but to qualify they have to pass a fitness test. So that nicely captures the targeted sector which is healthy, newly retired chaps, precisely the category the Church wants off its books.

Len studied the brochure Tom had enclosed. Its cover illustration showed a smiling bicycle-clipped clergyman standing alongside a bicycle before the Taj Mahal while surrounding him, three attractive sari-clad Indian girls smiled coquettishly. A loin-clothed snake charmer was in the bottom corner.

The brochure offered a fully paid cycling tour of India in groups of four, each with an Indian guide, as a reward for the retired clergymen's service. The cyclists would be accommodated in small hotels, as the brochure explained, 'to fully savour the real Indian experience.'

Len returned to Tom's letter.

We've had a wonderful response with 483 acceptances and the consultants are very optimistic of an eighty per cent plus initial strike rate. Their research shows the chance of surviving more than an hour riding a bicycle in Indian cities is negligible. But if that doesn't get them they say the food will as apparently the doss-houses they're putting them in are fairly disgusting with typhoid rampant, so overall it looks very promising.

There's also the prospect of an added windfall which could save the bicycle and guide costs. The consultants have chartered a dubious Dagestan outfit's thirty-six-year-old Aeroflot jet to fly them there so there's a decent prospect of the plane going down. The consultants with their usual thoroughness have insisted on night flights to increase the chances of crashing.

I've said it before and I'll say it again. Consultants are the most underestimated professionals of modern commerce. They really are doing God's work and the Archbishop and Church Commissioners are quite elated. If everyone had their standard of professionalism the world would be an immensely better place. Typical of their admirable diligence is that despite their projections they have a back-up scheme in place to take any survivors on to Laos. They've arranged a jungle walk in a location on the Vietnamese border infested with land mines. Currently they're negotiating a price with the Cambodian military to shoot the plane down on the flight home should there still be any survivors left, although in fairness, that was the Archbishop's suggestion. He's become quite captivated with the proposal and has promised a celebratory party at Lambeth Palace when the exercise is completed. I'll wangle you and Claudia an invitation. After all it was your idea which started this so you should be very proud. I'll keep you informed of the outcome.

Len folded the letter and brochure and put them back in the envelope. Recalling Claudia's peculiar behaviour when the subject had been first mooted he hid the envelope under some files in his desk's bottom drawer.

12

One morning during breakfast Claudia said, 'Claire's coming down this weekend.'

'Good show. We haven't seen her for some time now.'

'She won't be alone, Len. Philip Melcup's coming with her.'

'Philip Melcup!' Len exclaimed. 'Why?'

Claudia shook her head resignedly. 'Sometimes men can be so blind. They've been together for a year now. I don't know for certain but I suspect they're living together so try and be diplomatic.'

'Bloody hell. The cheeky bastard. I'll have something to say about that.'

'For goodness sake, Len. The girl's twenty-four. Anyway, it's a bit rich coming from you to adopt a puritanical line. Just be diplomatic. I talk to Claire regularly on the phone and I suspect they may have an announcement.'

'You mean she's pregnant?'

'No, you silly man. Anyway, let's just wait and see but try and remember the Victorian age has been over for almost a century.'

The couple arrived on Friday night in time for dinner and afterwards the four chatted into the evening.

On Saturday after lunch Claudia announced she was going riding with Claire. The artifice of this arrangement was obvious but Len said nothing. After the two women disappeared Len retired to the sunroom to read the weekend papers and as he anticipated, Philip came in.

'I was wondering if I could have a word,' Philip said.

Len put down the newspaper and waited.

'Claire and I would like to marry soon and we felt it a courtesy to, well, that is we thought we should mention it to you first and hopefully, as it were, have your blessing.'

'I see. But aren't you being a bit hasty? Claire hasn't finished her studies and God knows what you're doing and you've not known one another that long.'

'Actually we've known one another for over two years now,'

Philip replied. 'And we've been together most of that time. Also, Claire has only two months left in her course and she doesn't want to pursue a music career, at least not in a performing sense. She wants to compose music and she can do that anywhere.'

'And what about you?' Len asked sternly. 'What are you going to do? It won't be much chop for Claire if you're gallivanting about the world with this ocean business.'

'I've chucked all of that,' Philip said. 'To be honest I find it quite boring, at least in the actual things we do. Basically, most scientific research is unexciting so I'm going back to university to study aquatic biology. Then I thought I would undertake a complete analysis of the fauna of the Wye. No one's ever done it, at least not done it as I wish to and I can afford to. I'm quite independent from my father because of the Nobel Prize. I received one and a half million dollars for that.'

'What have you done with it?' Len asked.

'Claire introduced me to Tom. He created some sort of tax-avoiding device and invested the money in shares he said were ultra-safe. Anyway, I average one and a half thousand pounds each week from dividends so Claire and I are very comfortable, especially with her allowance from you.'

'But if the ocean stuff is boring, won't the river be also?'

'It's quite different. It's proper field research and I'm bound to find new things. I don't mean new creatures but perhaps something about the behaviour of the existing fauna that wasn't known before. Who knows? That often happens. It wouldn't be just mechanical sample measurements like I was doing in the Antarctic. But regardless, I'm not concerned that much about the new things possibility. Just recording how it all fits together and sketching all the different fauna really excites me. I've thought a lot about it and what will be most satisfying of all is producing a lovely book with nice paper and sketches I've done myself. I don't care if it sounds pretentious but my general objective is aesthetic rather than scientific.'

'But will anyone be interested?' Len queried. 'Who will buy the book?'

'Probably very few people. It doesn't matter. Libraries and universities might buy a copy. I could even have to publish it myself but I don't care.'

Noting Len's puzzlement, Philip continued: 'Actually, as far as I'm concerned it will be much more useful than what I was doing in the Antarctic, which was never more than tedious.'

'But you saved the world; or that's what everyone said,' Len exclaimed.

'Yes. Well I've thought a lot about that and to be honest I don't think it made one iota of difference. I've come to the conclusion that in the final analysis everything ultimately comes out in the wash regardless and it was all a lot of fuss over nothing. I've decided nature sort of looks after itself and if human activity occasionally intervenes in the normal ebbs and flows and changes of the global climate and ecology, eventually everything adjusts and sort of goes full circle.'

'That's all very nice in theory,' Len said. 'But this global warming stuff is serious, isn't it? What about the ocean rising and climate impacts we keep hearing about?'

'I've had lots of time to think about everything since the Antarctic business,' Philip responded. 'I've decided the global warming hysteria is nonsense. Maybe the earth is warming and maybe humans are causing this, but so what? Listen to the scaremongers and the one thing which comes through is their underlying misanthropy. In the context of the environment they talk about the human race as if it's alien to the globe. Yet by far the most environmentally destructive forces are earthquakes and floods and volcanic eruptions and typhoons yet they treat those as simply part of nature. Well, so are people and in each case change results from natural causes. Aside from that, there's a hell of a lot of the earth's population who would be very happy if their climate was a few degrees warmer. There's others who would be adversely affected but that's just an adjustment issue.'

'I see your point,' Len said. He thought for a time then added: 'I think I rather intuitively concluded at quite an early age that getting too fussed about things was pointless. Better to just go with the flow. I suspect Claudia views my approach as selfish and she might well say the same about your river plans, or at least consider them self-indulgent.'

'I can understand that,' Philip said. 'But so much scientific stuff, especially the discovery of new phenomena, just boils down to chance. What I know is, if you look then invariably you find something new and interesting and that's because nature is an ever-changing, continually evolving picture. That's why I now oppose the conservationist mentality. They try to freeze the status quo as if it's sacrosanct and ignore the reality of continuing birth, death and regeneration, which is the very essence of life.'

'So bugger saving the whales then,' Len teased.

Philip laughed. 'If it makes people happy saving whales then fine. That's a good enough reason. But they should understand there's no good biological or environmental reason to do so. Kill off all the whales and you'll save an awful lot more krill and plankton which they feed on. But no one cares about them and if you ask why not they talk awful tripe about intelligence; you know, the palaver about dolphins and gorillas and elephants having higher intelligence and therefore deserving special treatment. Yet these are usually the same types who espouse socialist ideas, which produce a pretty much un-Darwinian outcome in terms of human quality. Anyway, none of this concerns me any more, as I said. In a funny sort of way I now think what we were doing in the Antarctic was utterly pointless and if the Wyebury study is self-indulgent, so too was our Antarctic research.'

'But you got the Nobel Prize for that,' Len said. 'It must have had some merit.'

'I'm afraid that was all nonsense too. I'm rather embarrassed about it because it was so bogus. A child could have done what I did with the warm water phenomenon; honestly, it could have been anyone who discovered that. It's just that the others were away at the time. It's still a mystery why the temperatures rose so sharply then fell back to normal again but I don't care because what happened anyway is what I think always ultimately does. It just sorted itself out like I said but as always, humanity was blamed. You know, the fossil-fuel-burning line, which obviously was wrong given the sudden reversal. As far as I'm concerned it can remain a mystery because I don't think it matters.

'When they started making a fuss of me at the United Nations I tried telling them I hadn't done anything special but they seemed to be able to argue persuasively I had. Later I realised they were good at that sort of thing because basically they were politicians and were used to pushing people into doing or believing things, but somehow when they were saying it, it seemed logical at the time and it would only be afterwards, in bed thinking in the dark that I knew they were talking rubbish. For example, the Secretary-General of the United Nations said if I thought I had done nothing then why honour Christopher Columbus? He did nothing special just sailing a boat, but in accidentally discovering the New World he was first there so deserved his fame. They'd say things like that and it would sound plausible but after a while I realised that with the general despair at the time my role was a contrivance they needed. That is, they wanted heroes to be optimistic about. I know that's true because at the beginning when I was really embarrassed about the way they were going on about me I said to the Secretary-General that if they insisted on doing this then at least they ought to include Professor McLean.'

'So why didn't they then?' Len asked puzzled.

'The Secretary-General said that was an excellent idea so the next time I saw him, after I had been to Washington to see the President, I asked when Professor McLean would be arriving. He was rather cool to me and acted as if I'd tried to pull the wool over his eyes. He told me enquiry revealed the Professor had a beard and was under five feet tall and wasn't therefore an appropriate person to be a hero. I was a bit shocked but eventually I just got swept up by all the fuss over me. The Secretary-General came back to the Christopher Columbus example when I protested and he said Columbus didn't sail to the New World alone. He had a crew but no one honours them, and, he claimed, that's the way it should be for practical purposes.

'So after that I just, as you say, went with the flow although the disturbing thing was how few people understood what it was all about. At a cocktail party in Uganda I was congratulated by a Cabinet minister for causing the India-Pakistan nuclear war. They seemed very pleased about that. I was given all sorts of medals which had nothing to do with what I was up to, like the Polar medal and the Royal Geographical Society medallion and once in Gabon I was made an honorary general and given a medal for bravery under fire. I was made an honorary citizen in El Salvador and given an award for services to agriculture in the Yemen. In Estonia the president thanked me for lifting the world's temperature and showed me their plans for pineapple plantations. Our car was stoned in Venezuela by protesters claiming I'd caused the oil price to drop; all sorts of things occurred like that. By the time the Nobel Prize happened I was sort of used to being congratulated or thanked for things I had nothing to do with although later when I looked through the commemorative book they gave me and saw all the famous names of people who actually had done something great I felt a bit rotten.'

'Have you talked to Claire about this?' Len asked.

'Of course. That's why I'm changing careers and opting out of the limelight. It was her idea. Basically for the last year I've been a professional celebrity and now I feel too embarrassed to continue. Claire said not to worry about the past even if it is bogus. Just stop perpetuating it, so I have. Also, Claudia was very helpful when I discussed it with her.'

'I'm interested in that, Philip,' Len said. 'What exactly did Claudia say about undeserved honours?'

'She said I shouldn't care whether I deserved the award or not. Claudia claimed every economics Nobel Prize winner had received the award for a particular thesis, not one of which had stood the test of time after two decades. She also mentioned Kissinger. She said he bombed hell out of Laos and Vietnam then was given the Nobel Peace Prize for stopping doing it. Claudia's got a theory about it which she says she wants to tackle as a book project. She claims history shows most government initiatives ultimately produce an outcome the opposite of that intended. She quoted me all sorts of examples in economics and social policy and international policies and so on and said that most meaningful awards and titles and whatever are issued by governments and invariably are for the opposite of what they say. Anyway, I'm sorry to babble on like this, telling you what you already know.'

In fact Len did not know. Claudia had mentioned none of this to him and he was disturbed by Philip's revelations.

'Tell me, Philip. Have you ever talked about the Antarctic with Claire? That is, not your temperature thing but me being there. Does Claire know?'

'I nearly mentioned it once then I stopped as I knew eventually she would ask if I patronised the boat and I didn't want her going on about that. To the best of my knowledge Claire doesn't even know you were down there. At least, she's never mentioned it to me and I'm sure she would have if she knew. Nor's Claudia for that matter so I just let sleeping dogs lie. But I can tell you this. All the chaps were very grateful for you turning up like that. I hope you won't think it sounds patronising but I now think what you were doing down there was a lot more worthwhile than what I was, only I got all the tributes.'

'Not entirely, son, not entirely,' Len said quietly.

For a minute the two sat in silence. The thought occurred to Len that if Philip married Claire then eventually he would be Lord Melcup and his daughter would become Lady Melcup. And as he intended leaving Wyebury to Claire, it would once again become the Melcup family estate. For a few seconds he felt fate was mocking him and that his occupation of Wyebury was that of a temporary interloper. Then he recalled Tom's remarks about dynasties. What the hell; the coincidence of events was astonishing but in the final analysis didn't matter. As the boy said, ultimately everything seemed to go full circle. It was not in Len's nature to be fatalistic but somehow it didn't seem to matter that much.

Len's mood lifted.

'Have you mentioned the marriage to your father?' he asked.

'I've written to him,' Philip replied. 'He's still away with Lord Northridge on their worldwide salmon fishing expedition. They're somewhere in America now, according to the itinerary he left. But to be honest I'm not particularly close to my father so I don't suppose he'll care much one way or another.'

'If you're going to do this river study thing, then you and Claire might as well shift here,' Len suggested.

'Claudia proposed that,' Philip said. 'We'd like that very much. It's a funny thing. All I ever wanted was to escape Wyebury. But now, with all that's happened and what I now intend to do and also with you and Claudia here; well, it feels like I'm coming home in a sort of spiritual sense and I'm chuffed about that. Of course it wouldn't be for a couple of years until I've finished at university.'

Abruptly Len asked, 'Tell me something, Philip. Do you think Claire's an intelligent girl?'

The young man stared at Len puzzled. 'We get along very well. I've not thought about it. I mean, I suppose she is. I'm not saying she's not. Probably she's brighter than me. I don't really care,' he floundered.

'That's just fine, Philip. Forget I mentioned it. And tell Claire I'm delighted for you both. Now we'll have a pre-celebration drink to warm up for the celebration drinks when the others return.'

13

A letter from Lord Melcup arrived for Philip.

Dear Philip,
We're now in Bolivia ahead of the scheduled itinerary I left with you.

We were obliged to leave Alaska early following a quite scandalous incident. The fishing was first rate only to be ruined when an extraordinary thing happened. A Russian floating brothel, if you can imagine such a thing, anchored alongside a mining camp near our lodge and the endless noise meant absolutely no sleep. Lord Northbridge who as you know is our former Moscow ambassador, said it accurately reflected contemporary Russia in all its short-comings. Atrocities such as this make me proud to be English.

Consequently we're running ahead ten days and are staying in La Paz and driving each day to Lake Titicaca. Unfortunately the British ambassador has attached himself to us and his presence has rather marred our visit. He's somewhat questionable; a former Harley Street medical chap and not quite right. As Northridge said, the calibre of the diplomatic service has been severely diminished in recent years.

Unfortunately the local Indians fish for trout with nets and spears. It's outrageous and I've instructed the ambassador to lodge a complaint with the Bolivian government and have it stopped. I see no reason why these natives cannot be transported to the Amazonian region.

It's some years now since I've spoken in the Lords as nothing of importance has arisen but I'll certainly be raising this matter on my return.

I received your letter about your marriage plans. Not having met the girl I hesitate to comment other than to say it is no little consolation to learn she is the daughter of Lord Edwards. He is a man of first-rate character and it was a comfort to me when he took over Wyebury.

As for marriage, I have reservations. In my own case I rapidly concluded your mother was mad but eventually discovered her behaviour was in fact normal, once I encountered her friends and listened to my colleagues who were enduring similar conduct. As it transpired your mother and I were able to live together harmoniously thanks to Wyebury. The trick is to minimise all contact, which the size of the house enabled.

On my observation most chaps without that advantage eventually give up the ghost and lose their spirit under the relentless presence of their wives' irrationality. The constant clamour to change perfectly satisfactory furnishings, the squeezing of toothpaste tubes in the middle, the seeking of one's opinion and subsequent acrimony when it's delivered; all of these things which apparently are standard female behavioural traits are sources of unhappiness.

As a scientist trained in logical thinking you will find marriage more arduous than most chaps but if you follow those simple rules, that is to minimise contact and avoid expressing opinions, particularly when solicited, which seem to be those which cause the greatest offence, then you should be able to survive the distance. Ensure you have separate bathrooms and that hers has large mirrors. Women happily spend many hours just gazing at themselves, particularly during the awkward years between the ages of fifteen and sixty.

I can only wish you well and I shall look forward to meeting the girl on my return next month.

One other thing. I was particularly delighted to learn you will be living in Wyebury again. A long time ago I came to the conclusion that people fall into two categories in some sort of innate biological way. You know about all that chromosomes and genes stuff. There's inland people and coastal ones. Most fall in the latter category. Inland types are in tune with nature; the coastal fellows are in conflict. The inlanders are content, the coastal are restless.

It's cowboys and sailors, farmers and fishermen, philosophers and explorers, conservatives and radicals. Interior people are conservatives, coastal are restless and forever seeking to change things. I suppose our so-called progress is attributable to the coastals and their persistent discontent but if the goal of life is the pursuit of happiness then I'm pleased for your sake you're an inlander and have finally discovered that. There was a time I was worried and felt I had not done my duty by you.

Your loving father.

Philip put the letter down thoughtfully. He had always viewed his father as unworldly and out of touch and was startled by what he had read. Since deciding to return to Wyebury he had felt an inner contentment, which had pricked his curiosity. Now his father had explained it all perfectly. Also, the previous morning he'd had his first argument with Claire and astonishingly, it had been over her squeezing the toothpaste in the middle of the tube. Very soon it had developed into a blazing row. Later that day they had made peace when Philip offered to take her out to dinner, something to her annoyance he had constantly refused because of his fame and the embarrassing stares of other diners.

'Where shall we go, darling?' Claire had asked.

'You choose. I don't mind.'

'No. I insist you choose,' she had retorted gaily.

'How about Chinese then?' Philip had suggested.

'Oh no. Not Chinese. Let's go somewhere different.'

'Well, you decide then,' he had insisted.

'No, no. I want you to,' Claire had cried.

'How about Indian then?'

'Oh no; not Indian.'

'Then we'll go to the Marseilles cafe in Kensington.'

'Oh, Philip, not French. All that preciousness.'

'Italian?'

'I don't really feel Italianish tonight, darling; something more like Ambers would be nice.'

So they went to Ambers where Philip was pestered by autograph seekers and had a thoroughly unpleasant evening.

14

Three years passed after his return from the Antarctic before Len saw Andrew again. Tom periodically mentioned how busy Andrew was and Len had followed Global's rapid share price growth in the *Financial Times*' Canadian shares section. But otherwise he rarely thought about the Antarctic episode with so many changes affecting his life since his return.

Nevertheless when Tom telephoned to say Andrew would be in London the following week he leapt at the proposal of seeing him again. Claudia coolly declined his suggestion to join them so he drove alone to London and stayed at the Palmerston Club's president's apartment and that night the three had dinner at the club.

Andrew looked older but seemed more invigorated. His previous, confident manner had evolved into an aggressive assertiveness. He spoke enthusiastically about Global's past two years and its future prospects.

'Time was always going to be critical in maximising this situation; after all, Len, you hardly discovered a new industry; instead you simply found an untapped market with the oldest. So the biggest asset you had being first off the block was a monopoly but I knew sooner or later competition would rear its ugly head and we'd find ourselves in a price war.'

'You mean another ship turned up at McMurdo?' Len enquired. 'I'm not surprised. You remember I predicted that would happen when you asked to take the operation over. I always saw it as a oncer.'

'Oddly enough, no,' Andrew said. 'At least not the first year, which I must say surprised me too. It was so bloody obvious and there are never secrets in commerce when this scale of money is involved. Your operation was like shooting fish in a barrel and golden opportunities like that normally never last.

'No, we took the Olga Buskova back and had a fairly similar repeat run. I had a manager on board and after three weeks I left him to it. I expected to have to go down about once a month to sort out problems. As it turned out I only went in once more on a token inspection and everything was going quite swimmingly, so I let well alone as I was so busy everywhere else. I think the first time down there with you pretty much sorted out procedures and problems and of course I was in daily touch by fax with the turnover figures.'

'So what went wrong?' Len pressed curiously.

'It was when we returned again this summer,' Andrew said. 'This time we encountered unexpected opposition but not from a rival operator. It was bloody disturbing, I can tell you. This season there were more than 200 women at the base. Can you believe that? It's all this bloody equality nonsense. Initially when the feminist thing started women only took on men's more traditional activities; law, medicine, accountancy and so on. Apparently the turning point came about five years or so ago and at universities the bloody females started horning in on the remaining male-dominated activities like the sciences and engineering and geology and whatnot. There were even two women motor mechanics down there looking after snowmobiles. They're barging in on the more menial things as well.'

'But that's only about a tenth of the market,' Len said. 'It should still have been a goer.'

Andrew laughed mockingly. 'The reduced market was the least of my concerns. The problem was the extra supply competition and,' he added gloomily, 'they were bloody well free. It seems the women got fed up with the beards disappearing off to the ship all the time and one by one they began turning it up for them and once a few were at it, then very soon they all were. Fortunately by all accounts the relationships were mostly monogamous and also lots were fat and plain females; nevertheless it was quite a shock. Within two months our monopoly on supply was gone. We'd started with 130 girls and gradually reduced numbers until we had 100 although that meant lowering the waiting time from the three days we had with your original trip to only one. Striking the right balance between demand and supply was critical to maintaining maximum productivity. We still had a qualitative advantage by only keeping the really pretty ones; nevertheless it looks like the golden period is over. It's a very sad thing when you think about it; the declining moral standards. Our generations looked upon women with respect, not as tarts.'

'But the latest results are phenomenal,' Len said puzzled. 'Are you saying Global's had it?'

'Hell no. Actually, its best days are ahead. You really should buy some shares. Currently they're at twenty-two dollars Canadian but I can see that price doubling over the next twelve months based on earnings.'

Tom intruded. 'The Antarctic activity is now pretty small beer in Global's overall picture, Len. Andrew has expanded on a multitude of fronts.'

'I certainly have,' Andrew enthused. 'It's been damned hard work. For a start we hugely increased the girl business. The Olga Buskova is full-time now. It sails up to the Arctic circle at the season change. We've located a large base with about 3000 men in Alaska and it sits out the Antarctic winter there.

'Plus Zirovsky outfitted two Russian navy high-speed gunboats. They loaded up with a dozen girls each by using the Olga as a sort of mother ship and they charged up and down the Alaskan and British Columbian coast and serviced all the smaller mining and geology bases.'

'Surely that couldn't have been economical?' Len queried.

'On normal costings, no,' Andrew said. 'But we got the gunboats for fifty thousand dollars each a season, paid to Zirovsky. I think he gave half to a Russian admiral. Anyway, it went very well for a time until the US coastguard got upset at Russian warships in their territory. But of course they couldn't catch them so they called in the US navy and after one high-speed chase, the Americans started lobbing shells across the bow of our boats as they raced towards open sea. Well, it turned out the bloody Russians still had a stock of ammo on board. The captain of the one in the rear lost his temper, swung about, turned his guns on the Americans and knocked the bridge off one of their frigates. Killed a few chaps apparently. Zirovsky copped a lot of heat over it.

'It was actually quite an historic event because despite the history of antagonism it's the only time Russia and the Americans have ever engaged in actual conflict. Made me quite proud; part of history and all that sort of thing. Of course it was all hushed up. We lost that batch of girls as well. They were out of their minds with fright when they landed up in Vladivostock. Claimed they joined up for love, not war, and they all resigned on the

279

spot. God knows what happened to them. We're back in to this market again but now we zip across the Bering Strait from Vladivostock and use a Russian stable and all the guns have been taken off the boats.'

'But don't you still have problems with the coastguard and navy?' Len asked.

'No we don't. I had the gunboats painted white with a large red cross on their sides and the words "Christian Crusade Line" sign-written on the stern. I borrowed the brand from what you told me about your old franchising days. We gave one of the crew a false beard, a dog collar and a large Bible so whenever the coastguard looms up everyone stays below and he dons the beard and dog collar to pass off as a wet missionary type. Also, we got hold of a nun's outfit and one of the girls piles into that. They wave to the Americans and everything's fine. The coastguard thinks we're a do-gooding missionary service calling on all the outposts, which in a way I suppose we are, in fact.'

'Losing the girls is hardly a problem,' Len said. 'There's always a ready supply of those.'

'We literally lost a batch of twelve once,' Andrew replied. 'It was one of my better ideas. I'd read how the US government had forewarned the Shah of Iran after their satellite detected all the beards on the streets of Tehran. The CIA guessed something was up with all the mullahs coming into the capital and instructed their ambassador to warn the Shah. But the silly bugger thought the satellite story far-fetched and a week later he was history.

'After I read that Zirovsky introduced me to the right people in the Russian airforce and for only fifty thousand dollars they supplied us an army helicopter troop carrier and a satellite service spotting large numbers of beards gathered together in wilderness spots across Central Asia. They were mostly US mining and geology outfits and we did splendidly for a time, dropping in and charging them heaps. It looked like developing into a nice little subsidiary but it all ended in tears.

'The satellite spotted a bunch of 800 beards somewhere in eastern Iran. The helicopter dropped down, out popped a dozen naked girls and began prancing about only to find they'd landed in the middle of a prayer festival at some bloody sacred site. The mullahs stoned the girls to death, beheaded the crew and burned the helicopter. It was a damned nuisance losing the helicopter and the Russians wouldn't give us another so that was the end of that. They were quite unpleasant about the whole affair, not only for losing their helicopter but the incident caused a riot in Tehran and the Russian Embassy there was burnt down and a couple of the embassy staff murdered by the mobs. The way the Russians went on about it you'd have thought I did it deliberately. It was typical of so much of modern industry relying on advanced technology. Bloody good in theory but forever falling down through lack of the hands-on touch.'

'How's the parrot going?' Len enquired.

Andrew brought both hands up and covered his face in a gesture of horror. 'How's the parrot going? I'll tell you how the bloody parrot's going. It's in disgrace. For a start there's an arrest warrant out for him in Alaska. Christ that bird's caused some trouble.'

'Good God,' Len exclaimed. 'He was always a feisty bugger. Don't tell me he's back on the grog?'

'No; that's under control. What happened was this. The first time up in the Arctic we settled in nicely, much like at McMurdo. One day a black American geologist burst into my office protesting that the parrot had just called him a black bastard. I knew the parrot had a pretty good repertoire of abuse and bad language but I'd never heard him say that before so I laughed it off.'

'It's possible,' Len intruded. 'He was a fairly quick learner. Claudia taught him to say her name inside three weeks.'

'Anyway, this prick went on and on about it. Claimed he had a witness. So I asked him what he wanted me to do about it? Well of course being an American there was only one thing, namely money. I told him to piss off and sue the parrot if he felt that way and bugger me, effectively that's what he did.

'The next thing I received a letter from the Justice Department claiming I had breached some incitement of racial hatred laws. I wrote back facetiously saying they had the wrong man but I had passed their letter on to the offender. A week later a dead-head bureaucrat Washington lawyer turned up escorted by two state troopers. I telephoned an Anchorage law firm and an hour later a lawyer flew in on a seaplane. I've never seen anything like it. They all went at one another absolutely seriously.

'First our bloke argued the government had no jurisdiction. The parrot was an Australian national on an English-chartered Russian ship, he said. The Washington lawyer countered that was all irrelevant as it happened in American territory. So our man switched to the constitution and argued freedom of speech. The bureaucrat claimed the specific racial incitement laws overrode the generality of the constitutional assertions.

'All of this went on for about four hours then when they were leaving the bloody parrot shrieked at them to "fuck off" so the troopers arrested it for offensive behaviour and took it back to the cells in Anchorage. One of them actually recited a warning to the parrot about its right to remain silent before they carted it off.

'The lawyer and the pilot stayed the night on the ship and the parrot was brought up on charges, before the Anchorage court the next morning. We flew down in the seaplane for the hearing. You wouldn't believe it. They were all quite coldly serious.

'The parrot was fined fifty dollars for offensive behaviour and the bloody judge actually delivered a lecture about it conducting itself in a decent manner and warned any repetition would result in a prison sentence. It was quite surreal but at the time I got caught up with it all because everyone else was so serious.'

'What about the falling in love problem?' Len asked. 'Does that still occur?'

'Of course it does,' Andrew replied. 'But before our first return trip I interviewed candidates in Sydney seeking one to emulate Claudia's role. I advertised a seventy-five thousand dollars annual salary and was deluged with applicants. We took on an excellent woman. She was a forty-year-old spinster headmistress at a top Australian private school but she didn't last long. The Antarctic was spinster paradise and she was actively pursued by some of the older and divorced beards. After three months she was engaged to an American professor down there studying fish blood temperatures. Something to do with their antifreeze character-istics. Now she's married and living in New Hampshire and is headmistress at some plush private girls' school. Apparently they loved her jolly-hockeysticks manner and she's on twice the salary we were paying.'

'Well, it would certainly be hard locating another Claudia,' Len said. 'I shudder to think about the chaos had she not been there.'

'Actually we've got a cracker now,' Andrew said. 'We always change the stable between the Antarctic and Arctic legs and I go to Sydney to do the interviews with Rippin. So I re-advertised the operations manager position and one day in came a quietish middle-aged woman. Turned out she had been a mother superior in a nunnery and had suddenly seen the light and chucked it all in.

'I told her she was most unsuitable and she demanded to know why so I explained what the boat was all about. She brightened up and said it sounded the ideal job and that she had a lot of living to do to make up for her wasted life. She said she'd spent twenty years ensuring young women behaved in an unnatural way so didn't expect it would be too arduous maintaining control when they were behaving in a natural fashion. She's been a great success although I expect we'll lose her too. Apparently she's had four marriage proposals so far from the beards.'

'It's always amazed me no one's ever twigged about Global's activities,' Len said. 'To be honest, it's the main reason I've kept clear of the shares.'

'There's a very good reason for that,' Andrew said. 'No one knows. The operation is ostensibly owned by a Cayman Islands company with nominee directors and shareholders. It's untraceable. Incidentally, talking of twigged reminds me of that wowser character Twigg who harassed us on the first trip. I was down in Sydney about four months ago and he popped up in the newspapers. There was a photo of him entering a court handcuffed to a copper. Apparently after the near-drowning incident and women's underwear revelation he shot through to Australia and landed a job with the Boy Scout movement. According to the newspaper the scouting people were delighted with his enthusiasm, especially his willingness to take cub troops on weekend camps. He was up on about forty charges of molestation. Can't say I was surprised.

'Anyway, a day later the newspaper reported he was dead. Evidently the police held him overnight in a holding cell with two mass murderers and the next morning Twigg was found drowned with his head in the toilet bowl. The bottom had been blocked with a towel and the bowl filled with water. The mass murderers claimed it must have been suicide as they had slept like babies and heard nothing. There was the usual carry-on from some civil liberty types claiming the police had deliberately put him in with those cell mates knowing the consequences but no one else cared so that was the end of Twigg.'

'What you have to realise,' Tom intruded, 'is Global is now a legitimate scientific book and magazine publisher which is what's kept Andrew so busy. He used the share price premium to take over a multitude of scientific publishers through script swaps. Originally this was intended to provide a cover of legitimacy for the Scientific Books credit card disguise but once there were a couple of publishing houses on board it became really interesting and just kept going from there. Andrew discovered there's an enormous number of scientific publishers mostly run by wet buggers like the beards in the Antarctic. Properly managed they had huge potential so with our help Global started buying them up and more recently Global's moved in on the business magazine field as well.'

'It's actually a hot growth field and we're now the world's third biggest scientific publisher,' Andrew said. 'I've been busy cost-cutting by amalgamating lots of their administration, marketing and advertising activities under one roof. Also, I've combined a lot of the competing publications. We bought up eight penguin magazines and amalgamated them into just one; *The Penguin*. We've expanded the readership from penguin researchers to the entire zoology market by making sure there's plenty of new discoveries. To date I've handled that personally as a hobby. It's satisfied my creative urges.'

'What the hell do you know about penguins?' Len questioned.

'Not a bloody thing, old man,' Andrew replied. 'But I know what excites the buggers who do. Last year I took down some spray paint canisters and one day I wandered out, checked no one was about and painted a white stripe down the back of half a dozen of them. I've never seen such excitement. The penguin blokes were beside themselves about the new species. The fellow who found them first became quite famous in penguin circles and we helped it along with a cover story in *The Penguin*. I used a water-based paint that washes off after a couple of days so it's a bloody rare species. The striped penguins pulled in over forty new beards and they're desperate to catch one so I've decided to keep them scarce. I stripe three or four more about once a month, just when the beards are beginning to lose hope. I've created eight new species of fauna now. It's been terrific for business as each one flushes up fresh waves of beards coming in. Once I had Harding bring in a hydrangea in a pot. I planted it in a crevasse in the hills behind the base. Two days later a lichen expert found it and all hell broke loose. Within a fortnight twenty new beards had flown in to investigate. I worried about them taking soil samples and uncovering the ruse but as it turned out there was no danger of that. The beard who first found it roped it off so no one could get nearer than ten feet and his lichen party maintained twenty-four-hour shifts guarding it. Still, it was a nice little fillip for the boat with all the new chaps coming in. Which reminds me. I meant to write and tell you about it. Do you remember Paviour-West? I wrote to you about my beepers making his bloody leopard-seal colony turn their heads on command.'

'God, I'd love to have seen that,' Len said. 'I laughed when I got your letter. How did it all turn out?'

'It turned out better than you could ever have expected,' Andrew replied. 'You'll recall I was going to alternate the beepers. Well, I did that starting early one morning and I left them turning left and right every half minute for a day. That night Templeton came in. He was very upset and told me what had happened. Once the seals started the tennis match stuff one of the crew shot off to fetch Paviour-West. When he arrived he just stood and glared at the colony for about ten minutes without speaking. Then he started slowly walking towards them shouting insults at the top of his voice along the line that the leopard seals were deliberately taking the piss out of him. Templeton said he kept shouting out, "You ungrateful shits" and when he got there he started kicking them. Templeton says they're quite dangerous and Paviour-West was being tossed about when who should charge in but the Aussie leopard-seal weighing bloke Jensen who'd arrived the previous day for a new season's weighing. He laid half a dozen leopard seals out with uppercuts and rescued Paviour-West who was unconscious and they took him back to the base hospital. Two days later they flew him out on a Starlifter and since then he's been in a Bristol asylum which specialises in lycanthropic disorders. That's buggers who think they're animals. They say he's a whole new field of study as his disorder is an intense hatred of leopard seals. He spends all day planning expeditions to blow them up. The psychiatrists have given him four other patients who think they're owls and told Paviour-West they've been assigned from the navy and are under his command. Being owls they're quite happy to just sit there quietly each day while he lectures them on planned bombing assaults on the seal colonies. Apparently he's very happy. In pioneering all of this I almost feel I've contributed to medical science. We ran a story on it in *The Seal*.'

'So what about the beepers?' Len asked. 'Did you keep them going?'

'Just for two weeks,' Andrew said. 'I was intending to pick them up the next Sunday but that night Jensen came aboard and I had a drink with him. He told me he was back to weigh the leopard seals again to check for any differences and was annoyed to find Paviour-West had returned. When he rescued the Prof he had just wandered down to take a look at the colony. Anyway, he cut a deal with Templeton who had taken over as team leader. He agreed to give him a clear run for two weeks before he went in to start laying them out. Jensen and his crew spent most of that time on the boat so we did all right out of it. Actually it's Jensen's last trip. He told me his team ate a penguin on their first trip down and it tasted bloody good. They've located an ostrich farming entrepreneur who's funding them and they've bought land in the Falkland Islands to start breeding them as a delicacy. They've devised a marketing slogan, "A penguin in every pot." I'll be sorry to see Jensen go.'

'And the beepers?' Len queried.

'Well, I had a think about it and the next day turned on the left one and kept the leopard seals turning left at one-minute intervals for a fortnight until Templeton was finished. Then I picked up the beepers. Templeton went home and became quite famous in scientific circles for his discovery about leopard seals being left-handed. We gave him a cover story on *The Seal* last year and now he's a professor. As he's fixed up okay I'll put the beepers back next year and make the leopard seals right-handed. That will bring a huge influx of fresh beards which is bloody good for the Olga and also for the magazine as revisionist contributions always produce a great response.

'We're really doing well out of our scientific magazines as we've worked out the trick to expanding their readership tenfold on the normal specialist markets. It's actually quite simple. We employ a full-time apocalypse writer and he does an imminent-apocalypse article in each magazine at half-year intervals, centred around something pertaining to the magazine's particular field. The press love these stories and give them a good run and then comes a deluge of new subscriptions from the misanthropy mob. Left-wing academics and journalists; you know the types. They've been in a vacuum since socialism collapsed.'

'So the boat's still going along nicely then,' Len said.

'It certainly is,' Andrew replied. 'But it's not that significant for Global any more. All the girls do is provide a boost to the consolidated earnings. Now we've broadened into general publishing as well. We've landed Senator Fulton's autobiography. Also we're doing the memoirs of the former British prime minister. I've had a look at them. He's a bit scathing about the news media which may not be too smart if he wants sympathetic reviews. Tell you who I'd like to land though, and that's young Philip Melcup. Tom tells me he's your son-in-law. What are the chances, Len?'

'You're wasting your time,' Len said. 'He's had a gutsful of celebrity and attention. He's found what he wants at Wyebury and that's the same as me; tranquillity and anonymity.'

'Pity, that,' Andrew said. 'Actually, talk of the devil, we're actually kicking off our first book with one of this club's members, so my people tell me. Some old buffer called Professor Cone who gives this club as his address. I'm told he's written a sort of new-world-order book based on his lifetime's biological findings and we're at the proof-reading stage now. Haven't read it myself.'

In fact, unbeknown to the three men at that very moment, immediately above them in the library, the elderly Professor Cone sat wild-eyed with the proofs of his lifetime's work spread before him. There was a common theme to the chapters reflected in their titles including, 'Was Hitler Right? – A Fresh Consideration', 'Flogging – the Moral Solution To Unemployment', 'The Case

For Slavery', 'Total Sterilisation – An African Imperative' and 'Homo Sub-Sapiens – Evolvement Of A New Species In The Gorbals'.

'Andrew's been a cover story on over fifteen business magazines to date including quite a few Global doesn't own,' Tom said, bringing the discussion back to the company. 'Global's now a very respected commercial entity and deservedly so. And I'll say this. There's nothing unusual about it, either. In my experience numerous major corporates began with something a bit questionable. It's usually the easiest way to start from nothing.'

'Two more years with the Olga Buskova is about all that's left with that side of the overall operation. Its contribution to earnings is being constantly diminished by the growth in the conventional activities so even though its ownership is well disguised it's still a risk, which is why we'll probably sell it,' Andrew said. 'We could research other possible gaps in the girls market but if we find them then invariably they'll attract competition. We discovered a potential opportunity with offshore oil rigs but all that confirmed was what a unique opportunity the Antarctic was. The number of men on the rigs were enough to justify a medium-size boat but most were in locations requiring much larger ships to get there safely. Also, we couldn't just tie up like at McMurdo but needed the oil companies' consent, and we'd never get that. Basically the girls business is an industry with little organic growth potential so we'll be out inside two years. But it has spawned a successful new corporate so I'm quite proud of that.'

'Which is why Andrew is here,' Tom said. 'He's cashing up his options and taking over as a forty per cent partner and chief executive of my merchant bank so expect me on your doorstep a lot more in future when the salmon are running.'

Noting Len's surprise, Andrew explained: 'I've done my dash with Global. It was fun building it up but now it's basically repetitious and appropriate for the usual commercial dullards to manage. That sort of commerce is simply not my bag. Far better to be on the sideline backing all the winners as they come and go. Most commercial activity is a bit like a horse race in which everyone chooses a horse to back and then is stuck with it. But there's a special privilege role for merchant bankers allowing them to pick the certain winner just before the finish of each race.'

'It's a wonder you don't have more competition,' Len said.

'No it's not,' Tom said. 'It's no different in any field. Most people like the idea of being rich yet never bother trying to be. Most of those who get there do so simply because they actually make the effort. It's the same with everything. Look at the head waiter in this dining room. Arguably he's smarter than the Prime Minister but he probably thinks he's made it big simply by being top dog here. If you asked him whether he could step into the Prime Minister's shoes he'd think you were joking. But of course he could; a ventriloquist's dummy could. The bloody Prime Minister just does what the mandarins and advisers tell him. Under the modern political system a Liverpool housewife could run the show perfectly adequately. It's pretty much like that with commerce too. Success has nothing to do with intelligence; it's all about desire. The main reason the Prime Minister is the Prime Minister is because he wanted to be. Most people achieve what they set out to do but the vast majority set their targets far too low in terms of their capacity.'

'I'll tell you something I noticed in line with that argument,' Len said. 'When Claudia first joined me at Wyebury we made regular antique-shopping tours to fill the place. We must have visited hundreds of antiques shops in southern England and Dublin and one day it struck me that ninety per cent of their proprietors were putting on absurd airs and talking with ridiculous over-the-top plums in their mouths. But all the time I could see that desperate look in their eyes, fearful of missing out on a sale, and I realised that although many of them were fairly bright, the reality of their existence was that they were just simple little shopkeepers and rather pathetic, essentially living a bare-bones existence of pretence, too late to change and achieving far less than their individual potential. They'd made a bad call at the start and now were stuck with it. It's terrible waste when you think about it.'

'The academic world's the same,' Andrew contributed. 'Everyone thinks successful academics are brilliant geniuses. Well, I can tell you they're not, at least not the most prominent ones. The most successful are those who know how to work the system rather than actually doing anything innovative or significant. They write lots of papers and get them published. Most are guff and in the more precise disciplines sometimes quite fraudulent. But it doesn't matter because no one much cares. We soon woke up that even though half the stuff we publish is rubbish, it's actually good as it gets a bit of controversy going and everyone enjoys that. I once contributed an article under a pseudonym to *The Penguin* claiming evidence of penguins' cannibalistic tendencies. We got over 200 letters on that all saying it was bullshit so we published forty of them plus another ten I made up from fictitious researchers backing me up. The debate raged for over a year and circulation rose 20 per cent. It all brightens up dull lives.'

'Don't you remember the doctor on the ship the first year?' Len said to Andrew. 'Isaac. That was his name. Remember he used to say the same about medicine and we were both a bit shocked at the time.'

'There was an early nineteenth-century presidential candidate called Aaron Burr,' Andrew said. 'He once claimed all power was a bluff and by God he was right. Look at Tom's steak. Chances are the waiter accidentally dropped it on the floor before he brought it out. If he did, do you think they cooked up a new one? What you don't know doesn't harm you. They'd have just picked the lot up, reset it prettily on a fresh plate and all's well so long as they keep up the bluff and pomposity which goes with this sort of place.'

'I'll take my chances,' Tom laughed. 'But you're right. Do you know a survey by the consultants for our Church of England client showed seventy per cent of ministers don't believe in God? I was a bit puzzled at first and then they found out the same went for most of the parishioners. It's a classic metaphor for the broader picture. Everyone is role-playing and everything stumbles along quite happily but every now and then some goose gets up and shouts the emperor has no clothing, which is nearly always true but just causes disruption. I suspect that's why truth-telling radicals are always disliked. Telling people the emperor has no clothing has always been a loser's proposition.'

Len spoke up. 'Claudia once said the whole of American life rests on constant pretence, which is why she got tired of it.'

'Which is why it's so bloody successful,' Tom intervened. 'They all play the game and don't try and kid one another that they're not kidding one another.'

'There was a zoologist down in the Antarctic I used to talk to a bit,' Andrew said. 'Do you remember him, Len? Chap called Dr Tullett from Chicago. Sensible sort of fellow. Not wet like the others. He didn't have a beard. He was studying bluff in animals and was down there watching the behaviour of penguins pretending to be ferocious when their eggs or the young were being attacked by skuas. He claimed the higher you went up the evolutionary scale, the greater the need for bluff to survive. Things like dogs snarling to ward off much larger creatures like bears. He said you have amoebas at one end of the scale totally programmed and predictable and humans at the other end. But his main interest was to stratify people. Tullett reckoned people on the factory floor were without guile compared with, say, those at higher levels of society. The higher up you went, the more bullshit was necessary to preserve your position. He claimed it was an environmentally-driven biological issue rather than a sociological matter.'

'Which is why I like country life,' Len said. 'Plain and simple folk and total honesty.'

'Yeah. And totally dreary and not much fun,' Tom argued. 'And at the end of the day laughing counts the most and you have to be bright to do that even if there's a fair amount of blarney involved.'

The sound of a plate crashing in the kitchen interrupted the men's conversation. Tom beckoned the waiter. 'I've rather had enough now. Cancel my apple dumpling.' And the three men laughed conspiratorially.

Later in the club sitting room an elderly barman brought them coffee and liqueurs.

'I say,' Len said to Andrew. 'Now you're returning for good you'll need a club. It's not quite the done thing but as president I can fix a quick entry for you and Tom can second it.'

Andrew looked about the room. He saw the faded and battered furniture, the dingy 1950s lampshades, the threadbare carpet and the dreary Victorian oil paintings blackened by more than a century's tobacco smoke. In different parts of the room three elderly gentlemen, yesterday's men, were sprawled in their armchairs asleep, their heads lolling back and mouths open.

Newspapers lay spread across their fronts and scattered at their feet where they had fallen. At the bar sat a lonely figure, a prematurely balding young bearded man who periodically glanced wistfully about the room as if in anticipation of an imminent eruption of excitement. It was all quite dreadful.

'Well, I don't know what to say,' Andrew muttered.

'Say nothing, old man. Just leave it to me,' and two months later Andrew became a member of the Palmerston Club.

Epilogue

Sunning himself on the terrace Len rocked gently back and forth in his rocking chair and watched his granddaughter Jane canter across the lawn towards him and Claudia, who was ensconced in a wicker chair beside him reading a book. He was eighty-two years of age and at peace with the world.

The girl dismounted, tied the pony to a post and hugged her grandfather.

'When can I have a proper horse grandad? I'm too big for the pony. I want to go fast.'

'Only a year to go when you're sixteen. There's plenty of time ahead for all of that.'

'But it's so boring,' his granddaughter protested.

Already she was a striking beauty. Although widely admired ('A classical English Rose reflecting her lineage from two of England's most blue-blooded families', the caption had read in a recent *Country Life* magazine under a photograph of Jane at a horse show), at a certain angle her dark eyes flashed with an un-English glint reflecting the rich diversity of her bloodlines. Precisely, she was five-eighths English, one-eighth Polynesian and one-sixteenth respectively Norwegian, Gypsy, German and Mongolian.

At that moment Claire appeared. 'Come along, darling. The car will be here for you soon. Hurry inside and have your shower.'

'Oh grandad,' the girl pleaded. 'Do I have to go? They're all so boring.'

'Well, my dear. We can't always do what we want. Most girls would give anything to swap places with you. Not everyone gets invited to the palace to have tea with the young prince.'

'But why do I have to go every month? They're all boring, boring, boring.'

Protesting, she was led inside by her mother. Len continued rocking back and forth in the sun. It was a strange world and his had been a strange life. He thought back to his youth. In one lifetime he had gone from yob to nob. If anyone had told him back in the street-barrow days that his granddaughter would be lined up as a prospective bride to the heir to the throne... well it was all too extraordinary.

At that moment a Rolls-Royce bearing the Prince of Wales's emblem and flag drove up. A chauffeur opened the car door and a palace official emerged and approached Len and Claudia.

'Good morning, Lord Edwards. Good morning, Lady Edwards. A lovely day to enjoy the sun.'

Len rang the bell and a maid brought out morning tea.

'I must say, sir, the palace is most impressed with Lady Jane,' the official said. 'Such a charming young lady.'

'You'll have her back by seven,' Len said gruffly.

'Of course, sir. And if I may say so, she's considered by the palace to be a very intelligent young woman.'

For a few seconds the world stood still, then Len spoke firmly in a tone that brooked no argument.

'I'm very sorry but I'm afraid Lady Jane will not be going with you. Furthermore, she will not be available in the foreseeable future. Please give my apologies to the palace and His Highness,' and he rose and went inside to tell the girl the good news.